Run With the Hunted
First Omnibus
Books 1-3

Run With the Hunted
By Jennifer R. Donohue

Chapter One

Bits called our latest meeting when she sniffed out the job, but I chose the location: one of our local museums, free on Wednesdays. I arrive after a predictably disappointing date, removing that man's contact from my phone, and I find Bits sitting on a bench, a bouquet of snack bags peeking from her cargo pocket. It's possible she subsists entirely on vending machine food; I hesitate to ask.

"Hey Bristol. Their beverage restock isn't until tomorrow," she says when I sit next to her, smoothing my skirt. "I got one of those fizzy things you like so much, to try it, but it was the last one. You don't mind, do you?"

"That you took the last one, or that you opened a drink you're passing along to me?" I ask with a laugh.

"Whichever." Bits's existence is one of the perpetual slouch and shrug.

"No, I don't mind. I came from a wine tasting."

"Fancy. Was he second date material?"

"He was not. He had money, but not enough that it was sufficient substitute for things like charm or morals."

"Morals," Bits repeats, like it's funny.

"Yes, morals. He had no sense of how people ought to be treated." She nods, looking at the painting in front of us, a large, drab rendering of a fox hunt. I get the sense she already knows who my date was, and is unsurprised by the result.

Dolly walks in. If we are not opposites, then we are something close to it. I've taken care to cultivate my appearance, for the entrance I make. To ensure my makeup, my posture, my hair, are all done just so, I've pored over style guides and purchased pirated online courses from finishing schools.

When Dolly enters a room, people notice, but in a different way. In a checking for security, checking exits kind of way. Dolly smiles easily, big and brash and daring you to fuck with her. Dolly walks in like she owns the place, or will own the place, whether you like it or not, and her clothing is always off by at least a slight degree. Waistband slung too low, boots too heavy, t-shirt too tight.

"Y'all like the painting?" Dolly asks, at full volume and with broadened on-purpose Southern drawl, drawing short glances and slight frowns from the other museum goers.

I cross the room to Dolly and link arms with her, smiling serenely. "You're making a scene."

"Aw, fuck 'em," Dolly says, though she lowers her voice. "You want to stay here or get something to eat?"

"We could eat at the museum restaurant." I do not care to tramp through the city to whatever food truck these two would prefer to frequent.

"Have you seen those prices?" Bits asks. "I could pay rent for a month with what they're charging for salmon."

"Salmon has become rather dear."

"Not too dear, they farm 'em in all those rice fields they got in California now. It's just artificial inflation."

"Bits, I'll buy your lunch. You will not sit at a table with us eating whatever you have squirreled away in your pockets, it's far too much."

Bits shrugs. "If you say so."

We file through the museum restaurant. I get the salad bar, and Dolly and Bits order from the holo menu. We sit down to wait.

The silverware is surprisingly heavy, like picking up a handgun for the first time. I grind some pepper on my salad and fork the lettuce around to mix the dressing. Soon, Dolly's salmon and Bits's lasagna are brought to the table. "So what do we have?" I ask. Bits reaches for her pocket and I shake my head. "Just tell us, no holos here."

"An independent dealer, with legit certificates, is bringing a bajillion carats of diamonds into town for a private showing."

"By a bajillion karats, do you mean a very large diamond, or many small ones?"

"A combination, I think. A lot of high brilliance but small gems, but a couple of big ones too. Including one of those mythic 'biggest blue diamond ever found in Shangri-la' or whatever stones."

"If it's blue, it's probably Australian or South African," I say. "Go on."

"Invitations have been sent out to some upper crusty people. Some jewelers and some private collectors. An ostrich baron. An opera singer."

"An ostrich baron?" Dolly hoots, and I shoot her a narrow-eyed look. "Sorry, it's just we've been waiting so long for the ostrich boom to happen."

"Who's we?" I ask.

"The royal we. The world."

I look at her blankly and Bits takes pity on me. "Ostriches are more green than cattle. They need less land and have a smaller carbon footprint, so somebody could do double duty raising cheap lean meat and selling their allowance of carbon certificates."

"Okay, I'll ask. Why does everybody but me know about the market demands and environmental significance of ostriches?"

"We're just more practical than you, Bristles."

"Of course." I will not comment on the unwanted nickname; it never does any good. We eat in silence until the holographic check pops up. I tap my meal and Bits's to pay. "What kind of security do they maintain?"

"The hotel security is what you'd expect, cameras and rent-a-cops with walkies. They're not going to engage, just call police. Police response to that property is inside five minutes. They have panic buttons at the front desk, and in the security office."

"And what's their network security like?"

"They have guest wireless, but all the staff stuff, cameras and reservations, is hardwired. Server is in the basement. Staff is the weak link, they prop doors to go outside and smoke all the time."

"So we need security suppressed, we need to get in that room, and we need at least two exit strategies, yes?" I finish my salad, push the bowl to the side.

"Havin' a buyer lined up might be nice," Dolly says.

I wave my hand dismissively. "I might know somebody."

"These diamonds will all have identifiers," Bits says. "Little laser etchings. Sometimes it's a barcode, sometimes a serial number."

"Once they're in a setting, nobody will ever care to check that," I say. "Or, if it is checked, years down the line when somebody gets their engagement ring cleaned or something, it isn't our problem."

"That big blue one, somebody'll recognize." Dolly pushes her own empty plate aside.

"Maybe we should ransom it," I say with a wicked smile.

"I don't want the risk of that. Too many points of contact gives them that much more intel to find us."

"Nobody's ever even gonna see you, Itsy-Bitsy," Dolly says. "You'll what, sneak in that propped door, set yourself up in a towel closet, and tap into their datastream?"

"Yeah, probably," Bits says.

"Really, we shouldn't get our hearts set on a plan until we know more about the hotel, and the meeting," I say. "And how one gets invitations."

"I'm pretty sure their guest list is set."

"*Anyway*." Dolly rolls her eyes. "Broad strokes. You get the cameras handled, Bits, then Bristol and I make our way up to the room. We bypass the locks, we get the rocks in the bag, then we split."

"Split how?" I prompt.

"Bits can commandeer the elevators, make it so we can ride one straight to the basement. There's all kinds of fire doors in a place like that, and lots of alleys beyond. Won't take long to lose anybody in the city, and then regroup."

I nod. "Okay for a plan A. Plan B?"

"I trip the alarm systems, and everybody in the hotel empties out until emergency personnel clear it. You two can walk right out the front door and into a cab or something, and I can go out the way I came. We'll be long gone before things clear up."

"Do you ever long for a personal helicopter?" I muse, pulling up the holo menu and browsing the drinks idly. I don't want more wine. Perhaps something wicked like a milkshake? But no.

"Riot gear for this, yeah?" We all have riot gear, Dolly's name for it, though it is not my preference. Ripstop cargo pants with Kevlar in the knees and shins, turtlescale longsleeved shirts—thank you NASA for that particular technology—steel shank combat boots. Jackets or utility vests optional. Assorted face masks, with rebreathers and otherwise.

"The riot gear should suffice," I sigh. "Though I *do* think I'm going to see if I can secure myself an actual invitation to the event, in which case I'll wear one of my lined dresses."

"You won't want to take all those stairs in your heels," Bits says.

"I practically live in heels, hotel stairs won't bother me in the slightest."

"If you say so." Bits drums her fingertips on the table. "We have a shopping list?"

"Other than an invitation, I'm sure I have everything I need. Dolly?"

"Might need to top off my ammo stores, but that doesn't really concern you two. What are we thinking for transport, helicopter aside?"

"The lowest profile possible, it's the one time I don't want attention. Investigate the nearby side streets and alleyways for potential getaway vehicles?"

"Already covered," Bits says.

"Perfect! We arrive separately, do our parts, and depending on how the grab strategy works out, we leave on foot to meet the car, or a well timed cab. We won't be recognizable, and it isn't as though even that many stones will be too bulky to divvy up and carry easily. Simple."

"If you wanna borrow trouble, calling a job simple is the way to do it." Dolly pays for her meal. "Let's get out of here, all this culture makes me itch."

"Perhaps you should see a doctor."

Chapter Two

If you can imagine such a thing, I do have matters on my mind other than diamond heists. My dear friend Jules is flying in from Europe to review a show, and will be available for only a handful of nights. It simply will not do to let the occasion slide, so I find myself planning a party. It won't be extravagant; just wine and cheese and some manner of dessert, perhaps petit fours.

As luck would have it, while I am feeling out prospective diamond buyers, I learn that my dear friend Marquis in fact has an invitation to the showing in question. Marquis has a penchant for saying yes to every invitation, and an inability to be in two places at once, and I video call them directly. "Darling."

"It has been far too long," they say, getting their cufflinks into place. "What have you been up to, Bristol?"

"Such dreadfully boring pursuits, I won't even drag them all out before you. Though I will be having a tiny party in the next week or so. Perhaps you'd like to attend?"

"That does sound delightful." Marquis finishes their cuffs, looking at the screen intently. "I'm on my way to a show now, though. I haven't got much time to talk. Can I call you later? Or we can have coffee tomorrow?"

"Of course, I don't want to keep you."

"Good. I'll come around at ten for you. We'll go to the place beneath the aquarium, that we might have coffee and croissants in the presence of giants."

"In the presence of giants?"

"Well *a* giant. That old blind whale that I'm sure they just can't release anywhere, and so instead it looms endlessly over the cafe."

"Oh the poor thing, if we must. At ten, then." Marquis makes a kissy face and ends the call.

The next morning, I select my outfit with the care necessary to make it look thrown together. Polished cognac leather boots, knee high over black leggings, with a tunic length charcoal sweater and a large leather handbag, which complements the boots without matching them exactly. No diamonds in my jewelry, I don't have very many anyway, and I pull my hair back in a sort of messy bun.

"You're a vision," Marquis says, as we kiss cheeks.

"Oh please. My wardrobe doesn't begin to approach yours, for one." Marquis is wearing another of their signature tailored shirts, a different set of cufflinks, very dark washed skinny jean, and boots as well, but the kind designed to remain artfully untied instead of the slovenly way Dolly's sometimes do.

"One day, my dear, I'll get you on a runway," Marquis says.

"I'm not tall enough," I laugh, and Marquis hands me into the back seat of their car to cross town. Their driver wears a cap like the olden days, and thin leather driving gloves, and behaves as though he never hears a word we say. Sometimes it is a fun game to try and see if we can get a reaction from him, but this isn't the current mood. "You've been working too hard," I say.

"I am. It's so hard to get reliable help at the gallery. Are you sure you won't come work for me?"

"Oh, we would never be able to stay friends this way if I did. So I'm sorry, no. Though there must be some other way I can help." We arrive at the coffee shop, and the whale tank is a monstrosity. I wonder whatever possessed them to build it in the first place. We order our coffees and pastries and settle into a cozy corner table.

"This is more business than pleasure, then," Marquis says, sipping their tall and elaborate coffee drink, resplendent with syrups and a fluffy expanse of foamed milk.

"I do think the two can exist side by side," I say, wringing out the lemon slice into my espresso.

"Of course you do, and really, you aren't entirely wrong." Marquis blows on the foam on top of their drink, causing a tiny sinkhole. "But I know what type of business you do."

"Well yes. I hold you in the utmost of confidences; a girl can't keep secrets from her closest friends, it would simply drive me mad." I glance up at the whale, its inexorable pace. It reminds me of a dream I'd had in the midst of some childhood fever, where everything was moving but at a sliding freefall, not as quickly as it should be, but inevitable as death. Perhaps this was the wrong place to have come with Marquis at all, much less to discuss a successful diamond grab.

"Shall I guess what you want out of this?"

"If you'd like to make a game of it. I could just tell you."

Marquis smiles slyly. "No, I think I have it. Does it have to do with what else might be a girl's best friend?"

"It does." The whale flicks a fin.

"How did you know I'd get an invite?"

"It would be very crass for me to reveal my secrets."

"Of course." We sip our drinks in companionable silence. "You realize I can't be involved, so if you take my invitation, you yourself have to remain the picture of innocence."

"Of course. Putting you in danger is the last thing I want. And really, it'll be safer for my people if somebody is on the inside, counting noses and assessing threats."

"You just have an aversion to cargo pants." Marquis shakes their head, smiling.

"I haven't the hips for them, though I did just buy the most darling pair of black velvet combat boots."

"You'll have my invitation," Marquis says. "And yes, it is a help. That social obligation was a dreadful sword of Damocles, and I know you can act in my interests, which in this case is just making polite conversation and drinking bubbly. I had no intention of making any purchases."

"Yes, I'll make sure your reputation remains spotless. Thank you, Marquis."

"You're welcome, my dear." Marquis reaches over and peels a piece off of my croissant. "I shall notify the hosts you'll be taking my place, and send my invitation over to you."

"That sounds perfect." I look up; the whale has moved on to another portion of the tank and I can only see a swimmy white slice of the overcast sky up through the water. It's less of a relief than I thought it would be.

Of course, Dolly and Bits will be miffed that I've gone ahead and changed the plan, but I did warn them. Once Marquis and I leave each other, I send them requests to meet up after dark at a diner near to where Dolly may or may not be based. The sooner I might inform them, the better, that they might have time to air their frustrations before the job is at hand.

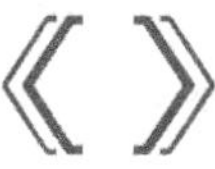

I DRAW LOOKS IN THE diner; it is a more working class establishment than I am used to and I seem misplaced. Only a few other people are here, some coffee-drinking political arguers at the counter, an older couple having the dinner special. I sit at a window booth with my thick ceramic mug of coffee and wait for the girls, who arrive together. I wonder if they spend much recreational time together, or if they were just engaged in all of their tiresome equipment checks. They slide into the booth across from me and the waitress appears with more coffee.

"So what's the new plan?" Dolly asks, sighing as she leans back with her arms folded.

"You can come up through a side door, I'll have already sabotaged the door lock and assessed private security, you burst in and pull the holdup."

"So you'll drink and hobnob with the rich folks while Bits and me do the work," Dolly says flatly.

I sigh slightly, trying not to think about the nameless stickiness of the floor beneath the soles of my boots. "I'll be keeping business relations smooth for Marquis, making sure the diamonds are what we thought they were and thus worth taking. I'm at most risk here, in that I'll be spending lots of time with both our victims and the authorities once they arrive. But by all means, Dolly, tell me again how your five minutes of shock and awe is far more risky and difficult than my role."

"If it's that bad, why offer to do it?" Bits asks. She's been putting one packet of sweetener after the other into her coffee, stirring, sampling it.

"It's worth the risk. I can handle it. And it's the way that makes Marquis seem blameless in this, and that's important to me."

"None of the rest of us were interested in involving Marquis," Dolly says. "Never even told us you were gonna."

"I'm sure I mentioned something to the effect." The waitress comes by with the coffee pot to top us all off, and Bits orders a stack of pancakes, Dolly some kind of hash.

"The circles you talk, you could've mentioned a pleasure cruise to Venus and we'd never question you. It takes its toll." She grins. She's still angry, but I've already won, of course.

"I didn't mean to make decisions without you and get anybody upset. It'll be alright, you'll see. And I have a line on a buyer as well. Bits, I've sent you the information."

"Received." She pauses a moment, looking at something in AR. "So are we set *now?*"

"Yes. We have a magnificent plan, cross my heart I will change nothing."

"If you say so," Dolly grumbles. "Though I swear, Bristles, if we agree to this and you call us tomorrow with another idea..."

"I won't, Dolly. Pinky swear." I smile and hold out my hand, and Dolly pushes it away.

"Sure, whatever. Bits, you're okay with this?"

"It's probably the best plan we've come up with. And by we I mean Bristol. I didn't have a better plan. It keeps us all safe, more or less, with minimal exposure. Dolly, do you even have nonlethal..."

"Yeah, I have a beanbag shotgun, and there's these weird compression gel things they have for handguns that I haven't tried yet. The magazines come preloaded. I'm surprised you even know about them, Bristol."

"I know about any number of things." I sip my coffee and stifle my grimace.

Chapter Three

I do not receive Marquis' invitation; the diamond sellers send me a fresh one, on actual paper with a digital chip in it which both verifies my currently claimed identity and plays a holographic display of the diamonds which will be offered for sale. I spend some time playing with the holograph, making the diamonds larger and smaller. The blue one really is breathtaking. And selling the lot, even at a cut black market rate, will be a tidy sum.

I dress with particular care, making sure the bionic earbuds are set properly, that there are no hitches in the turtlescale armor running like tulle through my just-understated-enough party dress. I have yet to be shot, and hope to continue that trend, though I would rather be protected than not. My stockings are not bullet or stab proof, but they can resist heat, flame, and chemicals. One heel sheaths a ceramic blade.

My gold jewelry was not my mother's, nor my grandmother's before her, though that's what I tell people about my simple pendant and chain, and dangling drop earrings. It's a pretty fiction. Where I come from, we have no heirlooms, no family touchstones.

I sweep my hair into a French twist. The hairpin has a tiny vial of pepper spray in the handle, and will separate into another blade if need be. I do hope there is no need.

I am not a gunner like Dolly, and I'm not an expert in knife fighting, but I have my tricks. Playing upon the unexpected nature of a sudden offense is a large part of my arsenal; nobody expects a girl like me to be able to fight back.

My purse contains the usual things, wallet with physical ID, a secondary phone to use for show, a variety of lipsticks, one of which is an explosive gel, my favorite way to manage small difficulties like door locks. My main phone is a slim and chic bracelet that Bits finagled for me, surrounded and camouflaged by other thin golden charm bracelets.

I stop at the hotel front desk with my thick paper invitation. The clerk scans the embedded microchip and directs me to the proper elevator. Once I'm alone again, Bits's whispery voice comes through my earbud. "Swanky. This must be where the mayor comes with his flings. Security is all contained with the building. The lines out are billing, emergency, and regular telecommunications."

"What does that mean for us?" I ask as I fix my lipstick in the elevator's mirrored wall.

"Nothing yet. Might make it easier to keep security away from you and Dolly. Well. Dolly. Or it might make it so if she gets caught—if *we* get caught—they can do whatever they want without the police ever knowing."

"Well." I don't have much to say to that.

"Right?" Bits laughs wryly. "So don't get us caught, okay?"

"I'll do my very best." I uncap the gel stick and work it into a wad. When the elevator reaches my floor it slides open with a pleasant tone, as though one had just climbed some serene mountain and hammered the gong at the top. The suite is at the entire opposite end of the hallway, the fire door halfway between the two.

I knock, and a very large man in a nice suit opens the door. The walls behind him are entirely glass, looking out over the city lights strewn like diamonds across the landscape. The other invitees are in various stages of being seated in a sunken living room, and I can smell the leather of the furniture from the doorway. "Oh, I do hope I'm not too late," I say in a very slight fluster, as though I've been rushing, and I make a show of juggling my purse and lipsticks about, pressing the gel into the doorjamb when that large man looks away in exasperation. "I didn't mean to keep anybody waiting."

The diamond seller is easy enough to pick out, classic briefcase cuffed to his left wrist. Also among the attendees are a trio of women so liberally draped in diamonds I can't imagine they're here to buy anything, and a handful of men in nondescript suits. It's simply the trend of men's clothing; the more expensive it is, the more plain it becomes. I do wonder if the ostrich rancher is attending, and which one he is. It seems gauche to ask; I shall have to consider shoes closely.

"Please, have a seat. May I bring you refreshment?" The barman is the right level of welcoming and attentive. Also armed. With a slight thrill, fear or excitement, I wonder if this diamond party is more than we had considered. But it is also the most appealing job we've had in a very long time.

"It might be wicked of me, but I would like some of that champagne, if somebody would share it with me. I'd hate to have a bottle opened only on my account."

"What are you celebrating?" one of the men asks. He's the right type, not too young, not yet old enough to start graying.

"Do I need to celebrate anything in particular? There's this lovely gathering, our beautiful view..." I turn to gesture, as the champagne cork is popped, and recognize one of the women from a gallery opening, I think. One of the other men is the opera singer. These are people with the means to buy diamonds, surely, though not the inclination.

"We may as well get on with it," one of the women says, turning to the man with the briefcase. She has no refreshments, and her shoes are a bit too serviceable to be partywear.

The man who'd spoken to me accepted a champagne flute, and I take my own and perch on the arm of his chair. He is *very* handsome, dashing and dark-featured like the old movies. "Just spectating, or are you a buyer?" he asks in a low voice as the man with the briefcase prepares the table.

"Oh just spectating," I say with a smile.

"Same. I heard the blue one was impressive, but those holos were on another level." He looks out of his element, and I try to picture what his element is. Yacht club? Board room? Neither seem to quite match.

"It was a very nice touch," I say.

"Will," he says, offering his hand.

"Chelsea." I clasp his hand in the barest of shakes, and he takes the invitation correctly, brushing the back of my hand with his lips. I smile and ignore Bits's snickering in my ears. Chelsea isn't my name any more than Bristol is, of course, but it's the fake identity I inhabit when dealing with people in legitimate business. Any of my accounts for the future are in another name entirely, offshore and DNA locked.

"I don't think I've seen you around," he says, and the corner of his mouth twitches. He's used to having better lines, I think.

"No, this was a rare opportunity for me." I lean in a little closer to him, catch the whiff of clean and oceanic aftershave from his neck and jaw. "This isn't one of those dreadful bidding situations, is it?" I ask, sotto voce.

"No, this is the showing. Any actual money will exchange hands at a later date."

"There's only so many ways to arrange shiny rocks on black velvet," the older woman snaps. "Any day now Richard."

"Yes, Mrs. Carter," Richard of the now no longer handcuffed briefcase says. "Ladies and gentlemen, if you would step over here into the better light, so you can view the color and clarity of the stones.

These here, the ones set in the briefcase, are the master stones against which you may check the clear ones." Then, with a small amount of ceremony which draws a derisive sniff from Mrs. Carter, he pulls the blue diamond from another compartment in the briefcase and lays it slightly apart. "With colored stones, as I'm sure you know, that isn't how the grading works. But you've already received the holographic information regarding the authenticity and grading of this particular stone."

Mrs. Carter, that overachiever, is already reaching for the blue stone. Her clothing is so gaudy it can only be designer, though perhaps she isn't dressing in a way that best shows her qualities.

"And the provenance of all of these gems are legitimate?" One of the other men asks. He fiddles with an e cigarette, as though he isn't sure if anybody would object to his using it.

"There are varying levels of legitimate, Nathan," Mrs. Carter says dismissively. I get the sense this Mrs. Carter intends to purchase the lot, and simply arranged this get together for the theater of it.

"Some more savory than others," he says.

"Do you really want to bring up blood diamonds here and now?" she asks.

"I suppose not." He puts the e cigarette back into its little leather case and tucks it inside his jacket pocket.

In my earbud, Bits says "Sorry, Dolly's almost there."

"Thank you," I say, both to answer Bits and to accept another glass of bubbly. The guardsman is to the side of the door, and at a glance seems mildly bored and mostly centered on Richard the diamond seller, which is curious. Perhaps if I could place Richard's accent, or Mrs. Carter's, it would be clearer to me. "Won't you have anything?" I call lightly. "It's hard to enjoy champagne with people who aren't imbibing. You're not lonely over there, by the door?"

"No, miss," he answers shortly. "No drinking on the job."

"Right," I say, both because it makes sense and because he sits to the right of the door.

"Thanks," Dolly says, finally online with the rest of us. "There are some interesting cars in the lot. Fancy ones of course, but I swear, at least one is unmarked government, which probably means it's more like three."

I look around the room again. That could be another explanation for Mrs. Carter; she's a spy, and every little bit of her appearance has been cultivated for the reactions received. Appearances are very important, and realities are hard to discern, socially, virtually. It occurs to me that my close companion's tie pin looks rather like one of Bit's littlest cameras, and from my vantage, I can see the curve his earbud. But if this is some manner of deeply shadowed government thing... I set my champagne glass down and try to formulate how to make my exit, how to say the magic words which will pull the plug on this job—and then comes the hushed noise which means the gel in the doorjamb has received its little remote electrical charge. Nobody in the room seems to register the noise.

Mrs. Carter is once again examining the blue diamond. The men have moved away a bit, so Will and I have a place at the table to look at the smaller, clear stones. They are remarkable, and I wistfully poke a finger at their bright hard glitter. They would make glorious jewelry in single settings or in an extravagant cascade across a woman's bared clavicle. They will more than likely live in the dark, in black velvet boxes locked away in a bank vault, or a hidden wall safe behind some country manor style paintings in their tiresome gilt frames.

And the blue one... I lean forward a little to get a better look. It's hard to even describe the color. Like the sky after a hard rain, thinned out and scrubbed clean. Mrs. Carter gives me a warning look and I give her an innocent eyed, polite smile before turning to Will. I don't get a chance to speak, though, as the door kicks in at that moment, striking the wall behind it.

Even prepared to see Dolly in her riot gear, it is a startling moment, and I jump and gasp with the rest of them, reflexively clutching at Will's sleeve. Dolly is swiftly in the room, sweeping it with her shotgun. She circles hard to the side when the door slams shut, the guard gaining his feet, knocking his chair over. "On the ground," Dolly says. She isn't yelling, but her gas mask dehumanizes her voice. "Keep your hands clear." The guard doesn't look at Dolly, he looks at Mrs. Carter, who is frozen with such a look of hate and disgust on her face that I can only study her for a moment. She seems affronted, not frightened.

Nobody moves for a very long time, and I wonder if I'll have to step in, but then Dolly racks her shotgun. Mrs. Carter nods. "Do what they say," she says, glaring daggers. The guard sinks to his knees, then lowers his front to the floor. She stares at the barman until he does so as well.

"Start bagging up the merchandise," Dolly barks at Richard, throwing a black duffle bag on the floor.

"It'll be okay," Will murmurs, and I wonder for a mad moment who he's talking to, then realize he's looking at me. I'm still gripping his suit sleeve, and he's put his hand over mine. I make a show of trying to take a deep calming breath, wide eyed, and nod at him. He smiles reassuringly.

Richard moves slowly, putting the diamonds into their velvet bags, into larger bags, and then as a man walking through deep wet sand goes to the duffle on the floor. He places the diamonds within and steps back. "I think you forgot one," Dolly says. "Maybe you should double check." Mrs. Carter still holds the blue diamond in her manicured, cocktail ringed hand, where it catches the light and looks like a trapped fairy. Richard looks at Mrs. Carter, and then at Dolly pleadingly. He starts to speak, his shoulders rising, and Dolly draws her handgun with her left hand to point at him, shotgun straining against its strap, still trained on the guard. She doesn't look at me. "Go on."

Richard walks back to the table even more slowly, and picks up the velvet bag for the blue diamond. He holds it out to Mrs. Carter. "I'm sorry," he says, almost inaudibly.

"There are ways to come back from this," Mrs. Carter says in a tone that seems, for her, strangely human. "Young lady, I hope you know what you're doing."

"Well, I'd hardly tell you if I felt unsure," Dolly says with a laugh in her voice. Once the blue diamond is in the duffle, she tells Richard: "Now zip 'em up nice, thanks. No sense dropping it all on my way out." The gas mask turns and seems to consider each individual thoughtfully. "Take out your phones and drop them on top of the duffle." Nobody moves. "Now!" she barks.

There are enough people in the room to overwhelm Dolly. I hope nobody will try. The phones are dropped, one by one, including the one from my purse. Dolly considers each person again, then moves slowly to the duffle. Letting the shotgun drop on its sling, she picks the bag up on her right arm. The big door guard comes up off the floor as soon as the shotgun muzzle is no longer on the invited guests, and almost without looking, Dolly pulls the trigger on her handgun and he drops, clutching at his neck, red-faced and breathing like a freight train, compression gel rounds bouncing to the floor. The movies don't really represent just how loud a gun is. Even mentally prepared for a gunshot, they still make me shaky. Thankfully, the earbuds afford quite a lot of protection, though there's still a distant ringing in my head.

Dolly backs to the door, still brandishing the pistol. "Anybody else?" Nobody else rises to the occasion. The other women are quietly weeping, and Mrs. Carter looks as though you could milk venom from her, like a snake. "Smart crowd. You'll find your phones, eventually. I won't even look at 'em. Have a good evening now." And then she pulls the door closed behind her; the explosive gel will keep it sealed for a time.

"Oh my God," I say, letting my knees waver. Will still has my hand, and puts his other arm around my waist, guiding me to his former chair.

"I'm going to check on Clancy," he says, and the fact that the big man's name is Clancy makes me laugh, and I try to put as hysterical a note in it as possible. Mrs. Carter looks at me, practically rolls her eyes. Good. Better to be thought a flighty young thing than a suspect.

"Call the front desk," Mrs. Carter orders the barman.

"Yes ma'am." He picks up the room phone, presses a few buttons, then shakes his head. "No ringtone."

"Does anybody still have a phone?" Mrs. Carter asks. Richard, sly Richard, returns to his now empty briefcase and pulls the bottom out, revealing a small folding model. "Call the police," she says. "There's still time."

"How will the police catch them?" I ask wildly. "The police won't see where they went! It's not like they'll still be dressed like a diamond thief by the time they're out of the hotel!"

"Reading you loud and clear," Dolly says in my ear.

"Calm down," Mrs. Carter says sharply. "Stop crying," she snaps at the women, who sniffle wetly and wipe their eyes.

"He's okay," Will says, to the room. Clancy is struggling back into movement already, and tries to shrug Will off when he makes the first attempt to gain his feet. Will holds onto him with startling ease and gets him standing. "Take it easy."

The pounding begins at the door. By the time the hotel staff gets the door open, police will have arrived—detectives and patrolmen and all of it. I settle in for a long evening.

Chapter Four

It is entirely typical for the girls and I to not have contact for a few days after pulling a job; Bits and Dolly think it increases our security. I put the heist out of my mind, for the most part, and concentrate on readying my apartment for the party. Marquis shows up early on the day of, while I'm getting dressed.

"Why didn't you call me about the other night?" they demand, enveloping me in a hug at the same time.

"The police said not to talk about it, actually," I say. "Oh, and I met somebody."

"You met somebody?"

"He was there too, and was very nice before, and very comforting after. The only person who got the slightest bit hurt was the large meaty guard, Clancy, if you can imagine such a name. And I think he was mostly embarrassed."

"You do find yourself in the most interesting situations," Marquis says. "What will you wear tonight?" they ask, watching me pin my hair up.

"The patterned mauve and white dress, I think. Unless you see something you think would be preferable?"

Marquis glances over the dresses hanging in my wardrobe. "The mauve and white is charming enough."

"I hoped you'd say so." I pull the door partially closed for modesty's sake, and step into the party dress. "Zip me?"

"Did you get to see the diamonds, at least? Was the blue one magnificent?"

"They were all magnificent. It was strange, though, it seemed like most of the people there were just set dressing, not there with the slightest interest in buying. They barely looked at the stones. I'm not certain of Will, either, whether he was an innocent like me or another prop."

"Your innocence is without question, I'm sure. When are you seeing this Will again?"

"In a few days. He's taking me for coffee. Not at the whale cafe, before you ask."

"I didn't think you liked it."

"No, not really. I'm surprised you noticed."

"You're an open book to me," Marquis says, and I smile.

"Why would I expect any less?"

It's lovely having Marquis help with the final setup details, and tweak a few of the things I'd struggled with. My apartment is not large, and I deliberately don't have much furniture, but there is always a better way to arrange things, especially through a gallery owner's eyes. We drink wine spritzers and fix each other's makeup, and then the food delivery arrives, all easily managed finger food.

My guests are all people in the right sort of scene, the beautiful people who are just artsy enough to be interesting, some of whom just rich enough to be very generous with it. They arrive at the proper stages of lateness, some bringing bottles.

An alert blinks on my phone while I'm talking to my dear friend Josie, a ballet dancer who's just come off tour. "Excuse me," I say. "I'm sorry, my neighbor loses her keys all the time."

"Of course," she says, and we air kiss before she's called over to another knot of people.

I finger wave at Marquis on my way out the door, keys jingling in my other hand. How delightfully kitsch is it that my building is still physically keyed?

Down the hall, the elevator dings and Bits gets off, slouching in cargo pants and a hoodie. By the way the hoodie bulks, she's wearing a bulletproof vest under it. "What are you *doing* here?" I hiss, catching her by the arm and pulling her into the doorway of the floor's vacant apartment.

"We've got a problem," Bits says. Her hands are balled into fists, still jammed into the pockets of her hoodie. "A big enough problem that I needed to tell you face to face, not in a digital message where we could be heard."

"What are you talking about? I can't deal with this right—"

"Stop being a prima donna for a second and listen to me. The diamonds. Remember how we talked about how each diamond would have a barcode serial marker on it, for authenticity?"

"Yes." I glance back down the hallway. It's empty, my door still closed. "Why?"

"That's not what's in the barcodes of these diamonds."

I look at Bits, but her facial expression is rarely of any help. I can tell she's scared right now, but not how scared, on a scale of spiders to snipers. "What do you mean? What is it?"

"I don't know exactly, I don't have the right kind of reader. But it's some kind of encrypted data, and they may or may not be able to track it."

"What do you mean? Like RFID?"

"Maybe. It's a good guess, anyway. So I put them in an aluminum case, to cut that off. And they're...someplace safe right now. But we need to sell them quick, if it's not already be too late."

"Too late for what?"

"They might know already who we are. Where we are."

I stare at her. Open my mouth, close it. I want to tell her not to be silly. But of course they already know where I am. They sent me an invitation. Down the hall, the elevator chimes as it descends floors. "Can they do that?" I ask finally.

"I wouldn't be here if they couldn't."

"Did you tell Dolly?"

"Yeah. She's in the car."

"I can't just leave! My apartment is full of people."

"That's good, you know nobody'll expect you to leave. You have a balcony? Go get changed and then come on."

"This is just unheard of. And no, no I don't have a balcony."

"Go." For once, Bits locks eyes with me, and her gaze does not waver. The elevator chimes again, on its way back up, and I turn and hurry back to my apartment.

"Is everything okay?" Marquis asks once I slip back inside.

"Just fine, darling," I say, smiling tightly. "I do need to make some adjustments, though. My underpinnings just will not stay where they belong."

"Isn't that a trial." Marquis sails off to speak with a man at the cheese and grape plate who wears tremendous spectacles which do not seem technologically augmented in any way.

I go to my room, blessedly empty, and shut the door behind me, locking it slowly and with care so that the little click isn't heard by those nearest. I shuck off my party dress and don my riot gear, rummage in the bottom of my closet for what Dolly calls the bug-out bag. I sweep everything from my vanity into my makeup bag and jewelry box and jam them into the bug out bag. The knock on my apartment door reverberates all the way to my bedroom and I freeze, every nerve alight.

"Don't worry about it," Marquis calls out, and I clap a hand over my mouth to keep from calling out, from stopping them. I open my window and toss the bag down to Dolly, waiting on the sidewalk.

Then I step back to my room door, velvet boots silent on the plush carpet.

Nobody seems to be alarmed, and there isn't much break in the conversations. I can hear both Marquis and whoever is at the door, though I can't make out what they're saying. I debate going back out to the party, trying to handle whoever is at the door. Dolly will be impatient, Bits is already in panic mode. I return to the window and look out.

When I selected my third floor apartment, I hadn't really considered a window exit. The neighbors have constructed a makeshift balcony just below me, however, a rickety eyesore made from chicken wire and pallets, and after a moment of psyching myself up, I stop thinking about it and climb out the window, hang by my hands, and drop. The balcony dips like a diving board and then holds, quivering. I climb over the edge and drop to the sidewalk, heart in my throat. Through the open window above, I hear a banging on my room door, an insistent pounding which suggests a polite knock was tried first. My wrist vibrates minutely beneath my glove; it's Marquis, I'm sure, and I hope they will understand. Dolly has me by the arm and drags me into the car. Bits is behind the wheel, gearshift already in drive, and starts moving before the door can close properly.

My wrist vibrates again, and again, and then it seems I hear a shout on the street, but I'm not sure exactly. And then Bits turns the corner down the block.

Chapter Five

"How long have you two had something like this planned?" I ask. Our safehouse is a refurbished shipping container in a sort of no man's land on the fringe of the city, between the river and several industrial parks which seem to be run entirely by robots and drones.

"I started to do it little by little once we started making money," Bits says. "We just haven't had to go to ground like this before."

"Who built it? You? Do we have to worry about other people knowing?"

"There are people who do this kind of thing, in many locations. I had it moved by drone freight after they built it."

"How do you even get wireless in here? This whole thing is beyond bizarre." I realize I've been pacing, stop. I read Marquis' messages over and over.

//Hey, open up.//

//Are you okay?//

//Wait, where are you?//

//What's going on?//

//Who are these people?//

//Call me.//

//Call me. I'm worried.//

//You need to think about what's going to happen.//

And last, but not least ominous: //They're willing to make a deal.//

"They won't do anything to Marquis," Bits says with her mouth full. There's a hot plate and enough instant ramen to choke anybody who cared less about the quality of their food than the quality of their gadgets. I think of the party food at my apartment, think about Marquis, who is probably one of my best friends in the whole world—or at least in town—and sigh.

"I certainly hope not. Marquis was on the original guest list."

"But if you think the whole showing was a coverup for the couple of people actually involved in whatever those diamonds actually are, then that won't matter and they'll realize it pretty quick," Dolly points out.

"In a perfect world," I say. *They're willing to make a deal.* "Bits, you still have no idea what the stones actually are?"

"They're actually diamonds. I just don't know what's encoded on them and haven't broken the encryption yet."

"Can't you hack it or whatever?" I wave my hand. I understand basic computer usage, my phone, household gadgets, I press buttons and they do what they're supposed to. Whatever it is Bits does when she puts that headset on is entirely beyond me, a completely different world.

"Well yeah, I'm working on it, but I need to figure out the right program, and then the right algorithms to start trying. At least the data seems static, like messing with it isn't going to erase it or do anything else terrible."

"All right, then what?"

"I guess it depends on what kind of a deal they wanna make," Dolly says. She flops onto her back on one of the fold-up futons. "They probably assume we don't have a way to find out what's encrypted on the diamonds, and they'll just offer us a chunk of change to go away. Not that I'm suggesting we work with The Man or whoever."

"More like they'll just find us and shoot us," Bits says. "Disappear us."

"I wish I knew who 'they' were, so I could refute that," I sigh. "And we just left Marquis there."

"If we'd taken the time for Marquis we wouldn't be able to have this conversation," Bits says.

"We need to—"

"We need to be goddamn careful," Dolly says. "We go out there, the crosswalk cameras will get us on the facial rec right off. Or an ATM. Or a car with a dash cam, anything."

"I'm amazed you haven't learned the benefits of these," I say, leaning over to rummage in my bag. I pull out a big square patterned scarf, large enough to cover my bare shoulders in a rain if I need it.

"I'm proud of you, learning anarchic hacker tricks." Bits grins.

"Oh, it's one of those things." Dolly doesn't like being reminded of what she already knows. I'd guess she probably has a dreadful hoodie.

"It's a matter of survival. I have several in the bag, we can each have one."

"Nah, you're the one who pulls off the starlet in a scarf look," Dolly says. "Okay, so what's the plan then? Or a first step?" We all look at each other.

"Well, I already contacted Bristol's diamond guy," Bits ventures. "Before all this went down. He might not want them now, once he sees the serial numbers aren't serial numbers." She looks down at her tablet, taps a few things. Her headset is still in its case; that's reassuring, if paranoid Bits doesn't think she needs to all-senses monitor our security situation. "We're still clear."

"If he might not want them, is it worth the risk trying to meet up?" Bits just looks at me. "Okay, or what about this: Is the fact that they're willing to make a deal an option at all?"

"It might be if we knew who 'they' were," Dolly says. "If this is Columbian drug lord shit, then no, there's no way we'll walk out of a meeting like that alive. If it's Americans recovering agent intel or something, then yeah, that's fine."

"You don't want to work with The Man but you still trust our 'Man' over any other?" I ask. Dolly shrugs, investigates the ramen options. "I think we've watched too many movies."

"What we should've done is gone to ground immediately," Bits says. "The sale was weird enough to begin with. Just a happy accident that you had a big party afterwards."

"The party has been scheduled for months," I sniff, shaking my head.

"They'll know that too."

Dolly throws her hands in the air. "Stop being so fucking ominous, Bits, they gotta have a reason to look and find out. They're not just omnipotent or omnipresent or whichever other one of those you wanna add."

"How do you know they aren't?"

"Okay. So I think we're agreeing to just try and sell the cursed things as planned?" I ask.

"Yeah, sounds like," Dolly says after a moment's pause.

"I'll message him again," Bits says. "And we should all try to get some sleep, it's late."

I'm awake in the dark for a very long time. Neither of the others make much noise, Bits fusses around on her gadgets for quite a while before all is finally silent.

Chapter Six

"I hope you know what you're doing, Miss Bristol," Baxter says. According to the peeling sign hung on his door he's a lawyer, but what Baxter really does is buy things.

"Have I ever given you reason to doubt me?" I ask as I settle myself in a seat, resisting the urge to spread a handkerchief there first. Bits places one of the little velvet bags on his desk.

"I can't say that you have, no. But this is a bigger haul than I expected from you." Baxter picks up the bag, pours some of the stones into his palm. His hands are improbably clean, nails trimmed and buffed. "How many bags of these did you say you have?"

"Four small bags like that, and then the pièce de résistance, a large blue stone."

"Lots of rocks. A big blue, you say? That one might give me trouble. We'll see." Baxter shakes his head, and spreads the diamonds in a velvet tray on top of his desk. He opens one of the drawers and pulls out a tablet with a sort of stylus plugged into it, which glows faintly green on the end when he clicks a button. "We'll find out together," he says. His eyes skim over Bits, and settle on Dolly for a moment. We're all still in riot gear, more or less, though I've unbuttoned my vest for comfort and rolled my pants legs. "Interesting cadre." I see no reason to answer. He fits a jeweler's loupe in his eye, and when he presses a button on that as well, it makes a small, high pitched noise. The lenses audibly adjust in the quiet room.

He spends some moments wanding over different parts of the diamonds and squinting, tilting his head this way and that. Then Baxter goes still.

Baxter pulls off the loupe and sweeps the diamonds back into their little bag. He shoves the bag, the tray, and both the wand and loupe at Bits.

"What is it?" I ask, getting to my feet even before Dolly does.

"Take it and get out of here. I don't even want to use equipment that's touched that."

"But what's wrong?"

"I've seen that encryption before. The stones aren't from Africa." I open my mouth to speak, but he screeches his chair back and comes around the desk, herding us out of the room like sheep, his arms spread wide. "Please, leave. Keep those in a Faraday box if you have one. If you don't have one, get one. Especially the big blue rock. I'll pretend I don't know anything when they come."

"Who's going to come?" Dolly digs her heels in, tries to pause on the foyer.

"I'm surprised they're not here already," he says, and slams the door hard enough that the sign falls onto the ground.

"Well that was...productive," I say, settling my scarf as we hurry down the cracked sidewalk to the car.

"I got some tech out of the deal, anyway," Bits says dubiously, closing her door behind her.

"Yes, we can read the information now, anyway. I've never seen him act like that, but I'm certain he'll be just fine. Baxter is used to getting rolled up with whatever investigations brush by him. I guess he got a law degree online?"

"Maybe he got it that one time he actually went to prison," Dolly says, pulling carefully into traffic. I twist in my seat to look out the back windshield past Bits, but no flashing lights or helicopters descend upon the block we've just left.

"It hardly matters now. We can wait for Bits to break the encryption and we can then decide what to do about them." Marquis hasn't texted me since last night, and it's taken all of my restraint to not text back.

"You really think the government is going to pay for them instead of just arresting us and packing us off to some mystical terrorist camp like Gitmo? Do they still have Gitmo?" Dolly asks.

"They say they don't, but whether they do or not isn't the point. There's always a Gitmo and there's always terrorists. It's integral to the nation's dialogue at this point."

"I swear, Bristles, you're involved in politics."

"She's not," Bits says quietly.

"I'm not, I promise. It's just politicians have the nicest parties, and like drinking around pretty girls while buying them drinks."

"Sure," Dolly says. Traffic thins, and Bits gets more and more edgy as we become the only car on the road. She looks around frequently, checking her tablet.

As we come to the last turn she says, "Cameras show nothing, and have shown nothing. Nobody followed us. But we'll have to leave after tonight."

"Yeah. Good," Dolly says. Once we're inside, she asks, "So what's the real problem here, other than that we stole a bunch of diamonds we can't sell? Is it Russia? Isn't Russia our ally?"

"Russia's always our allies, and then not, and then allies again. They just had a summit within the last couple of weeks. Nuclear power sanctions again. Trade sanctions, to do with human rights."

"Russia still uses old style reactors," Bits mutters.

"So what would be on the diamonds?" Dolly asks. "And were there Russians at the showing the other night? It didn't sound like it."

"I didn't think so either." Though my ear for accents could use some more work.

"Great, then it's some black ops bullshit we got ourselves in." Dolly shakes her head, but she's grinning, like this all has become more exciting than she could have hoped.

"Let's just get the data so we're aware of the decision we're making. I know a lot of people. *We* know a lot of people. We can find another buyer, I'm sure of it. Is that okay Bits? How long will that take you?"

"I have no idea," Bits says. She's already set herself up with a tray table at one of the futons and is in the process of scanning the first diamond, a plug running from the tablet to the loupe and then from the loupe to her headset. "I'll let you know when I think we need to move."

"I just want to know what kind of a world this is, where it's easier to move *diamonds* than *data*?" Dolly says. "Data's everywhere, speed of light, invisible."

"We're all living in surveillance states," Bits says. "And the diamond industry is one of the weird corners of it. Probably the certificates for these diamonds are real, and they had somebody like me layer the data into the etching. It's fucking elegant work."

"Of all the private diamond sales in all the cities in all the world," I say, but I'm the only one who's seen Casablanca.

We sit in silence for *hours*. Bits works with a concentration that cannot be broken. Dolly seems to fall asleep, and I occupy myself with magazines I've saved on my phone. It is with effort that I don't check the news, text anybody, call anybody just for the idle chatter of it. I spend so much of my time in idle chatter.

We all have a breaking point, though. "So it figures that I'm the one to bring it up, but are either of y'all bored?" Dolly asks. "I mean, other than the big ol' fearing for our mortal lives thing, this is kinda boring."

"It is," I sigh. "I can't spend endless time on the internet like Bits, and I'm not allowed to message anybody, and this is hardly a setup I can turn into a spa day. No offense."

"None taken," Bits says. "I've never had a spa day in my life."

"You should, they're absolutely divine!"

"Yeah I never have either," Dolly says.

"Bits, can't we do *something*? I know you don't want us to come and go to much—I understand that, I really do—but at least you've had the diamonds to occupy you..."

Bits pushes her headset up onto the top of her head, looks between Dolly and I. She hesitates, and I think she's going to make one of her very adult and reasonable arguments how, for safety and security's sake, we have to stay here and be as quiet as church mice, and we can just do something tomorrow once we change locations. I try to anticipate her argument, formulate a response regarding just how innocuous it would be for us to go to a convenience store, or even a food truck, something, anything in the world. The three of us are simply too small in this big city to be so easily tracked. In fact, with the diamonds all boxed up, they may never track us again.

But Bits knows we're up against the boundaries of Dolly containment. "So what do you want to do?" she asks finally. "Neither of you plays video games, or I'd say we can go to this underground arcade. It's dark out now, and they're safe people. I trust them. One last trip isn't going to be the dealbreaker."

"An arcade would be fun," I say. I can people watch in an arcade, at the very least, and Dolly can shoot things. "Do you mean standup machines that we put actual coins in."

"They're modified for tokens," Bits says. "But yeah."

"Fuck it, I'm in," Dolly says.

Chapter Seven

It's a relief to just be able to go out with the specific intent to have some fun and relax. Though we engage in criminal activities for fun and profit, I'm not exactly well suited to the stresses of being on the lam, looking over my shoulder at every move. I chose this, yes, but there are degrees. Bits drives by the light of the conveniently full moon and the light pollution from the looming city, and we don't see another car until she parks in a convenience store lot. Moths and other bugs of the night swarm about the LEDs, and when we get out of the car, our skin seems strange and blue beneath the abrasive light.

Bits leads us away from the convenience store, behind it and down a shadow-layered alleyway with fire escapes looming overhead. "So, this arcade isn't entirely legal," she says as we reach a yellow-lit steel security door. She knocks on the door and red shreds of paint come away on the knuckles of her gloves. Even though this is supposed to be a fun time, none of us relax far enough to take off our gear, not even me.

"I don't think any of us will even pretend we're surprised," I say.

"Not even a little bit," Dolly agrees. At least she's only carrying one gun, settled in the slide holster up her sleeve.

"That just means it's safer for us," Bits says. "Not a single person here is going to want to talk to any cops."

"What about feds or Russian spies?"

"I guess that depends on the deals they offer."

The door swings open, and what I can only assume is a bouncer surveys us. He's Clancy sized or larger, wearing a bulletproof vest and a sawed-off shotgun in a thigh holster.

"You girls lost?" He asks. His voice is falsely gruff, and I notice the laugh lines extending from behind his sunglasses.

"Come off it, Charlie, we're here to play." Bits shoves her anti-surveillance hood back.

A smile breaks on his face. "Bitsy, didn't see you there! Blondie here and the girl with the gun took up my attention. Where've you been?"

"It's a long story, Charlie. Maybe another time."

Charlie shrugs. "Well, come on in!" We file in, and he looks down the dark alley before pulling the door shut. As I pass him, I can see the glow of a heads up display on the insides of the sunglass lenses. The light in the hallway is intermittent, and the walls are all exposed studs, conduit. The whole building seems to hum.

"What's new?" Bits asks.

"Got in some pinball machines from a Japanese scrapyard, and a refurbished xBox with fighting games on it," he says.

"Which version?"

"Of xBox? That's not my department, you know that. Ask Lockhart."

"Will do." Bits leads the way down the hallway, the hum growing stronger. The fire door opens onto a metal scaffolded stairway, and the space below us glows like a nest of fireflies. Maybe this building used to be a factory or something, the floor seems huge and entirely open. Fifty or more brightly colored arcade machines are arranged in lines, along with pinball machines, skee ball, even one antique pair of dance pads. Christmas lights rope around many of the upright surfaces, and they have a little bar, with a popcorn machine, a fryer, and a hotplate.

As we descend the stairs, a knot of people close in near one of the arcade machines, their voices raised. Dolly starts to straighten her gun arm, and behind her, I put a hand on her shoulder. Another bouncer, this one far more sour looking, wades into the crowd and pulls apart two scrapping teens in ripped jeans, big stomping boots, and shirts with cartoon characters on them.

"No fighting!" the bouncer roars as he holds them apart like two cats that had gotten into a tangle. He thankfully relied on his hands for this; he has a shotgun too. "It's only a game. It's only ever a game. If you can't play nice, you can't come here no more." He gives them a shake, his tattooed muscles flexing. "Can you kids play nice?"

One of them nods, and the other one, the one with a bloody nose, manages a sullen, "Yes."

"That's good then." He drops them to their feet, and while they still stagger, off balance, claps them each on the back in a show of goodwill. The gathered teens around them keep them from falling, and then the crowd disperses again. The kid with the bloody nose wipes it on the back of his hand, then wipes his hand on his jeans, while the other boy walks off in a different direction.

"Is there anything in particular you want to play?" Bits asks, bright eyed but almost shy.

"When I was a kid," Dolly says meditatively, "they came out with a re-re-mastered console, an emulator of one of the first ones that they came out with in the 20th. There was a game on it that seemed so simple; you shot ducks like you were out on a lake, but if you missed, a dog—I guess it was supposed to be a retriever—would pop up and laugh at you. I guess TV's didn't work the way they used to, so it went away, and then they came out with the next generation of interactive TV's and somebody did the game again."

"Of course your favored video game is a shooting one," I say.

"Aw, come on," Dolly says, and actually looks hurt. "It's like, the first hunting game. Not a people shooting game."

"I don't think they have that one," Bits says. "Or they didn't."

"You two go on," I say. "I'll find a way to occupy myself."

"If you say so," Bits says dubiously, Dolly already urging her away.

I turn my attention to the people. The teens still trying to figure out who they are and what they want, the young professionals who, really, are in much the same boat as the teens except they're expected to be adults on a directed path by now. A few people who are older, silver starting to thread through their hair. I wander to the bar, drawn by the carnival scent of freshly popped popcorn, and ask for that and a water.

"No water today," says the slouching girl behind the bar. "You want a beer?"

"I guess," I say. I don't, but there is unlikely to be anything else I'd prefer to drink.

"You have cash?" The girl asks, still not moving towards the plastic cooler set on the floor behind her, leaking a thin stream of water across the concrete, or the popcorn machine.

"I do," I say. "Or I think I do." It is rare for me to have cash, actually, and I rummage in my cargo pockets, finally coming up with a wadded handful of bills, their denomination holographs flashing weak blue numbers around my fingers. "How much?"

"Ten." I count it out. "Not into the games?" she asks. I simply don't have the look.

"It's not something I ever got into. I love the atmosphere, though," I offer. The entire feeling here is of a surreptitious party, a joy that can't be scratched out.

"Yeah, Lockhart built it, more or less, but Charlie and Goose are necessary muscle. We make enough scratch to keep things going, somehow. I don't really know how Lockhart does it, to be honest, but sometimes I think the less I know the better."

"You're talking about everybody else, what's your name?" I ask, popping the tab on my dripping beer, licking the moisture off my thumb.

"Jane. I just work for the free tokens. Keeps me off the streets, right?" She shrugs and gave a short little laugh.

"You should give yourself more credit. A place like this can be intimidating, and yet you both work and play here. I think it's pretty wonderful."

"Well thanks for the pep talk." Jane walks off to help another customer, but her smile is a little bit different.

I find a chair and table. The popcorn is very good and the beer is a nice surprise, actually; some kind of artisanal craft brew I've never heard of. I pull out my non wrist phone to scan the QR code, and at that moment it buzzes in my hand. Reflexively, I answer it, voice only. "Bon soir."

"Is this the lovely lady I met in unfortunate circumstances the other night?" I can't place the voice for a split second, and then it clicks.

"If this is Will, then yes, it is! I'm so glad you called." A small cheer goes up from the nearby, larger crowd; apparently Dolly and Bits have reached some kind of achievement never before seen, and are still going.

"Is this a bad time? It seems loud where you are."

"I can still hear you, but give me a moment to get someplace a bit more serene. You know how those impromptu city parties can get; I don't even know who most of these people are."

"Well, I find it hard to believe there's anywhere you would feel out of place."

"Flatterer." I wander back towards the bar. Jane looks at me questioningly, looks at the phone, and then points at a door I hadn't noticed. I mouth 'thank you' and push through it into another dark hallway, keeping my toe in the opening so it won't lock behind me.

"Is it flattery if it's the truth?"

"Now we're getting metaphysical." I'm able to flirt emptily and with ease for a very long time, in all manner of circumstances, but Will's timing is disquieting. "But there must be a reason you called?"

"I wanted to know when I could see you again."

"Oh, I did hope you would say that," I say. "I do regret, I'm going to have to reschedule our coffee. Did you have something in mind next week maybe?"

"Just dinner in a nice restaurant."

"I think that would be very nice."

"I hope so." Will pauses, and that niggling unease just keeps rising. I shift my weight and peer out through the door back into the arcade. I can see Dolly from this angle, barely. I can also see up the stairs to the door where we entered. It seems to me the window in that door should be pretty dark. Or was there a light right at the entryway? I can't remember, and I should remember, but there's light there now, pale white.

"Will, I think I have to let you go," I say carefully.

"I'm sorry to hear that," Will says. "Are you alright? Do you need anything?" It seems a strange way to phrase things, a strange thing to ask.

"I'm not really sure," I say. "Have you heard anything more about...the other night?"

"Some, yes, though not from the police who talked to us. I may have spoken to Richard for a time, about the provenance of those diamonds."

"To Richard?" I ask sharply.

"To Richard. He'd have the best information, wouldn't you say?"

"Him or Mrs. Carter."

"Clever girl," he says and the sound in the background of his call changes just slightly, and I hear a fountain. Indoor fountains are un-

usual, but I can think of several in the city. Including at Marquis'
gallery.

"This might sound strange, Will darling, but where are you right
now?"

"Oh, at this little place downtown. Full of the most interesting
artwork at the moment. Some eclectic people as well. Do you know
it?"

"I think I might." I'm trying to keep my voice breezy. "Is it the
place down on Market that replaced the front windows with large
stained glass pieces?"

"That's the one! The gallery owner is most interesting. Marquis?
And I think Marquis knows you quite well."

"Why yes, we're very good friends. I was at the gathering the other night in Marquis' stead, as I'm sure you know by now."

"Yes, we're well aware." Will pauses significantly, and I wonder if
he practiced for this. "We're going to need those diamonds," he says.
"It's in your best interests, and your accomplices. You're in a great
deal of danger right now, you see."

"Am I? I'm rather alarmed that you've asked me for dinner and
then begun to threaten me." The light outside that upstairs door is
getting brighter. I tuck the phone between my ear and shoulder and
use my wrist phone to send Bits a message.

//We need to pull the plug. Alternate exit by the bar.//

"Chelsea, I'm not threatening you. I represent safety. But there is
a threat against you, from other interested parties."

"I see. You understand this is rather sudden." I see Dolly's posture
change.

"I do. But your position is very near to being compromised, if it
hasn't been already."

"And you say your people aren't after us, but rather a third party?"

"Yes. The party which is most interested in recovering those diamonds in the first place."

"And you're saying you can offer us help or asylum or something along those lines."

"In the immediate sense, yes. In the future legal sense, perhaps not. But, in order to have a future…"

"Oh, we were doing so well, and that was so very indelicate." Bits and Dolly are here with me in the dark hallway, and we let the door swing shut. It does lock. "Now, I'm sorry darling, I do have to let you go this time. Is this the number where you can best be reached?"

"It is, but I don't think you understand…" I hang up on him. The phone buzzes immediately, an angry hornet in my palm, and I shut it down entirely and drop it into one of my vest pockets.

"Who was that?"

"Will from the hotel room. He's with the ones who claim to be the good guys, and whoever the bad guys are, they're at the top of the stairs outside, waiting for some go sign."

"Oh shit, Charlie," Bits murmurs, her eyes going big and voice catching.

"With luck they tased him and left him outside," Dolly says. "Quieter and takes less time. Now let's get out of here. How do you think they found us?"

"I don't know, but we need to get to the car and then figure that out quick, because if they did it once they can do it again. I especially don't know why they didn't before now."

"Turn off all your devices," Bits says. She doesn't give me a look, but she may as well have. "Hopefully they didn't find the car."

We creep through the dark hallway, passing through spears of light from nail holes in the walls, and when the uproar of the raid kicks into a high volume, we run.

We reach an outside door, and Bits creeps out first, nearly silent. She comes back and motions for us to follow, and we go down another alley, until we once again come to the convenience store. I look back as we drive away, but the dark alleyways don't look any different from before, even as the first gunshots crack open the night.

Chapter Eight

The shipping container hideout and surrounding area seem normal, but Bits begins to pack. "Bits, it's three in the morning. A girl needs her beauty sleep." I try very hard to keep the whine out of my voice.

"We don't know how they caught up to us. And now we know what they'll do if they find us," Bits says, shoving a duffle bag into my hands. "We need to move now, because we have no idea whether this location is compromised as well. We power up zero devices until we get to the next place. Dolly, are you listening?"

Dolly, already packed, stands at the doorway looking through the peephole, her e cigarette dangling from the corner of her mouth. "Sounds good," she says laconically. "Nobody's on the road, if that'll settle your biscuits at all."

"It will not." Bits doesn't even crack a smile, seems on the verge of tears. I wonder how well she knows the arcade people. "I'll get us new burner phones. Keep your old ones, but I think that's how they tracked us, and that's why it took so long."

"Explain," Dolly says. Her e cigarette smells like cedar and something else I can't quite place.

"We all had our phones on us, any number of wireless devices. The closest tower that serviced the hotel would have records of everything that connected. It takes time to narrow down who would've been in specific rooms, but..."

Dolly nods. "As easy as that."

"Maybe I'm just making it sound too easy," Bits says.

"Perhaps it's that you make it sound very easy for the people with the right equipment and capabilities," I say thoughtfully. Bits does not make wild guesses; she can track me by anything I wear on a regular basis, from my earbuds to my bracelet phone. "Where is the next location?" I ask. "Perhaps a hotel? With things like a toilet and running water?"

"It is, actually." Bits finally stops her whirlwind, surveys the shipping container. "I think that's everything. Load up." Bits drives again; she's the one with the safe house algorithm. She's already hacked the license plate, so the holo displays another vehicle's. The tint of the windows is just enough to keep us from being instantly recognizable, but isn't so dark as to draw immediate suspicion.

"You've done this a number of times before you met us, I take it?" I ask.

"Yeah, kind of. My folks were survivalists, so pretty low tech. But once I started getting my hands on junked computers and rebuilding them, I couldn't stay out there in the woods anymore. I brought the paranoia with me, though."

I stare at her, mystified. "Paranoia about what, out in the woods? There aren't many people living outside cities anymore, are there?"

Dolly snorts. "There's plenty of people still living outside cities," she says. "Maybe not in the woods like Bitsy's folks, but there's all that real estate off the grid, and not everybody is a big fan of the way city things run. And there are things other than people to be worried about."

"You're a country mouse too, Dolly? Why haven't we ever talked about this?"

She shrugs. "It just never came up."

"Well." I am, for once, flummoxed. "I didn't mean for the two of you to think you couldn't talk about yourselves."

"It doesn't matter," Bits says. "What matters is getting out of this mess. Or managing this mess. Whatever you want to say about it."

We're silent for several blocks. I think of the things I would like to do instead of being driven to ground in the city. Moving freely about in the manner I am accustomed is high on the list. A nice long bath, with scented oils.

The hotel is a step up from a coffin hotel, which was my quiet fear. Check in is automated, and helpful robots handed us heated towels and snacks before we leave the lobby to go to our suite. "This was one of the very first robot hotels in the country," Bits says. "Japan had them for a couple of years before we did, and as always, we were happy to let them refine the process first before adopting it. There's another one by the airport, nicer for all of the business travelers, but then of course it's higher traffic."

"It's perfectly fine. I just hope there's a tub."

"Some have them and some don't."

The hotel is not multi floored in the traditional sense, but a number of split levels with long hallways, no stairs. The carpet is thin and lacks much texture, and is probably highly cleanable by whatever robot is designed for that as well. I can't imagine what a property this size must have cost, when it was built, though perhaps it had been in one of the early century recessions which drove the real estate market to its knees. There seem to be gardens outside, with little solar lamps. I imagine what it must look in daylight, perhaps overtures at Japanese aesthetics, with things like a koi pond and a little red bridge over it, stands of bamboo, thoughtfully placed shrines and vending machines for incense and other offerings.

Our suite seems very far from the hotel lobby, and I can see why once we're inside. I peel back the shade over the back window, and there's a whole separate parking lot out there, a property fence, and then a road beyond. Bits selected this suite for its means of escape. I am beginning to think perhaps I have not devoted enough thought in life to means of escape.

The beds are futons, though so different from the shipping container futons it's difficult to imagine why they would be called the same word. The mattresses are far thicker, the frames crafted with an attention to detail instead of just pipes welded together. Bits does a short tour of the room as we set down our bags, a device in her hand that I can't remember having seen before. It is *very* hard, trying to keep track of Bits's gadgets. "What's that for?" I ask finally, as Bits folds the thing up and puts it away, apparently satisfied.

"It checks for bugs. Listening devices, wifi detectors, credit skimmers, all of that. Nothing is here though. We can relax and go to sleep now."

"Aye aye captain," I say with a smile. I crawl across the first futon I come to, then sit up and take my boots off, dropping them to the floor. I'm tired, but not too tired to be decent. I unhook my bra under my shirt, wiggle my arms through the straps and pull it clear, dropping it on the floor as well.

"Tomorrow will be better," Dolly says. "We'll know more. Maybe Bits can find out who Will is, and who came to the arcade last night."

"I'm sure everything will be fine," I say around a yawn, covering my mouth. "I'm sure I can't hold another thought in my head right now, though. I hope everybody sleeps well."

It isn't a surprise that I sleep late the next day, or that Dolly does too. It is a surprise that Bits is up very early, slipping out to get new phones and who knows what other technology, but also coffee and freshly made breakfast sandwiches from a cafe whose name I don't recognize

"I figured you'd rebel sooner or later if we were just eating vending machine and prefab stuff," Bits says. "Though the vending machine just down the hall has that really good canned coffee, that you can have hot or cold, in like thirteen flavors."

"Canned hot coffee?" I'm curious but dubious, though I happily accept one of the takeout cups.

"Don't knock it 'til you've tried it," Dolly says, her sandwich already half gone. "And hey, we do have a tub."

"Oh good. I'll have a nice soak after we eat. Is there anything we can do to help you, Bits?"

"No, but thanks for asking anyway," Bits says.

"Maybe I'll take a walk around the grounds, investigate our vending machine situation." Dolly pulls out her ponytail and scrapes her hair back again. "How many other bodies do we seem to have in house?" she asks.

"Not very many. A couple of professionals, and maybe a couple of people having an affair, so all in all nobody that's going to bother us." Bits is already setting up the equipment.

I'm so tired of riot gear; I'll wear a dress and heels today, and it will be fine. I'll make it be fine. I can run in heels almost as well as I can in boots anyway; it comes both from practice and well-made shoes. Everything is practice. When not on the run, I practice conversation in front of my augmented smart mirror, tracking when I tip my chin, or widen my eyes, the degrees of smile. Gestures. Signature words. Before I knew more French, I used to intersperse French words into speech, but it never quite struck the right note.

I step into the bathroom and slide the door shut behind me. The tub is a step in whirlpool, more than I could have hoped for. I don't have much with me that can be considered bath oils, but there are a number of small bottles on the counter, and bath bombs, labeled roses and sandalwood, wrapped in a crackly imitation of cellophane, with golden ribbons, the whole thing designed to dissolve.

I have some indistinct plan of retiring to a warm and trendy place while I'm still young, though old enough to be taken seriously. I've never been to Morocco, but I've developed a fascination for it, hunting down articles, watching travel specials, trying the food when I can. I'm not certain what the exact allure is, but it's a name to hang a dream on, a place to yearn for the sights and smells of, the sound of people talking, the sight of sunlight on foreign walls.

My problem is I spend a lot of money, even as I'm trying to save money. I can access my savings account, but at great inconvenience, so the balance grows steadily despite myself. Riot gear is expensive, and parties, and good makeup, even without buying quite so many guns and gizmos like Bits and Dolly.

Relaxing into the perfumed water, I hear the hotel room door close. Dolly going for her walk, I suppose. Though really, if we were to be caught right now, maybe I would be relieved. I don't want to be on the run, I want to still be living in that gray area between legal and illegal, where I can have fun and live my casual life.

The bathroom door isn't kicked in, and Bits doesn't raise any kind of alarm, and I finish out my bath in dozy peace. The attached blowdryer in the bathroom is a compact ceramic one and surprisingly good, and I apply my makeup with the usual care. Bits has done something with our devices, to forward texts and calls without alerting any potential watchers that the old phones had been used at all, and I open my new phone to check my messages. I do miss my wrist unit; even with a stack of delicate bangle charm bracelets, my arm feels light, and I slide a ring onto my middle finger as well, to compensate, a heavy silver band made of an antique ornate spoon, scrolled seashells and just the right amount of classy tarnish.

I have a wide range of casual acquaintances, which makes for many casual invitations to come to a gallery, or a club, or an afternoon coffee. Marquis sent me a number of messages; hopefully they're all right and not just bait. A couple of exes had sent their usual things, gestures that they would be in town and would love to take me out for dinner.

And Will.

Will reiterated that he would love to take me out for drinks, dinner. It isn't just because we are somewhat entangled due to business—but the business end of things is very important, and he needs to speak to me further on that matter. Recover the package. He claims that neither I nor and my associates would be in any trouble, and I sigh. When has anything ever been that easy?

Chapter Nine

When I leave the steaming bathroom, Bits is in much the same position, cross legged on a futon and hunched over in a VR headset, surrounded by all the other accompanying tech. Dolly is still gone, the cedar smell of e cigarette remaining in her wake, and I load the little combo washer/dryer in the corner.

//Learn anything new?// I text Bits, thinking that it's better than speaking to her at this moment, but she answers me out loud without otherwise moving.

"Did you know that something like four of the Russian imperial family's Faberge eggs are lost?"

"I'd heard that, in fact. What's that have to do with our diamonds?"

"One of the diamonds has data that claims to reflect the location of those four eggs," Bits says. "Another discusses weapons caches after a number of disarmament treaties were signed." There is a long pause, and I have the time to set out my manicure equipment, the files, the cuticle cream, the polishes to redo French nails, when Bits speaks again. The blue diamond is on the table in front of her. "Did you know Russia had a system called Dead Hand, or Perimeter, which meant Moscow could respond to nuclear attack even if all of the command structure was gone?"

"I did not."

"It's still operational."

I pause, three nails into my left hand. "Still operational," I repeat. My grasp of the dates is fuzzy, but it seems such a thing would've been constructed early to mid 20th. For it to still be operational more than a hundred years later is chilling.

"This one has maps of the bunkers under Moscow. And there's another datacode, even further inside the facets, not just surface readable like the other ones. I think...well I don't know. I guess they wouldn't be launch codes. Maybe they're disarm codes?"

"For the Perimeter?"

"I think. I don't want to make faulty assumptions."

"What do other less impressive diamonds say?"

"Locations where subs were dumped in the arctic circle, though I guess they probably floated away by now, when the ice melted." Bits pauses, and I force myself to wait again, finishing my left hand and moving to my right, which is always a little bit more tricky. "Brand new planes that were built and then never flown, including a suborbital hypersonic jet meant to launch nuclear missiles."

"What is it with governments and their nuclear weapons? I thought the scorched earth approach had fallen out of vogue decades ago."

"It's all about perceived threat. Um. Mutually assured destruction used to be what people said kept everything safe. You bomb me, I'll bomb you, and then nobody can have anything."

"Just lovely. Simply marvelous politics."

"Well, they didn't have you yet," Bits says with a small smirk

My new phone buzzes, and I call up the message, careful of my nails. It's from Dolly.

//They have a fortune telling machine, come check it out.//

The phone buzzes again as a picture arrives of a neon AR spread of tarot cards.

If nothing else, it'll be a fascinating diversion. In the slummy apartment building where I grew up there was a woman who read tarot for people. The scarier the reading, the less she'd charge you for it, and people ironclad trusted her, but I'm still not sure any of her readings were accurate, or just what was bound to happen in the first place. She always knew I would leave.

//Where is that?// I reply.

//Right here in the hotel. Um. Take a left out of our door, take the first right, go through the water garden, and then right again.//

//Let me finish my nails, I'm almost done with my right hand.//

"Dolly found a fortune telling machine," I say to Bits.

"That doesn't surprise me," she says, her tone distant again. I assumed she saved the blue diamond for last, but she's moving the scanner over some of the smaller ones. "Go see it, and then bring Dolly back. We need to talk about whether we should call your Will and take their deal."

"He's hardly mine," I say, rolling up the manicure kit.

"He seems to have taken quite the liking to you."

"How would you—" I pause, staring at Bits's face, which is expressionless under the VR headset. Then I sigh and put my things away. "See you soon," I say, but Bits doesn't react.

A robot vacuum vrooms its way down the hallway, bouncing between the walls, beeping cheerfully when I step over it. There are a surprising number of windows as I walk through the hotel, shedding lots of golden morning light into the hallways. The water garden is quite lovely, little rainbows forming around the sprays, and a number of hummingbird feeders are interspersed through the space. The tiny, jewel-like birds flit about almost too fast to track. Or they're holograms or drones for the same eye pleasing effect; I'm entirely uncertain.

There are many, many vending machines through the hotel. Coffee ones, as Bits described. Clothing ones, for easily capsule-able clothing like bras, tops, underwear. I linger at the clothing ones for a time, then dig out a prepaid credit card. I've had a vending machine dress before and found it quite comfortable, in fact. This machine has a line of peacock patterned ones for a reasonable price, and I dial in my size and retrieve the plastic capsule.

There is plenty of food I don't want and won't eat, basic toiletries, and phones. I also get a little vial of hyacinth perfume from a French machine. I only had a little spray bottle of Chanel in my makeup kit and though the Chanel is my everyday perfume, I prefer to wear hyacinths when it rains, and I have a very strong feeling it will rain soon.

I turn the corner and Dolly stands there, e cigarette still glowing, in front of the fortune teller, labeled Madame Sosostris. I have a moment to wonder over the poetry of it.

"Have you tried it yet?" I ask.

"Me? Nah. Even if it is a game the idea kinda freaks me out."

"Oh, there's actually something in this world that freaks you out? How good to know."

"Like you thought I was some kind of machine."

"No, but you don't let us in very much, do you."

"I'm willing to say none of us lets people in very much. You seem to, but mostly it's just icing."

"Icing," I repeat, with a little bemused smile. It's the one I practiced when trying not to seem hurt, surprised, or angry. Dolly's right, though, in an unusually incisive way. I protect myself with layers of icing, pleasantness, decoration, that I expect others to freely consume. I keep the cake hidden for myself. "Well anyway, I don't typically have tarot readings, so this will be quite the experience."

"What's your fortune telling of choice then, princess?" Dolly asks, leaning against the wall across the hall from the machine. "Assuming you have one."

"Tea leaves or coffee grounds. The way Turkish coffee is made, and served, makes it my preferred tradition. You drink your cup of coffee with the fortuneteller and then they read your grounds. You can have it sweetened if you'd like—the coffee not the fortune—but milk does not typically enter the equation."

"Never heard of it," Dolly says. "Though I guess that shouldn't surprise me. Tea, yeah."

I shrug. "There are people who have a pack of cards passed down through generations. There are people who cast stones."

"I somehow didn't expect you to be into woo woo stuff like this."

"Some women like yoga, or pilates, or meditation. I like getting my fortune told."

"Do you ever do it yourself?"

"I pretended with a pack of playing cards when I was little, but no, I don't feel the spark."

"Interesting." Dolly takes another drag on her e cigarette.

I examine the controls. Madame Sosostris can do a number of different readings, from a basic three card past-present-future all the way up to the far more involved Celtic Cross. For the fun of it, I just pick three cards. I hardly want something involved with Dolly watching and smirking. It's also possible to select a preferred deck, but I just leave the default Rider-Waite set. Then I run my card, and the machine comes into further neon life, with an elaborate light show of shuffling cards before three are holographically drawn onto the front of the machine, their pink plaid backs an unexpected contrast. I've never given much thought to what the backs of tarot cards might look like.

The first card, labeled "The Recent Past," is the Chariot, which has to do with overcoming obstacles, and I give kind of a little laugh.

"What?" Dolly asks.

"Can you see it from there?"

"Not really. Won't mean anything anyway."

"Suit yourself. I thought you'd be more invested, considering you called me out here." The second card is The High Priestess, representing "The Present." The High Priestess emphasizes trusting one's intuition and keeping communication lines open, both sentiments I firmly endorse. And then the final card, "The Future", the Four of Pentacles, predicting the likely outcome: in order to secure wealth, we may be greedy or malicious.

Once all three cards are face up, the figures on them also stand up from the card surfaces, and the small holographs play out a little story based on the figures present and the meanings of the card positions. Dolly laughs, and the machine offered the option to save the reading to my device, and I select that, waving my phone for the data.

"Well that was something," Dolly says. "We'll see how things turn out, anyway. Greedy and malicious, it says."

"We *have* stolen a tremendous number of diamonds," I say thoughtfully. "Should we bring Bits some dreadful snacks, to raise her spirits? I don't remember the last time I saw her eat."

"That's a good idea. And I guess she has all the data read now?"

"I'm not entirely sure, but I don't doubt she'll be happy to regale us with all of that information."

"We just need some bullet points and an endgame, I think. Less of this hiding out shit, more collecting our money. I wanna get on with my life."

I laugh. "I'm not sure I've ever agreed with you more."

Chapter Ten

"Break it down, Bits," Dolly says. "Who're the players? Who're the good guys?"

"Dolly, there are *never* clear-cut good guys," Bits says. The headset has left lines on her face, and her eyes are droopy, out of focus.

"You've done an unbelievable amount of work for us, Bits," I say. "Don't you want to lie down first, have a nap, and then we can form a game plan?"

Bits takes one of the snack bags and shakes some chips into her hand. "Maybe. I'll tell you some stuff first. I did some digging online, deep web stuff, and I think whoever smuggled the diamonds might have been working both sides all along—a Russian operative feeding intel to other countries. Our original smuggler might have been in an artsy or performance crowd, and had access to high level bad guys, for lack of a better term, who might have been loose with their secrets and their phones and passwords and stuff."

"That's a substantial bit of information," I say.

Bits nods for a little too long, chewing more chips. I'm coming to the unfortunate conclusion that they are cricket chips, not corn chips. "So what we have are a lot of secrets that would have once been called Soviet, in the Cold War. Which is supposed to have ended, but I'm not sure it ever did, based on everything ever. I mean, it never got hot. But it never actually went away either. Maybe it's a shadow war?"

"That's a good thing to call it," I consider taking one of Dolly's e cigarettes, for something to do, or to soothe my nerves. That's what they're for, isn't it?

"And so the U.S. might have been the intended buyer for them. But after the original smuggler lost possession of them, it was to somebody who was more interested in selling them to the highest bidder."

"So here's a thing, did we hear about this job because diamonds are flashy and expensive, or because somebody was actually peddling the information?" Dolly asks. Bits shrugs with open arms, offers the chips around. I shake my head, Dolly takes a handful.

"I looked into Will a little bit. He's American. Born in Virginia, went to work in Washington after college."

"He was very nice when we were robbed by a ruffian," I say with a smile. "Comforting."

"He's easy on the eyes, I'll tell you that," Dolly says.

"He was very eager to meet when we spoke last night. I could definitely get him someplace public and see what we can get out of him. Discuss this deal of his."

"I wasn't going to ask you to, but..." Bits trails off.

"You do computers, Dolly does guns, and I manage people. I'll call him once we're done with our discussion."

"Bitsy, where'd you find this job again?"

"The tip was on a deep web message board, same as I've found a lot of our other stuff." Bits shrugs. "No way to know who posted it. Though even if I didn't hear about it online, Bristol would've heard about it through Marquis. They sent real life invitations. This whole thing is weird."

Dolly frowns. "Hey Bristles, you don't think Marquis...?"

"I think Marquis fit the appearance they wanted to cultivate for the sale."

"Okay, now I'm gonna crash for like, twelve hours. See if Will wants to take you out after that, so we can listen in and keep our eyes open," Bits says.

"I will. Sleep well."

She doesn't even kick her boots off, just puts the bag of chips down, curls up, and falls asleep. I wonder if some of the computer equipment might even still be attached to her. Dolly turns on the television, pokes at the remote until the sound routes through her earbuds instead of in the room. "I'll be here if anybody needs me."

"I think I'll make my call from that water garden. With all the hummingbirds."

"Turn all your shit off afterwards," Bits mumbles. "Just the call will give them a lot of intel, but maybe not enough to come knocking."

"Of course."

WILL ANSWERS ON THE first ring. "It's so good to hear from you," he says warmly.

"Good afternoon, Will." I've settled on a bench by one of the waterfalls, with a view of three hummingbird feeders. Maybe I'll be able to tell if they're real or not by the end of things.

"I trust everything went well last night?"

"We made our hasty retreat, if that's what you mean. I do appreciate the warning, though."

"You're very welcome." I wait. So much of a conversation depends on the pauses, on what isn't said. "So, I imagine you're getting tired of campfire food and would like a more civilized experience?"

"Campfire food?" I laugh. "Yes, it is dreadful. Civilization seems very nice about now. I'm not used to roughing it in any sense of the word."

"No, a woman like you enjoys reasonable comforts," he says. "And you deserve them. Luxuries, even."

"And now you're flattering me again."

"Do you have a restaurant in mind? You can choose wherever you'd like."

Wherever I'd like opens up infinite possibilities. I consider, and then name a newer place with a very experimental chef I heard about before all of this diamond business got started. "I'm not sure what the menu will be, of course. Though that's part of the adventure of it."

"Of course. I went to his mentor's restaurant in Chicago and it was an...experience. I guess the food was good. I had to get a burger after. The problem with all that gourmet stuff is they don't, in the end, give you very much food at all. They give you the idea of food. The notion that one day your stomach might be full."

"Will, are you a poet?"

"Some things make me wax poetic. Like burgers."

"Burgers," I say, rolling my eyes. He laughs.

"What can I say, I like things simple. And you do know what we intend to discuss over dinner?"

"Our possible future together? Perhaps certain luxuries?"

"Something like that." He laughs again. "I think we understand each other."

"Perhaps." He does seem very comfortable. Maybe he's overconfident, or maybe he has a file on me.

"So I'll pick you up around six?" Overconfident, then.

"I'll meet you there at eight o'clock. That's when the second seating begins."

"As you say. Until tonight, then."

"Until tonight." I hang up, turn off all of my devices. I'll redo my makeup, more elaborately. False eyelashes, a bolder red lipstick. I look up at the sky; I really should have checked the weather before calling Will, and I can't turn the phone back on now, but it does seem as though it might rain. I'll wear my hyacinth perfume, and my new dress. My turtlescale camisole will suffice, my usual stockings and hair pins.

I'm still planning, not daydreaming precisely, when Dolly comes to find me under the darkening sky. "Did you know Bits snores?" she asks.

"I'm sure we all do under enough duress." I am, in fact, confident that I do not snore.

"Depends on how I'm laying," Dolly says. She turn towards movement, and watches a trio of hummingbirds flit onto the nearest feeder and flit away again. "Are those real?"

"I've been trying to figure that out. I can't quite tell."

"They got robot bees and stuff now. Pollinators. Because so many of them died. They look like regular bees, I guess because they need to be the right shape to fit into flowers and rub up against the right stuff. Just making them discs or whatever didn't work."

"That's both sad and charming. I don't know anything about what happened with the bees."

"Back home we had a tiny little hive. But there was a big factory farm nearby with the bee drones. Robot bees."

"I thought that was what you meant."

"They tried to color 'em differently too, so it's kind of obvious when you see them, unlike the hummingbirds. Little articulate jewel toned robot bees. Though I guess there's naturally blue bees some places? Or there were. These ones didn't have stingers, though, that was a big difference. They still knew if you caught one."

"What happened if you caught one?"

"If it was just to see it, no big deal. The pollen gets stored in little leg capsules I guess, so just touching them doesn't ruin everything. But if you keep it from going home, or you break it on purpose or catch a bunch of 'em, they make trouble for you."

"The factory farm?"

"And the local government, since that's where a lotta the kickbacks came from. It's under some kind of FDA umbrella. What we learned in school isn't always what's true."

I try to think what "make trouble" means. Get ticketed? Then I realize Dolly said "had" a small hive. Not "has."

"Oh," I say.

"Yeah," Dolly says, dragging on her e cigarette. "That's not when I left home, but it wasn't long after. Couldn't get work there, and even though the bees made us so little, that income buffer was important. So now I'm here, and we do what we do."

"It seems amazing to me that we never asked each other anything before. Talked about why we were in this."

"What were we gonna do, have a slumber party and do each other's hair and nails while talking about boys and ruined families or whatever? No thanks."

"That isn't exactly what I meant."

"No, and that probably wasn't fair, so I'm sorry. But still. Who wants to drag all that shit out all the time?"

"I suppose." I stand up and brush off the back of my skirt. "I'm dining with Will at eight. I'll get ready early, and ride public transit around for a time, to muddy the trail, as the saying goes."

"We should keep eyes on you," Dolly says.

"By all means. I'll use my earbuds, as always, and you'll be in proximity, I hope. Here's the address."

"We'll manage it," Dolly says.

"You always do."

Chapter Eleven

Bits wakes up as I'm putting the finishing touches on my makeup and selecting jewelry. I'm surprised at how pleased I am with the new dress; some of it has to do with the low cost, and the fact that it's new. But it's subtly patterned in peacock feathers and goes with the heels I intend to wear, though really the entire point of a good workhorse pair of black high heels—with a stiletto in at least one heel—is that they go with just about everything.

"How dangerous do you think he is?" Bits asks through her yawn.

"I think he has the potential to be very dangerous. Coercive, perhaps, I can see him bullying me into a car or something, but not drugging me or having me shot or any of those things."

"Well that's...reassuring," Dolly says, squinting.

"Such is life," I say with a shrug, sniffing the hyacinth perfume and then applying it lightly to my wrists and the base of my neck. Put perfume where you want to be kissed, the magazines say. If my hair comes down at any point, or if Will stands behind me, the scent there will be intoxicating. "Where is the nearest bus, other than right out front?"

"Three blocks east," Bits says after a moment. "Here. New phone and earbuds. I already duped all your stuff, but you'll have to fiddle to get your settings just right again. I guess you can do that on the bus."

"I will," I say, slipping the phone onto my wrist. It doesn't fit just right with the bangles, the way the old one did, but it matches their profile pretty well. I'm certain nobody will notice but me.

"You're sure you want to do this?" Dolly's tone is softer than usual.

"It's fine. You'll be in the wings if I need you."

"Really, if that big guy in the hotel room is the only person I get to shoot, I guess we should still consider this a good job. None of us has even gotten shot at," Dolly says.

"Yet," I say with a little smile. "Let's not tempt fate."

The hotel's area of the city is full of industrial parks and mirror-faced office buildings, driverless automated vehicles, the occasional police patrol car. As I walk my three blocks to the bus station, I see the same police car four times, in fact. The fifth time, before the bus arrives, the officer slows to a stop at the curb in front of the bus station bench. I've already fixed my earbud settings, and have begun to idly search around in my saved music at a low volume, hoping to catch something with the right tempo to put me in the proper businesslike place.

"Do you need help with anything?" the officer calls, rolling his curbside window down.

"You're so kind to stop and check in on me! No, thank you, I'm just waiting on the six fifteen bus."

"I'm not sure I've ever seen somebody like you waiting at this stop," he says.

I smile, rapidly calculating what he could mean. Is he accusing me of being a prostitute? Is he just trying to flirt, but doing so very oddly? That's hardly appropriate. "It's certainly my first time at this stop."

"You came over from the hotel?"

"That's right. Having a little work retreat there."

"It's a nice place," the cop says. The radio in his dashboard mutters, and he bends his head to listen.

"He isn't a cop with a public history of doing terrible things," Bits says in my earbud. "If that helps at all."

"A little," I say softly, carefully, when I'm sure his attention is focused. "Anything else?"

"Not without a lot of dangerous digging that, at the moment, could draw far more heat than we need."

"An accident downtown might've delayed your bus," the cop says after several moments of consulting his equipment. The radio in the cop car crackles again, and then beeps a couple of times. "You take care of yourself. It can be dangerous out here alone for a woman."

"If you only knew," I say once he drives away, partly to see if Bits will laugh. Bits sort of snorts, her attention already elsewhere I'm sure.

The bus is automated and entirely empty. I pause before running my payment, and then go on with it. If the government, Russian or otherwise, hijacked an entire bus to get their hands on me, disembarking at this point will only delay the inevitable. I spend more time than I'd like on public transportation; the smells alone are enough to straighten one's hair. But I also resent paying for cabs and things, when the vast price difference could mean a new turtlescale piece, or another lipstick in my arsenal. The one I use on locks isn't my only variation on the theme.

The sidewalk is starting to speckle with rain when I get off the bus, all of the city lights blossoming dandelion halos around them. I wrap a surveillance scarf around my head and shoulders carefully, a black one this time with gold thread details and a tiny bit of fringe. I move in amongst the thin crowd and use the darkening windows to check for followers. None that I can tell, as I step into a department store. Walking straight through, the doors on the other side puts me onto a more opportune street, where I can catch another bus to ride for a few blocks.

"Looking clear," Bits says. "Except you did all that with your makeup and now it's raining."

"It's waterproof. I could go swimming like Esther Williams and be fine."

"Who?"

"Nevermind." I stop and looked in a mirror to be sure, but there isn't anything to worry about. "Time?"

"After the next bus, you should just take a cab to the restaurant."

"How are you tracking me, anyway? Or is that a silly thing to ask? You gave me this phone."

"Got it in one." This time, Bits does laugh.

"I don't suppose you have a window on my date?"

"Dolly has a vantage on the restaurant already, doesn't see any unusual activity. He isn't there yet either. The first seating is just clearing out."

"I'm surprised we're just not all linked up."

"Compartmentalization. Each of you tracks back to a different place, so we're not just a big glowing target for somebody to find."

I'm almost out of the department store when I notice a display of men's handkerchiefs. Not a major thing, but sufficient quality to catch the eye. I hesitate, go ahead and scan the code with my phone, tapping another prepaid account.

"A gift?" Bits asks once I'm back on the sidewalk.

"It's selfish to expect flowers but give nothing in return, wouldn't you say?" Literally everybody just walks around talking in this manner, though I've watched so many old movies, it still makes me self conscious sometimes. I still look around to see if anybody seems to be paying me more attention than they should, which is a difficult metric. I cultivate most aspects of myself to draw attention.

"I mean, you're not wrong."

The bus is another brief jaunt, though not solo this time. I cross the threshold for rush hour, and twenty or more people in suits are sitting or slumping in the bus seats, faces in their phones, or just staring vacantly.

I arrive at the restaurant at quarter past eight; perfectly acceptable, especially as I may have deliberately told Will the incorrect time. Second seating is at eight thirty.

"I was beginning to think you weren't coming," he says, stepping outside to meet me. He opens an umbrella, but a split second too late, and both of us get rained upon. I smile at the resulting waft of hyacinths.

"You worry too much," I say, and hand him the handkerchief box. His expression had changed just slightly when he smelled the hyacinths, and he seems entirely surprised by the flat box with its gray and white handkerchief inside.

"That's very thoughtful of you, Bristol, thank you."

"No more Chelsea?" I ask.

"I told you my name, it would have been kind to tell me yours," he says, offering his elbow. I rest my hand on it as we climb the steps to the maitre'd.

"Where did you fish up "Bristol?""

"It's what Marquis calls you," Will says. "Marquis is a very...interesting character. I don't suppose Marquis has ever been one of your suitors?"

"I hardly think that's an appropriate question for you to ask me about a dear friend. You and I have only spoken a handful of times, and you've only spoken to Marquis..."

"Just the once, to ascertain the beguiling blonde I'd met at the hotel wasn't Marquis, and to find out more about her."

"I'm quite flattered." I take a sip of water. "But I don't know anything about you, least of which if Will is your real name, or just one that you picked out of a hat to use in that hotel room."

"Is that how you chose "Chelsea?""

"It's a neighborhood in London."

"Of course." He fiddles with the items on the table in front of him, realigning the silverware after he folds the napkin in his lap, squaring the handkerchief box with the corner of the table. "Will is my real name," he says presently. Waiting people out must be one of his very best techniques. He keeps trying it out on me. "Though Bristol still isn't yours."

"No. But it's a true name, one I go by both for work and with friends." We aren't given a wine list, the glasses are simply filled. "My turn?"

"If that's how we'll play the game," Will says with a smile. I return the smile; perhaps he would relax if he thinks it was a game with rules, parameters. Boundaries he can find the edges of.

"Where are you from?"

"Virginia, born and raised."

"No accent, though." Granted, Dolly is my gold standard for this. Not all southern accents are created equal.

"No. Went to boarding school in the north, to my mother's delight and father's chagrin."

"Is she a northerner?"

"No, from Charleston." He says this as though it's all the explanation necessary, and I sort of nod, mystified. "Honestly, it's hard for me to make sense of your speech patterns," he says.

"Finishing school. Well, and some other places here and there." It's a relief that nobody seems to guess I am entirely a fraud, rags to riches, and not somebody rich who is slumming it for fun.

The waiter brings the first course, which appears to be a tiny forest built upon a piece of slate. A slow mist rolls through the trees, and the waiter lights a very small campfire on the corner of the slate. I clasp my hands and take in the little scene. The whole thing is entirely ridiculous, of course, but the workmanship is amazing.

"I'm afraid to eat it," Will says baldly.

"I know, I don't want to ruin it!"

"No, I mean I'm afraid to eat it. Like, this isn't food."

"Of course it's food. That's what, liquid nitrogen? Which probably means there's a sorbet in the middle there for us to cleanse our palates once we're done with the rest. And there's probably something we're meant to skewer and toast over the fire, so you haven't rescued me from campfire food after all." I lean forward a bit, hunting with my eyes, and then, experimentally, uproot one of the trees. It comes away easily, and the bark feels very slightly crackly.

"Well I did try." He skeptically watches me eat the tree in delicate bites. "But what is it?"

"Quail, I'd say. If it was ortolan we'd have been instructed to cover our faces."

Will selects his own tree and copies my approach, balancing it on his fork over the fire before chewing thoughtfully. "You probably already know this, but you're the most cultured person I've ever sat down with."

"I suspected, but it's still nice to hear." I pull another tree. The sorbet is visible now, and we must get to it soon. "Your turn."

"You came here alone tonight?" he asks. I arch a brow at him, look around. "I know you got here alone. I'm asking if your charming friend from the hotel is waiting outside. Or a sniper."

"The windows in this room aren't real, just elaborate light fixtures. Didn't you notice when we were outside?" I spoon up some of the sorbet. Lemongrass, I think.

"You understand, this isn't how interviews normally go. Typically I ask the questions, make the demands, and you act agreeably."

"The upset of the power balance is throwing you, it's natural. And can you really say I'm not acting agreeably?"

"It happens to everybody," Bits murmurs in my ear, and I finish my glass of wine to stave off the giggles. Will has reached the sorbet as well and doesn't seem to notice, and then the waiter puts the fire out and whisks away the slate and wine glasses.

"I wonder what they'll bring us next," Will says. "I've never gone to a restaurant where I didn't tell them what I wanted." I give him a particular smile, and he laughs. "That's it, the power balance thing again. This entire day, week, whatever, is an object lesson. I'm sure I'm really growing as a person."

"At least you enjoy your work," I say as a bowl is set in front of each of us. It looks like a regular bowl of soup, coconut milk with edible flowers, and is almost a disappointment after the majesty of the misty forest. "This is some of the best coconut milk soup I've ever had," I say after a moment, regretting my doubts.

"Even when you were in Thailand?"

"Oh, I've never been to Thailand," I say dismissively. "Hong Kong, though. Did you know, in Hong Kong, there are places that are a combination of gigantic swimming pools and fishing holes, where you can go any hour of the day or night to rent a pole and go fishing? You can have the fish cooked up if you want, if you catch something. You see gangsters there in the middle of the night. They need to relax too, if you can imagine."

"I did not know you could do that in Hong Kong. Or anywhere else for that matter, except an actual natural body of water. Gangsters, you say?"

"Gangsters, young professionals, everybody really. But the people who go in the middle of the night aren't typically law abiding locals."

"And how would you know?"

"I went to see the gangsters, of course." I saw it on a travel show that was actually more about food, but was also very culturally informing indeed.

"Of course."

"He's really never going to get to it," Dolly says in wonder. I'd missed her connecting. "He's really just going to treat this like a date the entire evening. Next time, I get to seduce the charming young man of the story." Bits laughs.

The next course is a plate of fish for each of us that seems entirely whole, head and fins and all. I stare at it blankly for a moment, distracted by the voices in my ears. I look up at Will. "I'm sorry, I didn't quite catch that."

"I said I do enjoy my work. Though I'm one of the youngest in the regional branch, so I'm constantly having to prove that I'm not just some punk kid who lucked into a good assignment."

"Does that mean the other day was very embarrassing for you? I am sorry."

"Not as embarrassing for me as it was for the gorilla at the door, anyway."

"Was he one of yours?"

"He was the courier's hired muscle. He just happens to be local talent." Will pauses, carefully dismantling his fish. It appears it was just cunningly put back together, which is a relief. The entire head is a rebuilding of other materials, not just an intact fish skull with eyes and everything. "But yes, he was ours."

"And here you are the, what, investigative lead? This is your first time on lead, isn't it?" I rest my chin in my hands and gaze at him. "That is dreadfully exciting."

"I'm glad you think so," Will says drily. "But we haven't really made much progress here."

"We're getting to know each other. We're having excellent food, or an excellent food experience, anyway. I'm certain you can be reasonably worked with. You have an idea of what you're after, I'm sure?"

"A few things, yeah." He fiddles with the handkerchief box again. I test myself, my eye for these things, looking at his tie bar; it does seem similar to the one he wore at the hotel, if not the same one. There's no reason to believe he isn't also wearing earbuds. When he pauses, maybe he's listening to his team members. What a farce this is.

"Well, what are you prepared to offer?"

"See, Marquis said to watch for a particular look in your eyes. He—"

"They," I interrupt.

"What?"

"They. Marquis uses the pronoun they. Marquis is not a he. Or a she."

Will recovers sooner than I expected. "They said that the look would be like that hard glitter when morning sun is on ocean waves, and I thought they were just being poetic, because to me it seems impossible to not be infatuated with you after even a brief meeting, but it's there now. That look."

"Poetics can still be truthful."

"So I see. And I believe Marquis was in a position to feel very truthful."

They want to make a deal. A flutter of unease, and I frown and shift in my chair. "Where is Marquis?"

"Marquis is safe. What do you take us for?"

"It isn't as though all of the masks are off, even when the gloves are, yes?"

"Yes." Will studies me for a long moment, and the waiter takes the fish away, mostly uneaten. "I'm not threatening you, or your friends.What we are discussing is larger than the individuals involved here. I imagine you became involved because you anticipated a payday. Well, we are prepared to pay. We just need to know the package is as intact as possible, all the pieces recoverable."

"All the pieces are recoverable," I say, hoping Bits won't prove me wrong. Silence in the earbuds.

"That's very good to know." The waiter sets glossy black spheres in front of each of us, and small pourable tureens of what seem to be hot fudge. "So then we can arrange..."

Will keeps talking, but Dolly is in my ears, louder than before, brisk, businesslike. "We've got a chopper incoming, which may or may not have to do with us, but the SUV's that all pulled up out front are definitely coming in there for one of you. Or both. They are *not* friendlies, they are openly carrying weapons. AR-15's looks like. I can engage, but there are too many for me to take all of them cleanly. This ain't exactly the best sniper roost I've ever had."

I keep my eyes on the dessert, picking up the hot chocolate tureen and pouring it over the black sphere. The blackness is darker chocolate, and it melts slowly away, displaying another garden scene within, this one including spun sugar lilies.

"They don't seem to be on Will's side," Bits says. "Their chatter isn't in English, and what I assume to be his chatter is. There's another radio network that's got personnel scrambling, and I assume that's whoever Will set up to be nearby. Both of you, take your exits. Now. Go."

I stand abruptly, chair knocking back, teetering on two legs, and then coming to rest again. I look at Will, who has also risen. Calculate. "Come with me," I say, and head towards the back of the restaurant, where I'd seen the holographic flicker of an exit sign when we came in.

"What the hell?"

"Trust me." I call over my shoulder, without turning. Could I hear heavy boots in the entryway, or was I just anticipating them? The creak of buckles on ripstop gun straps, the short slap of combat knife sheaths against a thigh or the small of a back. I leave the dining room rapidly, not running, and not all of the diners even bothered to look. Is Will behind me? He is if he's smart.

I turn the corner and there's the exit sign, across from doors to the kitchen, and I'm there in six steps, each one quicker than the last, high heels a staccato rhythm on the hardwood. Yes, those are his shiny shoes behind me. I slap my hands onto the emergency bar and a klaxon sounds throughout the building. LEDs flash at various emergency stations, and voices of diners begin to raise, even before I hear the front door explode inward in what has to be a cloud of splinters. It's a real wooden door.

We clatter down a concrete stairwell, and exit into a nondescript alley. I glance back briefly, past Will, to see if anybody else chose this exit as well. Even at this distance, there are raised voices, questioning, and other louder voices which are more strident, demanding, and I freeze for a split second when I hear a gun go off. I really need to become less gun shy.

Then Will has his arm across the small of my back and is urging me down the alleyway. There's a brief comedic moment where both Will's getaway car and mine are both there waiting. "Follow us," Will says finally. I nod, sliding into the backseat. No more gunfire behind us, I don't know if that's good or bad.

"You heard?"

"Yeah, we'll follow," Dolly says, and we drive off into the night.

Chapter Twelve

"So I hope this is the right choice," Bits says, holding the VR visor to her face; something seems to have happened to the strap.

"Well, they're not the ones shootin' at us," Dolly growls. There's a tear in her shirt and her ponytail is half fallen out, but she seems unhurt.

"I'm confident this is the better outcome," I offer.

"Oh, that's what you got outta you two making moon eyes at each other for three courses? Because it didn't seem like you were doing anything useful, from what I could hear."

"Moon eyes?"

Dolly makes a noise of disgust and waves her hands. "You know what I mean."

"Moon eyes," I say again. "Bits?"

"She isn't wrong," Bits says after a moment, picking her head up. The visor is still switched on, and colors play across Bits's face from below. "They didn't shut down their systems at all, and it looks like they called in cavalry to handle whoever it was that showed up in the SUVs. One agent was shot before they made it to their vehicles, but is stable. We're going to an undisclosed location, of course, but it seems like it might be on the industrial end of the docks."

"This is just really weird," Dolly says. "Why all that old bullshit about the eggs and submarines and Anastasia and stuff?"

"If an assumed lost Fabergé egg were to enter the market, the world would be in a clamor. Those items haven't been seen in more than a hundred years. It would be like if somebody knocked out an old wall in a coldwater flat in Liverpool and realized that the amber room was hidden behind it." I try to sound casual about it, but really, if I were to come into possession of something like a lost Fabergé egg, it would become the thing I was most private about in my life, a tiny jeweled thing which I could admire for my own pleasure and never tell anybody about. I hope that's the kind of person whose care those lost eggs have been in. I hope they're in a quiet room with drawn curtains and soft light to play off the facets of the jewels, and that delicate and caring hands occasionally open them to look at the marvelous treasure inside. I ache for such an opportunity.

"The amber room?" Dolly asks.

"Just another one of those magnificent things lost because of Nazis or war or both," I say.

Bits sighs, and then the brake lights ahead of us flash, flash again, and the car makes a sharp left without signaling. "What's our game plan going in here?" she asks, drumming her fingers on her knee.

"We want to be paid, we want to be safe, and we want our freedom," I say. "The same things we always want. Just because we think we might be dealing with actual big shot governmental good guys, or less-bad guys, does not change that in the slightest."

"There are times butter wouldn't melt in your mouth," Dolly says, but seems to intend it as a compliment.

"It's the only way to get by, sometimes. I assume I'll do the most talking?"

"Sure, so long as you get to the point, instead of endless small talk," Dolly says. We follow the car through a barbed wire topped chain link fence, onto what seems to be an abandoned shipping yard, containers piled high in the darkness, a few absolutely ancient arc sodium lights standing sentry at the perimeters.

We make the final turn, around one of the piles of shipping containers, and then it's searingly bright, big LEDs set up underneath a canopy that hides their light in a way I don't quite understand, but Bits probably will. There's big boats of indeterminate type nearby, and a few squat buildings, and I assume most of it is scenery to camouflage whatever the actual operation here is.

Dolly whistles aimlessly as we park and get out of the car, just a repeating run of notes, and I think about asking her to stop, and then don't. Dolly and Bits are both in riot gear, which is both amusing and perhaps appropriate; as I walk ahead and they come in on my flanks. They almost seem like bodyguards, though I sincerely hope none of this will come to that.

I wonder where Bits and Dolly have stowed the diamonds. I have every faith that while I was making my way across town, they were making sure the diamonds were someplace safe. It's actually very smart for me to not know that location just now. I can only assume Bits copied the files and has that encrypted and squirreled away in her systems somewhere.

Will comes to meet us. He left his umbrella at the restaurant, but I'd never even properly set my purse down. He does, however, have the handkerchief box, and that tiny thing makes my smile that much brighter "We approach the command center?" I ask.

"It's this way. This is all of you?" He looks at Dolly, then at Bits, then back to Dolly. "You did the hotel room amazingly clean," he says.

"I do take pride in my work," she says dryly, leaning into her drawl.

"And this is...technology and equipment?" Will looks at Bits again.

"You got it."

"Interesting. Very interesting. We've had a few days to speculate. But come on."

"Just to be clear, Will, are we under arrest?"

"What? No. You're free to leave any time you'd like. Though after what just happened I don't know why you might want to."

"I'm not sure why we'd want to stay. We still don't know who you are."

"That's right, that's true, I'm sorry. Come on." The other men in suits are out of the car, also stoic in the rain, but they just watch Will carry on. He leads us into a building practically in the water. I wonder when the nearest boat left shore last, and whether it ever will again. Everything within sight is weeping rust, and the way that boat's deck slumps towards the waterline, it seems like another prop, like more set dressing.

More people in black suits, men and women, are inside the first door Will opens, and he gestures us through. No obvious guns, but I pick out holsters as we breeze through. There are innumerable screens in the room. Hastily dimmed wall displays; tablets set on tables; on every agent's wrist, phones. They aren't all standing at attention, exactly, but they aren't busy at work either. They watch us cross the room.

The next room has wood paneling and no windows, as though a board room was transported from a skyscraper to this rundown building. I settle myself in the cushy chair at the head of the table, rocking back in it a little. Dolly and Bits follow my lead, and Dolly kicks her feet up onto the table with a grin. "Y'know, I've always wanted to do that in a place like this," she says.

"By all means, make yourself comfortable," Will says, not even hiding his smile. Heaven help him if he thinks we're *cute*. Dolly will eat his entrails.

"Your boyfriend is very nice, Bristles," Dolly says, and I smile at the little bit of pink that creeps above Will's collar.

"So what are we going to talk about, William?" I ask. Bits is working on her headset strap.

"Just Will," he says.

"I'm almost disappointed, but that's fascinating."

"Says the woman who hasn't told me her real name."

I wave my hand. "It's boring, I promise you."

"I'm sure."

"No, really. Names have a certain meaning and feeling. As children, we're named like puppies pulled from a cardboard box; it isn't necessarily going to bear the most cosmic weight."

"Well this took a turn," Dolly says, pivoting her chair towards Bits, who's holding the visor to her face again. She makes a distant noise of assent.

"We should get back on track," Will says. "I don't want your friends to get bored."

"We're bored already," Dolly says with a wink, and I sigh.

"Yes, business is business," I say.

"I'm glad you agree." Will stands behind the seat at the foot of the table, leaning his elbows on the back. "Now that we see what the other side is willing to do, can we cut to the chase?"

"Of course. I do apologize that you don't enjoy the banter. It's one of my few recreations."

Dolly sighs loudly and puts her boots up on the table again.

"Right. So. Where are the diamonds?"

"They're safe."

"They're easily recoverable?"

"More or less," Bits mutters, and at first I'm not sure Will hears her, but he bows his head slightly and rubs the back of his neck.

"That's good, I guess. And you've still got all of them? Haven't broken up the lot, sold or traded any?"

"We have them all," I say. It seems better for our safety that Will and his people don't know we're aware of the data. "They seemed more valuable as a set."

"That's more or less correct," he says. "Mrs. Carter would've been happy to carry that set away for herself. Maybe set it in a tiara or something."

"Mrs. Carter seems past tiara wearing age," I say. "Unless she's the leader of a small island nation that she rules with an iron fist in a velvet glove."

"She has a compound, anyway," Will says, perhaps a bit hastily. I smile, and wait. "Mrs. Carter, though, was working for foreign interests. She was a known authority to tap for this diamond sale. It would probably not surprise you to learn that the only reason they were for sale is that they were stolen from their rightful owners."

"And you intend to return them to their rightful owners?" I ask, tilting my head just a bit.

"Well, no." He clears his throat, then pulls out the chair and sits, still seeming a bit awkward. "No, the rightful owners are not to be considered allies."

"Ergo, Mrs. Carter is also not an ally."

"Correct. The purpose of the sale was to show off, ultimately. Espionage right under our noses. The seller, Richard, was an independent agent. He was paid handsomely, and in charge of the diamonds simply for his authority in the field."

"What a strange setup," I say.

"People like the ceremony of it. And figure nothing can happen, of course." Will muses on that for a moment. "Anyway. I don't know who you intended to sell the diamonds to, or if you tried already, but we are prepared to offer you each a comfortable sum in exchange for bringing them to us."

"I'm sorry, but why are they so important?" I ask. "Other than being remarkable stones."

Will clears his throat, frowning just a little bit. "Their base monetary value is a factor, of course. Nobody likes losing money."

"That's true, very true. And?"

"You know I can't fully disclose here," he says.

"Ah, girls, the diamonds have secrets," I say.

Dolly takes her boots off the table. "Can I smoke in here or what?" she asks.

"Go ahead," Will says.

Bits briefly pushes the VR headset up on top of her head. "You just told us they're more than they seem. This only increases the value," she says.

"Indeed." I raise an eyebrow at Will. "Last chance, I suppose, before we start writing figures on napkins. Or handkerchiefs, I suppose, as the room seems sorely lacking in a bar. Anything else?"

"There's nothing else you need to know about the diamonds," Will says evenly, but his frown, the unhappy quirk of his lips, that's the tell.

"All right, then. Get out your pen."

"Is this really necessary?" Will asks. He pulls a pen from the breast pocket of his very nice suit, and opens the handkerchief box.

"Are you hurt because you thought I got you a nice present for the sake of it?" I ask.

"No, I'm not—"

"We've got incoming," Bits says abruptly.

"How do you—" Will starts

"Hush. Bits, darling, what kind of incoming? We're in a port, there's a certain amount of traffic to be expected."

"A line of cars coming down the road we just took, in addition to one boat and something in the air, which might just be drones and not a chopper."

Will puts a hand to his ear, so yes, of course he has earbuds. He says, "It isn't a chopper, you're correct. Go out this door please."

"You've provided for this, one might assume?" I ask.

"Yes, but you're not going to want to walk on the decking in those heels," Will says.

"Everybody is so damned worried about my shoes."

Will holds the door impatiently. Dolly's already down the hallway as I pull my heels off and slip into a pair of folded leather ballet slippers from my purse.

The blandly painted passageway is yellow-lit, getting darker as Will leads us down several flights of stairs. Bits keeps her headset on and her hand on Dolly's back for guidance, keeping electronic tabs on whoever the interlopers are.

Surrounded by our breathing and footfalls, my eyes strain in the close darkness for light, for anything at all. It's dark enough and for long enough that I begin to see colors in the dark, like old-fashioned television static, and imagine shadows moving towards us, even though nobody else reacts to them. I was never afraid of the dark as a child, and it feels foolish to suddenly have that kind of fear now, but this is a profound and complete darkness that I was unprepared for. I try to to take stock, to set my focus on something other than the yawning emptiness around me. Dolly must have some kind of night vision in her augmented contact lenses and Will brought us here so decisively he must have something guiding him as well, so I'm the only one at the disadvantage, a position I sorely resent. I put my hand out straight, and encounter the smooth-rough fabric of Will's coat, still slightly damp from the rain, and the movement brings a waft of the hyacinth perfume to my nostrils.

"Watch your eyes," Will says just before opening a door into a hallway made out of white light.

"Where are we going?" It seems prudent to ask.

"There's a sub we can take. It's only a matter of time before the opposition is right here with us."

"A sub? Isn't this getting a little ridiculous?"

"This is already ridiculous," Dolly mutters. She never even got the chance to put her e cigarette away.

"They've engaged with your people upstairs," Bits says. "Though my connection is getting spotty." She pushes the VR visor up again and blinks at us.

"Communications from down here are typically bad," Will says. "And I guess that depends on your threshold for the ridiculous. I'll just ask again straight out, because we don't have time for anything else, do you have the diamonds with you?"

"Of course not. Why would we bring our only bargaining chip into a completely unknown scenario?"

"Right, excuse me."

The next set of doors are heavy steel and swing shut behind us with an ominous hollow bang, and here the concrete floor extends into walkways and gratings and water that smelled slightly brackish. Will slaps an honest to goodness big red button on the wall, and a klaxon sounds.

"Is that necessary or simply for effect?" I ask.

"Six of one, half dozen of the other," Will says. He gestures us towards one of the walkways, where the water boils up white and then a submarine breaks the surface, just like in all the movies. "Your chariot."

"And where are we going?" I ask again.

"Now this time, that's classified. We won't stay there long, you aren't prisoners, nobody's under arrest. We just need to assess and regroup. Someplace safe." Distant thumping briefly draws his attention, and a muscle in Dolly's jaw twitches. Water finishes pouring off the top of the sub, which lines up with the walkway. The hatch on top opens.

"Is this manned or remotely operated?" Bits asks.

"Manned. We'll see them once we're underway." We walk across the damp decking on top of the sub, and there's a ladder down the hatch. It really is a good thing that I keep flats in my purse, but for once in my life, I do feel the lack of riot gear.

Chapter Thirteen

Will briefly goes out of sight, presumably to converse with the submarine operators, and then leads us to a narrow galley with a small lounge. There's a couch, and table, and chairs, all just slightly too small for comfort. "I don't suppose anybody's hungry," he says. I shake my head.

"I could eat," Dolly says with a shrug.

"I'll see what I can do to make that happen." He rummages behind a partition.

Bits stows the headset. "I wonder if the car's all right," she says.

"Did you pack everything from the hotel into it before you left?" I ask.

"Nah, just some essentials, key items," Dolly says. "We didn't want to touch any of your stuff."

I stare at her. "So you just...left it? To be thrown out?"

"We're paid through the end of the week," Bits says. "It'll be there."

Will comes back with an armful of MRE's. "It isn't gourmet, but it'll be edible, anyway."

"I think our definitions of edible—" I begin, and Dolly interrupts me.

"It'll be calories, is what you mean," she says, taking one. "These don't require much explanation. They're always better with hot sauce, of course."

86

"I'm getting used to the fact that I'll probably never have a grasp of what you three know." Will shakes his head and sits down.

"Just think of it as a good way to round out your field experience." Dolly pulls the heat tab on one of the cans. "Complacency is dangerous."

"You're not wrong." Will examines the labels on a couple of the MREs, then pulls one open. "The gourmet experience was also a new one. I didn't actually go to that restaurant in Chicago, I just watched one of those chef shows," he says to me, a little apologetically.

"It isn't for everybody," I say.

Dolly laughs. "It isn't for people who are actually hungry."

"Appetites vary," I say with a sniff. "But, shall we continue our discussion? I think we were reaching figures."

"I've had word that we're supposed to hold off on that," Will says. "Other parties would like to be present."

"Oh? And after we've established such a magnificent rapport! What a shame."

"I'm sure they have their reasons." His neck does not redden. "It'll be fine. We'll be safe, we'll get a greater understanding of who our enemies are and what they're willing to do. Things will progress."

"If you say so." I cross my legs. The sub is very echoey, and clangy. Bits seems at loose ends without technology to reach for. "They seem willing to do quite a lot."

"Well. We'll also assess if both attacks came from the same party. All three attacks, if we include the raid on the arcade the other night."

"That was so stupid," Bits says. "We should never have made a mistake like that."

"You can't think of everything," I say, and Bits shakes her head.

"Something like that I absolutely should have."

"The fact that I could still call Bristol saved you some trouble," Will says.

"And the fact that you were able to call her is why we had trouble to begin with. Don't just say things to make me feel better when you don't even know me."

"Duly noted," Will says with an embarrassed smile.

"Thank you."

"Welcome to your view of the other side," Dolly says with a grin, moving on to another packet from her MRE. "Here's hoping it's educational."

"Oh, it already has been," Will says, with a brief glance in my direction.

"We're so pleased to have been a help to you and your organization," I say with a smile. "Is our secure and undisclosed location very far?"

"Not much longer." He checks his watch. "Another half hour, maybe?"

"And then we'll have our own fresh and educational view of your side of things."

"I hadn't thought of it that way." Will in fact seems slightly alarmed. I try to mentally construct a very short description of what I think our attribution in the case file would be, as if I know how case files are worded. A group of thieves? A group of well equipped thieves? A group of capable thieves? The thieves part has to stick, obviously. We robbed a great deal of diamonds from a group of wealthy and powerful people. For a brief moment, I again allow myself to think of how it would be to have one of those Fabergé eggs in my hands. Or just that blue diamond again.

Dolly and Will are finished with their MRE's by the time a tone sounds through the overhead speakers, and a woman comes on, saying "We're in the final approach."

"Finally," Dolly says, and I reapply my lipstick.

"Who will we be meeting here?" I ask Will.

"Mr. Harding is the lead here," he says after a moment's hesitation.

"Mr. Harding. Good to know, thank you. Is there anything else I should know about Mr. Harding?"

"I'm not going to brief you on my boss," he says with a disbelieving laugh.

I cap my lipstick and dropped it back into my purse with a shrug. "You can't blame a girl for trying."

He's about to comment, but then there's a rising sensation, and a little jolt.

"I feel as though we're approaching a Bond villain's lair," I say as we follow Will out of the galley and back to the hatch.

"We're the good guys," Will says.

"Everybody thinks they're the good guys." And then the hatch overhead opens, and more yellow light pours in.

We climb out of the sub and into another underground area, this one far less concrete bunker and far more natural cave. A tall man in a suit much like Will's waits for us on dry land. "Cut it close, didn't you?" he asks Will.

Will glances at Bits briefly before answering. "It turned out alright."

"Be that as it may..." His gaze rakes over Bits and Dolly in their riot gear, lingers on me in my date night dress. "You ladies have caused quite the commotion."

"It's a habit we've cultivated," I say. "Though we realized a little late that we were in quite a more complicated situation than we'd intended."

"Yes. It's interesting that you realized that before things got too far out of hand," Harding scowls. "It's almost embarrassing that this meeting took so long."

"We're used to being underestimated," I say smoothly. "And it's no fault of Will's that we anticipated contact. Really, what happened is our initial diamond buyer decided he wasn't going to touch the stones, which was unusual to say the least. And when we withdrew to regroup, things started to go a bit pear shaped."

"A pretty story, but there's more to it," Mr. Harding says.

"Why, of course there is. But are we going to stand about in a submarine dock all evening?"

He scowls again, for longer, then looks at Will. "This is your responsibility," he says, and turns.

We follow them into extremely dull-looking office quarters. We pause at a reception window and Mr. Harding berates the just-out-of-sight staffer for a few moments. I take the time to swap back to my high heels, folding the ballet slippers again and rolling them up in a spare handkerchief as an extra precaution against moisture.

The door buzzes and Mr. Harding stands back to let us through, Will taking the lead. He notices the noise of my heels on the tiled floor immediately, and if anything, his scowl abates just a little bit. I pat my hair briefly; my hair pins are still in place.

As we walk, Bits looks at door frames, corners, framed pictures. I'm not certain what she's checking for, but it's more than possible that Bits is also wearing augmented contact lenses. Or did Bits have the corneal augmentation surgery? She certainly didn't tell me about it. The notion of layering contacts with a headset makes me feel delicately nauseous; I'd put on a VR headset once in my life and fallen over immediately, a nosebleed ensuing. Bits is the one who inhabits that role, living a virtual life along with a real one.

"If you ladies wouldn't mind using this room while we debrief Will here, we'll be with you in just a little while. There are some vending machines, coded open access. If you need anything else, just knock on the door." Mr. Harding smiles then, a very trained and necessary smile, and I smile back warmly.

"That would be just fine, Mr. Harding, thank you."

The room seems to be an employee lounge, with a table and straight backed chairs in one end where the vending machines are, and a couch and more comfortable cushioned chairs taking up the rest of the space. There is a sparsely populated bookshelf, which seems to be made up mostly of cheap reprint paperbacks and some augmented magazines, the type with holo ads and video accompaniment to some articles, considerably less cheap.

"How does it look, Bits?" I ask, once the door is closed. She's already shoved the headset onto her face. I'm not sure when she fixed the strap.

"Pretty secure," Bits says. "We're probably not going to get ambushed here. Even if they tried, it would be a poor prospect. No fortress is impregnable or whatever, but this one is pretty good. I've read about facilities like it, dark place on the map. They're probably listening to us here—so hi guys—but it seems safe enough. Now to hope that Will makes good on his promise that we're safe, not under arrest, and that we will be worked with on this to recover those diamonds they want so badly."

"Good. So no surprises either."

"Not really."

By the time Mr. Harding comes back, Bits and Dolly are both asleep. Or Bits is still doing mysterious tech things, there's no real way for me to tell the difference without trying to talk to her. I spend the time trying to make sure my thoughts are in order.

Mr. Harding walks into the room and seems briefly thrown off that I sit serenely waiting for him, hands folded, ankles crossed. "I'm sorry, that took longer than intended."

"Oh, it isn't a worry at all," I say. "This space is quite relaxing."

"I'm glad you think so." He sits at the end of the couch nearest my chair. "Do I need to address all three of you?"

"I've been authorized to speak for the group. It's what Will and I were working towards over dinner, after all."

"Yes, quite." Mr. Harding clears his throat. "Quite the resourceful trio, aren't you? I suppose it isn't so unusual, in this day and age. But remarkable, yes."

"Well thank you very much." I smile. And I wait.

"As I understand it, you and Will were in fact at the point of coming to terms?" Mr. Harding seems to hesitate a bit each time he says Will's name, as though he in fact means to say Agent something instead, or Mr. something.

"We were, I think."

"I see. I'm authorized to offer half a million dollars for each of you, in the manner of your choosing. We can give you cash, though that'll make the boys in accounting shit their pants, the boys in security feel even worse, thinking of the suitcases just on the street while you choose banks or sew it up into mattresses or whatever else you intend to do with it."

"Half a million each?" I repeat. "That is rather generous."

"We think so, and we can get it to you as soon as—"

"I think it sort of seems to be worth more than the stones intrinsic value, wouldn't you say?" I ask idly.

"Why would you say that?"

"I did have a chance to look at them in the hotel room, after all, with the grading instruments present. Of course, the blue stone is its own beast."

"Exactly, the blue stone," Mr. Harding says. "I don't know very much about it, honestly. Me, I can't see the use for shiny things that seem to exist for the purpose of being shiny. I prefer useful things."

"Well, there are industrial uses for diamonds," I say. "But they're different stones entirely from the ones we're discussing."

"Very different, I'd think." Mr. Harding considers me a moment. He clearly thought I would fall all over myself accepting his initial offer. "What's your counter request, then?"

"I'd say a million each, for the sake of argument. Otherwise, I'd simply suspect we were being fleeced out of ignorance."

"A million each." Harding nods his head as he processes this. "That would be enough for you to retire on, live out the rest of your life, if you invested it responsibly."

"Or went to a country with a far lower cost of living," I say, thinking of places where the desert air meets the sea air. "I don't know about Bits and Dolly's goals necessarily, but personally, I'm averse to being shot at and pursued. The sooner I can normalize my situation, the better."

"I'm not sure many people prefer to be shot at, Miss."

"Bristol."

"Miss Bristol. I understand, your current situation is uncomfortable. You stepped into an unexpected arena, and there are forces at work here that not everybody is prepared to deal with. It's admirable you ladies avoided your pursuers so adeptly."

"We are quite the team," I agree. "Additionally, I want to make sure our amnesty is on paper and in your systems, signed and notarized by whoever necessary. We had no political intent in this action, and while obviously stealing in general is illegal, and stealing diamonds quite on a grand scale, we arguably kept the stones out of the incorrect hands until your organization had the time to regroup and liaise with us properly."

Another pause. "I'm sure that can be arranged," he says. Either I'm just shocking him time and again, which is hard to imagine, or he has some friends in his ears. I should always assume there are eavesdroppers, and speak accordingly.

"I think that's one of the most desirable parts of the deal," I say. "Will assured us we were neither arrested nor detained, and our freedom is very important to us, especially in the light of the payment agreement which I should hope we will reach."

"So money, your freedom, and freedom from prosecution on this particular event. Do I have it straight?"

"You do." I think furiously to see if I've forgotten anything else, but we'd meant to keep it as simple as possible.

"The amnesty would, I should hope, make it so our legal identities and passports and such function as expected, with no holds or hangups?"

"I should hope," Mr. Harding agrees. "An especially important detail, were one to retire to a foreign shore."

"The expat life is just so glamorous some places."

"I've heard that. Not for me, I love my country. But there's an appeal. Lower prices, carefree beaches, that kind of thing."

"I think we understand one another, Mr. Harding."

"You understand I need to run this past my superiors," he says. "Double the total amount, plus all the red tape with your amnesty."

"Oh, I understand. But, it isn't exactly as though we're going anywhere, is it?" I ask, gesturing at the lounge with a little laugh. Perhaps I ought to have asked for more.

"Not at the moment, anyway. You might want to get some sleep as well."

"Perhaps I will, though I do prefer a bed to other sorts of furniture. It's funny, sleeping in strange places doesn't bother me, but I do love my creature comforts."

"My wife, she can't sleep anywhere but at home. So she claims. Every time we're in a hotel, she goes on and on about this or that. As far as I can tell, she's sawing lumber, but she always says she couldn't sleep, gets a crick in her neck, all that."

"How dreadful for her."

"Yeah. For her." This time Mr. Harding laughs. Then he stands up, buttons his single button suit coat, and offers me his hand. I take it and shake firmly. "I'll talk to you in the morning. I'll send Will back here so you have a familiar face."

"It's most appreciated, Mr. Harding. How long do you think we'll be here?"

"It's hard to say. We appreciate your patience, of course."

"Of course," I say, my smile never slipping. How tiresome.

"Now have a good night. We're safe here."

It makes sense to be obsessed with safety, but making promises like that is the best way to test fate. There's no way to know everything, to track all the factors. You just make educated guesses and fling yourself into life's wayward currents. I give a little jump at the knock at the door, and then Will softly calls, "It's me, can I come in?"

I cross the room and pull open the door. "Afraid to find us in some level of indecency?"

"It's just polite," he says, and then I notice the folding cots on wheels in the hall next to him.

"Oh, you clever darling!"

"I did. Though you're probably the only one it bothers."

"Yes, I much prefer something resembling a real bed."

Will wheels the cots in, positions one and unfolds it for me. It's already up with sheets, and a folded scratchy green wool blanket. "Army issue, I'm sorry about that. They do utility, not comfort."

"It's fine, I'm sure." I slip my heels off and line them up next to the head of the bed with my purse, pull the pins from my hair. I take a moment to peel away the false eyelashes and swipe at my face with a makeup removal cloth from my purse, peering into my compact mirror to make sure I get it all. "I'm so dreadfully tired that I won't notice to complain."

"I'll be right here if you need anything," he says, browsing the sparse bookcase. He takes one of the magazines and sits at the table.

I curl up on my side, hands pillowed under my cheek. For a folding army issue cot, it's more comfortable than I might have expected, and I fall lightly and comfortably asleep to the scratch of Will paging through the magazine, tiny holo sounds occasionally reaching my ears.

Chapter Fourteen

It isn't often that I wake without some natural light in the morning, and it's disorienting. Will still sits at the table, his tie pulled loose. Dolly's there with him, working through another MRE, one of the pulp paperbacks propped in front of her. Bits is still in much the same position on the couch, with her VR headset on.

"I had hoped for a hot breakfast," I say, sitting up and stretching my arms.

"There might yet be hope for that," Will says.

"I bullied him into getting me this, I was starving."

"You must be, to eat those."

"Aw, they aren't so bad. Don't have to worry about it spoiling like fresh food, or anything getting into it. Sealed and shelf stable. Not terribly interesting, but a little hot sauce goes a long way."

"I always wondered about that little vial on your keychain. I always just assumed it was cyanide, in case we were ever captured." I slip into my heels yet again; the dress seems remarkably unwrinkled.

"Nah, the cyanide is in one of my molar replacements," Dolly says with a crooked grin, then drains the last of her coffee.

"So what's our plan for the day?" I ask. "Will we have another handler? Or will we at least be directed to a more amusing holding room while you men stomp out there and save the world?"

"You're stuck with me for now," Will says.

I wonder how long Mr. Harding will keep us waiting, if he'll try that tactic again, but then the PA system crackles and a detached female voice says, "Will Scarlet and guests, please report to conference area D." Bits gives a start and pulls her headset off.

"Shall we?" Will asks, finishing his coffee and standing.

"When *will* they let you sleep?" I ask. "I would have thought it was preferable to have you well-rested, reflexes and judgement intact."

"I'll sleep when I'm dead," he says. I have a terrible shiver of foreboding. "Hey. I keep telling you, we're safe here." Will looks as though he wants to take my hand, or put an arm around me, but he does neither.

"Ever hear the saying whistling past a graveyard?" Dolly asks, when I seem disinclined to answer, a rarity in all of our association together, to be sure.

"Yeah, why?" Will puts their books back on the shelf.

"Just thought it might apply here. Come on, let's not keep people waitin.'"

"I'm afraid they will have to wait, I absolutely must step into the ladies' room and fix myself before we have any sort of business meeting."

"You look fine," Will says, and I look at him, smiling pleasantly, until he sighs. "It's along the way."

There are numerous unmarked doors we pass along the way, and then the stereotypical pair of restroom doors, male and female. No gender neutral bathrooms in this organization.

We girls go in with no comment to one another, leaving Will to linger in the hall. I lay paper towels out on the counter, though it does appear to be a very clean facility, and pull my little travel make-up kit from my purse. I'm done nearly before Bits and Dolly are, and as an afterthought, I use the barest whisper of a spritz of the hyacinth perfume, before packing everything back up and hanging my purse in the crook of my arm again.

"It's like magic," Dolly says. She on occasion does her makeup with what is essentially a black crayon, but is very casual about it either way.

"I could teach you," I say, as always, and as always Dolly just laughs and shakes her head.

We rejoin Will, and after some more walking, reach another generic conference room. I am becoming inured to the fact that the meeting places with this organization will not, in fact, have alcohol available. But what really grabs my attention is the presence in the room besides Mr. Harding; Marquis.

"You wicked man, you didn't tell me Marquis would be here," I say, leaving it up to Mr. Harding and Will to decide who I am addressing.

I close the distance with three swift steps and Marquis catches me by the arms before I can embrace them, staring into my face. "I was so worried," they say. "You just disappeared. You just left me."

"I'm so sorry about everything," I say. Oh they're angry at me. They have every right to be so very angry with me. "I was worried about you too, but I just couldn't message you, we were barely staying ahead of—"

"I've been here since the night Will called you," Marquis says. "They wouldn't tell me anything."

"I'm so sorry," I say again. I'd hoped for a happier reunion than this, especially in front of strangers. "Are you okay?"

They shrug and let go of my arms. "Mostly bored and frustrated. Worried sick. But you look just fine. New dress?"

"I hate to interrupt the reunion, but we're going to have a person from financials in here, a notary, and another operations supervisor. Yes, before you ask, this conversation is being watched and recorded, to make sure we're making the deals we said we would. It protects all of us. Do you feel properly apprised of what the plan is moving forward?"

"Yeah, sounds great," Dolly says. She's already planted herself in one of the chairs. "We heard the recording of last night's conversation, what you an' Bristol hashed out seems just fine. Is Marquis gettin' cut into all of this?"

"Marquis has made their own arrangements," Mr. Harding says. "We'll move you to what we hope are more pleasing or entertaining accommodations until the rest of the situation is resolved, after which everybody can go home."

"Fine then," I say, sitting next to Dolly. Everybody finds chairs, the additional personnel shuffling in as Will sits on the other side of me. On impulse, I take his hand briefly, squeeze it, and smile when he looks at me.

Papers are passed out to each of us, depositions practically, and I do in fact take the time to read the entire thing. Bits did as well. Marquis. Dolly, however, only takes out her e cigarette, and gestures with it as if to say "this alright?" When nobody stops her, a sweet cherry pie smell lightly puffs through the room.

"You're not reading it? You trust your compatriots that much?" Mr. Harding asks.

"I do," Dolly says, and blows a smoke ring. "Haven't led me wrong yet."

None of the information about the stolen stones references anything about hidden data, or indicates in any way that they're more than just diamonds. Bits and I glance at each other, and I raise my eyebrows just slightly. Bits blinks once, slowly. She has copies.

"Problem, ladies?" Mr. Harding asks from his seat at the head of the table. None of the other staff have spoken, and I wonder what sort of deals this room has witnessed.

"There is the question of delivery," I say.

"Pardon?" Everybody in the room looks up.

I plant my finger on the applicable line. "It says here that upon signing, we will deliver the missing package in full. As stated, we are not currently in possession of the package. It's in a secure location. However, that location will be burned for us immediately should we subsequently be chauffeured in SUVs and black helicopters and whatnot for your recovery's sake. That is not acceptable to our business model."

"You'll notice we do not really indicate the illegality of your business model or the means by which you came by the package," Mr. Harding says. "We could make those adjustments as well if you'd like."

"And nullify our agreement in its entirety, as it predicated upon the amnesty and the payment these documents also indicate." I smile.

"That's why I let them read it," Dolly says to the room at large.

"Disappointingly, my documents discuss no packages, so I feel safe signing them. Unless as a show of solidarity I ought not?" Marquis asks, and I feel wildly relieved. They aren't so mad at me that we won't move past it.

"No, darling, go right ahead if you feel like you're all set. Our agreements shouldn't affect one another's."

"They are entirely separate," Harding says, and one of the notaries nods. Mr. Harding continues to study me, and I do not waver. "It says staff accompaniment, does not specify number of staff, or describe the vehicle type. It satisfies the agreement for Will to accompany you."

"I think that is a generous interpretation of the papers you have given us, Mr. Harding, and if that is the spirit of what this agreement is, I am more than happy to sign it."

"Is that okay with you too?" Mr. Harding turns to Bits.

"Yeah. Looks good." She shrugs, still reading, but doesn't bring up any other issues once she's finished.

"It's a good thing you all were so willing to be reasonable," Mr. Harding says. "Pens are there on the table, Marquis will receive pay-

ment and transportation immediately. Will is empowered to distrib-
ute payment once the package is in hand."

"Splendid," I say, but I use a pen from my purse. It isn't often that
I hand write something, and I have a particular pen that I feel shows
off my penmanship the best.

Chapter Fifteen

When they let us leave, three days later, we don't receive anoth-er submarine ride. Instead, we take an elevator for an inter-minable number of floors to the surface, and then up from there, wordless and off-rhythm muzak plaguing us for the duration.

//Can I hack it and change it?// Bits texts me.

I smile thinly and shake my head. //Best to keep some cards up our sleeve, just in case.//

"So I don't really get where the threat went," Dolly says.

"What do you mean?" Will asks.

"We fled here by cover of night and water, by the skin of our teeth near as I could tell. We could smell the cordite. And now in three days it's just kinda...done?"

"Our people have worked to confuse the signals they've been us-ing to find you. The various satellite tags which identify you as you have been replicated hundreds of times across the city and increas-ingly beyond. It makes that method of search useless, unless they have unlimited personnel and resources."

"Not necessarily," Bits says as the elevator doors ding open and we escape our canned music hell. "The right algorithm could knock down the false positives in almost no time at all just by comparing the movements against the original sample. Then they'd have a much narrower scope to search, and if each individual they had on it took a vector, they'd drop it even faster."

"So how much time are you saying we might conceivably have?" I ask.

Bits shrugs. "A couple hours. Or thirty minutes. It depends on the quality of their equipment and personnel. Or I could just be paranoid and everything will go according to plan."

"I am so fucking glad you said that," Dolly says, looking up at the sky.

"I knew you would be."

"Look, there are other reasons it's done now. Let's...let's just get in the chopper," Will says.

"To where?"

"Ladies' choice, I guess. To one of our motor pools, or back to your car."

"Our car is all right?" I ask.

"Last I knew it was. When the opposition swept in, they gave the vehicles a cursory search and scan, but they know what they're looking for, obviously, and how best it could be hidden."

"Well, they think they do," Bits says.

"Why you wicked girl, whatever do you mean?" I ask. "You didn't actually leave the diamonds in the car?"

"Well, no. But you'll see."

"Well I know the suspense is killing me," Will says. "So have any of you ridden in a helicopter before?"

"Got my license to fly one," Dolly says.

"Really?" Will turns to stare.

"Dolly manages our vehicular needs," I say, gritting my teeth just a little. I'd previously mentioned a helicopter and she hadn't said a word. "And firearms, if such a thing becomes necessary."

"That detail had somehow escaped me," Will says. "The vehicle thing, not the firearms. Your car is so—"

"Unassuming? That's on purpose." Dolly shrugs. "Besides, it gets good mileage. Has one of the best and longest lasting batteries on the market."

"Especially with a little tweaking," Bits says. We settle our headsets and the rotors spin up. Dolly is not permitted to pilot.

A helicopter ride is interesting enough on its own, but we're over water for far longer than I anticipate, and I do get a teensy bit bored. I'd have preferred a night flight, with the city stretching out beneath us like jewels on velvet, dark buildings looming, encasing everybody's tiny lives within.

The shipyard does, in fact, look much as we left it. It was almost a disappointment, little sign of explosions or gunplay or our hasty exit, save for the fence in one area is a twisted ruin. The car is there, little dark sedan, just where we'd parked it. Windows intact, doors closed, trunk shut.

"I almost expected to never see the car again," I say once the helicopter is silent.

"It would've been a shame," Dolly says. "After all we put into it."

"I call shotgun," Bits says.

"I never get to sit up front," I say to Will.

"You never call shotgun," Dolly says, pressing her thumb to the lock until it beeps and unlatches all the doors.

"Excuse me, I didn't grow up 'calling shotgun.' And what's the other one you go on about?"

"Punch buggy," Dolly says.

"Punch buggy?" Will asks, eyebrows raised.

"VW Beetles? That they've made since the 20th? Apparently one exclaims punch buggy and punches the nearest passenger in the leg or arm."

"I'm really glad my brothers never knew that," Will says. "Not that there were many beetles where I'm from."

"There were like, three or four versions, but they kept making the original style in Mexico for decades after everybody else stopped." Dolly starts the car. "I'm not really sure why. But people would go south of the border and drive them up. Hell, they might still do it. And where I'm from, the weather's good for cars. So. Lots of punch buggies."

"Your childhood must have been amazing," I say dryly.

"Got real good at not hitting like a girl," Dolly says. "Because my brothers're the ones who taught me."

"What about you, Bits? Any punch buggying in your household?" Will asks. Bits has the VR headset on, her head tipped back against the seat rest.

"We didn't have many road trips," she says distantly. "And I don't have any brothers. Lots of cousins. Turn right here."

"We came from—" Will starts, and I lay a hand on his arm.

"Just let them." From the way his suit moves, and the slight crackle, the inner right pocket is where he has our documents. I envision manila envelopes, one for each of us, each containing a passport and a pay chip and a copy of our amnesty agreements.

"You don't know either?"

"I was out with you, remember?"

We drive for twenty or more minutes, then pull into a bus station that looks like it hasn't been used since the original bugs were rolling off the line. Grass grows up through the cracks in the pavement, and the perimeter fence has sagged into a metal haystack in the weeds, as though the big bad wolf huffed and puffed and blew the house down.

"We're clear," Bits says, and Dolly parks just around the back and cuts the engine.

"I don't get it," Will says. "Why an abandoned bus station?"

"Well. This isn't a hangout. It isn't along a well traveled road. There may or may not be some serial killer rabid dog bogeyman kinds of stories about this bus station in particular."

Dolly muscles open the half unhinged door, which to my eye seems as though it was last opened before any of us were born. It's bright inside, not like a closed building at all, and when we step through the opening, we look up at the clear blue sky through a tremendous hole in the roof.

"Everybody's up on their tetanus shots, right?" Dolly asks.

"Actually, yes," I say. It only seems prudent.

"Yup," Bits says.

"It's regulation," Will says.

Dolly laughs. "Geeze, folks, I was mostly jokin'. But it's good to know we're all covered." Bits keeps her headset on, but every once in a while lifts it and peers around at the real world.

"I never would've guessed you were into urban exploration," I say, picking my way through the broken tile, the roots which have heaved themselves up from the dirt below.

"It has its uses," Bits says.

We reach the wall of bus station lockers, which are improbably pristine, unbent, unrusted, and most of them with their keys still inserted. Dolly catches my eye, then grins and winks before producing a key, orange plastic fobbed, from one of her many, many vest pockets. Bits takes out a similar one and goes to a locker near the middle, surrounded by other doors missing keys. Dolly goes to a locker near the end, near the women's room, the big long sign hanging off of one rusting, weeping bolt. Each pull out a green enameled, workman's style thermos.

I rummage in my purse for a lipstick to apply while watching the proceedings. "That was dreadfully clever. Is that all of them?"

"Yup," Bits says.

I turn to Will, smiling. "Isn't it grand?" I ask, and I step in towards him. Reflexively, he puts his arms out, and I put my hands on his lapels, stand on tiptoe, and kiss him full on the mouth, lightly at first, but then he closes the circle of his arms around me, and we lean in together for a blissful moment.

He breaks the connection first, moving as though he stumbled while taking a step, but we're both standing still. I slip a hand inside of his suit coat, pull out the envelopes. "Wha—" he starts, and then his voice fails him. Dolly and I guide him to sit in one of the bolted-in bus station chairs that remains.

"I'm sorry, Will, I know you intended to keep your end of the bargain. We simply couldn't trust Mr. Harding and the rest of them, though." I raise my eyebrows at Bits, who opens the thermoses and selects a couple of the black velvet bags, dropping them into one of those silvery signal-blocking bags she keeps on hand. "These are the dangerous ones," I say. "The ones with nasty locations, and launch codes, and all that Dead Hand business. These others, while very interesting, contain no threat to anybody. They're simply too lucrative to let go. You do understand, don't you?" He just looks at me mutely, betrayal writ large in his brown eyes. I pat him on the cheek as he tries to speak again. "I haven't killed you, if that's what you're worried about. Either your compatriots will find you, or you'll recover and be able to call them."

"We done here?" Dolly asks.

I take out my last handkerchief, carefully blot off all my lipstick. "I should think so."

"Whenever we get used to a place..." Bits says as we walk out to the car, headset hanging around her neck like flight goggles. "Time to move again, I guess."

Epilogue

Though I have never been religious, I always pause and turn my head in the proper direction when I hear the call to prayer waft through my silk-hung windows, borne on the sea breeze towards the stunning blue waves, the world beyond. It is deeply beautiful to me, and I respected it. Perhaps one day I shall convert to something, perhaps not.

There's a light rap on my door. "We've got some early birds," Suzette says. She's the first friend I've made here. She's from Paris, and she loves party nights as much as I do. My little apartment is much like the one I last had in America, without much in the way of furniture, but perfect to fill with people and drinks and hors d'ouevres.

"I'll be right out!" I return my attention to the cosmetics arrayed on the table in front of me. I've already put in my diamond earrings, hung a thin golden chain around my neck, the barest whisper of precious metal against my pale collarbones. The night promises to be clear, and while my hand hesitates on the Chanel, I pass it over for the sandalwood rose, spritzing my inner wrists, the hollow of my throat, the back of my neck. I apply my lipstick, blot, take a moment to look at myself in the mirror. I admire the speckled light reflected onto my skin from the Fabergé egg set there on a little pedestal, risen above the other bits and baubles. I draw a finger along the edge of it, for the pleasure of it, then stand.

I imagine Will is going to show up any day now, and it remains to be seen if it is with or without the cavalry. I switch off the light as I go to meet my guests, leaving the torn-open air mail envelope to fuss a little in the breeze, with its stamps upon stamps, forwarded and forwarded, until it reached me here on this foreign shore.

Run With the Hunted 2:
Ctrl Alt Delete
Jennifer R. Donohue

Chapter One

There's a dead pixel in the sky. Once I notice it, I can't ignore it. My eyes keep dragging up to look at it, no matter where I am or what I'm doing. It's an itch I can't scratch, a smear on the lens of my immersion. Plus, I don't know how long it's been there, and that bothers me.

The moon is always somewhere real-time appropriate. They tried the stars, in beta, but it took far too much bandwidth and nobody wanted a project like that. Now most places, it's flat black at night, sometimes cloudy. Just the moon. Sometimes a comet, if one is visible to the naked human eye real-time. It's ridiculous, what people bicker over when given the forum. Not a surprise. Just ridiculous.

So now that's my pet project. I spend my time adding stars. My personal night sky is a complete one, and when I have the time or the urge, I go through the old Hubble and Cassini and Kepler photographs, so if I want to spend time virtually lying on my back on a mountain or rooftop, just looking at all of the stars mankind had ever heard of, I can do that. I upload it to the public servers, little by little. My VR immersion rig is built from the best one money can buy, but the others are catching up. Managing the data better, with solid states and local nodes and the new fiber infrastructures.

I sometimes go to Carnivale in Venice at night time, since VR's the only place you can visit Venice anymore, the crenellated buildings all scanned and then rendered true to life, buildings which aren't standing in Venice anymore, sucked into the mucky lagoon or swallowed up by the waves or what have you. The twinkle lights, the gon-dolas. Everybody there is always all dressed up and masked. It adds another dimension, the party plus the game of IDing human or pro-gram. It isn't easy like it used to be. On impulse, I stop a man in a giraffe mask and, through my unicorn mask, ask "Do you see that in the sky?"

He looks down at me, and then up at the night sky, shakes his head. "See what?" he asks. He's human. I'm good at the Human or AI game. I'm not good at dealing with people in real life.

"Nevermind. Bug hunting." He nods and goes on his way. A SpaceX constellation shimmers by, reminding us all who we have to thank for worldwide internet.

My nose itches and I wrinkle it distractedly. Next would be to find somebody in the same VR node as me, using the same service provider. Theoretically. Except my VR node is just mine, paid for in an isolated jungle in Mexico, my rig built by hand piece by piece and hooked up to the local fiber after greasing appropriate political palms up the ladder, through intermediaries. Intermediaries are much bet-ter than me doing it. This could be real bad.

I move off the street, out of the crowd, and start my immersion exit protocol sequence to boot out of VR. It's been awhile, actually. Longer than a public protocol would've allowed. Public protocols existed for a reason, I'm happy to acknowledge that. But really they're unnecessary limits. Turns out, when you have the money for it, anything's possible.

The Carnivale around me fades away, the sounds and smells first, then the sights, like an old fashioned photograph un-developing, and I'm left temporarily with the flat gray haze of the non-waking state. It's drug induced, meant to be a body-brain buffer between the shock of VR immersion and consciousness, or vice versa. It isn't nec-essary if you're just upright using a VR headset. It isn't necessary if you're still just living your life.

Do I feel a needle sliding into my arm? I'm cotton-mouthed, not quite conscious, unable to protest. I like being more awake before the post-immersion wake-up meds.

After a moment, things come into sharper focus. The room's still dim, but ambient sounds return, the hum of servers and their water coolant, a compressor somewhere. Breathing, my own and somebody else's. The flat plastic smell of the carpet, still pretty new, mixed with the antiseptic smell of the medical equipment for VR immersion, the IV rig, all of that. The grass and gun oil smell of the intruder. I open my eyes slowly; eyelids tend to stick, especially after so long.

Dolly grins down at me. "Hey Bits," she says. "I wasn't sure tapping your machine with a hammer was the best way to get your attention, but I guess it got the job done. Hope I shot you up with the right stuff once that light turned green."

"Oh Jesus Christ, Dolly, what're you doing here?" I ask hoarsely. "And why didn't you just message me?"

"Well actually it's a good thing, 'cause it looks like you're here all by your lonesome. Empty IV bags aren't good for anybody." She drops a needle into the sharps container; it's really just B vitamins. I think.

"There's failsafes," I mutter, looking at the IV tree, but Dolly's right, those bags are empty. I rub my eyes. "How'd you even find me?"

"Oh you know. I got my ways," Dolly says, like that even means anything.

"Why'd you even find me?" I try.

"Well. I gotta find somebody."

"I'm not working right now, Dolly." I try to sit up, fail, and Dolly steadies me against the back of the cushy immersion chair.

"Yeah, Bits, I can see that. But I got something I need your help with. Lucky I actually know how to get you back on your feet."

"I'm starving." Starving not starving. I can't eat real food right away.

"You stink too. How long were you under?"

I reach for the data and it isn't there. "I don't...I don't know."

Dolly gives a low whistle. "Shit, Bitsy. Isn't that inadvisable in the extreme?"

"The benefits of having your own setup." I look around. The overhead light is out, burned out, because the one in the hall is on.

"Well let's get you hosed off and fed. Then I'll pull out my list."

"List. On paper." I rub my eyes again. They alternate between watering too much and not enough. This probably isn't the longest I've gone, but it feels like I was immersed for a long time. The chair massages muscles, mitigates some of the effects of immersion, but there's the sleepwalking stage of returning to real world consciousness, the inner ear disturbance of becoming upright again. Headaches, sometimes.

Dolly laughs. "I do everything I can on paper, Bitsy."

"Why didn't you just call Bristol?"

"Don't worry, this is in your wheelhouse." Her tone is off, I think. I can't tell. "Let's get you to the shower."

Chapter Two

Dolly's always been stronger than she looks. She supports me down the hall without breaking a sweat. I don't know how she's so strong, I could never carry her. She gets the shower running, locates shampoo, conditioner, pulls out towels and a bathrobe and smells them, shrugs. I remember my nose itched in VR, reach up to scratch it. My fingernails crackle with dry blood, but nothing hurts. Nosebleed maybe, mosquito maybe. "It seems like you've done this before, Dolly."

"Maybe I have. You steady enough to get yourself hosed off?"

"Yeah." I don't want Dolly to help me shower, that's not really where we are in our relationship.

"Alrighty. I'll look for your kitchen."

My stomach does a slow flop and I yawn to stem the nausea. "I'm sure that'll sound good when I'm more awake. Or in, like, two weeks." There's protocols. Vitamins. Meal replacements.

"It will." She pulls the door most of the way closed and walks off, whistling.

I drop my clothes on the floor, yoga pants and tank top, take a breath, and step into the spray. The water's too harsh at first, a thousand needles, and I stand off to the side, just letting it warm my skin.

Eventually I just go numb, and I fumble the bottles of shampoo and stuff. I'd buzzed my hair before I went under, and it's at a plush length that's soft and nice to touch. Eventually, or maybe it's quick, my fingertips go pruney, and I turn off the shower.

Going barefoot to the kitchen, every step feels new and tender. It doesn't really smell like cooking, but it doesn't smell like burning either. My nose just hasn't really kicked back on yet; sometimes my senses don't quite do what they're supposed to once I'm back in the real world. Takes some time to boot back up.

The coffee pot is steaming, almost full, and Dolly's head and shoulders in the refrigerator. "You still like your coffee sugar no milk, right? 'Cause your milk's way off."

"Right." She sets it in front of me, and the mug between my palms is far too warm at first, and I hold it gingerly on the butcher block countertop, perched on a stool.

"I don't know why you do that to yourself," Dolly says, watching me from the corners of her eyes. She's wearing her riot gear, I realize.

I shrug; it won't be a productive argument. "I thought you were gonna cook or something."

"Oh yeah. Gotta see if your eggs float first."

"If the eggs..."

"If they float, they're no good. If they don't, they're fine." Dolly gets out a glass bowl, slops some water in it, and slides the eggs from the carton in it. One of them floats, and she frowns and puts it back in the carton. The others don't, and she cracks them each, one-handed with surprising adroitness, into a skillet heating on the stove.

"Why are you in riot gear?" Should I be in riot gear?

"I told you." She glances at me, pokes the eggs. Did she? She could've. Time's skippy and gappy after a long immersion.

"I can't eat just regular food right away," I say. I can't decide if the eggs smell amazing or not. I can't decide if I'm amazed Dolly can cook or not.

"I know but you don't have any of that protein goo. Eggs are the best you've got here, buildin' blocks of life and all that. You don't even have the right vitamins in the cabinets, just some C. You should probably still take that." And Dolly loosens the lid and slides the plastic bottle across the butcher block.

"Didn't leave to get more after the last time," I say. Which seems like it is and isn't the right answer. I'm forgetting something and I have such a headache.

"That was dumb," Dolly says, back turned. The vitamin C goes down with effort, one of the pills sticking sideways a second, flooding my mouth with the sour almost-vomit taste. I drink more coffee, washing it away with the sweetbitter. I always have trouble swallowing vitamin C.

"It was."

"You get obsessed with that digital nonsense. Get too much in your head." Dolly slides a plate in front of me, then gets herself a cup of coffee. Sunny side up, the edges gone lacey from the heat. Golden tortillas, buttery. "Think you can keep any of that down?"

No. "I don't know yet."

"If you can't, don't push too hard. We'll get outta here tomorrow, next day, get you some protein slurries. Unless you got some squirreled away that you also forgot about."

"I don't know." When did I last have to say I don't know so many times? I shake my head, but that's a mistake, as the world around me tilts, shifts, rights itself. "Where are we going? Why are you here, anyway?"

"We're headin' to California first," she says around a mouthful of tortilla and egg, some yolk running down her chin. "Anyway why'd you pick Mexico?"

"The climate and the exchange rate."

"Climate's nice, you're right about that." Dolly's already done eating. I look down at my plate, at the glistening eggs, think about how the yolk will slump out when I puncture it with a fork, and I burp a sour, vitamin C tasting burp. I shove my plate at Dolly. "You sure?"

"Yeah, I'm sure. And it hurts worse to throw up when you're empty."

"I wouldn't know." Dolly tucks into that plate with equal gusto, then gets up for more coffee.

I try again. "Dolly, why are you here?"

"I told you, something we gotta get done. It's kind of urgent, but I don't know the timeline."

Just perfect. "And I told you I wasn't working."

"Yeah, are we gonna sit around repeating ourselves, or are we gonna talk like grownups?" She pushes away her second empty plate. "You care if I smoke?"

"No. Or, I don't know yet."

"Fair enough." Dolly slaps her pockets until she pulls out a pack of cigarettes, cheap plastic lighter tucked into the wrapper, pulls one out, lights it. The smell of tobacco is sort of soothing, actually. Makes me think of...somebody. My father? My memories have a way of being scrambled, especially after time in full tactile VR immersion. It's expected. Dolly is being uncommonly patient, actually. Though doesn't she normally smoke ecigs? Not this much, though. Not one after the other, constantly.

"So what's the job, Dolly? What's the plan?" It's amazing Dolly hasn't already launched into it, pouring out the salt shaker and drawing diagrams on the butcher block with her fingertip, leaving the cigarette just kind of stuck there in the corner of her mouth.

"We have a friend in a tight spot. Need to bust her out."

"Out of where? A prison, I assume, from the way you're saying it."

"Something like that."

"So a black site then."

"Maybe? Once we know where she is it'll be easier."

"Stateside? Mexico? Elsewhere?"

"I'm. Um. Not sure." Dolly drags at the cigarette, not looking at me. I'm used to Dolly being rock solid. Evasive isn't unusual, we're all pretty shaky on the concept of honesty. But there's something else there that I can't track, under the usual Dolly brashness.

"What do you mean you're not sure?" I get myself up this time, to pour more coffee in on the sugar sludge in the bottom of my mug. The ring of my spoon against the porcelain is very sharp. I feel like I'm not really seeing in color right now, everything infinite shades of gray.

"It's probably stateside. We were supposed to rendezvous. When that didn't happen, I poked around, reached some dead ends. Drew my logical conclusions."

"Then came here."

"More or less."

"No, you said you went to Bristol first."

"Did I?" Dolly is quiet for a long time, jiggling one leg, smoking. She did, didn't she?

"So what, then?"

"Well. I need you to do some tracking, first off."

I sigh. "The easiest way to do that is reimmersion." That's inadvisable. If Dolly even knows that. She knows weapons, that's for damn sure. Cars. Geography, military protocols, including, evidently, some VR immersion ones, but not enough to lecture me.

"Good thing we didn't leave yet," Dolly says with a crooked grin, getting up and running her cigarette butt under the faucet. She comes and collects the plates, washes them, half whistling that same tune that I don't recognize. She does that a lot sometimes.

Chapter Three

Despite Dolly's rush, she doesn't let me re-immerse right away. I totter around my dim abandoned estate on tender-soled feet, Dolly smoking almost constantly and hovering at my elbow. The floor's all tiles, polished coral, no carpeting. Most of the windows are shuttered, so it's cooler in the house, even though the only room with actual environmental controls is the VR room, for the rig and medical stuff. When we step out into the courtyard, it's like stepping into a mouth. The jungle, evening closing around us, is close and damp. Birds I don't know the names of make their strange cries in the trees.

"The locals here don't put worms in their tequila," I say to Dolly.

"No?"

"No, they put a scorpion in each bottle. It makes me think of Macbeth."

"Why's that?" Dolly lights another cigarette.

"Everybody talks about Lady Macbeth's mad scene, out damn spot, but Macbeth has his own mad scene too. He says at one point, my mind is full of scorpions."

"I like Shakespeare," Dolly says.

"You do?"

"I guess mostly the fighting. Shakespeare's bloody." She laughs and drags on her cigarette. "You're sure you're okay to do this? You don't wanna sleep?"

"It's okay. You said it was probably urgent, I'll go back into immersion."

"If you're sure." Dolly shifts uneasily, gun belt creaking. "I don't want to push you past—"

"It's okay. You asked, I'll do it." Maybe then she'll leave me alone. Probably not.

I REMEMBER DOLLY SAYING something about taking a hammer to the rig, and pause to examine the machines. There's a ding in the casing of one, a hammer lying on top. I pick it up, hold it a minute to gauge my strength. Since my immersion chair is the best money can buy, I've hardly lost any muscle mass.

"Dolly, seriously?"

"Like I said, I didn't know your wakeup protocols and it seemed like the fastest way. Was I wrong?"

"Not exactly. Better than unplugging me I guess."

"Which would do what, anyway?"

"Probably nothing. I assume I'd wake up eventually."

"See, it's that assume word. We don't like that assume word."

"It's like how in the olden days you used to wait for your computer to tell you it was safe to turn off. Or you used to manually eject a drive. It probably wasn't necessary, but better safe than sorry, right?"

"I know they don't think it's safe to immerse for six months."

"Another reason I came here. People were more likely to leave me alone, between the cartels and the tigers."

"Are you talking about the riddle, or literal tigers?"

"The real estate agent seemed worried about literal tigers. I haven't seen any."

"Christ, Bits." Dolly stares at me, frowning.

"What, did we finally find something you're afraid of?"

"Nah, I just wouldn't've left the AK in the Jeep if I thought there were tigers. Gimme a sec."

"I can't believe they still make those," I say when she comes back.

"This particular one is a more recent knockoff," Dolly says, leaning it up. "Hard to argue with a workhorse like that. I mean, there's more modern analogs, caseless, ammunition AR overlay, all that good stuff. But, can't hack an AK with one of your VR dealies. And you can't pull an AR enabled firearm out of a puddle and still expect it to work right, so there's that."

"There's that," I agree. "Though there are some waterproof AR weapons."

"Yeah, but they're not AKs."

"You can't convince me you have brand loyalty."

"I don't. Lots of folks do, but I wonder if it's more superstition, like using the same shoelaces all the time."

"You don't use anything all the time. You don't even care what kind of cigarettes you smoke."

"Exactly." Dolly grins.

"So you're...reverse superstitious?"

"Anti-superstitious? Whatever. This isn't a movie; no sense only using a rifle you named or some stupid shit like that, right?"

"Right." I settle back into the VR chair, pull the helmet down over my head, feeling the wires spider into place through my hair. A shaved head isn't necessary, I just like doing it, especially before a long immersion. "So who am I looking for?"

Dolly hesitates. Dolly never hesitates. "Bristol."

I jerk upright, the wires scrabble-tightening in my hair. "What? What do you mean Bristol? What happened? Why did you take so long to tell me?"

"Shh, shh now, calm down. You're all fucked up, you needed time. Even this is pushing it, but I dunno how long we can wait anymore."

"Why isn't she in Morocco?"

"Well that's a million dollar question, right?"

"Dolly." I was ready to be sick before we ever started this conversation and now I close my eyes, clench my jaw.

"I know, I know, I'm sorry."

I take a deep slow breath, let it out. "Okay. I can't just search the internet at large for Bristol, especially not after the scrubbing work I've put in. Give me a waypoint."

"Well I think it's likely that the county sheriff in Montana who arrested her has probably contacted DHS by now."

"Homeland. Of course." And of course I can't say no. And of course...I want the challenge. Hacking Homeland. "What the fuck *happened*?"

"Well I think she thought getting caught by as small a fish as possible would keep the big fish away the longest."

"Yeah but—" I have too many questions and they bottleneck where my thoughts meet my voice, so nothing comes out.

"Time's wasting, Bitsy. Come on, run me through your protocols."

I show her on the console what to hit to cue my logoff sequence. I can do it myself anytime I want, but emergencies are emergencies. Then I close my eyes and start my login sequence. I wonder for a sec if maybe it won't work, if I'm too saturated or too agitated and the autohypnosis will just fizzle, leave me awake and in the real world with my scalp tingling. The brain-computer interface implant can only do so much sometimes.

I open my eyes in Texas. Or at least the official Virtual Reality architecture of Texas, the Lone Star State. The DHS mainframe is in Texas, I guess in what used to be army property, and army buildings almost always look the same. To me, anyway.

There's regulation height chain link fence, with razorwire along the top of it, and what looks like people in uniforms, patrolling with dogs in bulletproof vests. It seems particularly mean to shoot a dog.

It seems sadistic to do it in Virtual Reality. What, you want to know if they programmed authentic dog in pain noises?

I stroll up to the gates, fiddle with the lock. People make a big deal when they refer to something as military grade, but in my experience it tends to mean the same quality as everything else, if not slightly under. It just costs more. It isn't actually coded better, and I'm in without any trouble. Nobody notices. The patrolling 'personnel' are automated anti intrusion systems, not in-person, VR immersed hackers. Or whatever the alphabet soup government calls them. Tiger teams, that's the old fashioned term. Maybe they still use it. It's the one old fashioned thing I like, the vocabulary from the first days of the internet.

Everything's neatly labeled and with clear direction, that's a military grade truism, and plain old records is as good a place to start as any. I flip to subheading DHS arrests, sorted by most recent. There's a file for supply rig hijacking with inventory from the rig, but the numbers just kind of swim in my brain and I shake it off. Too much, and not Bristol. They raided people ordering pressure cookers. Deportation targets. I look at the date and can't make sense of it, if it's sooner or later than I think it should be. I shuffle through to subheading prisoner holdings. Subheading prisoner transfers. Run her aliases. If a small-time sheriff arrested her and transferred her up the chain, county to state to federal...Bristol, Madison, Chelsea, Florence, Paris, Devon, and we have a winner. She's somewhere in Kansas, transferred from locals in Montana. And not for long.

I look up. The records section is coded to look like an old fashioned storage room, metal shelving, cardboard boxes, signs on the walls. Or maybe all records storage rooms still look like this in person, if they're kept analog. We've all seen pictures of the National Tracing Center. But the signs on the walls are different now from when I got here. Glowing? Did they change color? I head for the exit, thinking about those coded German shepherds in their bullet proof vests. I don't know if the color shift means a change in threat awareness level, but I've got what I came for.

Technically, I can exit immersion from the facility, but exiting from free space is preferable. Technically. So far as protocols go. Because I follow protocols so closely. The door behind me opens and I freeze in place, the copy transfer of Bristol's file ticking off its last bit of percentage. There's a member of personnel in the space here, and I'm not keen to find out how DHS counters hackers. You hear horror stories, of course. Recursive hypnotic viruses that leave people fucked up so you can't think can't sleep can't—

"Excuse me, ma'am, I'm going to need to see your credentials," a voice says, close. Shit.

"Of course, of course," I mutter, initiating my countdown, fumbling as though I have lag and my security packet is on the way, 3-2-1, golf-tango-echo—no, no that's wrong and then I'm shaken up, distracted, and can't restart the protocol, fuck.

"Your credentials," the voice repeats, and then I'm facing another woman of similar height and build, if our avatars are at all representative of our real selves. "Or we're going to have a problem."

"You seem to be suggesting we don't already. What's your rank?"

"Corporal."

"Well, Corporal, are you in the habit of accosting everybody who enters the records room?" I ask, abandoning the exit protocol for the moment, shifting rapidly through my falsified credentials. I skimmed a sergeant's last year, year before, when me and Dolly and Bristol had the business with the diamonds, because you just never know when having officer credentials will come in handy, even cross agency.

"Considering it's my job, yes, yes I am. It's protocol to ask for credentials, for credentials to be presented, for the handshake, and for parties to be on their way. I apologize that this seems to be a foreign concept for you—" the Corporal is struggling to capture my attention, to trap me in the immersion, backtraces already running, for all the good it'll do her. My signal reroutes all over the place.

"Sergeant," I say with a certain amount of smugness, presenting the credentials, real ones cobbled together with updates and enough of my own bioreadings to make it that much more authentic and confusing.

"Sergeant," the Corporal repeats, sounding mystified. She scans the credentials, and steps back.

"Everything is in order then, Corporal?" I ask.

"Yes, ma'am. You understand that I—"

"Yes I do, Corporal. There's no need for this incident to go any further. Just doing your due diligence. So few people do more than lip service anymore," I say. The exit door is so close.

"Thank you, ma'am. Have a good day."

"You too, Corporal." We salute each other, and I feel ridiculous, and she fades back into the code of the records room. I leave out the exit door, go down a featureless hallway that makes me wonder why the fuck somebody coded it, and then I'm back under the VR Texas sky again, once again at the end of my immersion exit protocol, 3-2-1, golf, tango, foxtrot, oscar, and then I'm sitting up in my rig in Mexico, tearing the headset off and saying to wide-eyed Dolly "Pull the plug and get the hammer."

"What?"

"Did I stutter? Pull the plug and get the hammer." My immersion exit is short, precious seconds trimmed away, hacked off, until it's that little packaged phrase, tricking my brain into waking up in my body again instead of in the machine. If that Corporal in Texas decides she's not so sure of me after all, she's sending a red alert directing resources at locating my signal. But it's ridiculous to be so worried about that, I'm so careful. Tracing me would take literally hours, I'm sure of it. But still.

"You're the boss," Dolly says with a shrug and a curious grin. She sticks a cigarette to her lip and lights it as she leaves the room. I turn sideways in the chair and belch sourly. My stomach doesn't seem like it's moored properly.

By the time Dolly's back with the hammer, I've recovered enough to pull the plugs on all of the VR gear, pull the hard drives on what I'm keeping and bag them, jam them into carrying cases. I always have to be prepared for these eventualities, though I don't remember who taught me that. I remember the smell of cigarette smoke, or is it gunfire? Pain spikes in my temples and I make a mental note to chase those thoughts later.

"You're sure you want to do this?" Dolly asks.

"Sure. I don't expect unmarked helicopters in the next twelve hours or anything, but better safe than sorry, right? Another wakeup, and we're blowing town, you already said."

"I didn't know if you'd need more time. I've never seen you in such bad shape."

"Not many people have." We let that hang for a minute there between us. Really, I'm not sure if I've ever seen myself in such bad shape either. "Okay I packed what I need. Everything's unplugged, but that doesn't mean some things don't still have juice. Be careful."

"So that means you got it, you found her."

"Yeah, yeah, Bristol's in Kansas right now."

"Right now?" Dolly is kind of swinging the hammer in her right hand; there's something about a hammer that makes you want to swing it.

"There's an interrogation team coming in four days, and she'll be moved after that, but they didn't have a point B. So, that could mean a lot of things. Release amongst them, I guess."

"That's our Bits always seeing the silver lining," Dolly says, in the least silver lining voice I've ever heard, and then she hits the VR immersion rig with the hammer. I imagine she does it as hard as she can, judging from the scream of metal and how far some of the shards go.

Chapter Four

"Fucking Kansas," Dolly says, an hour later on the veranda.

"I'm sure Kansas has nice things going for it," I say, sipping my protein slushy. Mangosteen, a fruit the Queen of England once offered a hefty sum for, delivered fresh from Asia. I read that on the inside of a vintage Snapple lid.

"Yeah, sure. They probably wind farm the hell out of it. Isn't that where a lot of astronauts came from?"

"That's Ohio."

"Really, do you know what my main problem is with her being in Kansas?"

"No, Dolly, tell me."

"It's so flat." I just look at her. I should know why she thinks that's bad. I used to know why she thinks that's bad. "It's flat. It's hard to insert on a military facility anyway, but a flat one? They see you on approach. They see you coming thirty miles away. It's terrible."

"Then we hijack the transport."

"If there is transport and they aren't just gonna put a bullet in the back of her head in the basement."

I've never seen Dolly this kind of agitated. Not even during the diamond thing, when we thought maybe both the American and Russian governments were after us for scary Cold War nuclear codes. No, Dolly was still her grinning fucked up, southern belle, devil-may-care self. I should feel more amped up, but everything is muffled, distant.

"Well, step one, we get back stateside," I say. "We hook up with people you know or people I know. DHS'll think she's too valuable to just execute. Or, they won't know what they have and just shuffle her around."

"Yeah. Maybe." Dolly stands at the edge of the veranda, looking out across the courtyard towards the jungle. "I almost wish we would see a tiger," she says.

"I know what you mean."

"I heard someplace that a tiger won't attack you if you're looking at it. So people in jungles where there's tigers, sometimes they wear masks on the backs of their heads, so they've got faces there too."

"I didn't know that."

"Makes you wonder why something that big and deadly is worried about you just looking at it."

"It kind of does." Maybe tigers are just lazy.

Dolly lights another cigarette, still looking at the jungle. Her AK is slung on its web harness, barrel against her leg. She always looks most at home when she can open carry.

"Of course, breaking into a federal clink is crazy," Dolly says. I blink at her. Time passed somehow. She doesn't have a cigarette anymore and it's raining.

"Yes, it is. But crazy never stops you from doing anything."

"You know me so well."

"We just need to get there and then we'll see how to do it." I normally want far more of a plan than this. Contingencies. Alternate approaches. This isn't even a plan. We normally want more than a plan.

"True enough." She's quiet for a minute. "Anything we can do to get you tuned in faster?"

"No. Unfortunately my implant doesn't have any kind of fast acclimation programming. It was on my list." I could tinker with the implant, maybe. If the problem is the implant. "Something to work on on the road, maybe."

"Yeah, maybe. Funny, the things the brain can do, ain't it?"

"Yeah, funny."

"Not, like funny ha ha."

"What you think to laugh at and what I do aren't always the same thing."

"Isn't that the truth. You hungry yet?"

"No, I'm not hungry yet, you bottomless pit. You can eat if you want. I'm just going to sit out here and wait for tigers."

"Fair enough. Holler if you need me."

"I will."

Dolly clomps inside, untied boot laces clattering on the tile floors. She's whistling again. I hold my phone in my lap, but I don't feel the impulse to fiddle with it just yet. I should. There's so much to look up. The borders, if anything's going to affect our crossing, Nebraska. But I just stare off into the jungle, listening to the slowly pattering rain, which also sounds just like the wind through the leaf laden branches, except there isn't any wind, just the rain. I shake my head. That kind of circular thinking is too easy to get trapped in when you immerse in VR a lot, and especially right now. I set the tablet on one of the little end tables and walk out into the courtyard, the gravel prickling the soles of my feet, the rain pattering onto the crown of my head, my shoulders, my arms, trickling warm down my skin like sweat I didn't work to shed. I tilt my head back and let the rain fall like tears on my face, and maybe I'm crying. I should be crying, I'm so goddamn scared for Bristol, I know this intellectually, but even so, I can't really react.

I go back inside before I'm soaked, trailing my fingers along the walls until I stop in front of one of the few decorations I added, an ugly painting of an old fashioned English hunting scene. Men in red coats and white breeches on horseback, hounds coursing, a fox running. I reach up and lift it off the wall, heavy in its dark wood frame, and it slips out of my hands, drops straight to the floor. The red coats seem very bright, throbbing off the painting, but nothing else does. Dolly appears near me, impossibly fast. "You okay?"

"Yeah. Gonna need money, right?" I nod at the wall safe that the painting covered.

"I guess?" From the look on her face, she looked for it and didn't pick the right spot.

I spin the dial, left right left, then press my palm to the biometric scan, where it tingles for thirty seconds, and then beeps and hisses open. I've got a variety of currencies. Bundled U.S. dollars, rolls of gold coins that a number of countries will take, and the keychain authenticator for one of my offshore bank accounts.

"We need to keep this small, I don't know where you have people you trust." Or where I do. Lockhart's still okay but not near Kansas.

"I admit I was probably jumping to conclusions when I said they'd probably just shoot her."

"Probably." I don't like talking about this. "They don't seem to know who she is yet. They don't know about the diamond business. But they must think she knows something they want to know, and they must have a reason to have her mobile." Back when we first got together, started doing jobs, I hacked agencies one by one and erased things in our digital records. Fingerprints. DNA from cheek swabs. I altered descriptions and overwrote pictures and voice and video. It isn't impossible to connect dots across the years and make a case regarding who each of us is, the internet is forever after all, but I did my damndest to make it as impossible as possible.

"They always think somebody knows something. Do you want another smoothie?"

"No, I don't want another smoothie. You're taking very good care of me, Dolly but right now I want to know a little bit about how we're going cowboy rebel against the United States Goddamn Department of Homeland Security to cut Bristol loose of whatever it is you got yourselves into."

"Well we had a job," she says, and then my head fills with static. When it clears, I'm sitting on a wooden stool in the bathroom, lights bright white, too bright, Dolly still talking and the electric razor humming over the sides of my head. It's how I prefer it, rather than the allover shave, though I've walked around with both.

"Thanks," I say to Dolly. A cigarette burns on the edge of the sink.

"You're welcome. You're all in and out, is that normal?"

Negative. "It'll pass."

"I know it will. But you've got a long time to make up for."

"You keep saying that. It isn't the longest I've gone."

"Isn't it? And what's the longest you've gone?"

Was it a year? "I can't remember."

"Do you remember anything I just told you?"

"You and Bristol were doing a job."

She frowns, reaches to pick up the cigarette, take a drag. "No. *We* had a job. All three of us."

So after we separated in Berlin. After Bristol went to Morocco and I came here and Dolly went...wherever it was Dolly went. "And whatever we did got Homeland on us."

"You don't remember?" She's watching me in the mirror, razor silent, loose hair scratchy on my neck.

I try. But reaching for the memories is like trying to get a piece of eggshell out of cake batter; I think I have it and it slips away, again and again. "I don't remember," I say, and I realize I'm breathing a little too hard, sweating a little. "Something went wrong though."

"Take it easy. Yeah, yeah it did." She takes another short, hard drag on the cigarette, puts it out in the sink. "And if I try to tell you again, you're just gonna reboot again. Which is pretty freaky, gotta say."

"Try living it." I've never had it this bad. Sometimes it's just how the real world is, a little bit here and there. Glitches like everything's digital. Time speeds up or slows down and you miss things or you see everything, more than is humanly possible. I had to have been counterhacked. Something in my equipment got screwed up, and I didn't know, and it was wrong for months. I immersed like that. Who knows what I did, what it did to me. No wonder I didn't recognize the date.

Chapter Five

The border crossing into California is no sweat, Dolly says. I don't remember it. Evidently we stopped at some point and put our questionable gear in the box. I probably would have worried more about it, if I could have gotten my thoughts to focus on it at all. Instead, I keep looking at the ocean, once we can see the ocean, and I think about the plans the military had to train and weaponize dolphins. Or had the military actually accomplished that? There was that super weird experiment in like, the 1970s with the partially flooded house that the woman lived in with the male dolphin, but that was more of a communications experiment than a weapons one, which was weird too, because it seems to me that we actually did establish a good interspecies communication. Maybe it was more like the 1990s that they were using dolphins to defuse bombs, or that they were putting lasers on them or whatever. Dolphin codebreakers. I can't help myself and giggle.

"What's, uh, what's goin' on Bitsy?" Dolly asks. It's dark out and we've just pulled into a hotel parking lot. It looks like...oh what was that movie, with the murders?

"Just tired and thinking about things. I'm sorry."

"Well, I'm toast. You're okay with sharing a room, I assume."

"Yeah, though you throw elbows in your sleep," I say.

"Yup, separate beds," Dolly says. "Sit tight, I'll talk to the friendly front desk clerk."

Hope he doesn't want to murder us, I think. Though honestly, any desk clerk that breaks into a room with the two of us would get more than they bargained for. Well, that breaks into a room with Dolly. But Dolly is more than a handful for most people. Meaner than a rattlesnake, when she wants to be. I don't know where I learned that saying; probably from Dolly herself.

"Bitsy, come on," Dolly says, and I get the sense she's been repeating herself for awhile. She's being far more patient than I thought she had in her.

"Sorry. I didn't think you'd be so fast."

"It's okay. You can get that bag, at least? I'll grab the duffles."

"I can carry my duffle," I protest, mostly because she expects me to.

"It's not a big deal. Come on."

We walk across the parking lot and I realize about halfway across that it isn't gravel or dirt, but shells. Oysters maybe or clams, or maybe just whatever got dredged up. Maybe it's sand dollars and it wrecked the mermaid economy for that decade, plunged them into a Depression. I stifle what I just know would be a crazy kind of giggle. Dolly's worried enough already.

"What did the room set you back?" I ask as Dolly unlocks it with a key, not a keycard. It has an oblong plastic keychain with the number on it in black letters.

"Don't worry about it. Not like I don't got the money."

"You didn't blow it all on guns, booze, and muscle cars?"

"I did not."

"Dolly. I might be disappointed. Maybe a racehorse?"

"Negative." Dolly pops the snap on her handgun and goes rapidly into the room, flicking the lights on, checking the corners. It's clear and seems clean enough, the carpet and comforters smelling of cleaner and detergent, a faint amount of sand squeaking under Dolly's combat boots on the bathroom tiles.

"Well if you didn't blow all your money then why were we doing a job?"

""Some things in life, I do for the thrill of them, Bits. Or because I feel like I have to. You got anything like that?" Dolly asks, with her knife's edge smile.

"I guess I do," I say. "Bristol though?"

"If nothing else, we're thick as thieves. As the saying goes." Dolly says, sitting on the end of her bed and untying her boots. "You hungry?"

"Not yet. Order what you want."

"I hope you don't mind, I stole the blender from your hacienda, and brought a cooler full of protein, so we've got you covered."

"Why would I mind?"

"I dunno. I've just always been one of those ask forgiveness, not permission kind of people."

"I'm surprised you didn't bring more of the food, honestly."

"Didn't see the logistics of it, honestly, all that raw meat. The tigers'll get it. Or somebody else'll get wise to the fact that you've cleared out and head up there. Whichever."

"News travels fast," I say.

Dolly paws through the nightstand, then turns on the AR TV and looks up local delivery on the internet. "Thai, Mexican, Ethiopian, Chinese, Taiwanese, Japanese, Korean, Indian, Cajun, Jamaican, Nova Scotian, French—"

"Nova Scotian?" I ask.

"Yeah. Looks like mostly seafood?"

"You know you really just want tacos to go with the tequila you brought. Going through the choices is for funzies."

Dolly laughs. "I do. But maybe I was hoping something would catch your fancy."

"Just get the damn tacos, Dolly."

"I'm getting the damn tacos. Geeze you're pushy."

I lie back on the other bed. "*I'm* pushy," I say to the ceiling. I think about the VR headset in my bag. The AR contact lenses.

"Yup, pushy and a chatterbox. Just always runnin' your mouth, Bits, it's real hard for anybody else to get a word in edgewise." Dolly is flipping through the channels at a rapid pace, almost faster than I can really follow. Spy movie, car race, weather, politics, home renovations, golf, game show, war movie...

"Well I'll just have to work on that, Dolly. I'm glad you brought it to my attention."

"Hey, we're all works in progress, right?"

"I guess." Dolly stops on some music channel. Ten hours in the car and I still feel like I'm moving, stationary on the bed. That two-lane highway that headed north from Mexico is well kept but hard traveled, so it doesn't exactly maintain a glassy fresh-paved condition. There are some roads, all over the world but I think at least one in California, that if you drive in a certain lane at a certain speed, the asphalt is grooved in such a way that the tires passing over them played a song. I fell down that YouTube rabbit hole once, and during one of my immersions went all over the place to many of those locations and drove over them, in an electric sports car with the top down, the wind through my hair. I didn't visit the California one, though.

The tacos come and Dolly pays, her boot laces rattling against the legs of all the furniture in the room. I think maybe I'll just melt into the bed, my limbs so leaden, my eyelids feeling like those bibs they put on you in the dentist's office. Dolly runs the chain and the bolt on the door, and then sets the rustling paper delivery bags down somewhere. She's still for a moment, then comes and pulls my boots off and drops them on the floor, and I slip into a sleep that feels dreamless but isn't, not quite. It's just filled with a view of looking through the windshield at the highway through my new sunglasses as we drove north under a blue sky.

Chapter Six

"We need to call somebody," Dolly says in the morning. "We aren't gonna take a transport just the two of us, much as I'd like to be that badass."

"It'd be a good story," I say. The coffee maker is going and Dolly's eating a cold taco, watching the news in not-English.

"Atta girl." Dolly grins and balls up her taco paper, gets up to pour coffee. "How you feeling?"

"I don't know."

She hands me a mug and I slide my sunglasses on, take a sip. Dolly put the magical just right amount of sugar into the coffee. On the news, some celebrities are doing...something. Some world leaders are going...somewhere. I can't remember right this second who the president of anywhere is. "I think Nicky is the pony to bet on."

"Nicky...Nicolai, the guy we met in Paris? Your Russian friend?"

"The one and the same. He happened to be...well, I won't say in town, we ain't in a town. In the general vicinity. And he might know some people we can pick up along the way, get a temporary crew rolling."

Nicolai is one of those citizen of the world looking types, and you can't quite nail him down until he opens his mouth and you heard the Russian in his voice. Well, Bristol nailed him down, when we met him in Europe, but apparently she'd spent some time in Moscow because of course she did. He has a good tan, but that could mean he has a natural tan or he likes tanning or he got genetically modded to look like that.

"I brought you girls some vodka," he says, when he shows up. He kisses us each on the cheeks, me first and fast before I even realize that's what he's doing, Dolly slower.

"And we've got tequila with a scorpion in it, so if you wanna swap, we can do that," Dolly says, lighting a cigarette and offering him the pack. He looks at it, and makes a face, shaking his head.

"Dolly, you'll excuse me for saying you have no taste."

"I will. I have no taste on purpose. If it doesn't matter what I'm smoking, it means I can always get a pack of cigarettes I'm happy with."

"While that's perfectly defensible, it also prevents you from taking joy in the things you like," Nicolai says, pulling out his own pack of cigarettes. He looks at me right as I take a bite out of a coffee wafer candy bar. "She gives this same explanation for beer, and everything else."

"Except guns," I say with my mouth full. Eating candy doesn't feel like real eating.

"Except guns," he agrees. "Dolly has the most snobbish taste possible in guns and ammunition."

"Does that make up for it?" Dolly asks.

"It makes you a pain in the ass, my friend."

Dolly laughs. "I've been told that more than once."

"I can imagine," Nicolai says. "Now what's the job?"

"We need a few operators to hit a convoy and extract a very good friend of mine. Ours." Dolly says, smoothly, without batting an eye. She must've practiced in her head.

"Sounds like a good time," Nicolai says. "When will this party begin?"

"Couple days. In Kansas."

"A state I've never seen." He shrugs

Dolly grins, plops into one of the wooden chairs by the little table. "Interested in attendin' the party, are you?"

"Only if somebody else can bring the beer. Honestly, she drinks swill," he says to me despairingly, and I can't help but laugh. "What's your part in this?"

"The same as in Paris. Equipment and communications." I remember Paris, at least. It was before the diamonds.

"I'm happy to hear that."

"Thanks." I finish my candy bar. Paris was easy. No shots fired, hardly any blood pressures raised, everything just smooth sailing, smooth talking. Who was the other person working with us in Paris? I can't remember. Somebody Bristol knows, a woman from South Africa or Nigeria, who split her time between there and Paris.

"So you know some folks then?" Dolly asks.

"I can make some calls. I know some people who might be on board."

Dolly blows a smoke ring. "If they're not?"

"I know other people, in Detroit, if the first group doesn't work out."

"It's DHS. Probably a small group, definitely covert."

"You do get into the most interesting difficulties, Dolly," Nicolai says, and I wonder what their history is.

"You still in?" she asks, still smiling, but her eyes narrow just a little, watching him. Her cigarette is in her left hand, her right hand resting on her stomach as she slouches back in her chair. It's no coincidence that her pistol is holstered there on her left, unsnapped. And if I noticed that, Nicolai has to see it too.

Nicolai smiles and drags on his cigarette, his posture changing not at all. "What do I care, if it's DHS? They aren't omnipotent, they can't track us to the ends of the earth. Especially not with Bits on comms and equipment. Especially if they're keeping it quiet."

"You know what to look forward to, if we get collared," Dolly says.

"That's the risk people like us take, with the life we lead," he says with a shrug. "I'll call my people. They'll want to be paid."

"They'll be paid," Dolly says evenly, stubbing out her cigarette in the clamshell ashtray.

Chapter Seven

Dolly goes out to get cigarettes and something for dinner. She does not say what she is purchasing in either of those categories. Nicolai goes for beer and then occupies himself with phone call after phone call, walking up and down the entire sidewalk in front of the motel, talking and smoking and occasionally gesticulating. The front desk clerk look out the window at him a couple of times, and I message Dolly to remind her to go over and pay for adding a guest to our room or whatever.

I put in my AR contacts, and then I get the blender out of the Jeep and make one of my smoothies. I drink it in a chair on the sidewalk outside of our room while looking at the glimmer of the ocean across the highway and across a further expanse of beach. I look at the passing cars, their flickering broadcasts. I glance at Nicolai when he comes past but I leave my phone in my pocket. His calls aren't my business. I can do it with just my implant and contacts, sometimes, but no. I might be starting to feel something like hungry. Maybe. It's still hard to tell. Some kids come by on skateboards, yelling to each other and using the parking lot railings as something to do tricks off of for awhile, and I watch until I suck bottom on the smoothie.

Dolly pulls into the parking lot right as Nicolai hangs up his fifth or sixth phone call, and carries a cardboard box full of takeout boxes.

"What'd you get to eat?" I ask.

"Somali. Peanut chicken, among other things."

"Sounds good," I say.

"You bitch about things I pick out and then bring back Red Stripe," Dolly says thoughtfully, popping the top off one on her forearm. Dolly is a source of many of those sorts of tricks.

"I like Red Stripe," Nicolai says, looking at me in appeal.

"If you get Red Stripe actually in Jamaica, you get the recycled bottles, so the glass is all dinged up," I say. "They send the fresh bottles out of country."

"I didn't know you ever went to Jamaica, Bits," Dolly says. I can't really tell what her tone of voice is.

"I've been to a lot of places," I say. "With and without you and Bristol." In person and in VR. I went to Jamaica, not long after the diamonds. I went to a lot of places, various banks, Jamaica, Cape Town, Hong Kong, Berlin, all over the place, put money and data caches in safety deposit boxes, so if I can get to a place, I'll always have means.

I remember sitting under the umbrella at my hotel in Jamaica, trying to figure out what color blue I'd call what they painted the little individual cabin roofs, almost like it was one of those Greek islands with the white buildings. They used copper to make that blue, had always made it like that, maybe since the Renaissance. I remember ordering Red Stripe because I'd heard of it but also because it was local, because it had a color in its name.

"Bitsy, come back to us," Dolly says with her signature grin, Titanium White. They probably aren't her original teeth. Not a whole lot of people necessarily have their original parts, in this world of tomorrow, with cybernetic organs, lenses for eyes, prosthetics. Teeth are a logical progression, considering how few insurance companies, for however few people had insurance, actually offered dental care. Mine are fake. Bristol is happy to declare that she's all original parts.

"Sorry," I say. Too far in my head after too long in immersion.

"Are you hungry?" Dolly asks. She doesn't say 'yet', but it's in her voice.

"Kind of. I had a smoothie." But she's handing me a paper plate of the peanut chicken, rice, and greens.

There's a little bit of a flinch, just around his eyes, when Dolly calls him Nicky, but I don't know what to do with that. Bristol would.

1928. That's when Red Stripe was first made.

I eat about a quarter of the food on my plate before I stop and take stock. So far so good, but I'm done.

"So did you get ahold of your people?" Dolly's asking, leaned forward with her elbows on her knees, already finished with her second plate, drinking her second beer.

"I did," Nicolai says. He sits back very straight, holds his disposable bamboo knife and fork the European way, like Bristol.

"Which did we get, Texas or Detroit?"

Nicolai clears his throat and sets down his plate. Crosses his knife and fork on top of it with precise movements. Wipes his mouth with a paper napkin. "Neither."

"Neither," Dolly repeats.

"Not for money, drugs, guns, none of it," Nicolai says.

"Buncha pussies," Dolly says, leaning back in her chair and lighting a cigarette. "Guess it's you and me after all, Bits. And you, Nicky, if you're in. I'll pay you for your time and whatever ordnance you can give us, anyway."

"Ladies, I will help how I can. But an outright assault, we just can't do that," Nicolai says.

"What about Marquis?" I ask.

"What about them?"

"Well they've known Bristol..." I trail off.

"Last I knew, Marquis was very politely no longer returning Bristol's calls," Dolly says.

"I guess I can't blame them." Money isn't everything, after all. "Don't you have people?"

"Already contacted some of them when I was lookin' for Bristol to begin with, and tracking you down. Retired is one of them popular words," Dolly drawls, in that particular way she has when lividly angry and doing things more slowly, so as not to self-immolate. I haven't seen her like that very often. Titanium white.

Chapter Eight

"Okay, so how are we gonna do this?" Dolly asked. "Assuming it's just the three of us."

"We identify Bristol's vehicle, I compromise it, and we get her out. They don't want attention, it looks like they'll be using cars, not armored transports." How many cars, I don't know yet. And if they're networked together I can exploit that and probably get all of them at once.

"You make it sound so easy." Nicolai sifts through the stuff on the table for the bottle opener, pops the cap of his next bottle of Red Stripe.

I shrug. "It's not a real plan, is why. It's a hypothetical."

"But you are confident you can just, what did you call it, compromise a vehicle?"

"Oh yeah, that's no sweat for Bitsy," Dolly says. "Sometimes she does it for fun, just for practice."

Nicolai looks at me. "You do?"

"I do." His new regard makes me uncomfortable. Even now, a lot of people are still pretty unsure what hacking can do, and I'm not really in any hurry to quantify that for them.

"Can you show me?" he asks.

"I guess." I glance at Dolly, who drags on her cigarette and shrugs.

"What's the harm?"

"Nothing, I guess." I pull out my headset.

"Does my car need to be on?" Nicolai asks, rummaging for his keys. "Because I can—"

"Modern cars are never entirely off," I say distractedly as my headset boots up. I have a pretty good catalog of the most popular vehicles on the road and what can be compromised, on the spectrum of benign to malicious. It varies further based on conditions. Sometimes it's as simple as using salt to fool the autodriver; we did that on an eighteen wheeler once.

Nicolai's car is a forward-slung electric six speed that a company nostalgic about the Ford Mustang started putting out in the last decade. Nicolai's car is, ostensibly, fairly secure. Earlier, I noticed the little programmed icon of a lock; built in antivirus and antimalware, both good stuff. I virtually reach out into the parking lot and tap my electric fingers on the car. Nicolai has satellite radio subscriptions, GPS, autodriving that he hardly uses. Interesting. How does autodriving work with the manual transmission? It has to be both, then, so probably six speed clutchless shifting.

I magnify the floating line of code I need. I can see it through the virtual window, tinted just a micrometer darker than is probably legal. I fiddle with that code, twist it back on itself like an old fashioned wire coat hanger, and the doors unlock.

"Go sit in the car, Dolly," I say. I can hear myself, of course. Hear them in the room. The visor isn't full immersion, but interacting with the real world while working in VR is like working on dual monitors, with one of them behind you and uses tank commands instead of the elegant code.

"It's locked," Nicolai says. Dolly only scoff-laughs, and I hear the scrape of the chair, the clomp of boots as she goes outside. A few moments later, a dismayed sound comes from Nicolai. I'm not sure why he seems so sad, actually. If we're going to do this thing, I need to be a competent hacker. Maybe he just hadn't considered his stock antivirus antimalware could actually be bypassed.

"Good enough, Bitsy. come on back to us," Dolly says, back in the room next to me again.

I don't really want to do it, but I close my eyes, pull off the headset. No exit protocol necessary. "That easy," Nicolai says, shaking his head.

"Bitsy's just that good," Dolly says in what's meant to be a consoling tone. "Not just anybody's gonna be able to hack the Nickymobile, don't you worry."

"Until a moment ago, I was more worried about it being named the Nickymobile. Now, I am less sure."

"Dolly's mostly right," I say. "Not just anybody with a headset and a smartphone is going to be able to hack your car."

"But you took hardly any time."

"Also true." Practice makes perfect.

"And it's off. Or the ignition is off."

"Correct." I'm tired, and getting a headache. Really, this should be funny. It's like I performed a magic trick for him. I wouldn't even need to put the headset back on to just turn the thing on right now, with my phone, or with my contacts and implant. I could honk the horn or flash the lights, but I resist the impulse.

"I toldja she was good." I'm so glad that she isn't celebrating more loudly.

"So that's a good baseline?" I ask.

"I would say so, yes," Nicolai says, a combination of gloomy and relieved.

"I'm going to lie down now, then."

"You okay? Do you need anything?" Glimmers of nursemaid Dolly again. It's just so *weird*.

"Just tired and a headache. Right now, I'm going to drink some water. I don't think I drank enough water today. And I'm going to go to sleep." I'm just not the kind of person that tylenol or aspirin works for.

"Should I..." Nicolai was already starting to get up.

"Don't bother, I sleep like a rock,"

"More like a hibernating bear," Dolly says. "Rocks don't make the noise you do."

"Maybe they do, just really slowly. Geologic age snoring." I go into the bathroom, close the door, and drink three cups of water. I stare at myself in the bathroom mirror while my stomach gurgles and I wonder if I'm going to lose what had actually been a pretty nice dinner. My first solid food other than candy in however long. But other than a slow roll, some flip flopping like a fish right when it feels the hook, my stomach holds steady. Good. I brush my teeth with the teeny tiny toothpaste and toothbrush provided. Nicolai and Dolly are pretty quiet when I come out. Maybe Dolly filled him in. Maybe not.

"I mean it," I say. "Keep planning. You know what I can do, Dolly."

"We will, don't you worry," Dolly says. "Just get your rest."

"No doubt," I say. My head hits the pillow, and I think of VR and the night sky and the line between sleeping and waking blurs away into stars.

Chapter Nine

I wake up and don't know where I am. Silvery moonlight comes through the thrown-open motel room curtains. Dolly sleeps sprawled on her stomach in her usual way, like a cast aside toy, and has one arm flung over Nicolai, who sleeps stiffly on his back like a vampire expecting to rise from the grave. Then I remember.

Bristol. Leaving Mexico. Nobody to help us. Red Stripe. The room feels very close, as though all the exhaled breaths of everybody who has ever slept here are still trapped.

I get up and go out into the parking lot barefoot, leaving the door ajar. I can hear the sign buzzing at the side of the road, can see the puddle of yellow light from the main office spilling onto the crushed oyster shells. Hardly any cars are here. It really could just be a murder motel and we'd never know, unless we get murdered too. I slept in my AR contacts and my eyes are dry; I feel every millimeter of every blink.

I pace up the sidewalk to the hallway of vending machines, bounce away from their constant whining hum before it catches me, white on white noise static that I'll never escape, it'll shake my skull apart. I walk almost to the office, back to the room again. I think about the real metal key that Dolly has for our room and wonder if they have a computer in there, or just a big ledger book that people sign when they arrive. An old fashioned no-tell motel, in this day and age. I stand looking at Nicolai's car, next to Dolly's Jeep. He must have locked it again after I went to sleep.

"What's up?" Dolly's behind me

"I woke up and couldn't stay in there anymore."

"Want a ginger ale?"

"What?" I turn to look at her. She's looking at me with something like compassion.

"A ginger ale. To calm down." Dolly gestures towards the vending machines with the cigarette she's about to light.

"Are you making fun of me?"

"Nah. I just didn't know if it was your stomach or what. And if it was an or what, we got stuff to add to the ginger ale."

"If you think I'm going to drink tequila and ginger ale..."

Dolly puts her hands up, leaving the cigarette on her bottom lip. "Hey, I don't judge."

"I know." I take a deep breath, count to five, let it out. If Dolly of all people thinks I need to calm down, I need to calm down.

Dolly leans against the wall by the room door and blows a smoke ring. It drifts ghost like across the parking lot towards the highway, towards the ocean, and I lose track of it. Breathe. I guess I've been sweating because it's cooling on my skin now, in the breeze, the headache in my left temple barking like a bored dog. Oh how am I going to do this? How are we going to do this?

"Tell me something about the job that went bad."

She shifts her weight, surprised, and her eyes catch the light from the motel sign. What's the expression on her face? Guilt? She's probably just tired. "Are you sure that's a good idea?"

"Just a random fact in the middle. Give me a stepping stone."

She's quiet, paper on the end of her cigarette crackling, exhaling sighs of smoke. "Yeah, I get you. Gimme a sec." I wait, counting my breaths, which don't feel so restricted anymore. "I picked the job, I guess I should say that."

Guilt, then. Weird. "We always trade around." Dolly acting like anything less than confident is almost scarier than not being able to remember what happened. Not being able to hear and retain what happened.

"Okay, yeah. Bristol wasn't in Morocco anymore because the more she traveled, the more of an electronic trail she was leaving to confuse pursuit. And before you say that you can help with that, she just wanted to globetrot and have her little adventures and overwrite their data. She was only gonna ask you as last resort."

I wait, don't feel any worse. Don't feel any better, either. Of course there was going to be pursuit. We all signed very nice amnesty contracts and then made off with both the money the contracts promised us and the diamonds that *we* had promised them. "Okay, makes sense. That isn't it, though."

"No. Just testing the waters." She takes a final drag, flicks the butt into the parking lot and there's a tiny spray of embers when it lands. "We were visiting sites. Looking for a place I'd been. Um. Trained, I guess. And—"

"You needed a file," I say, almost remembering but not really, and a sudden wave of dizziness hits me, just as hard as if I was standing on the beach and a real wave broke. Dolly catches me when my knees buckle, and I grab her arm with both hands, trying to steady myself.

"You're all gooseflesh now. Come on, back to bed. Don't go wandering in the night, okay?"

"Okay." The idea of walking back into the room doesn't stuff the breath down in my throat anymore. "We're leaving in the morning, right?"

"Right," Dolly says, but her tone says we won't if she thinks I can't.

We crawl back into our beds and I don't think I'll be able to sleep. I watch the color of light change, listen to Dolly's breathing slip into sleep breathing, listen to Nicolai's not-quite-snores. But I do drift off because the next time I open my eyes, Dolly's standing in the doorway smoking and humming to herself, while watching Nicolai do something with his car out front. "He's still spooked about your digital wizardry," she says without turning. I don't know how she knows I'm awake.

"A lot of people get that way. He has to have seen it before, right?"

"Right? You wouldn't think a guy like Nicky'd have his head in the sand, but here you go. He might talk to you about hacker-proofin' his ride."

"There are some things I can do for him."

"That's good. Lie, if you gotta. Otherwise he's gonna whine halfway across the country and back about how somebody's gonna hack his car and drive him into something, or something."

"Well. They could."

"Yeah, but why bother?"

Nicolai comes back in, also smoking. And people think my VR habit is bad. "You slept well?" he asks.

"I had my moments. You?"

"We'll be better prepared the next time we find lodgings," he says carefully. "There will be enough rooms, or enough beds, for each of us."

"Sorry to offend your sensibilities," Dolly says. There's only so many stops we can afford to make, timewise. She stands and surveys the room for anything we might've left. "Are we ready to roll?"

"How long is it from here to Kansas?" Nicolai asks. "And which car goes first?"

"Nicky, buddy, you really asking me that?"

"Sorry, Dolly. Of course you'll go first. But how long?"

"How many miles to Babylon?" I mutter, and Dolly gives me a sidelong glance.

"What now?"

"It's an old poem. Nursery rhyme. Whatever. How many miles to Babylon, three score miles and ten, can we get there by candlelight, yes and back again."

"Yeah, but does anybody ever remember what a fucking score is?" Dolly asks as we get into the Jeep.

"No, I have to look it up every time," I laugh.

"Dolly..." Nicolai says carefully.

"Christ, Nicolai, it's like, twelve hours or twenty or something, I don't fucking know. We'll drive until we get tired and get a motel again. Calm your tits. Driving across the United States takes far less effort than driving across Russia anyway, and we don't have to worry about the KGB."

"The KGB isn't—"

"Well whatever the fuck took its place, meet the new boss, same as the old boss. Bits will set up communications between our cars, won't you Bits? You got those little satellite walkie things you can program on a private network?"

I don't know why I haven't thought about earbuds before now. Or anything. "Oh...yeah. Give me a sec." I rummage in my bag for the walkies, then pull out the VR headset again. I don't need it for this, strictly speaking, but I like using it. It'll make it faster. I set up the connection, each unit absolutely only talking to the other, encrypted. I hesitate a moment over the password, and make it 3scoreMiles&10. Nobody'll have to enter a password ever, but being prepared for eventualities is always part of the game. We'll network earbuds eventually, but I guess waiting is just another natural step on taking things easy. I should get eye drops from a vending machine. Or maybe I should just not sleep in my contacts. There's an eye implant now too, I just read about it.

"Here, stick it on your windshield. Don't make that face, the adhesive won't last once the unit is removed. Flip that button to make it voice activated, then you won't have to worry about settings, just talk when you want to talk, and it'll broadcast when we talk."

"And here is where I find out that Miss Bits can be bossy as well," Nicolai says, taking the card-sized walkie.

"That's us, a pair of bossy bitches," Dolly says, grinning. "Didn't know she had it in her, didja?"

"I did not."

"Well, let's get this show on the road," Dolly says as I slap the walkie on our dashboard. Though I guess it's a drivie, in this context. I run our route into the GPS and Dolly looks it over, makes a noise of disappointment. "I was kinda looking forward to getting my kicks on Route 66."

"Well, we'll have to get somebody arrested in a more convenient location, then. Or break into Area 51."

"Is Area 51 real?" Nicolai asks. These cheap little walkies still have pretty good audio, I'm always surprised.

"Like, do they have aliens and the remains of a crashed spacecraft there real, or is it a real government site real?" Dolly wants him to ask about aliens, she really does.

"I take from your tone that I don't really have a right answer," he says mournfully.

"Aw, don't feel too bad, Nicky."

"Thank you, Dolly. Thank you for being such a stalwart friend." She laughs so hard, I think I'm going to have to reach over and take the wheel to keep us from crashing and dying before we even leave California, but Dolly keeps it on the road. She always keeps it on the road.

"No problem. Now we'll try to push 'til eleven anyway, then get brunch like the fancy assholes we are, and maybe Bits can do a status check on the projected convoy."

Chapter Ten

We have our brunch closer to lunch, in the kind of no name place that Dolly has an affinity for seeking out. The menus are augmented with holographs, spinning pictures of each dish with the ingredients list and allergy warnings, and I spend probably too long fiddling with that just for the pleasure of it, after the waitress brings waters and a coffee pot.

"Bits, gotta pick something," Dolly says after awhile, and I get the sense that the waitress has probably circled back around a few times and been waved away.

"Sorry." I pick French toast with a side of bacon, because eggs are horrific to me right now. Dolly orders a full on lumberjack spread, bacon, eggs, sausage, toast, all of it. Nicolai orders eggs Benedict, but even as the waitress leaves to put in the order, he mutters that he's probably going to be unhappy with it and should've picked something else.

"Well, now's the time," Dolly says.

"No, no, I might just be pleasantly surprised," he says. "I don't like making trouble for the kitchen."

"Alrighty," Dolly says, but she rolls her eyes and I stifle a laugh. There aren't a whole lot of other people here, though more filter in as we wait for our food. Lots of truckers, and lots of family vacationers, by the looks of it.

I wonder where the closest actual town is, and if locals ever come here to eat, or if they just come here to work. We're just off the highway somewhere in the middle of Arizona, where rock chimneys jut up out of the desert hardpan, and the mountains purple the hazy, distant horizon. The waitress sets the plate down in front of me and I jump. "Sorry, honey," she says, squinting at me.

"It's my fault, I wasn't paying attention."

"Gonna only get more jittery, you keep downing coffee like that," Dolly says, already shoveling food in her mouth. "Plus we'll have to make a bajillion rest stops."

"This is my last cup," I say. How many did I drink already? One at the motel. Two here. Three? Coffee doesn't make me jittery, why would Dolly say that?

I poke at my French toast; nicely browned, dusted with powdered sugar. The syrup decanter on the table is unlabeled, but there's a 97% chance that it's flavored corn syrup and has nothing to do with maple. Maple syrup costs more per gallon than gasoline, maybe we should hijack a maple syrup truck when this is all done. Is that classy enough for Bristol?

I look over at Dolly, mentally play the "where's Dolly's gun?" game. She isn't in full riot gear right now, so in a tank top and jeans, it's hard to hide one. Maybe an ankle holster? She definitely has a knife, anyway. I've lost track of which states are open carry; we might be allowed to go strapped all the time and just aren't. None of the truckers are carrying.

I watch Nicolai fork into the poached egg on his plate. The yolk oozes out across the Canadian bacon and English muffin, mixed with the sunny Hollandaise, and a surprised smile crossed his face. "I'm happy that I was wrong," he says after the first bite.

"Well that's good," Dolly says, half done already. I start eating. There's no way I can finish this, but Dolly probably can. The French toast doesn't taste like anything, not even after I douse in it syrup, but it isn't the French toast's fault. I'm starting to get afterimages of things around the diner, particularly if they're shiny, or silhouetted against light, like Dolly, who sits facing the door but with her back against the white curtained window. And the AR contacts don't help.

"I'll be right back," I say, and stand up unsteadily. Dolly says...something...but I can't really hear her as I make my way to the bathroom, jaw clenched, breathing through my nose. It's single occupant, the door hanging open, and it's through sheer willpower that I close the door firmly but quietly, lock it, and then lean my forearms on my knees and throw up the French toast and all that coffee and then continue heaving until tears are streaming down my face but nothing else will come up. At least my hair is short and I don't have to worry about that too.

My vision statics out when I flush and then stand upright, and I hope I don't just pass out on the floor right here. I wash my face with the flat fake floral hand soap and dry off with the scratchy brown paper towels. There's a certain smell those brown paper towels always have when they're wet. I rinse my mouth and dig into my pockets, hoping for a tin of mints, a piece of gum, something. Nope. It's okay, they sell stuff like that at the register. It feels like my eyes are minutely shifting from side to side, but I can't see in the mirror to see if that's real. The static still hangs in my vision, and past experience tells me what kind of headache is breaking over me like a wave.

A knock at the door. Kind of brusque, maybe it isn't their first knock.

I clear my throat. "Just a minute," I call. I pull the door open right as a woman, holding a little girl's hand raises her fist to knock again. We look at each other for a long moment, and I feel like maybe the woman expects me to apologize, but I can't find the words, or the right facial expression, and eventually the little girl just shoves past me and the woman follows.

Dolly meets me partway across the room. "You okay?"

No. "Time will tell," I say. I want to crawl under a table and put a blanket over my head and shake until I pass out.

"Nicolai paid, so we're ready to leave if you are."

"Thank you, Nicolai. I just want to get some mints."

"If you say so," Dolly says, hovering.

"And then I'll hop into VR, get some more intel while we're on the move, like we said. Make it that much harder to track me." She eyes me dubiously, but relents and goes outside.

They do have mints. And painkillers, but not any kind that'll help me, so I just chew three mints before I jam the rest of them in my pocket and go outside. The parking lot is so very bright, and I close my eyes and fumble with my sunglasses, dropping them twice before just giving up.

"Bits, are you sure you're—" Dolly starts.

What does she want me to say? We don't have the luxury of me sitting this out. "You keep asking me that. We need to know what's happening to Bristol and neither of you knows how to do this." Eyes squinted almost closed, I get out my VR headset and lean my head back on the seat. Dolly's still talking, maybe to me, maybe to Nicolai, but I'm already focused on the virtual, looking for the coordinates of the Kansas location from the files I copied. I can play back what she said later, see if it was important.

Things are very flat in Kansas, and the sky seems very big. There's a lot of buildings, old and new mixed together, and the street in places is brick. Train tracks, the old kind, not for a monorail or hyperloop. The building I need is concrete, of course, that institutional block that's been so cheap and popular for so long. The fence around it doesn't have razorwire the way the Texas facility does, but I have the overwhelming feeling that security here is a lot tighter. I take a couple blinks to make sure my avatar is appropriately nondescript Army, with appropriate at-a-glance credentials. This facility is far more subtle with its visible security levels, no patrolling people or programs visible. I pass through the gates unchecked, approach the front door.

It's keycard locked, but I know how to bypass those in person, and VR is life's digital mirror. I want to avoid tripping every alarm, avoid causing the slightest suspicion. I'm on high alert for any communications, changes, anything to do with me cracking this and entering the domain. The last thing we need is for me to screw this up, to screw anything up.

This would be easier in full immersion, without my real life ears receiving data, without my head throbbing against the gently rocking car seat, the sun hot on my hair, tasting mint and I-just-threw-up. But I take my time and double check my work at every step. Then I'm in, cautiously continuing through the server halls, admiring the coding, dipping into data here and there. I copy the list of vehicles in the motor pool, and the list of what's requisitioned for near future transfers. I send that to Dolly's phone to keep her busy. She doesn't typically mess with me when I've got the headset on, but she's worried and worry makes people make mistakes.

Next I locate the holding cells. They probably neutralize the language. Kind of like when they say "enhanced interrogation"; pretty much everybody knows that means a particular range of unpleasant things.

Fuck, my head hurts. My left temple feels like it used to be an egg, but that egg broke and the yolk and albumen are running down the side of my face in liquid pain. There's a throb to it, a long and steady throb, and I try to concentrate on my breathing while taking the programmed stairs down to the programmed basement.

It's a waste to have personnel hanging out trying to watch for little changes in code. It's improbable anybody will notice what I'm doing. I can't say I've never been caught, but I can count the times on one hand. At least one of the times was deliberate; I was working with another hacker and diverted attention off the higher value target and onto me instead.

There are more people in holding than just Bristol, and my digital ghost passes three occupied areas before reaching her. She's got a TV, and even a remote, but the remote is locked to five channels, without power and without volume control. It's tuned very slightly too loud. She doesn't have earbuds in, or contacts, or I'd be able to send her a message. No camera into the cell, or I'd be able to see her. I'm scared to see her.

Her file is on the door and I make a copy while I scan through it quick. Height, weight, still no good ID. Transfer date is pushed to three days from now, instead of tomorrow like the original files. Recovery time, before the exchange is made. I feel a deep terrible chill. Mostly they've just done environmental manipulation, too hot or too cold, the TV thing, not letting her sleep. Mostly basics, mostly physically harmless, and I can envision Bristol doing social backflips to get these people to see her as human, to have empathy, to take pity on her and make that connection that would stop them from hurting her. But yeah, they still hurt her anyway.

There's a side note about her teeth being all intact. I wonder if I'm going to throw up again.

A frustrated note from one of her handlers, because they have her on a light level of sedation that will normally lower a person's inhibitions, make them inclined to be talkative. Not so with Bristol. Or rather, she's talkative but on zero of the topics they have an interest in. I imagine her discussing this year's Paris fashion show in excruciating, exquisite detail. I can hack Bristol's door, but there isn't anywhere for her to get to. We aren't in Kansas right now, and there are a lot of armed personnel in that building. Bristol is relentlessly hopeful; or at least I have to assume she still is. That she looks upon this as a temporary inconvenience, another experience to write about in her little locked leather-bound diary, memoirs that she says she'll publish when she's old and it won't matter anymore.

I make myself read the details again. They hurt her, but not enough that she needs medical attention. She'll be operational, when we stop the convoy. They've got a note about her belongings and I scan that. No diary, that's good. It looks like she had her purse, her coat, her phone and earbuds. Purse full of makeup and actual paper ticket stubs and fashion magazines, folding flats, an anti-digital surveillance scarf, and a dress from a capsule vending machine. Bus station locker key. My breathing feels funny and I do a scan to make sure I'm not compromised, our location a beacon for law enforcement in a fifty mile radius. But no, my equipment is secure. I'm still 'standing' in the hallway outside Bristol's holding cell. When the files are done copying I walk away. How many people are here anyway? How many people can they hold? It seems like a lot. Domestic terrorism is such an easily manipulated idea.

There's another exit here and I check it over carefully to make sure it's a real thing and not an 'alarms will sound if opened' trick door.

It's so bright in VR outside that I recoil and have nowhere to go, my head already against the Jeep headrest. I pull the headset off, squeeze my eyes shut again almost immediately. My ears pop-squeal into white noise, and there's a hand on my arm, something on my face. Something wet on my face. Am I crying? Poor Bristol.

I bring my hand up and it's swatted away, and Dolly's voice pushes through my hearing fuckup, clear as day. "You got a gusher, see if you can hold this here. If you can't, keep out of my way." I hold a cloth against my face. A bandanna, probably. Or one of those digital scarves. It bothers me that I didn't run into any cybersecurity measures. Are they just that much better than me? Am I just that much better than them? I can't make either option make sense.

Dolly must've gone away for a little while, or maybe she sent Nicolai away, because then she's nudging something cold against the back of my other hand, and I crack my eyes open enough to see a to-go cup, a straw. I fumbled at it, and Dolly just sticks the straw in my mouth. It's sugared-up iced coffee and I must've told Dolly about how sugar makes things bearable, about how coffee or hard drugs are the only things that touch these headaches for me.

"You okay?" Dolly asks, when I sit up a little straighter, take the cloth away to squint at it. That's blood all right. I sniff and scrub at my nose, looking around but I can't remember for what. Oh, my sunglasses, on the dashboard. With them on, I'm almost able to bear the world. "Do you want to ride with Nicolai? His car has, y'know, a roof. Windows, tinted."

"I don't really know," I say. "No."

"About which?"

"Either." I drink some more coffee, first happy to have it and then sure it's the biggest mistake ever as my stomach curls on itself. I turn my head away from the straw. The ice rattles as Dolly jams it into a cup holder. We aren't in the diner parking lot anymore. "Where...?"

"We relocated to that truck stop right off the highway, to gas up and get road snacks and other incidentals. Plus, I had a feeling this would be good for you. Nicolai is very good at following instructions, luckily, so I didn't have to leave him babysitting you. He doesn't seem to be very comfortable with the sight of blood."

"I'm standing right here," Nicolai says from outside my field of vision.

"Yeah, not like I forgot," Dolly says. "I'm just fillin' Bits in. She missed you goin' a whiter shade of pale."

"You have to understand the further implications I read into the sudden fountain of blood coming out of our friend's face, I was concerned for her. I don't faint at the sight of blood. I would be a terrible businessman in this particular venue if that were the case."

"Yeah, you would," Dolly agrees.

"We're wasting time," I say.

"What's our deadline then?" Dolly asks, banter gone. I wonder a lot just how thin that banter veneer is, how much of the joke and swagger is part of the put-on dangerous woman image that lets her interact with normal people. Dolly is definitely the most genuinely dangerous of us three. Me and Bristol can both handle ourselves in our own ways, but Dolly gets this extra sparkle when things are particularly thrilling.

"Well, we've got more time than tomorrow. Transport is in three days. But none of the records say where she's going, just that she's being moved." I close my eyes again. If I can just focus on this for a little while, run the logistics, it'll at least keep the pain at arm's length. Maybe. At least I can still think.

"But she's okay, you think," Dolly says.

"I think she'll *be* okay. Bristol is resilient."

"You mean she's still gonna be pretty." She's joking but not-joking. Bristol's cultivation of appearance, of expectations built on her beauty, is something that she's worked on like somebody who sharpens knives for a living. It's all on purpose, it's all calculated.

"Also that."

Chapter Eleven

Back on the road, Dolly mutes our end of the conversation on the walkies. "You mentioned enhanced interrogation," Dolly says.

Did I? "I did." I can see no upside to talking about this. I can't bring myself to look at the files again right now, to see what exactly that meant for Bristol. My head feels like one of those plastic 3D puzzles with the big chunky pieces, and like the pieces aren't fit together right.

"Look, I'm not going to get all MKULTRA on you, because fun as that is to drop into conversations, it's got nothing to do with that. But somebody somewhere along the way figured ways of partitioning the brain using hypnosis, right? Even from yourself?"

"Oh. Yeah, right. I know that." Some people call it brainhacking, which I don't think is the right terminology to use exactly, but nobody asked me.

"Well. It's something I've got." I think I'm not really surprised. She's looking at me expectantly, like she's never told anybody—but no, that's not it. She's waiting for me to static out and reboot again. "Like, I know how to do it. And there's. Other stuff. That I can't access myself."

"But what's that got to do with Bristol?" I should've asked something else but I can't.

"She knows about mine."

Oh, great. That's the best. "A smart enough interrogator can feel along those barriers."

"Also true. But it takes a long, long, long time. Kind of like...a dictionary hack?"

"I get you." It can. It depends on your setup. I imagine Dolly and Bristol holed up in a hotel somewhere, Bristol doing her nails and Dolly breaking her guns down like praying the rosary, practicing their autohypnosis. But I was there too. I clearly have something walled off too, but the way I react when I get close to it isn't how I think these things normally work. The more I think about it the more the throb in my head looms again, the more my thoughts are scribbled out with a black marker.

"So how much..." she trails off, takes a breath. "I guess if her files said she talked, you would've said something."

"Oh, Bristol has talked a lot. About all kinds of inane and inconsequential things. Her interrogator put a note in the file complaining about it."

Dolly laughs, loud and surprised, and I'm in too much pain to even flinch anymore. "That's just perfect, isn't it? We shouldn't expect anything less."

"We shouldn't." I can't keep my eyes closed because it makes me feel worse, but I also can't look at her. I try to fix my gaze on a distant point on the horizon. Isn't that what you're supposed to do if you're seasick? There are things Dolly can't access; that means somebody has passwords, there are passwords, passcodes, passphrases, and this is where I lose the string again and either nod off or pass out.

I dream about concrete walls with bright green moss growing in the cracks. I dream about a squarely spiraling hedge maze that has a pit in the middle. I don't know what's in the pit, but it's loud and it's angry. I'm afraid, but not of what's in the pit. What's in the pit is mine, and I have no reason to be afraid of it, but as I try to get to it, I keep tripping on my untied shoelaces. Bristol is whispering in my ears, telling me about the beaches in Morocco, the seashells that you can find there, little pink ones like fingernails and big white clamshells and sometimes, if you're lucky, you can still find the spiraling chambered fossils of ammonites. I put an ammonite to my ear but I don't hear the ocean I hear static, overwhelming static, and one of the walls of the maze just falls apart. Then I hear Dolly, talking about how sure, getting replacement muscles hurt, but it hurt less than having to replace an entire arm, and it was lucky we made so much money on our jobs, because that meant her arm was like a real one. Bleeding edge cybernetics, so real that they bleed, she says, laughing and holding out her bleeding, torn-up arm, glittering with shrapnel that's seashells.

When I wake up, it's 5:30 am, my AR contacts dryly glued to my eyeballs but still reading, in an unfamiliar room. Dolly and Nicolai are talking somewhere, bickering. I push myself upright, and the room wavers, spins, resolves. Does Dolly have a fake arm and I forgot? What happened to her original arm? Does Dolly have fake muscles and that's why she's so strong?

"Morning sunshine," Dolly says. A covered tray is on one of the tables; room service I guess, but the coffee maker is part of the wall, steaming and ready to be poured.

"Morning," I say. "Did you sleep at all?"

"I did. How'd you sleep?"

"Okay." I'm looking-not-looking at her arms, bared in a tank top. They look like they match but that's part of it, right? Having enough money so everything looks the way it should. She does have a scar on her left shoulder I don't remember, thin and pale and curving back down through her shirt. I'm surprised I didn't notice it when we were spraying each other with sunscreen on our drive up from Mexico. No I'm not. Dolly has a lot of scars.

"Here, sit down, have some coffee. I didn't order you any food, but they've got a blender if you want a slushy."

"I don't want anything," I say, and she eyes me skeptically, then dumps coffee in the blender with ice and sugar.

"Bits, should you check on our timeline?" Nicolai asks.

"Give her a fucking minute," Dolly growls over the blender.

"I'll do it," I say, because I'm supposed to. And it isn't like I need much encouragement to get out the headset, not with the building tension of whatever it is we'll have to do in order to get Bristol out of trouble, not with how I constantly feel in the real world right now. "It'll be fine," I say, reassuring Dolly or myself.

"Mmmhmm," Dolly says, in very much a 'you're a grownup who can make your own decisions even when they're terribly wrong' kind of way.

I've already got the headset powered up, though, and am slipping it over my eyes. I'm in Texas again. No, Kansas. I walk through the gates again, the front door again. I can see other code activity this time, and I'm careful to behave within expected parameters, get past where there's now a guard, automated or staffed, just inside. My coded clearance disguise is good enough to not trigger any alarms that I notice. Every time I do this, I get a better sense of their limitations and protocols. Security is only as good as the space between the chair and the keyboard, as the saying goes.

The motor pool is actually staffed with security. It's the Uncanny Valley game again; I can't say what exactly makes me realize the patrols aren't automated, but I know for certain that they are staffed. The records are automated, though, and I grab a capture of the next seven calendar days. In fact, just to make sure, I go a few weeks back and grab that data too. Maybe it'll line up with Bristol's original arrest, I don't know. I don't remember, from the files, and Dolly's been doing a lot of things, but synchronizing our watches isn't one of them.

"Is everything in expected order, ma'am?" a voice at my elbow asks.

"Yes, it seems to be," I say, glancing at the personnel member. That's the thing about military avatars, they always display their rank.

"Thanks for checking in on me, Lieutenant. Sometimes I get lost in all these records. We understand the need for redundancy, of course, but..." I trail off with a wry smile.

"Of course, ma'am. It can be overwhelming." The Lieutenant salutes and continues on, only to stop again when another officer enters the motor pool area.

I noodle around with some more records, then notice the motor pool's connection with the rest of the server at large. Military grade indeed. Nobody just casually standing next to my avatar can see what I'm looking at, but if one of those security personnel decide I'm acting suspiciously, or if somebody deeper in the data structure does, all sorts of alarms will go off. If I just put a little line of code here, and here, then I'll get pinged when the convoy leaves.

It isn't like anything can actually hurt me in VR. There's the possibility of backtracing and drone strikes, that happens and nobody's a fan. But the problem with making the virtual as real as possible is your mind sometimes makes your body think that things are happening. And there's the hypnosis thing. Oh shit the hypnosis thing.

"Not trying for a vehicle above your pay grade, are you Captain?" The other officer, major, hasn't really neared, but near and far are relative concepts in VR.

"No sir, double checking a vehicle I already turned in."

"Good diligence," the major says, and right when I think it's the end of it, he continues, "I don't want to hear about mileage discrepancies because somebody's running a side project out of here."

"Sir?" No system alarms have begun, but my fight or flight is ramping up, shaking my concentration. This conversation is no good.

"Like this operation," the major says. "Do you know anything about this operation?" The major gestures at the files I just copied, the two vehicle prisoner convoy. "Almost too small to be a real thing stateside. We don't use only two vehicles for anything."

"I can't say I'm familiar, sir. It isn't my project."

A security officer passes us once, twice, and then is joined by another just as I'm stepping away. I should've stepped away sooner. An alarm goes off, and I flinch, but it isn't for me. The major's uniform pixelates. Tracers are going back through his connections, all that streaming code, automated systems faster than human thought.

"Excuse me, ma'am, I'm going to have to ask you to return to finish your business another time," one member of security says to me. "This guy isn't supposed to be here. We've had a few hacker incursions lately."

"That's fine, Private, thank you for your time. I think I've gotten everything straightened out." I leave the motor pool, hesitate. Should I try to help the other hacker? Why are they asking about Bristol's convoy too? I ping what I can remember of his connection, a tiny little ghost ping following Homeland's backtrace. Also in Kansas. I really wish I had a good way to get information out of Dolly, or information out of Dolly that I can stand to hear without my brain turning into soup.

I pull the headset off and Dolly's already handing me another bandanna. "Thanks."

"What's up?"

"Convoy is going to be two vehicles. I grabbed some personnel files but didn't look at them yet. Somebody else was hacking the same info at the same time I was, and got caught."

"What does caught even mean in this context?"

"Not a whole lot if you're me. That guy, they know where he is, which means I know where he is. I'm not sure if they're just going to scoop him up or strike him or what."

"Well, where is he? Anyplace useful? We're low on helpful bodies here. Might be somebody we can bring aboard."

"Maybe. I feel bad seeing that and just walking away, anyway."

"Nicolai, you're awful quiet. Don't have anybody else workin' this on the side, do you?"

"I do not," he says.

"Well," Dolly says, shoving the coffee icee she just made at me, with that particular grin. "I guess we might as well warm up by drag racing Homeland."

Chapter Twelve

Dolly breaks 110 as we cross the Kansas state line, the wind around the topless jeep tunneling past the upright windshield with an unbelievable roar. Maybe in a panic, maybe sensibly, I fight the impulse to just crouch in my foot well and wait for us to either reach our destination or for it to be all over when a deer decides to step onto the highway at the wrong second. Nicolai initially complained about the sudden change in plans, the mad dash from the hotel, but Dolly ignored him. His muscle car can beat us, no question, but he's letting Dolly take the lead.

"How far did you say, Bits?" Dolly yells. It takes a few tries, and damn it, I should've put in earbuds when I woke up.

"Cut north here and maybe thirty miles?"

"And you're sure Homeland'll be onto him too?"

"Pretty sure."

"And what's their timeline?"

"Christ, Dolly, I don't know where their nearest drone site is, or personnel. I don't know enough about how Homeland operates to—"

"What?" Dolly yells.

I pull the headset up. The nearest real base, as opposed to the weird black site where they've got Bristol, is three hundred miles away. "For a drone, hour and a half. Personnel, much longer. If they follow the speed limit."

"Ping the guy. Tell him to be ready."

"Like he's just going to run out into the parking lot and hop in the back," I yell. Everything about this is ridiculous, down to the last detail.

"He will if he knows what's good for him."

She isn't wrong. I ping the connection I had for the guy, but he's smart, he already pulled the plug. I follow the code, look for other nearby connections. He's in a motel, was using their regular wireless. I find the router; the phone line is still separate from the internet, imagine. It's digital, though. I find his room and ring the phone. One ring, two rings. If it was me, I wouldn't answer the phone. If it was me, I'd already be gone. Six rings, seven. I'm about to hang up when the line opens. "Hello?"

The VR headset doesn't have a mic but voice to text is practically human, finally. "Hello, Major. Can I assume you want evac?" I text, and the phone spits it out dutifully in a voice similar to mine. Uncanny Valley in everyday life.

"Who is this? Why are you calling me? Did you say Major? Are you seriously trolling me right now?" No audio either, of course, just scrolling text on my end.

"I'm not the one who got caught. Do you want an out or no?"

"You were also...you were the one...fine, yes. Tell me when and where."

I check the GPS. Ten minutes, unless something terrible happens. "Ten minutes, edge of the parking lot. Turn off all your equipment."

"Okay." He hangs up, and I pull the headset down around my neck, look at Dolly.

"Look, I know you wanted more personnel or whatever, but there's no guarantee this guy will work well with us. And he was sloppy." Why am I arguing? It's not like I want to just leave him.

"You just want to be the only hacker," Dolly says.

"I just don't want to get killed by an amateur." I dig around in my bag for the shrink wrapped earbuds, link mine up to my phone and the walkie, lean over and plug one into Dolly's ear. She takes the other one and settles it without swerving even a little bit.

"I agree," Nicolai is saying. "Dolly, are you sure you want to add an unknown element at this point?"

"Buddy, the convoy hasn't left yet, we got time to get him and we got time to vet him. If he seems like a clown we can cut him loose or leave him in a culvert or whatever, I don't care. But if there's a chance he's going to be a help, a real help, I wanna take that chance. So, I'm sorry for the unplanned detour, I know plans are very important to you, Nicolai. But this is what we're doing."

I sigh. She isn't wrong, we need more people. "If nothing else we can find out why he was looking into the same data as me. Seems like a coincidence is unlikely, right?"

"I'm not sure I believe in coincidences," Dolly says. "Here's the exit?" She doesn't wait for an answer, just slows to a clearly far more reasonable 55 miles an hour for the off ramp. "Where's the motel?"

"Left," I say, gripping the door handle. At least if Dolly rolls the Jeep, our deaths will be quick and merciful. At least my head doesn't hurt right now anymore.

A tall skinny guy...no, it's a girl, angular featured and in an oversized jacket, with a backpack. She's standing on the grassy expanse between the motel parking lot and the road, her head craning anxiously this way and that, towards the highway and the other way. The other way is where the drones will come from, I think. They're sure to be scrambling now, hustling in this direction between 85 and 110 miles an hour. Or more, depending on the make and model. Or less. There are laws about what drones could be used on American soil of course, but if none of this was on the up and up to begin with, those laws are kind of out the window. Like Bristol's interrogations. Her detainment, I think, is probably justified. But that isn't the point.

Dolly doesn't even really come to a complete stop, just kind of skid-slides up to the shoulder doing twenty and the girl's already running and throws her backpack into the back first, then as the Jeep fishtails and the speedometer dips below ten, gets in herself. It's a fairly adept hop, a swift folding of lanky limbs. Dolly steers into the slide, and loops back down the road to the highway onramp again. I lean back, set of earbuds in my fist, and I loop the kid into the walkie signals.

"Your equipment is powered off?"

"Yeah, I did that as soon as we hung up," she says. "Who are you people?"

"Don't matter right now. Buckle up, buttercup," Dolly says.

I glance back; I've always been a terrible judge of age, so can't tell if she's a teenager and just inexperienced, or mid-twenties like us and careless. "What's your handle?"

"Null," she says after an uncomfortable pause.

"I'm Bits, this is Dolly. The guy in the other car, when you see him, is Nicolai."

"Bits?" she asks. "Just Bits?" She's suddenly wide eyed and excited in a way totally different from terror at Dolly's driving.

"Yeah, why?" I turn back around before I get sick in her lap.

"You're the one who hangs the stars in VR," she says. "You're a fucking ghost story."

"I'm a ghost story?" I ask. It hadn't occurred to me what other hackers thought of me. Or if they thought of me at all.

"Yeah. Private node, long immersions. Nobody's been able to track you, not even close, but there's code devoted to seeing how long you're online for. And every time you go offline, there's a big rumor mill about that. Especially this last time."

"I didn't know."

"Classic Bits," Dolly says, laughing. "So what, she's a VR legend?"

"She is, yeah. I guess that makes it make more sense now, how you found me so easily. Both online and in person."

"It's not like I'm the only one in the world who could've accomplished that. Especially with the way you had your protocols set up."

"I thought my protocols..." She stops. I glance back at Null, and her cheekbones are sunburn red. "Maybe you can teach me."

"Oh God," I say. Dolly's just whooping laughter over this.

"It's like an old kung Fu movie, where the cocky hero is accidentally schooled by the master and then seeks to be educated," she says.

"Yeah, Dolly, just like that." I roll my eyes. "Yeah, I guess I can teach you."

"Wait, that's it? You're internet famous and that's all you're gonna say about it?" Dolly asks.

"What else am I supposed to say about it?"

"I dunno. Anything. Literally anything."

"I...well it's not like it's a *good* thing, to be internet famous. It's kind of better if nobody'd ever noticed me at all."

"I think that's part of why too. You just do things, you don't showboat or claim credit," Null says helpfully.

"The stars," Dolly says distantly.

"Yeah, the stars. In the VR immersion, there aren't any stars. Weren't any stars. Just the moon. It bugs me. It's not like the mainframe doesn't have the processing power for it. They just didn't want to put in the work. So I did."

"The stars," Dolly says again, shaking her head. I'm so glad she's going a more normal speed now. "Bits, you do always surprise me."

"What, you don't think the stars are important?"

"I guess I don't really think about them. And I definitely don't think much about virtual reality."

You can say that again. "Wait, Null, why were you looking at that data?"

"For the upcoming transport?" Null asks. "They're planning on going to a site that was decommissioned in the late 90's, early century, and there's a lot of tech there that people have speculated on for a long time, but nobody's been able to get in. It's offline."

"But why do you know about the transport to begin with?" Dolly looks at me, a little enough twitch that she could've been checking the mirrors, but I catch it.

"It was a total fluke, I'm into old tech and I was poking around looking for other stuff and there was a flagged association with this arrest file. And then the convoy is really weird and—"

"Old tech," I repeat, because it sounds both totally possible and also a lie and I'm rapidly reaching my saturation point. I can't see what Bristol would have to do with old tech. Unless it has to do with data from the diamonds, but she didn't talk about that at all. And doesn't really care about most of it. Just the Fabergé egg. I wonder if she just left it in Morocco like an abandoned puppy.

"Well I guess it's lucky that we found you," Dolly says, like she doesn't at all believe it, but what else are we gonna do. "Bitsy, maybe check what we're looking at?"

"Yeah, I'll do that," I say, pulling up those personnel files I skimmed. Six DHS staff, even gender split. Maybe one day I'll get my shit together about what military ranks mean, or maybe it won't really matter in my life anymore, but a female Captain, former Army, is the highest ranked person tapped for this. The personnel will be in pretty standard body armor, each have a sidearm. No weapons on the vehicles. "Hey, do you have a gun?" I probably should've been paying better attention.

"A gun? No, I don't have a gun." Null's voice cracks, and her eyes widen, and I try to decide if she's really just a teenager after all. Maybe a runaway. Well, worse people than us could've found her.

"Do you know how to use a gun?" Dolly asks.

"I've been to the range with my dad," she says after a second. "You don't think we're going to have to shoot people do you?"

"There's no 'we' shooting people, kiddo," Dolly says. "We'll give you a taser or something."

"But everybody else is going to have guns?"

"Probably. I think I've got a vest that'll fit you, or maybe Nicolai does. Nicky, you're quiet again. You know that makes me nervous."

"I just did not see where you needed my input," he says. "You seemed to have covered the bases."

"Is he Russian?" Null asks. She didn't quite seem to know how loud or quietly she could talk with the earbuds.

"Da, comrade," Nicolai says dryly.

"You got a spare vest or not, Nicky?"

"I have one that might suit, yes, I only saw our new friend briefly."

"Wait can...can somebody explain what we're doing?"

"We are hijacking that transport you found so interesting," Nicolai says.

"Oh."

We whip past a 'speed checked by aircraft' sign and I check again. Still nothing in our vector. I cast my net wider, and there are the blips, those little connections of the remote drones scrambling to Null's motel. They've still got about twenty minutes, and right as I cycle away, the first ground vehicle comes into that vector as well. I hope they just find Null's empty room and leave things alone without detaining anybody or anything. Hotel staff put up with too much shit as it is.

"Dolly, hey, what's the plan after we get Bristol?" Things are crackling on the edges of my vision again. The top of my head is just going to come right off. "Is it one of these old tech places like Null is talking about?"

"We don't need to worry about that right this second, Bitsy."

I look at Dolly, hands at ten and three, eyes on the road. "You could've just said no. That's not a no."

"You are correct."

"This site has the potential to have much lucrative merchandise there," Nicolai says.

Is that true, or is that what Dolly told him to get him on board? "I really need you to tell me the truth, here," I say.

"I have never lied to you," Dolly says, looking at me steadily for a moment. I believe her. We don't lie to each other. If only I could figure out what's wrong. I look at the scar on her shoulder and try to decide if it's old or new. "And I tried to tell you everything when we were still in Mexico, remember?"

The static, the pain, the buzz of the razor on my scalp. Tigers. "I remember." Nobody says anything for awhile, and then I get a little bell icon in my AR. It's the tracking code I left on the transport vehicles in the motor pool. "They're on the move now," I say.

"Motherfuck." Dolly makes a face, looks at a mile marker as it whips past. "Light up the route to our rendezvous. Not like we needed time to plan or anything."

Chapter Thirteen

"Nicky, you got a taser or a stun gun or something that our new friend can use?"

"You are aware of my stock, including a number of actual guns that—"

"I don't mind the taser or whatever, it's okay," Null says quickly.

I'm not sure how up for ambushing and shooting people I am, actually. I think of the gunshots going off like fireworks in my skull, even though noise isn't really a problem for me. Lights are. The wrong thoughts, apparently. I think about Bristol getting as far away from me and Dolly as she can and then getting arrested on purpose. Was Will that close on her trail? On ours? What were we *doing*?

"I got beanbags for my shotgun," Dolly says. "So we can do that if we want." She looks at me. "You got rubber bullets?"

"No," I say. "I don't know." I've never had to draw my gun during one of our jobs. Wait, that's not true. But I've never had to take the safety off.

"Nicky, how many tasers we got?"

"I only have two," he says.

"Oh, are they the ones we dueled with that time?" Dolly asks, laughing.

"They are."

"You two dueled with...you know what, never mind. It's fine." I wish, suddenly and strongly, for water. I should drink more water, hydration helps with all kinds of things. Though rest stops are rife with surveillance. Everything is.

"I want to hear it," Null says in a small voice. This poor kid's going to bail out of the back next time we slow down. Not everybody's equipped to handle Dolly. I hope she knows the right way to roll.

"It ain't exactly a common thing, taser duels," Dolly says. "At least not in my experience."

"Shocking," I say, leaning over to see if there's bottled water under my seat. I'm going to regret this when I sit back up again.

"Well, you spend enough time around enough rich Russians, and enough bottles of vodka get consumed, some wacky shit is bound to happen. And this one time, we were in a pretty nice place too, weren't we? Bristol was there. Wherever the Russian Riviera would be considered, the Adriatic Sea or Black Sea or someplace, on somebody's yacht, everybody very drunk, and I don't know how the topic came up but it turned out Nicolai had a case that had matching tasers in it. The kind that shoot out the little line that sticks into a person, and then shocks 'em. You know?"

"I know," Null says.

"So we did it old fashioned duel style, two of us back to back, and paced it off. It was a yacht, okay, but not twenty paces big, I forget what we did instead, me and Nicolai. Were you here for this, Bits?"

"Nope." I sit up, sway a little against my seatbelt with the head rush. No water. I think I'd decided to go to Tokyo or something where I could have actual fun; boats and bikinis are not within my interests.

"Anyway, we paced off and we turned, and actually pulled our triggers at the same time, but Nicky missed and I didn't." Dolly grins. "But we were already dressed for swimming, so once he was done twitching on the boat deck, we all went for a swim and everything was fine."

"Sounds like a blast," I say. It does not.

"Well, maybe we'll do it again sometime," Dolly says.

"No, no I will not," Nicolai says. "But you are welcome to use the tasers."

"You're a pal, Nicolai, thanks. So yeah, Null, that's you settled. Maybe Bits will want one, too, I dunno." She glances at me and I shrug. The pain has shifted more into pressure across my cheekbones and wrapped around my temples, like somebody lined my VR goggles with barbed wire. "It's not like DHS will shoot to wound," Dolly says. I maybe lost some time again.

I rummage in my bag, and find a couple of candy bars, no water. "Can we stop? I'm dying of thirst."

"We're kind of on a timer here Bitsy," Dolly says, her tone strained enough that even I notice.

"I know." In AR I pull up the moving dots of the transport, two cars, and our moving dot. The area where we hope to intersect; we need to get there before them. I'm tired and my head hurts and I'm so thirsty I want to cry.

"Okay we'll stop and I'll run in," Dolly says finally. "Unless anybody else needs anything?" Nobody takes her up on it. Dolly's off the next exit, through a gas station old enough that you still need an actual key for the outside bathroom, and then we're on the road again, a shrink wrapped flat of bottled water squeaking awkwardly into the space between the front and back seats. I break the cap twisting it off, and spill some water in my lap, but then it's coursing over my lips and tongue and it's so sweet and cool and good, like I've never had water before in my life, only heard legends of it while I lived out in a desert. I drop the empty bottle between my feet and drink another one, a little slower but not by much, some dripping down my chin.

"Don't worry, I'm done," I say, before Dolly does anything to stop me from taking another.

"I'm sorry we can't give you more time," she says, in an uncharacteristically serious tone.

"We have the time we have," I say, feeling so detached from the world around me that in that moment I experienced no worry, no regret. I'm just not thirsty and have such a headache that all I can do is float in the timestream, since I'm not in the datastream.

And then there we are in a turnoff, waiting for the two transport vehicles to come down the road. Everything is flat, flat, but this seems to have been some kind of highway department maintenance site. Dolly does a final check of everybody's weapons and shoves a ballistic vest at Null. She's in her riot gear, and I'm in my riot gear, though I don't remember doing that when I got up this morning. There's a pole barn here, a few other buildings I can't really pinpoint the exact use of other than maybe storage or housing a water supply, and the hulking rusting out remains of a broken down snowplow. Both of our vehicles are visually hidden from the road, but Nicolai's car has a signal so we better hope DHS isn't running a scanner. I can only assume Nicolai has dragonscale, or a vest.

"You've done this before?" I ask Null as we get out our VR gear. Null's headset is practically factory stock, the kind a phone gets slotted into, little wireless keyboard in her hands.

"Hacked a vehicle? Yeah. Not one like this, though. It was a normal car. I did it just screwing around, seeing what could be done."

"It's a lot like that. Tougher security protocols, though. So if you can't get the one on your own, come and back me up, and we'll pair up to hit each one separately."

"Got it," Null says. She licks her lips, makes sure her earbuds are settled. She looks both nervous and excited, and I hope this isn't a huge mistake. Another huge mistake. There've been a few.

"All right then. We'll get our connections now, make sure we'll have control, and then do the hard shutdown when they're at that mile marker right there. Dolly and Nicolai will move in first, we'll make sure the communications stay down, and physically move in after."

Null looks at me a little oddly. "I got it. Dolly just went over it."

She did? "Just making sure. It doesn't hurt to be redundant."

"I'd rather hear it twice than mess up." She pulls her headset down.

There isn't much here that shows up in VR. There's an AR pinball machine booted up in the pole barn; must've been some kind of employee lounge. I can imagine snow plow guys hanging out there in shifts, sleeping on an old orange couch and just brewing pot after pot of coffee as the drifts keep piling up. It's kind of wild that the plow is still here, somebody could've stolen it and sold it for scrap by now. We could use it to block the road, interrupt the convoy, except they'd see it way too soon. My mind is caught on the plow, like when you bite the inside of your cheek and then bite the same place again over and over, accidentally. Or trip over the same spot in the sidewalk, the same break, even if you've been walking past it for years.

Dolly would love a snow plow plan. But a snow plow plan will get people killed. I don't say anything. Anyway, we have guns. I don't say anything.

//Can she handle a vehicle hack?// Dolly messages me. //Her goggles look like the kind of VR that grandmas get at the grocery store to play solitaire with.//

//She says she's done it before.// She'd hacked the same facility as me with those 'goggles', I don't remind Dolly.

Null and I virtually walk out to the mile marker where we want the vehicles stopped, past the ghostlike blips of Dolly and Nicolai's online equipment. And we wait. I watch the flagged vehicles come near, watch the little surveillance drones. These drones are automated and only record surveillance data, so that's good. The predators would have to deploy from a base, if the communications reached there. If. Which they won't, if we do our jobs. Normally I'm not worried. The walkies on all personnel rout through a dish on each vehicle, so if the vehicles are down, communications will be down.

I don't see anybody who looks like cybersecurity. I've got my VR in all around vision which I'll pay for later, the way I feel, but right now, I'm in it to win it. Bristol's in the second vehicle, I see now, but I'm in charge of the lead one. I prod the code gently, try the protocols I know already, run them through the dictionary hack program I modified for military hacks specifically, and after a moment I'm looking at the vehicle data. Personnel (female officer driving, three more men, one passenger side, two in back), weapons loadouts, GPS, connections to the base, destination coordinates. No place I recognize, I screencap it all and save it to search later. There's something throwing off a signal that I don't quite recognize, but it isn't communications and it isn't a weapon.

"You got it, Null?" I ask. This is a big ask for somebody we just met.

"I have it. You want to swap, so you've got her vehicle?"

"Yeah thanks." We do the handoff, and then I'm looking at the other vehicle's loadout. It's seriously different. All nonlethal, no repeat of that additional digital device, GPS tracker on Bristol. Probably her ankle. I got to work on that; Null had left it alone and I'm glad. On the walkies, I say "Kickoff in three, two, one," then I hit my virtual switch that ties everything in the targets together. Their satellite goes down, steering locks up, all of the engines slow. Front doors lock, Bristol's door unlocks, her GPS bracelet spoofing continued forward momentum. We'll have to manually remove it.

I steal a look at Null's work, for peace of mind I have to, but it's good. The vehicle stopped or is stopping, all of the doors locked, and as a bonus, the AR connection between their guns and their contact lenses are jammed. They might not even know it yet, that their biometrics and aim assists are off.

Distantly, I hear Dolly whooping. Nicolai's got to be with her, or covering the vehicles, or both. I watch everything that I switched off, that Null switched off, and so far everything's copacetic. So far, no other signals came online either, and I slide my headset up for a second to get a look at the real world, eyes squinted almost closed as I do.

The funny thing about bulletproof vehicle glass is it doesn't really shatter. The front passenger of vehicle one is hammering on their windshield with a gun butt, looks like, which when you think about it will screw up all their calibration even if Null hadn't already thrown them a whole bunch of static. The driver already has her seatbelt unfastened and is pretzeling herself around to try and kick out the windshield, I guess. Maybe she's yelling at him to help. It looks like she is. The first kick doesn't clear it and she's crunching up for the second.

Nicolai stands with his weapon shouldered, just waiting for a target. Dolly's at the rear vehicle, already has Bristol out, and is fastening her in a bulletproof vest that makes her look like a woman in a business suit from the 1980s. Too big, but it'll stop what they're carrying, anyway. She isn't dressed in anything like her normal clothes. It looks a lot like hospital scrubs. And her hair is—

The windshield of the second vehicle is kicked out, and one of the guys slides off the hood and turns. Dolly extends the sawed off shotgun with just her right arm and squeezes off a round. It discharges with a weird noise that makes me think—hope—that Dolly loaded the beanbag rounds after all, and the guy folds up onto the pavement. The other one takes cover where I can't see, but Dolly's got her pistol out and uses the backseat as a step to hop up onto the roof of the car. She's practiced that. She walks on the roof to the front, aims down, and squeezes off three rounds, or maybe the pistol is a three round burst, I can't remember now. Is she whistling that song again? I have a feeling those are regular rounds. It seems like too little too late to be worried about shooting people, but I still feel a momentary twinge, a sudden big deep hollow in the pit of my stomach as things start to stretch out and slow down. And then Nicolai cries out and I turn to him like I'm underwater, like I'm dreaming.

He staggers back, clutching at his chest, but he's still standing. The vest took it. I've had bruises from being shot in armor before, but I'll take bruises over literal holes in me. I've never actually been shot in my flesh bits. Dolly has; she has a scar just under her right collarbone, and when Bristol exclaimed over it at first sight, Dolly had been super casual, saying if the bullet was bigger, or a little bit higher or lower, she would've ended up in a box. Or test driving one of those cybernetic arms so many people are excited about. Dolly has a lot of scars, and any explanation of them come with so much brag, there's no way to tell what's true and what Dolly's running her mouth over. Her arm though, her arm, and—

A bullet passes so close by my face I feel the air move as I stand there with my thoughts and my hand on my holstered gun, and that, *that* finally yanks me back to the real world with the fierce sharp focus of the combat adrenaline dump and that familiar drilling hot pain in my left temple. Null's running, though, Null tases the man from the front car, leaving him a jittering pile of person and equipment on the bumper of the car. I don't see the officer. The other two personnel from the front car are still in the back seat, still wrestling with seat belts and windows and bulky equipment, and trying to climb up front and also get out the windshield. The windshield trick is a good one; emergencies are varied, though. They take up a lot of brain space.

Dolly is yelling something, either at me or at Nicolai, or just yelling to yell. Null retreated again already, pulled her headset back down over her eyes. Then I see the officer.

That piece of equipment, that signal I couldn't figure out in virtual space, now it clicks into place. It's one of those prototype cloaking devices, the next step up in camouflage gear, except it's too clunky, too expensive to produce in any kind of volume. The officer, when she got out of the car, must've flipped the switch and then just flattened herself on the asphalt. Smart; the less varied the background, the better the device was going to be at replicating it. But the officer moved, not very much, but enough to maybe pull the rifle off the tased guy on the bumper, and my eye caught the shimmer in the air as the camo device tried to keep up with the movement. It's good, it's very good, but I just spent however long immersed in code, and when you're doing that you bet you keep your eye out all the time for irregularities like that when you're in VR immersion. I raise my gun and fire.

The device doesn't cloak the blood that spurts and begins pouring from that shimmery spot in the air. The device doesn't dampen the sound of the officer crying out in a cracked and raw-edged voice, and when she falls back, partly against the vehicle, the device can't track her movements as she thrashes in pain. For all that, I can't tell where I shot her, and I look around, sick and shaky, because there are at least two more guys I need to be worried about I think. It's not like me to lose track. It's *my job* to keep track.

Except there aren't any more, one already groaning and subdued, the other still enough that I assume he's dead. Dolly is a preternaturally good shot, and has joked more than once that she should just get a job in Vegas doing one of those old timey Wild West shows, except she'd be bored out of her skull and only be able to take it for so long.

I holster my pistol and leave it unsnapped, like I'm going to quick draw it or something if I need to. It's very quiet now, except for the officer's choked sobbing, her attempts to communicate with base. I have a quick peek in my headset and Null still has all comms locked down, including the little drones, which are resting now on the road. Dolly grinds one drone, then the other, under her boot heels as she clears weapons from the personnel, and then goes to the rear of the front car. "Pop the trunks," she says, calm as can be. Before I can do anything, Null has the trunk open, obscuring Dolly from view. Bristol stands off to the side, reloading a pistol. Nicolai stands next to her, quietly saying something, and Bristol looks at me for a moment before nodding, wavering a little on her feet.

Dolly pulls something the size of a cooler out of the trunk and hauls it over to the officer, who looks like she's glitching. It's like VR and the officer has something wrong with her code. I feel unsteady myself, but there's nowhere to sit down and we can't stay here. There's only so long we have before somebody comes looking for them. Dolly closes her eyes and feels around, and then the active camo switches off and the officer isn't a glitch anymore. She's a woman in cargos with a bullet proof vest and a sidearm, splattered with blood. My bullet went in above the vest, in that soft spot where the collarbones meet. I can't understand why she isn't dead already, because even though she's got a hand pressed on that spot, the blood's still pumping between her fingers. From the look on Dolly's face, she isn't really sure why either. But she rummages in the kit like she's going to try to help, and that's what unfreezes me.

I go to Dolly's side, drop down on my knees. The world does a too-far drop with me, shimmers at the edges, resolves. "What can I do? What are you going to do?"

"Well, they got this expanding foam that fills up wounds, that might do the trick. Or she might be done already. I'm no medic." Dolly breaks the top off the tube, shakes it briskly. "Gotta move your hand," she says to the officer, who looks up at her with glassy eyes and bloody foam flecking her lips, and for a second I think she's dead anyway. Then the officer moves her hand, eyes slipping closed, and Dolly sticks the nozzle against the wound and presses the button. It makes a noise like coating a slice of pie with whipped cream, and the foam is white. It reddens rapidly in spots, but the blood stops. Dolly picks up the officer's wrist, feels it for a moment. "Still hanging on." She pulls a pack of syrettes from the kit, separates one. "Painkillers," she says to me, and flicks the back of the officer's hand to make a vein stand out before sliding the needle in and depressing the plunger. The officer's face tightens, and then she relaxes on the ground.

"So I didn't kill her?"

Dolly blinks. "Not yet, anyway. Once we're ready to clear out, you can hit the big red panic button in their comms and medical will scramble for her." Dolly pulls a black box the size of a paperback book off of the officer's vest and hands it to me. "She's the only one wearing one of these, thank Christ. It's shitty, but still the best one of those we've seen yet."

"I've never seen—"

Dolly slaps the first aid kit closed and shoves that at me too, getting up. "Throw that in the Jeep. I figure you want to be out of here in ten, you think?"

"I think ten minutes might be too long," Bristol says from somewhere behind me. Maybe the other side of the car still.

"Five then, we're almost done." Dolly grabs me under the arm, pulls me up. "You okay?"

"Yeah." I'm not a new kind of not okay, anyway.

"The Jeep's just past the snow plow corpse," Dolly says. She pulls the officer's sidearm, picks up the rifle the officer had gone for. The tased guy is starting to recover, trying to close his twitching fingers on the rifle that isn't even there anymore. Like taking candy from a baby. What a weird saying that is. Who gives candy to babies anyway? "Grab one of the zip ties outta my pocket," she says to me, then she shakes her head. "Nevermind, go to the Jeep. Null!"

"I can do it," I say, but Null's doing it already, and then Dolly's got the guy face down on the asphalt next to the officer with his arms zip tied behind his back. "Now, it's not actually that hard to get out of zip ties," Dolly says. Nicolai comes, takes the first aid kit out of my hands. "You just gotta know the trick of it."

We stand, watching the guy a moment. "Which he doesn't," I say. Do I?

"Correct."

"Don't forget to pull their credentials," Bristol says over the headsets. Did Dolly give her earbuds already? Were hers just in her recovered belongings?

"You honestly think I'd forget a thing like that?" Dolly asks.

"Of course not," Bristol says with a laugh in her voice.

We're back at the Jeep and Nicolai's car in four and a half minutes, dog tags and portable drives in a foil lined bag, active camo prototype in one of my cargo pockets. Null has her VR headset hung around her neck like me, keeps looking at the people, the cars, back to me every once in awhile, chewing her lip.

"What's up?" I ask. Bristol is in Nicolai's car, Dolly leaning in on the door and talking to her.

"I've never done anything like this before," Null says. "I've only ever just looked at things.

"We all start somewhere," I say, but I've never actually shot anybody before today. I've shot *at* them sure, but missed.

"I would dearly appreciate it if somebody would remove my unwanted accessory," Bristol says.

"Oh, sorry," I say. I should've been on that already. I grab my little tool case, crouch to look at the GPS tracker. I pull my headset up for a moment to make sure there isn't anything I'm missing, a dead man's switch or panic broadcast or I don't know what. We're so close. But it's clear. I shake the goggles up on my forehead and twist the final corrector, and the bracelet falls heavily to the ground.

"Alrighty then, back in the saddle, buckaroos," Dolly says. "Bitsy, just hop in here, Null come with me."

"Okay." When I'm not focusing on the job anymore I'm so exhausted I'm not sure I could've even walked to the Jeep. I crawl across the back seat of Nicolai's car. My ears are ringing, and I don't know when that started or if it will ever stop, and I just feel like I need to catch up with myself.

Bristol's kind of glassy eyed when she turns around to look at me, but I think that's from chemical restraints. "How do you like my hair?" she asks, running her hand over her buzzed scalp.

"Oh Bristol," I say, sad and sick. She always spends so much time on her hair. The whole package. Even in pajamas Bristol doesn't look as undone as she does now, so barefaced that it's like she's an unfinished painting.

"Bits, darling, you aren't crying are you? You aren't thinking about how limited by my hair I was! This is a stroke of genius, actually. Now I can look however I want. There are wigs in any style you can imagine. They really only helped me."

"Sure, it's like they set you free," Dolly says dryly over the headset. "It's ironic, just like that song."

"But the song—" I start to say, and Bristol laughs.

"Has been discussed to *death*," she says. I know the song but I don't know the song but who cares anyway. We saved Bristol, we did it. I don't know where we're going now. Dolly had a plan, did she tell me a plan? Wait I copied their maps.

"Bits." Dolly's been saying my name over and over for awhile, I guess. Trying to cut through the static.

"Yeah?"

"We're far enough out, call the ambos for them." Bristol is still looking at me and I slide the VR visor down so I don't have to think about what look should be on my face. I lie back on the plush leather of the back seat. We've covered more miles already than I realize, and the connection is choppy, but I delete the code that brought down the convoy's communications, hit their panic button for emergency services.

"Done."

Nicolai is being awfully quiet. I wonder why. Probably starting to feel the bruises under his vest.

"Roger that," Dolly says cheerfully. Bristol should've gone in her Jeep, they could've gossiped about me all they needed to without bothering me about it. Nicolai turns on the radio, or maybe Bristol does, some kind of old but new techno jazz, instrumental. I could sleep forever, I think. But no, of course I can't, the rocking car stops soothing me after awhile and starts making me feel like I'm gonna throw up.

"Who's our new friend?" Bristol asks quietly when I sit up and pull my visor off. Her hand is on the walkie mute.

"We picked her up earlier," I say, not sure if that's right, but Nicolai doesn't say no. "She was hacking the same place I was, at the same time, and they caught her."

"Convenient," Bristol says.

"Bristol, she's just a kid," I say. But should I have thought about this more? Dolly should've thought about it more, anyway. I have been unwell.

"I'm sure it's fine."

"She's been very helpful," Nicolai offers.

"Especially when nobody else was, I imagine," Bristol says.

"We tried to..." I trail off. I don't need to tell her this. Walkie channels open again, I say "I hope we're finding a place to hunker down."

"Just putting some pavement between us and them, and then yeah, we'll find another off the beaten path gem like the ones we've been purveying. Sorry Nicky."

"It's to be expected," he says.

Chapter Fourteen

I didn't know so many motels with burned out signs and unpaved driveways existed, and yet here we are again. Dolly has a special knack for finding them, I guess, the way Bristol can always find a place to eat that serves authentic espresso. Weird little not quite superpowers, and I try to think about what I think mine is and think about Null saying I was a VR legend. Dolly and Nicolai go off to get food before we think about what that kind of decision might mean for the rest of us, and Bristol gets in the shower. She has a bag that Dolly must've gotten for her from a bus station locker. I must've lost time again, blanked out during that stop.

Null sits cross-legged on one of the beds, pretending to look intently at her screen. She looks at me sometimes, looks away. She wants to talk about what happened today and I want to do that for her, be a mentor or whatever, and I can't. I'm lying flat on the bed on my back and the bed still feels like the car on the road. I curl over on my side again and just hope that it'll stop before I have to go in the adjoining room and throw up. Dolly left the connecting door open, anyway. My head hurts and doesn't hurt, sometimes fine, sometimes like my skull is a butterfly tacked to velvet, like my headache is a dying fluorescent bulb. I try to decide which it'll stop on, when the flickering stops, hurting or not. It used to be not. Hurts me, hurts me not.

Then Dolly and Nicolai are back, Dolly's boots untied again somehow, if she ever tied them in the first place, talking too loud for me to sort words and I just shove my head harder against the pillow. Dolly clomping out again, coming back as Bristol exits the bathroom in a cloud of steaming rose scent. "They're out of fucking ice, can you believe it?"

"I'm amazed they provide the illusion of having ice to begin with," Bristol says, like a cartoon cat who doesn't like getting her paws wet.

"What do we need ice for?" I ask, sitting up, regretting it.

"Your head and the warm booze Nicky had in his trunk," Dolly says, looking at me critically. "We should take the party into the other room."

"Maybe it'll help if I eat," I say. It never helps when I eat.

We eat—well they eat—and somebody puts on old movies on the crappy motel network. Probably Bristol. Black and white old movies, not even early aughts.

"So what now?" I ask. "We got Bristol out, we all go home now?" Bristol shoots Dolly an accusing look.

"Not exactly," Dolly says. That sparkle's still in her eyes.

"What do you mean?" I say at the same time as Bristol says "You didn't tell her?"

Dolly sighs, elaborately. Nicolai looks uncomfortable, or maybe he just never looks comfortable, and I look at Null, who is just watching and listening avidly, like she's taking notes.

"Every time I tell her it doesn't work," Dolly says.

"How can it 'not work', what does that mean?"

"It means it doesn't work, she just can't." Dolly kind of flaps a hand and finishes her drink. "She can't hear it without like, rebooting."

"Rebooting?" Bristol's staring at me now, her eyes luminous under too much forehead. There wasn't a wig in that bag Dolly brought, even if there were clothes and cosmetics and rose scented shower stuff. There probably aren't wig vending machines.

"She tries to tell me some things, and I hear white noise, and then wake up again doing something else." I wait, but for once, Bristol has nothing to say. Maybe she's still coming off the drugs they were giving her. She probably shouldn't be drinking, but it's too late now.

"Dolly, you can't expect her to *work* like this!"

"I did just fine," I say. I did a good job. I also just want to go someplace dark and sleep for a thousand years, so why should I even argue about this? I should just say I can't do it. Mission accomplished.

"You did, Bits, there's no faulting your work. I only mean—"

"I know what you mean," I say. She stops talking and quirks her lips, glances at Dolly. "Okay. Tell me the story again."

"I thought you just said hearing the story reboots you?" Bristol asks. Dolly's looking at me though, squinting just a little.

"Something changed," she says. Not really a question.

"I think maybe," I say, thinking of the dream with the wall coming down. Maybe my subconscious is running its own dictionary hack. "How's the arm?"

"Purring like a kitten," she says, flashing a grin. She pauses, nods, hands me the tequila. "Okay."

"Okay," I say, and swig from the bottle. I always forget, tequila isn't my favorite.

"So we were tracking down the leads on some of our diamond data. Looking at the older cold war stuff, the stuff we thought had to be decommissioned. And we found a program that sounded really familiar. To me, anyway."

"Why would you know anything about a program?" I ask. I take another swig of the tequila, hold up the bottle to look at the scorpion in the bottom, its tail half curled. It looks like it has little hairs on its claws, but they're probably called something other than hair.

"Not a computer program, darling," Bristol says. I wonder if she knows she's touching her head behind her ear, where hair would've been, but every one of Bristol's gestures is on purpose.

"More like project, I guess," Dolly says. She keeps looking at me, waiting for me to static out and reboot. I'm in kind of a neutral state, no real headache though I'm sure it's waiting, no white noise whine in my ears, though I'm sure it's waiting too. "Way back then they didn't really have cybernetics yet, just the ideas of it. From crazy scientists, I guess, and books and movies. But like, the Russians have almost always had the idea of super soldiers, right? And America never likes being beat out by anybody, much less the Russians."

"But this was Russian intel." I had the diamond data all backed up; normally I could search it up quicker than they could explain it to me.

"Russian intel about an American program."

"An ongoing American program," I say, without realizing I was going to say it.

Dolly nods eagerly. "At a lot of sites across the country, most of which are decommissioned."

"So we were looking for the places that were payday versus actual live fire engagement," I say. I'm remembering, not-remembering. I can't remember what comes next until I say it, like rereading a book that I last saw when I was three. There's something I'm forgetting, something Dolly doesn't want to say in front of Null, or maybe she's just trying to feel out where the new boundary of my difficulty is. Same.

"We were, yeah. And some of 'em, I knew about and some I didn't and we were mapping it out and matching things together. We were kinda looking for the one that I remembered. For something more, um, personal. Than just a payday."

"The one you...remembered." I wasn't feeling so great anymore. I wasn't holding the bottle anymore, Bristol had it, though she definitely hated tequila and only drank it if the social situation required. Dolly didn't notice, either deliberately or because she's Dolly.

"Lots of places, the government, or I guess maybe it was private corporations on government contract, brought in locals to work on. Promised them a paycheck, that their families would be looked after. By then, that was the only chance some of those locals had at a future, and they took that chance."

"You were one of them."

"Me. My brother. Some of our friends." She takes the bottle from Bristol, takes a swig. "Some of us, by the time we were done, were sent off to other places, and mostly didn't know what happened to each other."

"So is this a payday or revenge?"

"Both. Neither. Ain't nobody gonna feel bad for what they did to us. Hell, I mostly feel fine about it, physically. It's the rest of it that I got the problem with." Weirdly, I remember her talking about bees. Corporations and their bees, locals and their bees. It's hard to imagine Dolly as a farmer, a beekeeper, anything than what she is now. What is she now? What am I?

They keep talking but the static overtakes me like an avalanche, like the ocean, and I'm pulled under.

Chapter Fifteen

I dream of the hot green seething trees around my villa, that encased it in flickering shadows even at noon. I dream of tigers. Tiger cubs, playing in the clearing just down the hill, where the old owner landed helicopters. Fully grown tigers, and they're normally solitary, aren't they? Nosing open the door, once it rained enough, and dried enough, and the door swelled off its hinges and my sad eyed real estate agent couldn't find a new buyer. Tigers prowling in the hallways, maybe pursuing rodents, catching mice, like if people hunting for potato chips was a thing.

I walk past the tigers in the hall, to my VR immersion room, to find the server stacks intact again, the hard drives in place, LEDs blinking briskly. And I'm there in the chair again, all of the little pads connected, the mesh over my head for the neurological impulses, the visor over my eyes, the IV settled in my arm. I stand over myself, looking down. Looking at the displays on the machines. Looking at my immersion-slack face, not so different from sleep, I guess. And then, as I watch, rivulets of blood began to come from my nose, and from my eyes beneath the visor, from the corner of my mouth.

Then there's a grumbling in the room, the chuffing, coughing noise that tigers make, and one pushes me aside, pushes standing awake-me aside, and goes to prone VR-immersed-me and begins to lick the blood off my face. But a tiger's tongue is very rough, rough enough to lathe flesh from bones, and so my face begins to come off, in blood dripping layers, the VR visor clattering to the arm of the chair and then the tiled floor, dragging on the end of its cable, the mesh hanging up in the tiger's teeth until it chuffs again, face and nose wrinkled, and tugs it away. The tiger keeps licking and my skin keeps coming off.

When I come fully awake, I'm almost on my feet in the now-dark hotel room, the sheets and blankets tangling me up. Mostly dark, the blue-gray light of dawn seeping around the window shades. Somebody has their hands on my shoulders...Bristol. She's saying something, maybe I'm saying something, everything is white noise and bright lights in the corners of my vision where I'm sure no lights are on. I sit down on the bed so abruptly that Bristol stumbles, shoulders into me, the most graceless thing I've ever seen her do. Then she sits on the bed next to me, breathing hard. Dolly stands in the doorway between rooms, sawed-off shotgun in hand, adjoining room lit behind her and Nicolai saying something in Russian that I can't sort out. Or don't I speak Russian?

"Bitsy what the fuck?" Dolly says.

"I had a bad dream," I say, which seems so childish and stupid. My mouth has the heavy copper taste of blood in it, and my face is wet, but when I wipe it, no blood comes away on my hands, they're just wet from tears, sweat.

"I can see that," she says. She flicks the safety on the shotgun, which strikes me as really funny. Sawed off shotgun, but with a safety. But I can't find the energy to laugh, and also probably that's good because it would be far more alarming if I just start laughing now. In the dim room I can see the orangey striped tiger, the blood blotting out the white between the black stripes. I can hear the heavy tearing sound of its tongue lathing, the rain-like patter of blood on the floor. I shudder, and Bristol shifts, seems to hesitate, and puts an arm around me. Dolly comes and sits on the other side of me, does the same thing.

"I've never heard you make a noise like that before, Bits," Bristol says.

"I'm sorry," I say. I'm still crying, I realize. Just seeping tears. Tears, not blood, hot on my face.

Dolly kind of gives me a squeeze. "Nah, we needed a wakeup call at dawn anyway, more or less. This way we can get all situated and ready to roll out. Sound good?"

"Yeah," I say, a few moments of sorting out Dolly's sudden shift into businesslike. Maybe not so sudden. Maybe Dolly hadn't actually been sleeping, and was just mentally running the scenario all night. That is very much like her. And this is honestly the most I've seen Dolly care about something, the most sustained focus I've seen her give something. Even after the diamond heist, she'd been more relaxed. Though 'relaxed Dolly' is still also 'ready to spring into action Dolly'. Like a tiger lounging in the sun.

"Was it a VR dream?" Null asks quietly. I'd forgotten about her.

I hesitate. "More or less." I wipe my face again. "I dreamed about Mexico, and tigers. At my place there."

"Mexico," Null says, in a musing tone.

"She had herself set up in an old drug lord's villa," Dolly says, her voice light and easy as always. "Problem is, there were rumors the guy had pet tigers that he just turned loose before he bugged outta there. Probably just rumors. But enough to make you wanna carry a gun all over the place."

"Tigers? Yeah, wow. That's scary."

"I never saw one," I say. "Or even heard one. It probably wasn't true."

"Probably," Dolly agrees. "But clearly it's a risk you were willing to take."

"Clearly." I squeeze my eyes shut, open them again, hoping to banish the afterimages of stripes, luminous eyes, white whiskers turning red. "Is it okay if I take the first shower?"

"Of course," Bristol says.

Hot water is a mistake, all of my sinuses throbbing like I've been beaten about the head. Cold water has its obvious downsides too, but I chatter my way through a thorough scrub down anyway, my head in such crystalline pain that I think it'll shatter at any second. But now I can think straight, at least for those seven minutes, and I think of whatever decommissioned site we're going to down in Louisiana, a part where hardly anybody lives anymore after hurricane after hurricane came roaring up through, Cat 5 and bigger, levies gone, cities gone, so much overrun swampland and forest. So much kudzu. So many feral hogs. It's the perfect place to keep going with clandestine stuff, especially if you're picking your 'volunteers' from a population where doctors are scarce and you have families needing to be seen to.

We pack everything in the Jeep, everybody in the Jeep, except for Nicolai. "Decided not to come with us after all?" I ask.

"I have a different role," he says.

"Safer, and yet somehow more lucrative," Bristol says. "Not that we lack for funds, mind," she hurries to add. She isn't used to my being confused all the time, missing information. Join the club.

"It was a pleasure spending time with each of you," Nicolai says stiffly.

He drives away before we do, and it's hard for me to not just keep tabs on his vehicle. But I don't want him backtraced if our operation goes sideways, again, and I uncouple his walkie from our network and try to put him out of my mind.

We make a couple of stops, bathroom breaks, breaks to get out of the car and walk around and stretch, so Bristol and Dolly can get away from each other for five minutes. One of the rest stops has a wifi booster, and I make short work of their security, slapping my VR headset on and getting right down to the fiber optic connection like somebody coming out of the desert going for their first drink of water. Apparently I've searched for super soldier black sites before, but not in conjunction with Louisiana, and I do another broad search, file grab everything I can find to scan through when the connection drops again. I toe into the dark net for information too, though what I immediately find looks like a lot of tinfoil hat nonsense. Still, I grab that too, because who knows where I'm going to find some truth, something to tease out of the wreckage of human reasoning and follow to a useful source.

I pull off my VR headset at the same time Null is doing the same. "Hey, let me look at your setup. I told you I would."

"Thanks." Null hands it over almost shyly.

It's matte black plastic; most of this stuff is, not unlike the active camo box that I've still got in my pocket. I should give that to Dolly. There's black electrical tape reinforcing some of the seams where the thing's been pried open, probably to add more RAM, a bigger processor, things that even an out-of-the-box unit purely for kids to play video games on won't have, but can accommodate. It's a bitch getting everything to fit back together, I remember that from my first one. Everybody remembers their first VR headset, pried apart, cobbled back together, tool-scored, tape-gummed, with its occasional hitches and starts in processing, a troublesome proclivity to disconnect and power cycle if you didn't get the soldering just right. The head strap is some kind of web material, an imitation of what military belts and straps were made out of, comfortable enough for awhile, but also the kind of thing that lets the buckles slip their adjustments incrementally as time goes by.

I run my thumbnail under the tape, find the tabs, pop it open. The soldering jobs are very good, actually, and all the components more or less jigsawed together just as one would like. The RAM's a little wiggly, and there are two cut rate graphics cards working together to try and do the work of a midrange one. The heat sinks are well placed, and the fans (because there are fans and not a liquid cooled system) are very small, really smooth running. I look at them, try to figure what kind of equipment they'd been pulled from. Maybe a video game console, maybe some kind of remote kids toy like a robot or a drone.

"Hardware looks pretty good, considering," I say.

"My budget screwed me, of course," Null says with a shrug.

"That's how it is for all of us. But you do really well with your equipment, which means you'll be amazed at what you can do with a decent headset, something that's better out of the box before you make your adjustments. Which, again, are very good."

"Thanks," Null says, and she's a little pink on the edges again, though this time from pride, I think, not embarrassment.

"It's okay if I test drive it?" I ask. She already said so, but it's just what you do. The etiquette of looking over other people's equipment.

"Yeah, go right ahead." Null's pretty good at sounding casual, but I can only think of the first time I had an older veteran hacker who was willing to look over my rig. It was nerve wracking and exciting, and I wanted both to get complimented and to get pointers on how to get past whatever bugs were hindering me, the hang-ups I still had no matter how much I'd tinkered and scanned and adjusted.

I slip the headset on, boot it up. Even on my head, the fans are very quiet. Maybe the kid likes the fans, maybe it's a budget thing. I'll bring up closed system liquid cooling; it's less able to be interfered with by random signals, or magnets or whatever. Not all that hard to do, either, with a couple of parts.

Connectivity out here is bad in the first place, but Null's signal is strong, then rapidly declines, and then spikes again, something my rig isn't doing. Something I could probably adjust, maybe something I could replace from my kit of assorted tools and parts, the stuff you keep around just in casies. I don't have a viable replacement for the video chip, nothing that would fit in Null's differently shaped headset, and that's a shame. The colors are a little off, but I'm not sure if that's a settings issue, Null's preference, or just my brain going weird again.

I do some general internet things, check movie times in Los Angeles, look at the space elevator construction webcam. There's a sandstorm in Dubai, obscuring most of the camera view, but I can still see the bright yellow construction vehicles, their headlights piercing the gloom.

I pull up maps, pick a random location, Seattle, and walk around for a few minutes in the VR. Null doesn't have the all-around vision toggled, opting for 180 instead. Even with the headset, the feedback is good, the sense of walking motion appropriate, not mismatched. It's raining in Seattle, because of course it is, and I don't opt to pull the available umbrella. Cold raindrops fall on my scalp, on my shoulders, but the rain feeling isn't quite right, and that's the fault of the haptics. I open a few more things and then stream a music video too while all of it's going, and there's some sluggishness, some hitches, more of those spikes and lags. The wiggly RAM tries like hell to do its job, but I wouldn't run like that any longer than I had to.

I shut down what I opened, pull the headset free of my head, take a second to acclimate to the world around me, the sunlight.. "It's good, overall," I say. "Most of your problems are hardware, like I said. Have you thought about liquid cooling?"

"Of course I've thought about liquid cooling, who hasn't? But you see the space I'm working with, and the odds and ends I have jammed in there, those little fans were the best I could do for the time being. If I could get liquid cooling—"

"You could improve the video card, and then I think there would be space for you to improve the haptics too." I don't mention the connectivity spikes. I have a weird feeling that I don't know how to address.

"Oh hell yeah!"

"You nerds," Dolly says with a laugh. I jump. I forgot we were all in the Jeep together. "You're all the same."

Chapter Sixteen

We're in Louisiana and kind of circling around to where we want to go, or to where Dolly wants me to go, before she sends me a file. God knows where she stores anything, and I didn't know she had any wireless storage on her. Maybe she just keeps it in an envelope until she needs it, pulls it out, puts it away again. It makes sense that she didn't give it to me before now, I probably couldn't have handled it.

I lost time again; Bristol is wearing a wig that she didn't have before, gleaming auburn like one of the foxes in my painting, sleek and straight and probably just long enough to put up in the French twist that she likes so much, if you can do things like that with a wig. I have no idea.

There's fast food bags on the seats between me and Null, and drinks in the holders. Mine is the iced coffee, I assume, and when Dolly glances back, sees that I'm with the world again, she reaches down in the console between her and Bristol, pulls out a rattling white bottle, and tosses it to me. "Got some good stuff," she says. "Proceed with caution."

When did she get some good stuff? Where? "Thanks," I try to read the label and my eyes just slide right off the teeny tiny words and numbers, and I finally just take one, my iced coffee really more luke-warm by this point and I wonder why until I look out the window at the not-quite-paved-anymore road, the huddled green forms of what were once houses overgrown with trees and bushes and kudzu, grasses so long that they bend and mat together under their own weight. It's the kind of grass you'd want a machete to walk through, both to clear a path and to fend off, I don't know, wildlife. Poisonous snakes and feral hogs and whatever other dangers were in the used-to-be inhabited deep south. People still live here, in places, I know that. But they're the kind of people who decided they didn't want to leave their land, they didn't want to move into the suburbs, or the cities, and deal with everything that entailed. Population and surveillance and police and the constant inundation of advertising and news. I mean, I ignore a lot of those things pretty well, even when I'm not on-purpose getting around them in ways that said police would be less than happy to know about. My own version of roughing it; inhabiting the modern world, but embracing the digital beyond what most normal citizens ever do. A step beyond, not a step back. "How much longer? Do you want to tell me, so I can try and check it out?"

"Couple hours, maybe, depends on the roads." She glances at Bristol, or maybe me; hard to tell with her sunglasses. Is she hesitating, or concentrating on the road? Is she hesitating because of Null? Dolly never hesitates. And what's *my* problem with Null? She's just a wet-behind-the hacker ears hacker kid who got into a target way over her head. "We're making a rest stop at the next likely place, though."

"That's good." I feel like so much of the last...week? Has it been a week? Has been made up of rest stops and driving and drinking various things and then having to stop again. Maybe it's the normal amount of stops and I just didn't notice before, my head in VR all the time, sifting through files, surveilling the sites and likely sites, getting a sense of what we needed to avoid in order to all come away from it successful and alive. We'd had such a good record of that until whatever screwed up my head.

The gas station isn't really a gas station anymore, so Dolly almost drives past it, until Bristol says "They do have lights on. And an open sign." She pulls the Jeep around and parks, and cuts the engine, and we all get out and stretch. It's the time of year when everything seems to be more green than anything real could be, and bugs I don't know the names of scream in chorus from the grass, and from the trees. Cicadas, some of them, I'm sure. It must be a nightmare trying to keep this patch of land clear, whether they intend it to be a parking lot anymore or not. Everything grows aggressively right up to the edges, and there's grass and Queen Anne's Lace shoving up through cracks in the pavement. There's a barbecue grill off to one side, but I don't smell anything cooking.

"Well let's just hope they're friendly," Dolly says. Null, almost to the door, pauses like it hadn't occurred to her that they might not be. Dolly laughs. "I'm sure they're friendly, kiddo, it's okay. I even left the AK in the Jeep."

"The AK?" Null asks and I think, hasn't Null seen it? Why didn't Dolly use it when we hijacked Bristol's captors? But I guess that would've been dumb. It's not a weapon known for its accuracy. Dolly just laughs again and kind of claps Null on the shoulder and walks into the place without taking her sunglasses off like she's a movie badass, and we trail in behind her. Bristol comes last, doing some fiddly thing with her makeup in a little compact mirror. If I didn't know it was a wig, I wouldn't know it was a wig.

There's a guy kind of near the counter, and two just-older-than toddlers playing with toys near the back, and his smile doesn't seem too guarded when the little bell rings over the door and we all walk in. I wonder when his last customers came through. I wonder how he gets supplies. From people like us, probably. I get a not quite memory, an echo, a digital ghost, of Dolly talking about hijacking autodriving eighteen wheelers out on a highway someplace. Salt. I remember doing that.

"Bathroom?" Dolly asks before any pleasantries are exchanged, and he smiles a little and points, and we split off to browse. Just like civilization. The kids don't really pay us any attention; either they're too absorbed in their game, or they were really drilled not to talk to strangers. I look for digital signatures in AR, a wireless booster, cameras, even just a cell phone, and I don't see any of that. Not like my internet connection is great, but it's still there. Thanks SpaceX.

I find some coffee drinks I've never heard of and the caffeine can really only help at this point. Weirdly, they have a display of the types of brain vitamins I'm supposed to have been taking, and I grab a couple of bottles. Do I have cash? I poke around in my pockets and find some rumpled up bills, their little holo-AR numbers jumbled and pixelated. In a city they might not even take these, but here, the guy behind the counter doesn't even blink, just counts and counts me back my change.

There's a broken-down lottery ticket machine, and after I take my vitamins, I kind of lean on that while I wait for everyone, with an area map pulled up in AR. It's looking familiar, based on some of those maps that I pulled when I grabbed a bunch of those military files, and I start flicking through those, looking for the one that I remembered.

Distantly, I hear Dolly's laugh, loud and brash as always, and think we're probably about to leave. We should be. It's like I can feel a clock on us now, an urgency to get this done. I find the map I remembered and it isn't quite the same as here, but it's close, and I wonder if it's pre-the last biggest storm. I overlay the two, wiggle them around. It's possible the place we want is underwater now. It's possible it's one of those kudzu mummies off on a road that isn't a road anymore, all the trees swathed in Spanish moss and alligators sunning themselves on the broken up driveways. Maybe there are cougars or panthers or whatever; didn't there used to be wildcats here? Well, Dolly has an AK. I've got a gun. Bristol...well I guess she'll need a gun 'cause she's unlikely to just Disney princess charm animals into not attacking us.

I save my work, close the windows. It might be the caffeine mega dose, might be the vitamins, might be the good stuff, might be wishful thinking, but I feel like my headache is diminished. I feel more normal. Or maybe I just think I feel more normal? There are so many variables at play. I see Null giving me what I think is kind of a weird look but think no, she probably either isn't looking at me at all or her look is entirely normal.

And then she glances away when I notice, so it was definitely a weird look.

Then I think of a saying in our circles, that it isn't paranoia if somebody is actually after you.

It'd be stupid to assume people *weren't* after us, after what we pulled last year. Maybe Null is part of a team watching for us to resurface.

We're walking back out to the Jeep, Bristol still chattering, Dolly laughing once in awhile, and I'm thinking that Null's headset really only needs to connect to the internet and VR in the most basic of ways, and if she's on their side, whoever they is, homeland, or whatever, they can just give her signal all the permissions she needs. She doesn't really need to hack anything, and that leaves room for her equipment to—no, I looked at her equipment, there was nothing weird in there. Nothing I haven't seen before. But her connection fluctuating like that, it meant something and I knew it but I didn't know *what* it meant. Except that she's been with us for days now and very definitely knows who we are and whoever she's working with knows exactly all of that as well.

Without thinking, I purse my lips and whistle that little tune that Dolly's been repeating since she woke me up. Dolly's head whips around like she's a dog who just heard the treat bag rattle, and our eyes lock. I tilt my head, just a little, at Null, who's walking just ahead of me. Dolly gives the barest of nods, and she and Bristol climb into the Jeep first. I can only hope that they have a rapid furtive conversation before Null and I get there, and that they clue me in. We're in the final approach, and we've had to handle this kind of thing before, but I can't imagine we're going to get away with it as easily as we did with Will.

Chapter Seventeen

I send Nicolai a message to warn him. It's bad luck, that every time we need help beyond the three of us, we've been compromised. Marquis, I think, ended up with a very good deal, and is safe and happy somewhere, but they probably would've been safer and happier right where they were in the first place. At least Nicolai was actually kind of in this life to begin with. It wasn't entirely our fault.

Null hadn't sent out any messages since we stopped, that I noticed. How many did she send out before? Did she just have a constant screen-shared connection with handlers at some HQ? Was there a satellite HQ, a roving van that hovered closer to us than we ever would've considered, ready to swoop in and...arrest us. I guess. Take us away to a place like where they had Bristol, where nobody would know, and nobody would care what happened to us, as long as they got "results" for whatever actual government agencies—not shadow agencies—they reported to.

And like, I'm not confused that they consider us criminals, of course we are. But legitimate lives were long-ago made too small to be bearable and this is what we chose for ourselves instead. But it doesn't mean we're not still *people*. It doesn't mean I don't believe in a little thing called human rights.

Oh wouldn't that stick it to them, if I backtraced Null and blew their operation open by leaking it all to a legitimate news source. People who operated from physical studios, and who had money and clout and public support. I could only assume it was the same government agency (but name undisclosed, wink wink) that helped us out with the diamonds thing, who we then double crossed, which was mostly Bristol's doing but it's not like we three didn't all agree to the idea. We had our cake and ate it too, some faster than others. I take a sec, check my accounts; yeah, I've still got money left, in the ballpark of what I thought I did. I check in on Null's activity again. She tried to trace what I was doing, I think, but still hasn't unsnarled my vpn, my proxy servers, my reroutes. She just knew I was connected to the internet, and that there was activity on my connection. I cycle my passwords, because fuck her dictionary hack if she's running one, and I try to focus on a plan. A plan for whatever this location is, and for dealing with Null.

I imagine Dolly would have a very succinct suggestion for dealing with Null. Maybe it'll come to that, maybe it won't. It didn't with Will. She suggested it then, for sure, and Bristol smoothed it out instead. Dolly always likes simple, though. It's not that I don't like simple; I just understand that it doesn't always work out like that.

I also understand that I probably haven't chased away the headache forever, especially if whatever's wrong with me isn't to do with just being in VR for six months, but to do with whatever cost Dolly her arm. Or did that happen even longer before that? I don't have that information at hand in my brain. I could message one of them and ask. We've got enough to worry about.

We roll down green tunnels of country road with Dolly and Bristol bickering pleasantly in the front seat. I sigh and lean back in my seat, slide my VR headset on. Null doesn't say anything, has been quiet since the last rest stop, actually. Maybe furiously making final plans with her handlers or whatever. Maybe just tired. Maybe not a spy after all. Guess I'll find out.

Because of Null's lag spikes, she doesn't even notice me waltzing into her system. Or if she does, she's better than I'd thought. You judge a person on their equipment, you have to, and what if she was a tried and true professional and embarrassed to be running the rig she had, not proud that she accomplished as much with so little? Too many options. I don't read people face to face good enough for this, that's Bristol's job. Even Dolly's better at it than I am. I poke around in her task manager for a screen sharing app, a direct uplink app, anything like that, and I find both. Great. Jesus I wish I was in my right mind. I backtrace, save the IP address elsewhere in my systems so I can revisit it later. I have to cut her connection. I have to tell Bristol and Dolly that I'm doing it, and why. Beyond that, I don't want any decisions to be up to me.

It is and isn't an easy thing, planting malicious code. It's harder with another hacker who's seasoned, but it's easier if they're using unfamiliar equipment, and equipment that's deliberately lowballing their abilities.

Her stuff doesn't black out immediately; I want it to do a slow fade, kind of mimicking her spikes, until after one of the low times when the connection bottoms out, it just doesn't come back. Weirdly specific, I guess, but I already have a little program that does close to that. I make the necessary tweaks and take a minute to flick through her file registry, what little there is of it. She doesn't even have any *music*, I really definitely should've known. I set the program running, then message Dolly and Bristol: //Null is a plant, I don't have full info yet but I'll bet her people and Will's people are pretty close. I'm cutting her headset's capabilities, she'll probably squawk about that pretty soon. Not sure how much damage she's done.//

It's a fun little program, actually, malicious without actually hurting anything. It isn't ransomware, and all your files are still there. You just can't connect to the internet for awhile. It times itself out again over seventy two hours, or can just be deleted from the registry, if you can find it. If you can tell it apart from all of the other legit registry programs that it ghosts itself to look like.

I back off my connection with Null's headset, and not long after hear her cry of dismay, that kind of soft, frustrated noise we all make when technology stops working but, by all rights, it should be working. Or it was working and now isn't and you didn't do anything. Should I check out that IP now? Maybe not. I pull my headset down, so it's around my neck and I almost don't have to squint, the tree cover is so thick. "What happened?"

"I've got nothing here. Are you still okay?" Null has her headset in her hands, the reset button held down.

"I was, yeah. Not great, but had a couple bars." I pull my headset up again like I'm checking, and I do check for new connections, for drones, lurking vehicles or what have you. We're clear. "Yeah, still operational."

"What the *hell*," she mutters. I wonder how old she really is, if she's working with a government agency. Most of the people we saw last year were so *young*, or maybe they just all look young, and do those rich-people fountain of youth blood transfusions or something. Wouldn't that be a hook, live forever, just work for this shadow agency. Government vampires.

"Bits?" Dolly actually sounds worried. I blink and the Jeep is stopped. She's turned around in the driver's seat, one hand still on the wheel, seatbelt straining. Even Dolly still wears her seatbelt.

"Yeah, yeah, I'm okay, sorry. Got sleepy I guess," I say lamely. I only lost about twenty minutes this time but I guess I was pretty far gone. Bristol is turned around too, actually. Null's attention is split about 70/30 between her headset and me. It occurs to me that I should've assumed she had contact lenses too, but it doesn't seem to be the case. She'd be blinking alternately, I think, or rubbing at her eyes, if not outright just touching her eyeball to shift the lenses. Ask me how I know. Just thinking about it makes me blink a little more. I'm sure that's not reassuring to Dolly. "Are we there yet?"

"Not yet," Dolly says, a frown briefly quirking her lips, furrowing her brow.

"I'm fine," I say, eyes wide and earnest even as I'm starting to see flickers in my peripheral vision, because I'm fine right now, that's the truth. It'd be really nice to have a good twelve hours without a migraine. Without a headache. Maybe we can get through this. Once I get through this I can sleep for another six months, and I'm more than starting to think that the long VR time isn't the problem here. "Let's get this show on the road."

"Sure thing," Dolly says, putting the Jeep in gear again, though Bristol looks at me longer.

"We'll have a spa day after this," Bristol says in a voice that's a particular sort of kind-but-critical, the voice that says I don't drink nearly enough water, nor moisturize my skin enough.

"Sure thing," I say. It wouldn't be terrible. There are worse things.

Chapter Eighteen

We get closer to Dolly's undisclosed location and Null gets more frustrated with her equipment. She tries to hide it, increasingly badly. I'm not sure what's occupying Bristol's thoughts at this time; for all I know, she's catching up on social media scandals that occurred for...however long she was incarcerated. I saw it in her file, but my mind slides away from it like trying to read in a dream, so I let it go. She's here, she's fine. She's a better liar than all of us, but we never lie to each other. She's fine.

I slide my headset on, double check my proxies, and then go investigate the address of whoever was attached to Null's headset when I torpedoed the connection. I'm sure they're on high alert. I would be. They don't know if she lost connection just because of where we are; the hurricane-ravaged south that has little left in the way of infrastructure except in pockets where some people decided to fancily and flashily rebuild, with habitats and seawalls and other high tech weather resilient structures. Only certain types get in, of course; those who can afford to live there, and those who get paid to work there.

But Null's people haven't sent any response yet, if they even intend to. There aren't any active drones in our proximity, there's no police who have peeled off from their regular patrols and are inbound. I'm sure whoever Null was reporting to is still sitting in their cushy neo cold war bunker and trying to raise the connection, maybe trying to access any local cameras to see where we've gone, maybe trying to connect with a satellite to focus on our location, but good luck with all the tree cover and the off-green Jeep that Dolly had to've picked for exactly this reason.

She did; I'm staring at code and then I've got a flash of memory, a waking dream, her and I in a used car lot where somehow the guy only had dialup and was more than willing to take the cash that she counted out to him. Broken pavement and faded plastic garlands of flapping flags, gray sky, broken glass right in against the curbs, like that's as far as they swept it and there was no point trying to do anything more, a quarter machine full of little white squares of gum that were rock hard and didn't even smell minty anymore. The salesman whose voice was too loud when it didn't need to be, whose suit was more expensive than it needed to be. He was the only one there, did all the paperwork himself on a typewriter that was older than all three of us put together. Faxed it off to nowhere, for all I know, on a machine that wheezed and screamed like the phone line was haunted by trapped souls. He probably sold to a lot of desperate types. He probably wasn't used to somebody like Dolly.

Dolly went over the thing from bumper to bumper, crawled under it, leaned over the engine for I don't know how long. Guns and cars, those are Dolly's purview, and especially cars that have as little computer stuff in them as possible. If any. This one didn't have any, a retro rebuild on a modern Jeep chassis, maybe by whoever sold it or traded it to this used car guy. Maybe by somebody else. She added the lock boxes underneath after, aluminum to block wireless signals and scans. There's a couple of places where guns are hidden, I'm sure, and I wouldn't put it past her to have a sniper rifle broken down and stowed in the roll bars.

Does she actually have one stowed there? Did I help her do it? That seems likely.

When did she buy the Jeep? Where were we? We were getting ready for...

But it's gone again and I'm left looking at security protocols that look pretty much exactly like the protocols that I saw last year when we were fleeing...whoever...(probably the Russians, or an unnamed Russian agency) into the arms of whatever this unnamed American agency is. With all of those diamonds. Everybody wanted those diamonds, us included, I guess. More for the payday than anything else but I'd be shocked if Bristol didn't keep *any* to wear. It's so satisfying, to be proven right. But scary too, in this case, because these people have resources. Money and guns and personnel and helicopters. Contracts with us that were promptly broken. Whoops.

Null doesn't know where we're going, so they can't know, even if they have their guesses. I don't know where we're going, though I think maybe I do know. I think we went to one of these places. I think Dolly's been on this trail for awhile, and then I spent six months in VR, not realizing that something had gone terribly wrong. I think Dolly and Bristol put me there, hoping I'd be okay.

I pull off my headset like I'm breaking the surface of water after sitting at the bottom of a pool on a bet. I blink and look around. No time skip this time, I'm here and now. No headache, yet, though the flickers are still in my vision. "Are we there yet?" I ask before Dolly can ask how I am; I'm tired of people having to ask me how I am.

"Five more minutes," Dolly says. Null laughs oddly.

"Are you okay?" I ask Null.

"Still not connecting," she says, gritting her teeth just a little. Sweating just a little. It's hot here, yeah, but she's panicking. I don't think we're going to hurt her. She's not on our side, I realize that now, but we're all on our own sides.

"So what's our game plan?" I ask because it's weird that we haven't talked about it. Or maybe we did when I was in a fugue state. "Just get in, grab whatever, get out? That's a little weird for us."

"It isn't our usual fare, no," Bristol doesn't turn around this time, I think she's playing with her phone. "There are some items in particular that can only be found at these sites. Or, found most easily at these sites. And we're in a particular position to find these locations."

"Gotcha," I say. Did we talk about the diamond heist in front of Null? Probably not. No reason to. Dolly has so many other things to brag about, that clusterfuck of an adventure doesn't need to be on the table.

"There's probably gonna be surveillance even," Dolly adds. "Bitsy, I think we packed your hoodie in that bag you got between your feet, Null..."

"What do I need?" Null says, and that's her biggest mistake; there isn't a single hacker who doesn't know about digital surveillance and what to do about it.

"I have a scarf she can borrow," Bristol says smoothly. "They take up so little room, I always have a bouquet of them in my purse nowadays."

"Thanks, I just wasn't ready for all of this," Null says in a rush.

"If we had the time, I'd take a look," I say and we both kind of shrug.

"Okay so there's probably gonna be a keycard lock, I should mention that," Dolly says.

"And do we have—" I know the answer.

"Nah, why would we?" Dolly grins, glances at me over her shoulder. "You can handle that." I can handle that, of course I can.

An overwhelming sense of déjà vu settles over me as we finish bumping down the green tunnel that was once a road and pull up to a tall chain link fence, the top of it still shiny in the daggers of sunlight that slice through the canopy. The grass is tall, hide-a-tiger tall, and the screaming of cicadas or crickets or whatever is louder, higher pitched. Dolly gets out with a set of bolt cutters that she was keeping God knows where and cuts the hank of chain that's keeping the gate closed and pushes it open. Bristol slides over and drives the Jeep through. I didn't know Bristol could drive stick. She's in riot gear too, and I guess for once didn't complain about doing it. She was so proud when she found those velvet combat boots. Null's just in jeans and a t-shirt, essentially. And the hoodie. Then I remember she's still got the ballistic vest Dolly loaned her and I'm relieved; then I remember she's one of the bad guys. Or rather, one of the not-us guys. We aren't really good, are we?

I take a deep breath, hold it a sec, let it out. Then we're all getting out of the Jeep. I've got my phone out and I'm looking around for the cameras.

The stuff for the keycard reader is in a flat pack toolkit in one of my cargo pockets and I practically sleepwalk through disarming it. It wants to send a signal to...somebody...to say that it's been accessed, and I cancel that. The cameras are probably motion sensors, probably recording and broadcasting any time there's any movement, but if this is a mothballed site, what's the likelihood of somebody having eyes on that feed 24/7? Proportional to how recent our last site visitation was. I don't have that information; I mean, I do. I was there and Dolly's told me over and over, but I've still got that block.

The door buzzes and kachunks open. I hum Dolly's little song as I slip inside and find a security panel a few steps down the hallway, flip it open and find a place to plug my headset into it, trusting Dolly and Bristol to come in and cover and all that. I remember doing this, in the other place, a weird overlay of memory and present action, and without thinking, punch in some numbers. The panel turns green, chimes gently, and I pull my headset up to watch the data stream by. Nobody's been here in a long time, not inside. Once a year, looks like, a walkthrough for infrastructure and security testing. Nobody assigned here. Just this level, two garages.

Bristol is talking and I think maybe Null is asking questions but their voices are kind of a smooth background murmur, no particular words sticking out as I find the code for the camera directives, find the memory banks where recorded activity is stored, and watch the last thirty minutes or so on 10x speed before wiping our arrival and looping a previous recording of some feral hogs trotting through the grass outside the fence. They must check the perimeter more often, with how often it storms, with the wildlife and the vigorous foliage. Nothing on schedule this week or even this month, though. And it is April. There's something about finding that out that steadies me.

Why would the same code work in two places? Personnel maybe. I look for an inventory sheet, forward it to Dolly and Bristol's phones. The code, the numbers are swimming in front of my eyes and I pull down my headset and see the hallway lit by its low energy back-up lights, the way it was when we came in, and I see it lit only by our bouncing flashlight beams, the way it was at the other place. It was a different place, right, and not here? The not-gas station guy didn't look at all like he recognized us, unless he's set dressing, an actor, somebody Dolly knows from before we all got together. We don't hit the same place twice, that's stupid. We wouldn't steal the same diamonds twice, would we? Bristol might. We kind of did. I guess not; they never truly left our possession once we took ownership.

I stumble a little, over an uneven tile that isn't uneven when I look at it again, and Dolly catches me by the arm while looking at her phone. My head still hurts but I kind of don't care. I wonder why I never just keep my own bottle of pills around. The good stuff. Probably because VR wouldn't be my only bad habit then.

"This way, isn't it?" Bristol asks. Null seems to be keeping close to her. Maybe my one lucid non-tech thought of the day, I wonder if Null thinks that in a bind, she can take Bristol hostage and get herself out of here. That won't work out well for her. Dolly just nods, takes point, and I follow right behind her. I resist the impulse to hold onto her belt to steady myself; I've done it a couple times, if we were on the move and I was using my VR goggles. It works well enough but isn't advisable. Add it to the list. This is still better than working at a convenience store, or getting an internship or whatever, and hoping to be allowed to have a life that's good enough, that I'm happy with.

Not all of the security measures are linked to that panel, that would be dumb, but many of them are linked to the motion sensors of the camera, which both sense that we're moving but don't see anything unusual, and so are super confused about whether everything is fine. Most of the stuff is just as simple as doors locking down, but they've got some weaponized drones too that we need to watch out for, either for me to hack or for somebody to baseball swing out of the air. Or shoot, I guess. I don't think any of us has a baseball bat. I don't have a baseball bat. Maybe Bristol should have a cricket bat or a field hockey stick or something. A blunt weapon, but make it classy.

"Where are you thinking, Bitsy?" Dolly asks.

"Me? I thought this was your rodeo."

"Oh, it is." Oh, I get it. She's just trying to keep me engaged.

"Physical records is down the hall."

"Good old fashioned paper files, gotta love that perfume right, Bristles?"

I can practically hear Bristol roll her eyes. She didn't put on perfume for this, I only just now noticed. "Old books is the perfume people like so much, Dolly, not manila envelopes and tiresome government records."

"Oh right right." Dolly opens a door apparently at random and I turn around because it's like I can *feel* Null cringing behind me. "Not the stairs."

"There are no stairs," I say, and then I cringe myself when I look because it is suddenly so bright, like we're outside again, but no, just a flood of natural light through skylights which are probably those transparent solar panels. I think the lifespan of those isn't great, so they're probably just normal windows again by now. There's a grid of drones parked on the floor, though, ready to take flight, but all still in standby, little red lights on them blinking to show they're fully charged.

Dolly looks at us and laughs. "Boo!" she says, and shakes her head, pulling the door shut. "They'll just stay sleepin', right Bitsy?"

"Right," I say, but I don't know why I'm so sure. Then I remember I fixed them to stay just sleeping, that's why.

If I stick this out, I'll know what happened. I'll be fine again.

We keep going.

This place isn't so big that it'll take a lot to go through. The stairs are lit by red backup lights that are actually kind of soothing for me, or at least don't make my head feel worse. Most of the rooms on this top floor really are decommissioned, just full of rolling chairs around fake wood conference tables, monitors that aren't plugged into anything, lockers all hanging open and empty, dry and dusty bathrooms.

Dolly turns a faucet handle and nothing happens, not even a rattle from the pipes. "Makes you wonder about their fire control," she says with a wink.

"They probably have condensed aerosol fire suppression, with all the tech that they had," I say. "Actually that's probably on its own server and backup generator so that if—"

"Bits, sweetie, she was making a joke," Bristol says, her hand on my shoulder. "Though non-water fire suppression is I'm sure *very interesting,* and we can talk about it another time."

"It is," I say. Normally this would be funny, me giving a detailed response to Dolly banter, but we're all tense, we all have our role, and I'm sure we're all hoping nobody misses her cue. Especially me.

Null can miss her cues I guess. She's probably missed a few already. They've probably got some kind of tracker on her. We didn't check that out, unless Dolly was just so sneaky that I didn't notice.

When we find the records room, it isn't much larger than a regular office but jam-packed with filing cabinets, and Dolly just starts rooting around. "I'd offer help, but..." Bristol trails off.

"It'd ruin your manicure," Dolly says, her grin flashing in the indistinct light. "Just gotta find the right...vector or year or whatever, and we're golden."

"Why is it paper?" Null asks, the first she's spoken in a really, really long time. Guess she didn't figure out how to get her internet back.

"You can't exactly remote hack a file cabinet," Dolly laughs.

"Yeah, but we're here and they left everything."

"Because who would *bother*," Bristol asks, wrinkling her nose a little. If she had white gloves on, she'd be drawing lines in the dust all over the place and tsking. Dolly's still laughing, but more quietly than her typical bray, a file folder open on her forearm as she skims it. Except I feel like she's looking at a clipboard, and remember sunlight. A big door, with a separate lock. The smell of old rubber and engine grease.

"Did you find what you're looking for?" I ask. I feel like I'm aware of a ticking clock.

"Yup. Yes I did." She takes some of the papers, folds them in a square, jams them in a cargo pocket. She claps her hands together, making us all jump a little in the quiet. "Alrighty, on to looting, our favorite part!"

"Wait you're not going to—" Dolly takes my arm, leads me stumbling out of the room before I can finish.

"I'll explain as much as you want me to right now, but you gotta consider that's the difference between Null walkin' outta here and not," she says in my ear, barely louder than breathing. "Because she can't know what this says. That'll be the difference between you 'n' Bristol walkin' outta here or not."

Chapter Nineteen

"Where shall we 'loot'?" Bristol asks, quirking her lips a little, but I don't know what's funny. For some reason, everybody's looking at me.

"Um," I say, pulling up my headset, looking at the map. Maybe I will just hold Dolly's belt and let her walk me. The pressure of the straps make my head feel a little better. Or that pill is making me feel a little better. Or I don't know, the less I'm talking, the better. "Looks like this place is pretty much cleared out. Another drone room, and it does look like all the drones are nonlethal. Or they have been so far."

"Oh, they the kind with the little tasers?" Dolly asks.

"Yeah. And little onboard systems to dial for emergency. They're smart enough to tell the difference between intruder and fire and stuff." Dolly already knows. I scroll through more information but there's no way I can read enough while we're just standing here to truly understand where we are. Those empty rooms are labeled classrooms. There's more probably empty rooms labeled clinics. Isolation rooms. Drone rooms. Mess hall. Command. Garage. And...second garage? That's so *weird*.

Somebody, probably Dolly, starts walking me while I'm doing this, and I'm not really paying attention until Bristol says "No, I will not" in such a tone that I pull the headset down again.

"What? What's wrong?"

"Dolly is disgusting, is what's wrong." Bristol is shaking her head, Null is just wide eyed and Dolly is grinning, eminently pleased. Her natural state. She's also holding some manner of military ration, still sealed by the looks of it, and not recently. Probably within the last fifteen years anyway.

"I just said that the date's still good," Dolly says with a shrug. "And wondered what the dessert was."

"You'd totally eat it," I say.

"Of course I would. It's food, ain't it?"

"It is not," Bristol says, and I remember her delight at that gourmet restaurant. And she's been to lots since; I guess it's easier for her to just pretend she's never been hungry than to remember anything from that time. I don't really blame her. I do wonder if anybody ended up paying that bill, though.

"Okay Bitsy, c'mon, where to?" Dolly asks. I blink; I don't know where she put the MRE and I don't remember when she lit a cigarette but I blink again and there's no cigarette. The MRE is still gone.

"The armory," I say. "Though I don't know if they left anything worth selling."

"Maybe they left a few museum pieces. Or the kind I'd like to add to my personal collection."

"Yeah maybe they have an early-aughts AR or something," I say.

"They never did start making those again," she says thoughtfully. "Probably for the better."

"That bad a gun?" Null asks.

"That bad for society, more like." Bristol may as well be tapping her foot and rolling her eyes. She isn't, but maybe she hears that ticking clock too. Honestly, she just hates spending time in dusty military holes. Who can blame her?

"This red light is creepy," Bristol says as we walk down the hallway. More déjà vu, she said this last time, or in the other place. Dolly's whistling that *song* again.

"It's so your night vision isn't fucked," Dolly says as she reaches for the next door. I get an overwhelming sense of dread, that movie theater impulse to yell.

"Don't go in there." I say it, but keep myself from yelling it. When's the last time I yelled anything?

"What's wrong?" Null sounds...relieved?

"Nothing this time," Dolly says, hand still on the door but paused to look at me. "There was last time, though."

"Last time?" Null says, but I'm not confused, finally. Things are clicking into place for me. Last time. Last time, the other one of these, Dolly didn't find what she was looking for in records. And then things started to go bad, to slide slowly sideways. I messed up hacking the inventory computer that they had, trying to figure out what was there besides the rifles and grenade launchers and prototype energy things, which we knew didn't work well and had a habit of failing spectacularly and we left alone. The security on the computer was twisty, it was more than a usual algorithm, and I tried it, flubbed it, tried it again and got it. But the damage was already done, I already felt off.

"Dolly, we need to talk about—" but she's already opening the door I didn't want her to open and I never pull my gun but I've pulled my gun again and—

Nothing happens.

Dolly looks so damn smug but I'm so relieved I don't even care. Bristol almost looks bored, and maybe she is bored, who can say. She probably would rather be catching up on her messages and planning her next party. What kind of payday are we even looking for here? And why would any of us need it?

"Not now, Bits. See, it's clear." Just dust on the floor, and dust on the empty shelves and racks. Dolly's right, there's nothing. She even walks around the room with her arms out while we watch her and nothing happens. But it makes me think of the active camo box, and that isn't in my pocket anymore. I don't know when that happened.

"I believe we ought to hurry more than this," Bristol says. "I'm certain Nicolai is in position by now."

"It might really help me if I knew what this was," Null says but kind of quietly, so we'd have the option to ignore her. "Especially if you already got what you needed, Dolly?"

"What, you don't like walking around places like this?" Dolly asks.

"Not particularly," Null says as we continue. Dolly looks at me and shrugs, like 'what's her problem' and I laugh because what else can I do.

It's like we're clearing the rooms in a video game level, just making sure we haven't missed anything. I almost expect to see ammunition and medpacks just on the floor when we go down the hallway to the final room, the thing that looked like a garage but not a garage on the map. So very irritating and inconvenient for whoever ran this program to not label their maps, but I guess they knew what the rooms were so why bother. Like how in the olden days in Britain there used to be three spices that got set out on the table, salt and pepper and something else, except nobody ever wrote down the something else because why would you? Everybody knew. I think about that sometimes. Salt and pepper and...Savory? Rosemary? I wonder what size the holes on the shakers were. Or if they were shakers. Didn't people use salt cellars for a really long time? A salt cellar and a pepper mill and—

There are footsteps in the hallway behind us except there aren't. It's just my memory overlap again, welling up, glitching in flashes. Us running, us with Null and nobody running, Dolly slapping a new magazine into her gun, Dolly's gun still holstered. Sparking drone parts scattering across the institutional tile floor, the smell of burnt electronics and gunfire.

There's another layer of security here, of course there is. Not a retinal scan (those are always a bitch to circumvent if you don't have a live eye with appropriate security clearance), just another keypad on its own circuit, not even as hard as the first one. Dolly probably could've just talked to it with a paperclip, the way some basic car computers can be adjusted. Funny how paperclips still exist.

Then the door buzzes and Dolly shoves it open and there's more light again, this time because part of the roof caved in under the weight of kudzu and neglect. There's so much sunlight after the dark hallways with their soothing red that for a second it feels like my eyes are just full of TV static and I think I might just fall down from another migraine right there like a cut-string puppet. But my eyes adjust, and the pain doesn't come again. It's just full of leaves and vines and grass in here, and we startle up a flock of black winged birds when we start to walk through.

I look around for shimmers in the air, expecting...what am I expecting? Active camo like the officer in Bristol's convoy had. But there's nothing. Why did we walk through this whole place if all Dolly wanted was a handful of papers from practically the first room we came to? But then I realize what we're walking past, what this whole garage is actually full of, and I stop and grab a handful of the vines, pull. Null actually gasps.

It's power armor, not huge bullshit anime style power armor that's tall as a building, but stuff a person could get in that would make them eight, nine feet tall. The edges don't make sense, all angular and weird, like those airplanes that are built to deflect radar. Imagine a unit of these, invisible to radar, marching onto a location. I stare into the dark mirror of the closed-face helmet that I just uncovered, remembering one with a shattered visor, with the arm sparking and broken, dripping hydraulic fluid and blood. I remember somebody's raw voice, Dolly's, yelling "God damn it Bits! What's wrong with you?!" I don't know what Bristol was doing. Finding our exit,

I guess. I don't know how we got out, I can't remember how we got out, and what I remember now is my ringing ears and the smell of burning, snow that just wouldn't stop falling, no it's burning paper, maybe burning other things but there's no bullets flying anymore.

I pull off more of the vines like shucking a cob of corn, the suit shining in the sunlight, and I reach its power source. Nuclear, a surprise and not a surprise. Something like that isn't enough yield to go critical, but it doesn't mean that a bunch of them together didn't make a big enough boom all the same. Oh I can't take credit for that. That's what Bristol was doing, actually dirtying her hands with grenades or with C4 I can't remember which it was now, and it isn't important right this second. We, I, tripped the security; there were lots of automated turrets with lots of lethal rounds, and we blew up all of those suits of armor and dragged ourselves away from the smoking aftermath before human personnel arrived.

We went there looking for the papers, the physical files, that pertained to Dolly's defunct super soldier program, and hoped to also have something to sell in the process because old habits, right? What we got was a hurt Dolly—a very badly hurt Dolly—and a very messed up me. Hypnosis as a thought-virus, I guess I should've learned more, sooner, about brainhacking. And it's a good thing we sold all those diamonds plus stole that government money last year, because cybernetic arms still cost a lot, especially ones that just look like normal.

I blink to reset, look around. Bristol isn't actually bored, that's just the cultivated look on her face, so her actual watchfulness isn't apparent. Dolly's leaning against a non-kudzu'd wall with her arms crossed and an unlit cigarette hung on her lip. And Null is just standing there, watching, waiting, so expectant she's ready to come out of her skin. "Why are we all just standing here?" she asks. I don't really have a good answer for her.

"Will these work?" I ask Dolly, even as I put my hand on one and feel it humming, faintly.

"They will. But we're not doing anything with 'em right now, that's Nicky's job."

"So that's it? You just came here for some papers and you're going to leave?" Null's voice cracks just a little and I can't tell if she's upset, in disbelief, or what.

"Sure are. Call it disaster tourism," Dolly says cheerfully. "We ready to roll?" she asks me.

"I think so." The papers. The hypnosis. There's a phrase that makes it so Dolly doesn't feel pain, a phrase that makes it so Dolly will kill targets indiscriminately. It took a lot for me to decrypt the map of the sites in the first place. There's more, and none of those phrases were ever stored electronically. But Dolly is Dolly and wants to stay that way. I wouldn't have her any other way, though I think Bristol might not mind having some level of control.

But Null. Dolly hits the big red button that opens the garage door and we walk out to the Jeep, Null right there with us. Then it's just me and Bristol and Null, and I don't know where Dolly is. The last time we had to shake a government asset, Bristol kissed him with special lipstick and we just kind of left him at an abandoned bus station. None of us are really in a kissing position here. Null is messing with her equipment when her phone rings and she startles, drops it.

The gunfire comes from nowhere, a shimmer in the air that I only just barely see, the muzzle flashes interrupting it. Null kind of shudders backwards and then collapses with a coughing wheeze and in the held-breath post-gunshot silence, even the bugs quiet, I can still hear her breathing. I expect it to stop every time I hear her take a breath and then I notice the rubber bullets on the ground. Oh. Her phone stops ringing and the pause is too quiet, all those screaming bugs silent. Then the phone rings again.

"I know, I know, we just keep leaving witnesses but," Dolly shrugs. "C'mon, we gotta go."

"You just had to be so *dramatic* about it," Bristol says.

"Like you're one to talk. And I wanted to use the camo thingie."

"We're going to have incoming," I say, once I feel like I've caught my breath. "And we'll have to ditch the Jeep."

Dolly shakes her head. "I really liked that Jeep."

Epilogue

I've got about a million messages that I'm skimming to make sure they're okay to delete. Lots of spam, there's always lots of spam, but there's listservs and group chats and newsletters and all the digital detritus that just piles up if you're not on top of it. And I wasn't keeping good track for...awhile, even after Dolly came and got me. I didn't realize I wasn't, and I also apparently didn't spend six months in immersion, but I thought that was the truth when I said it to Dolly. It wasn't six months but it was still...awhile.

I wonder now if my real estate guy actually said anything about there being tigers, or if my brain mashed up Pablo Escobar's hippos with military tiger teams. I don't ask him about it when I message him to clean the villa out and put it on the market. From what I can tell, nobody ever went there. Probably nobody was ever even able to trace me, but I don't want to visit and find out.

Sometimes I still catch myself whistling that little scrap of hypnosis song; it's the kind meant to help you focus, and even though I wasn't conditioned the way Dolly was during her super soldier program, it helps. And of course it makes me think of Dolly and her deconditioning, and the look on her face when the kill command words didn't work anymore. That's about as far into brainhacking as I'm ever going to get, and having been brainhacked once, I can say I'm not interested in revisiting the situation ever again.

Eventually, I reach inbox zero and pull off my VR headset. I have a plane to catch.

**Run With the Hunted 3:
Standard Operating Procedure**
Jennifer R. Donohue

Chapter One

Right about when I find the right car, my robot dog's legs freeze up. Should've included it in the equipment breakdown last night; the desert grit out here doesn't agree with it at all, but I figured I had a little more time. The trip to Chiba is a long haul and a long wait once you're there. It's only the one guy who fixes 'em.

"Sorry bud," I say, and it blinks its luminous blue eyes at me and wags its tail.

The car's battery is dead, that's good. Means no security's gonna start blaring, painting a target in the local map. I can just break in old fashioned way, give it a jump with the handheld kit, and by then it'll figure that I'm supposed to be here and we can go on our way. When the cars still have power, Bits can cut the security and remote-start them for me, but that takes some of the fun out of it.

"Who are you talking to?" Bits says in my ear.

"The dog." Of course nobody's around; I'm just off a highway out of town, near one of those concrete block type of apartments that I'm not sure anybody's ever lived in.

It's not a super rare car I'm breaking into, a Jaguar but not limited run. People like buying the car of their dreams here, and then waking up and going home. I like taking the cars before the police impound them and selling them to somebody in the street racing circuit, after Bits hacks the keys and fixes up the registration records for us.

This one's in okay shape. Tires full, all dusty but the windows are closed. They're not always closed, sometimes you come out here and they've got a whole desert ecology on the inside. I slide the slimjim down in the driver's door, fish around, pop the lock. The keys're in the ignition, that means I won't have to hotwire first, fix later. I pull the hood release, tap the dog's head when I walk past it again. It does the quizzical hound head tilt that all the dogs we ran when I was a kid would do, if they were thinking about something. I guess the robot dog has more to think about than they did, and probably less. I'm not sure how good its sniffer is, for instance. I know what the specs say, just haven't seen it in action.

I check the fluids before I clip on the cables. Stuff's low but not awful; we got this one in the sweet spot. Not so tip-top that it's some kind of bait for a police sting, not so rock bottom that it wasn't worth it for me to walk out here. It starts like it has morning-after regrets, gravelly and hoarse, but it starts. I feel that. I unclip the equipment, put it and the dog in the passenger seat, walk around once to make sure all the lights light. I swap out license plates. "How we looking, Bitsy?"

"All clear," she says.

"All right then, see you in a little while." Seems like anytime I'm driving around here, there isn't much traffic, which doesn't make much sense. There are so many people here. I even sometimes just go a cafe or whatever by those tree island things they built, to watch the cars.

"Okay. Dinner's ready."

"Is it, now." She doesn't answer, probably got lost in the stars again or something. We kind of swap around with whose turn dinner is, every once in awhile go out with Bristol, who doesn't live here, but doesn't *not* live here. She skips around when she's inclined, which is a lot. It's a good leaping-off point for plenty of glamorous locales or whatever. I wasn't thinking about food but yeah, I could eat. I also want to get this car in the garage and Bits hooked up to its brain, and

I want to get the robot dog broken down to see if it's grit, or something else.

I've probably only driven a Jag about five times, this trip included. It's a nice ride, a little too nice. Sometimes I do want to feel that connection to the road and not like I'm flyin' along on a cloud or something. Get too comfortable is when you make mistakes. I check my mirrors the way church people cross themselves. But nobody's following me, I don't see any cars more than once, I see a few cops but they're just doing normal cop things, no sweat. I pull into our garage next to the range rover, cut the engine, and get out to watch our street surveillance for a few minutes. That's normal; the way we work sometimes, paranoia's healthy. Still nothing, though, and I unpack the car before going upstairs.

Dinner tonight means that Bits ordered from a few delivery places; falafel and fast food and pastries apparently. The bags're all spread out on the counter, still closed, and she's sprawled on the couch, headset on. The TV is on too, tuned into some international news station, captions scrolling by in like five languages. There's a certain amount of background noise she likes running; hell, I do too, but I think we got different reasons for it. Mine's to do with coming from a big family, hers is to do with appreciating static like it's music.

"Hey the falafel place does cakes in jars so I got a bunch," she says, not moving.

"I'm gonna take the dog apart first, I'll eat later."

"Bristol's coming over later."

"Is that who the pastries're for?"

"Yeah, she's out to dinner right now."

"Perfect."

She sits up then, as I start down the hall, pushing her headset up. "What's wrong with the dog?"

"He stopped walking."

She makes a face. "Is it the sand, you think?"

"I'm hoping."

"Well, Chiba's always fun." Tech guts wonderland for her, she means. Some people travel places for street food, religious sites, art, Bits likes going places where she can rummage through bins of old tech and see what she can build. Sometimes it's like she's making stuff from the future that never happened, instead of the future we got. Less there to occupy me, though, especially with how jumpy Japan's gun laws are. Hong Kong, though, there's some good fun there. And who knows where Bristol would want to tra la la off to. Providing we go as a unit, of course. We all got our own tastes.

"We don't know yet that I need to go to Chiba."

"No." She shrugs, and I shrug, and I take the dog to my room. My workbench there is mostly for guns, but I've taken apart engine components there, and the robot dog. The garage is too small to really work in, it's a weird little building we're in that makes me think of row housing except it's freestanding. Like all those places back home that dried up and died out after the industry left, and they took down the houses one by one, sometimes built brick supports for the people who wouldn't vacate. It's hard, getting people to leave home, no matter how bad home seems to outsiders. Unless they're the type that never loved anything about home to begin with, like Bristol.

I stroke my hand over the dog's back, power him down. There's a little pattern puzzle to lift his backplate off and give you access to everything, so you don't do it accidentally. And yeah, there's some grit in there, but the problem looks to be the more fiddly bits of the drive train. It's more complicated than a drive train; all four legs move independently, in all the different dog gaits, but that's what it amounts to. I blow the grit out with some canned air, poke around to see if I can fix it anyway, and then figure I'll leave things in the hands of the professional robot dog fixing guy. There's too many circuit boards and chips and nice solder work in there, and even though

I can mess around with basic ones thanks to Bits, these're above my paygrade.

Chiba it is, then. Maybe it's in the backyard of wherever Bristol wants to send us, because that's a lot of what we talk about when we get together, what we're gonna do next. I think we're all pretty set on funds, but they don't last forever, and it it ain't a great idea to get lazy and fall too far out of the game. I message the robot repair guy to get the ball rolling; no telling how long the wait'll be, any way you look at it. I leave the robot dog shut down. It won't know the difference, that way. Won't have to wonder why it can't walk.

I go hose off, since Bristol's like as not to comment on whether I stink, and by the time I'm done and dressed, I hear her high heels coming up the stairs. TV stays on though. She'd love to have device free dinners or whatever, but Bits likes having that little line of analog interference if somebody's driving past waving around listening devices. Can't say as I disagree.

Bristol's pink-cheeked like she went for the third drink instead of stopping at two, and bright eyed like she just won at her favorite game. She's got a bottle of wine with her, no surprise; she thinks none of the rest of us have any taste.

"What's the verdict?" Bits asks, like Bristol wasn't chattering about this or that, and Bristol pouts a little, picks up the remote to change the tv.

"Outside my expertise. I sent the guy a message."

"Whatever are you two going on about?" Bristol asks finally, channel now to her liking and rummaging for a corkscrew in the kitchenette drawers.

"The robot dog's busted."

"Oh darling, I'm sorry." She pauses, and I just grin at her, hard. She doesn't give a fuck about the robot dog. "Is tonight bad, shall I come back?"

"Nah, let's get things going."

"I *did* hope you would say that, and this little thing I've heard about might just help distract you from your dog worry."

I frown. "Like, 'cause we're getting to work or—"

"Because it has to do with *dogs*!" Bristol doesn't talk about animals much. Now that I think about it, I've never seen her interact with a single one, not even the robot dog. Not even somebody's way too expensive cat that lounges only on pillows and eats paté or whatever. I'm real sure she's never even ridden on a mechanical bull in a bar, and most of them don't even have heads. That kinda weirds me out actually; I've even seen Bits pet a dog at least once. Or look at a bird that flew by. Not Bristol.

"Dogs? Bristol, you don't *like* dogs. What're we gonna do that has to do with dogs?"

"I have never said that," she says primly, finally getting the cork out of the damn bottle and pouring one of those stemless unbreakable wine glasses half full. They're probably not actually unbreakable, but I haven't gotten bored enough to try it yet. Probably if you shoot one or run it over or whatever, it'll break. Video's probably online already, another missed chance. Shootin' stuff to see if it breaks. How it breaks? When it breaks. Everybody online copies everybody else anyway, I could find a niche. "And are you aware that there is a very exclusive, highly competitive market for some types of dog?"

"Breeds," Bits mutters, but not loud enough to interrupt.

"I may have been, yeah," I say. Not really, but it's not like I never been to an animal auction before.

"And do you know how much the most expensive dog has ever auctioned for?" We both just look at her. Bitsy's lookin' it up I'm sure, but there's no sense stealing Bristol's thunder at this stage of the game. "Five *million* dollars, just last year. Before that it was two million, around the turn of the century. They actually had quite the downturn after that for quite awhile, I'm not really sure what caused the resurgence. I'm sure it's a little like the stock market."

"Totally just like it," Bits says, somehow with a straight face.

"They what? Dogs? You're losin' me here, Bristles."

"Oh the breed of dog, I'm so sorry. The Tibetan Mastiff." She looks at us as though it's a big reveal, and Bits and I look at each other. Bristol sighs.

I give it a shot. "But so what's the deal? Like, if the Tibetan Mastiff market is so boom and bust, shouldn't we've bought low to sell high?"

"If we actually wanted much to do with those animals for any length of time," Bristol says and I just bray laughter. Like I said.

"But who would want that?" Bits asks, hiding a smile.

"Exactly! What I propose is much simpler."

"Y'know, Bristles, you always *think* that..." I say.

"One of my contacts in Tokyo can put me in touch with somebody who will pay three million dollars for a specific one of those dogs that is to go to auction next week. However, they can *only* pay three million dollars, so they want to hire somebody to just...scoop the dog up for them."

"Scoop up the—now I'm no dog expert, but most of the time, a dog's got mastiff in the name it's a pretty big dog."

Bristol waves her non-wine holding hand. "It's a *puppy* how big could it be? And we know how easy it is to get into places and walk away with all manner of things. This would probably be the easiest three million dollars we ever make."

"I dunno, the Paris job was pretty easy." Plus the appeal of bein' able to say the Paris job.

Bristol rolls her eyes. "And significantly less than three million dollars."

"In today's exchange," Bits points out.

"Yeah we're not exactly strapped for cash," I say. "Not enough to do something you hate."

"I wouldn't ask us to do something I *hate*." Bristol's starting to get pouty. "I'm not a monster, I don't hate *puppies*."

"You probably haven't spent much time with puppies, they're the monsters." I laugh and she sighs gustily. "Okay, okay, fine tell us more. Where's the dog now? Where's the auction gonna be?"

"The auction will be in Macau, I don't know where the dog is right this second."

"Macau? You sure you don't wanna just do a little casino job instead of this dognapping thing? That's what all those movies you like are, right? Casino jobs?" They're fun movies, anyway. Too big a team though.

"We don't have enough people for a casino job," she says, sipping her wine. "No I think this will be good, a little diversion from your gearhead games, and then we can come back here, I think, or do whatever."

Come back here meaning the location isn't burned yet, yeah. But... "Bristol, is somethin' going on that makes you want to blow town for a little while?"

"I don't know what would make you ask that." She looks at me with big innocent eyes. "I've heard of a job I think will suit us, in a location that's favorable. Macau is rather near where you take the robot dog for repair, isn't it?" I shake my head. It's closer than here but it ain't exactly next door. Bristol sighs. "Fine, but you would have been leaving town yourself in a few days anyway, wouldn't you?"

"You got me there." She isn't lying but she isn't telling the truth. But, good enough for now. "Bits, what do you think?"

"It sounds easy which means something terrible will happen," she says cheerfully. "Let's do it."

Chapter Two

The thing about flying is you have to do it without a weapon, and I hate traveling without a weapon. I do always know how to find one once I'm where I'm going, and I think about this every time too. I learned in school a million years ago, or maybe Bits saw it on the internet and showed me, that squirrels don't exactly remember where they've hidden stuff. Squirrels just know the types of places where stuff is likely to be hidden. And that's how it is for me; it isn't that I got guns hidden globally, I just figure out where guns are likely to be hidden. And I return the favor, hide new stuff when I'm flush, say thanks to whoever when I'm in need. Let the circle be unbroken, by and by lord, by and by. And especially lately, I been flush a lot, so I restock those places. It's like little free libraries.

Plus, nowadays, you go to the right places, you can get enough parts 3D printed that're innocuous enough by themselves but put 'em together and you got a handgun that walks right through security scans. Not great when just anybody can do it, there's a lotta folks out there just want to hurt people for the sake of it, and there's no way to trust that equipment the way you can with actual brands. Real brands, you know if something's a piece of shit that's gonna melt by your seventy fifth round, or that you can leave in a puddle for six months, slap a mag in it, and fire it without even shaking out the barrel. I guess I'm glad I can reach for the tech when I need it. If I was a computer nut like Bits, I'd probably set myself up with a buncha the printers, do a bespoke gun boutique, but I don't got the patience with the electronics or the eye for design. I can fix motors and maintain my equipment, and that's all I need. The robot dog would say otherwise, I guess, but I *didn't* get the talking version for a reason.

My Japanese ain't great but most people at the airport speak English. Hell, it seems like most non Americans speak more than one language, English included. My school was barely a school anymore by the time I got there, it's not like we had language classes, and it's not something I pick up easy the way Bits and Bristol do. I try, though, and I smile big, and even out in the street, seems like most people like trying to help the big dumb American who isn't an asshole. Especially if they recognize the carrying case for the robot dog. People get real sympathetic then, which is kinda weird, since I know there's only so many people had access to this model, but when you're a legend, you're a legend, and the guy in Chiba is a legend.

It's pretty much impossible for him to be the same guy in Chiba that's been there since the early oughts when the first kind of these robot dogs were breaking down and there was only one guy left, and that occupies my thoughts a lot. Did the shop get passed to him, like when a venerable sushi chef passes the restaurant down to his son that he's trained his whole life, once he's absofuckinglutely certain that he can do the job right, knows every aspect of the craftsmanship? (I watched a documentary okay) I guess maybe. Not like I know enough Japanese to ask, and besides, seems like it'd be rude. It's none of my beeswax. I give him money, he fixes my dog, and that's all we need to be to each other.

Anyway, plane food's garbage and that's me saying that, so it's gotta be real bad. It'll be an easy thing to stop for street food once I drop the dog off. Chiba's got a famous monorail, and even though it's a ride, that's what I take from the airport just for the sake of it. I don't like taking the trains stateside, not the hyperloop either. Other places, it's one hundred percent the way to go. In America, I just always want the great American road trip, I guess. Like sure, as a nation, we were historically *really* into trains, but then the car happened and then the highways happened and freedom is the open road, blah blah blah. The open road ain't so great if you've got a flat tire or drones after you, but it's the risk I take over and over again. Beats old fashioned action star running on the top of the train bullshit. Which isn't to say I wouldn't if I had to. Maybe I'd want the equipment for it, though. Like magnet boots. Are the tops of trains magnetic? Guess you wouldn't wanna risk that on a maglev train though.

At some point, probably in the 'oh god we're really fucking the climate here and we're actually going to do something about it' frenzy, a lot of cities, worldwide, went back to what they once were, trollies and trams and people on foot. Definitely after the pandemic. But no cars means the roads can be narrower, means there's a lot more little businesses, and a lot more people in the streets, which I think are made of that kinetic rubber stuff that gathers power and transfers it to the street lights, the air conditioners, the surveillance.

It's cold enough that it's fine for me to wear a hood up, and at this point all of my hooded things have the flashy material in the fabric, to fuck with the cameras. I think all of Bits's clothes in general have that. And Bristol loves those 1900s starlet going for a ride in a convertible roadster scarves. Plus I feel like she was chattering about her foundation or some shit having stuff in it that was transparent to the naked eye and didn't affect her look, but fucked with being photographed. She does love being photographed; she does not like bein' in custody. None of us do, but she's the one with the most recent taste of that. She went on to Macau first though, to get a sweet suite with a view that she prefers or something. Maybe get in some spa time.

We all traveled separate. I'm a little surprised, not-surprised, that Bits didn't come with me, actually, but I figure she just wants to worm her way into all the security soon as possible. Anyway, international like this, it's better to arrive separate, but stay in touch. If she wants, she can probably be in any of these cameras to see what I'm up to. Or hack the little toy drones that this street vendor guy has, to have a look around. It's weird, after this time, to just be walking around without somebody here watching my back. I'd probably never *say* that to Bits and definitely not to Bristol, that I like having them back me up. We work together well, each doing our part. We don't need to say it. We just keep on doing it.

My connecting flight to Macau is in four hours, so I don't have a whole lot of turnaround time. Don't need to find a walkaround weapon while I'm here, I'm just like any civilian who wants their goddamn robot dog to just work the way that it's supposed to. I get to the shop and it's the same as it's been my other two trips. How many Americans make the trip, I wonder? Still. It's not like I'm Bits and just want to be as invisible and unmemorable as possible, I don't care about that, but it's a thought that I put on the shelf in my mind, that if any of the pissed-off government agents looking for any of us happened to come here, I could be identified, and that'd be another pin on their map.

Because I messaged ahead, they have the work order all filled out for me, even have some diagnostic guesses in English, and I'm able to tell them which ones I already tried. The young man who goes over it with me blinks a lot behind his glasses, and seems very thoughtful. I'm not the kind of person you want to have a misunderstanding with, even though I'm definitely on my best behavior here. Real polite, please and thank you, though there's no reason not to have manners in stores and things. Service staff, they don't deserve whatever bullshit's happening in your life.

//How'd it go?// Bits messages me when I'm back on the street.

//Fine as can be expected// I say. //It'll be ready by the time I'm back.//

//Is this...does this seem weird?//

//Bristol's job? Sure does, but you were all for it.//

//I was worried you were getting bored.//

//Oh you'd know if I was getting bored.// I grin, and somebody on the sidewalk moves out of my way a little more vigorously than they needed to. Whoops.

//No I mean, I noticed you were getting bored and I was worried about it.//

//You didn't say anything!//

//It's hard to say some things,// she says, and fair enough.

//We'll talk about it at the hotel.// I think about it. //We'll have what, a day or two, between us and the auction? Plenty of time to figure logistics and get more out of Bristol. Maybe this dog has a diamond collar or something, and that's what she really wants.//

//You'd think she'd have had enough of diamonds.//

//Bristol? Enough of diamonds?// I laugh, and some people turn their heads and look at me. Too loud again.

//Well remember, she won't wear them until she's *old*, which sounds like she stole it from a movie.//

//She did steal it from a movie, we watched it, remember? And she thinks 'old' is forty.// I go to one of the ramen vending machines instead of a stand; nothing's wrong, that I can tell, but I just have a feeling that I shouldn't spend any more time than I need to, not now that I've been getting people's attention. No telling who you might run into. Maybe a friend, maybe not a friend. Or maybe not a friend anymore. I burn as few bridges as possible, a lot fucking fewer than Bristol, who I think maybe set her whole old life on fire before she walked away without turning back like some kinda action hero. But it's been a couple. Plus you never know when the government'll change its mind about not needin' you anymore and just whistle Lassie Come-Home and because of whatever they programmed you and injected you and implanted you with, you just gotta do it. As far as I know, I'm all good and deprogrammed, especially after that last roadtrip stateside, but that's kinda the whole point. You don't actually know.

That tension goes away once I'm back on the train to the monorail so. There's something to be said for following your instincts. Or I just imagined the whole thing, and it'll never matter.

Chapter Three

I'm one hundred percent certain that literally anyplace else in Macau is cheaper than the Venetian. It's damned impressive, I'll give 'em that. A Michelin starred restaurant, of course, Bristol loves that shit. Chock full of suites, that's good, the more breathing room we can give each other when we're on a job, the better. They've also got a big goddamn shopping mall with a McDonald's and a Uniqlo and a hundred other things and I'll bet that just sticks in her craw to see. They're really committed to the whole aesthetic, though, It occurs to me that maybe Bristol picked this place because she thinks Bits'll like it. Like, there's a place with an Eiffel Tower right down the street, she could've picked that and didn't. One of these days I'll have to ask her how many Eiffel Tower proposals she's gotten.

I take the elevator up to the top floor, because I guess she couldn't resist the notion of going all the way to the top. The hotel is real quiet, not like every cheap joint I've picked. Must mean that the walls are thick enough to actually have real art hung on them, or real copies of real art, maybe even with wood frames instead of woodlook recycled plastic, and the carpet is plush enough that even when I try to stomp like a fairytale giant, my footsteps are swallowed up. If there's people sittin' and looking at the security cameras, they're probably laughing. Or Bits is already in the machine, and they're just looking at a loop of the last time the hallway was empty on repeat, with the timestamp advancing the way anybody would expect it to.

She always erases our footsteps behind us, like when horses are dragging branches in an old cowboy movie.

I get to our door and don't even have to wave my key at it, it's unlocked, and I push it open to a room nicer than I've ever owned, with a view across the city to the harbor. I wonder if all those windows open, and honestly pray that it never matters; this is pretty far up, and there ain't a lot that I'm afraid of, but it doesn't mean I wanna free climb down the side of this bitch either.

Bristol is pacing back and forth on the phone with somebody, speaking French and making faces so that her tone of voice comes out right. Like, everybody knows that when you smile on the phone, people hear the smile in your voice or whatever, but she takes it to a whole 'nother level. Bits is swallowed up on one of the couches, cushions galore, and the window-sized TV is tuned to the weather channel but has a feed of local news layered over the bottom corner. TV's've been doing that about forever now but you hardly ever see anybody use the in-picture thing. I drop my bag from a little higher up than I need to and Bristol turns and raises her eyebrows at me. I grin and wave, and she rolls her eyes and vanishes into one of the rooms, the door closing, whisper-quiet. This whole quiet hotel thing is gonna get to me real quick.

"How was your flight?" Bits asks.

"It was great, I got bumped to first class after Chiba, so they gave me drinks in a glass like a real grownup. Lemon scented hot towels. Dessert." I flop on the couch next to her, put my boots up on the coffee table. I probably should've grabbed something outta the minifridge first. Or no, those things cost a bajillion dollars. But I didn't notice any vending machines either. There's a point at which hotels class themselves outta having a vending machine on any of the floors and I just think that's really sad. Probably no ice machines either, they're all in the rooms. Places really lose character when they take out those little common area touches, capsule everything off. "We got a timeline yet?"

"Yes and no? The auction's just a few blocks away, and the objects being auctioned, which are not all ridiculously expensive dogs, have been arriving for a week or more. Bristol's trying to figure out if our target is here yet." She glances at me, smiling a little.

"Well is it?"

"Yeah."

I laugh. "Well did you tell her?"

"You know she doesn't like being interrupted on the phone." She laughs too. Of course Bits would have the intel; once she had access to the auction catalog, I'm sure she was tracing the dog's owner, the dog's handler, the dog's seller, the flight manifests, so many numbers that it just makes my brain swim but she's really in her element.

"I think we're all a little bit jumpy about that. How many times have good things happened when Bristol was on the phone?"

"I'm sure plenty, but the bad ones stick out."

"Ain't that the truth." I get up and look out a window; 38 floors. I wonder if hotels still have that superstition about having or not having a thirteenth floor; I didn't notice it when I was in the elevator and it would be too weird for me to go back out and check. Maybe that's a Western thing anyway, different cultures have different lucky and unlucky numbers. Different lucky and unlucky colors. And animals.

"Dolly, hello! And here we gather!" I wonder sometimes what Bristol's original accent was, because the way she talks now isn't how anybody talks. Not outside of old movies, like that one I found and then made Bits watch with me because the main character was just one hundred percent Bristol, she had to've seen the movie and done it on purpose, there's no other explanation. But that's part of the point. We don't ask each other for explanations like that. We're the people we are, not the people we came from. Just some of us changed a little more than others, I think. I don't think I changed much at all.

"We sure do! And we're starving, actually. Were you getting us room service?"

"You're always starving." She comes and perches on the edge of one of the overstuffed chairs, and I lean way over and pull a bottle of water from the minifridge just to watch her flinch a little. She's real good at hiding it. But also I'm sure there's only so much real money we're paying for this place anyway. And there's only so real money seems, after awhile.

"Fair enough. What's our plan?"

"Well, I have secured my place at the auction," she says.

"Oh your paddle number?"

Bits snickers and Bristol stares at me. "My what?"

"Don't you get a little fan or paddle or something that you wave when you bid? That'll have a number on it."

"I don't...think they call it that, no."

"So you don't have one."

"Nobody said anything about *paddles*, no." She's fun to rile up, but I gotta be careful not to take it too far.

"Okay okay so you're going into the auction through the front door. Then what, you're just gonna pretend to have the cash or whatever to outbid everybody for the dog?" It's possible that she just actually has enough money saved to outright buy the dog, but if that was the case, then we wouldn't be here and laying out a plan to steal the dog and collect a smaller paycheck than its pricetag.

"Yes, and then once I have access to that back auction area, where the goods are kept, I can let you two in and we can make off with the animal."

Carefully, Bits says "Don't you think that's making things a little more complicated than they need to be?"

"Well we need to make sure it's the right dog, don't we?"

"They probably number 'em or something." I open the fridge again and look at what's in there. Lots of little snacky things, absolutely none of it prefab like an American hotel that would have like, Snickers bars and stuff. White Claws. "Collars? Tags? Chips?"

Bristol waves her hand. "Regardless, yes, that's the plan. We'll have to rent a car of course, and be careful of the interior color, to mitigate the dog hair."

"And then we're taking the dog right to your buyer?"

"Well of course, it isn't as though we have anywhere to *keep* it. And I don't know the first thing about keeping a dog."

"So just a grab and go, that's not so bad," I say. Other than Bristol's insistence on being right there with her face in the action. I'm going to have to take a little walk and get some equipment. Bits and I share a glance, and I think she has more ideas than just about the color of the upholstery. Which, good, 'cause so do I.

Chapter Four

"She just always has to be *seen*," Bits says later, when Bristol is out auction shoes-and-dress shopping and we're eating fast food that we snuck off to get.

"It did work for the diamonds thing."

"Yeah, it's worked for things. But we *really* don't always need to be so high profile. We don't always need to have any kind of discernible profile. We could try that."

"Just in and out the back door with the dog after hours? Before or after the auction?" I guess I don't really have what people call a palate, but damn if fresh hot french fries aren't one of the best things in the world.

She shrugs. "Before for a lot of reasons, but also if Bristol's sudden appearance alerts INTERPOL or whatever, we can already be packed and leaving."

"Makes sense. Really, I just always assume Bristol's sudden appearance is gonna cause a problem, whether people know her or not."

Bits laughs. "I think she thinks that about you."

"Prob'ly." I laugh too, eat some more fries. "We gotta be prepared for her to be dramatic about this, like it's the ultimate betrayal."

"I think that's a risk I'm willing to take," Bits says thoughtfully. Bristol dramatics are just part of the package; there's no harm in it. Hell, she's as solid as any one of us, getting arrested on purpose and giving me time to go plug Bitsy into her rig in the hopes that her brain would stop coming outta her ears. And so I could get a new arm slapped on. Only some of that is exaggerated. Goddamn that was scary. Like. Top five. Just that whole bucket of snakes. I been shot, stabbed, lightly singed, shocked, partly drowned...but that's my first actual loss of limb. The skin's real skin at least, they tank grew that and grafted it on, so I don't have to worry about dust getting in or whatever.

And maybe it's better that I can't access my arm's biomechanical innards just to tinker around a little. Tempting though it is, even I know it's not really the best idea. I can't even fix my own robot dog. Tempting. Though actually the idea of opening a little door or whatever in my wrist or forearm so that I can get to fuses and stuff kinda freaks me out. There aren't fuses. It actually runs though my own generated bioelectricity or whatever. There's a manual that I've kinda skimmed. I know some people kinda hack them anyway, somehow, override the controls so they can get more strength out of them, or speed. It's tempting. Not the kind of decision you want to make in the middle of crisis, or the kind of thing you can just flip a switch on and get results. I don't think. Where is that manual? Maybe I should get a spare to tinker with first, get comfortable with it, then get a door put in.

"Okay. So we get the layout of the place, we figure where the cameras are. We pull the vehicle around, get inside between security sweeps, get the dog, get out, get back here. Much simpler. Much less risk. Plus, I still got that camouflage we pulled off that fed or whatever. When we recovered Bristol." She hesitates just a sec, then nods.

"Oh good. And I've got the layout of the place." She swipes the file over to me. "And I've got the auction catalog, but Bristol still has to tell us which dog's the right one."

"There's more than one dog at the auction? I assumed it was mostly gonna be art and shit."

"It is, but there's three dogs."

"You said the dog was here though?"

Bits blinks. "Yeah. All three dogs are here."

I take a sec to look at the pictures of the dogs. They might be puppies but they're the partly grown style of puppy, not the tumbly ball of fluff style of puppy. "So, what do you figure the point of stealing one of these guys is? Can't breed it legally, like registered, if you don't got the papers right?"

"Maybe breeding isn't the point." Bits looks off into the middle distance for awhile, probably reading something in AR. I always assume she's got at least three screens going at any given moment. Maybe one of those set it and forget it kinda games. Maybe she's keeping track of bitcoin mining, though I dunno where she'd have the rig for that set up. It wasn't at her place in Mexico. I think she sold that anyway. But I'm just making stuff up in my head to pass the time. "Anyway, if she doesn't tell us, I can just hack her email or whatever to see."

I frown. "I don't wanna start doing shit like that to each other. We'll just ask her. Show dogs always have weird names, don't they? She'll wanna giggle over that."

"Yeah maybe. You're probably right." Bits looks at me again. "Sorry. It just seems so simple sometimes. Like, a lot simpler."

"No harm, no foul." I clear the garbage, stuff it into the too-small garbage can, like the hotel people expect the rich folks using the suite to not generate very much garbage at all. You'd think they'd know better, dealin' with rich folks literally all the time. Rich folks throw everything away, and this is just paper stuff and there still isn't enough room. Makes me wonder how often room service comes up, actually. "Hey we should hang a thinger on the door. Do not disturb, no room service, whatever."

"You're right."

"And anyway, I'll bet the room is no pets." I keep a straight face until Bits kind of tilts her head quizzically and then I start snickering.

We're both laughing when the door chimes softly and Bristol comes in with an armful of shopping bags.

"I'm sorry to have missed the joke, darlings."

"Aw, it's not a big deal," I say. "Was this just an excuse for a shopping trip?"

"Everything's an excuse for a shopping trip," Bits says, and Bristol pouts.

"I'd prefer if you two didn't gang up on me."

"Sorry Bristles," I say in an approximation of sincerity. She inhales, nostrils quivering visibly, and then smiles. Practiced, serene.

"Thank you, Dolly."

"Show us what you got?" I ask, not 'cause I really care much but because it'll perk her up and make her chatter about all kinds of things, guaranteed. And she does, and me and Bits pay part attention to that and I pay part attention to looking at the stuff Bits forwards me, a rental car company first and then intel on Tibetan mastiffs. Male or female, depending on how close to full sized, we're lookin' at something like seventy five to a hundred and fifty pounds, which is like a person but not unmanageable. I've wrangled more weight than that, especially since the body mods I got courtesy of Uncle Sam before the program ended and we all scattered. Even before my fuckin' arm got blown to pieces and I got a new one, just like the original only better.

"What do you think?" Bristol asks finally. She doesn't really care what either of us thinks, but it's just in her programming.

"I like the shoes with the red," I say. The shoes have red soles, like she walked through paint, or a whole lotta blood. Maybe there's some symbolism there; we only know so much of each other's stories, by design. "And that blue dress."

"Thank you," she says, smiling. "I've wanted a pair of shoes like that for a long time, actually."

"Why'd you wait? Not like you didn't have the money." That's like me craving a particular gun and not getting it. Not that I worry overmuch about brands, just functions.

She smiles a little, shrugs. She has her answer rehearsed and it's real funny to realize and watch that in action. "I suppose not, but it just didn't feel right before now."

"So happy to be able to share this joyous occasion with you," I drawl on purpose and if we were little kids she'd stick her tongue out at me.

"You could use a new pair of shoes, you know," she says huffily, packing her things away again.

"Yeah but I just got these ones nice and broken in," I say, looking down at my scuffed boots, raveling lace-ends, and Bits laughs. "Anyway, wouldn't want to steal any of your thunder, Bristles." She looks at me and I grin wickedly, waiting for her rebuttal. She fights with herself about it, visibly, and then takes her shopping bags to her room.

"Careful, she'll come up with a plan where we all need to dress nice," Bits says.

"She can come up with whatever plans she wants, doesn't mean we're doing 'em," I say. Bits makes worried "she'll hear you" eyebrows at me but honestly, we had a great plan for the diamonds that she reworked for the hell of it, and claimed that it was in the interests of making things quieter and safer. That's all me and Bitsy are doing, trying to keep things quieter and safer.

Chapter Five

Bits and Bristol're asleep when I go for my supply run. Well. Calm late night stroll. Seems like a lotta places, the only people out are taxis and rideshares and people stumbling home from bars or whatever. Taking a bus, which I also do. Here, though, there's a twenty four hour life, especially with the casino. They do some kind of road race here coupla times a year, and it's amazing they make it as glitzy as they do. Macau and Monaco, but here I think they have a motorcycle one and now a bullshit hovervehicle one but that stuff's still mostly prototype and not really in general circulation, in a way different from just not having enough money keeps stuff out of people's hands. They really hover, they're not like those self balancing skateboard things from the early aughts.

Nobody seems to pay much attention to me as I walk, and I don't get that feeling I had back in Chiba. I still gotta mention that to Bits, but I'm sure she's already doing whatever internet magic it is that she does to see who's where and who's talking to who and about what. It's always reasonable to assume we're on somebody's docket, at this point.

There's a lot more drones here than in other places, not just traffic cameras, but their patterns're predictable and recognizable, if they're just on auto. I don't see any that aren't. I can hear parties going on, some engines revving. Active race or not, some people like to speed run city streets at night. Can't say I've never done it, and it can be a way to make some fast cash.

I make my likely stops, collect a few things that fit in pockets or hidden holsters, nothing traceable that I can tell but I'll have Bits check that too. Ammunition, and a good workhorse handgun, a 1911 style that's god knows how old but taken care of so well that I almost don't take it. This is, or was, somebody's baby, a natural extension of their arm. But I need it, so I do take it, and hopefully I can leave it back where I found it after this. Hopefully it doesn't have to find its way to the end of my arm through any of this. A pair of tasers that looks like they've been fooled with to give off a bigger zap. We've already all got our riot gear, at least we don't need to worry about getting that together again from scratch. What variation Bristol wears of it is another story, but she's a grownup, there's only so much I can do about that. Riot gear sure didn't keep me from losing an arm.

As I circle back to the hotel again, I stop at a 7-Eleven for some junky heat lamp food that I can eat in peace, without Bristol's complete and utter disdain. 7-Elevens are an interesting place, same brand in Macau as in New Jersey as in Tokyo as in Paris, they're good at keeping things familiar, but there's only so familiar they can stay past a certain point. Okay maybe there isn't a 7-Eleven in Paris but I've made my point. And I love it, really I do. There's a Japanese restaurant across the street with a sushi bar and everything, but by the time the other two're eating breakfast, Bristol would turn her nose up at overnight sushi. Bits wouldn't mind, but Bits likes 7-Eleven just fine too, and I grab her some snack food bags with labels in varying languages. Cricket chips and seaweed snacks and something with cheese, I think.

The clerk is playing a game in AR, I know the signs after all this time with Bits, and besides, they've got the glasses for it. They ring me up without looking at me much, which is probably also just a self defense mechanism of working at a place like this overnight. The clerks at off-highway places back home had that same look, always. Maybe clerks at places like that in general. Lord knows they're thankless, low-paying jobs. But a job's a job, sometimes. You can't always do what me and Bits and Bristol do. Maybe they get health insurance. Most countries got laws about that kinda thing nowadays. Huh. Wonder if I have health insurance. Probably my replacement arm's better than health insurance would've gotten me anyway. Or I got it sooner, anyway; VA takes forever.

I grab the bus back over the bridge, take in the sights. Mainland China is right there, and there's a twisty-looking skyscraper that has a light show on the outside of it. The colors and patterns change something like ten times, and I wonder what that looks like from the inside. Probably like nothing, it's probably just color-changey on the outside, not like living inside an aquarium. I'm the only one who gets off when the bus stops, and I take an indirect walk back to the Venetian, eyeing the other casinos and idly thinking about what a real casino job would be like.

The cage is always in the middle of the floor, that's not gonna work when things're open unless you're a comic book villain. The vaults, those movies covered vault stuff. I'm not super interested in vault stuff. We could hijack an armored car, that'd be workable. That's happened, in the real world, and people've gotten away with it. It's happened in the movies and gone horribly wrong, of course. Wouldn't be an interesting story if stuff didn't go wrong. Anyway, money's *heavy*, and I'm sorry to say there's only so much of it we could physically handle quickly. Bristol might be stronger'n she looks, I dunno, but Bits definitely isn't.

Also, one of the other hotels in town has a ferris wheel on the roof and I'm kinda mad at Bristol for robbing us of that opportunity. Maybe she's ferris wheel averse. Maybe she got engaged to her one true love on top of a ferris wheel and then tragedy struck, and that's why she's so familiar-but-distant with people now. Probably not. My brothers used to try and scare me and my sisters when we were little, shaking the cars on the ferris wheel when we were at the top, except I didn't scare. My sisters, though, they'd shriek and beg the boys to stop, and we'd all be laughing and the operator down the bottom would yell at us to stop. After awhile there weren't many fairs that came through with rides, but we went to every damn one. Every, *every* fair, even if there weren't rides and funnel cake and rigged games, just barns of animals to look at that the 4H-ers threw their whole damn lives into, coming to school ragged on every edge during lambing season, after mucking stalls, after...doing whatever it is you do to care for pigs. The ones raising chickens and things were pretty okay.

We never did livestock. You can't really count bees as livestock, I don't think. But we had bees and were shadetree mechanics for about forever, did some scavenging all over and machined parts besides. We being my family. We check in every once in awhile, those of us who're left. We're doing okay. Nobody's been home in a long time. I thought about swingin' by when we were doing the decommissioned sites thing but then that went so far sideways we didn't know up from down. We being me and Bits and Bristol.

All's quiet in the hotel lobby when I walk back in. I forgot a reusable bag, normally I'll have at least one rolled up in a pocket but not while I'm flying I guess, so I had to buy one from 7-Eleven and just flaunt my shame to everybody. Everybody who cared, anyway; the lobby was empty of people to turn their noses up at me. The night shift dude wasn't even there, but he was when I left, and I had a paranoid moment that something was very wrong but then I heard a door close, and another one, and he appeared from some behind-the-desk door to find me standing there in his nice lobby in my combat boots, holding my 7-Eleven bag, and we had a long moment of looking at each other before I grinned at him and said "Have a good night" and he nodded and said "You too."

I guess it's not paranoia if you've got people after you on the regular. Still though. I take the stairs, not the elevator, all the way up. I stop and stretch at the landings, do pushups at a couple of them, run up some of the flights. Nothing says we're gonna be cooped up for awhile, but I get the feeling we're gonna be cooped up for awhile, and that's no good.

I forgot to check for the goddamn thirteenth floor again.

There's no sign anybody's done anything in the suite while I've been gone, and I maybe expected Bits to circulate a little bit because god knows what her internal clock's doing, but I hang the 'Do Not Disturb' on the door before I set the bolt and then jam a doorstop underneath. Then I hit the hay.

Chapter Six

We're getting about to auction day and Bits and I know the layout of the auction place, we know the pattern of the security patrols, we know how many people are there on the late shift, but we still don't know which goddamn dog it is. In the catalog, two are male, and one is female, and from their pictures I'm not sure I'd even say they're the same type of dogs, but dogs're hardly my specialty. And even if they were, it wouldn't be Tibetan Mastiffs, it'd be like. Catahoulas or Redbone hounds.

"We could just ask her," I say.

"I could just break into her phone," Bits says. It's on the counter of the suite's kitchenette, an unprecedented abandonment, while Bristol's at one of the spas. I think that's where she is, anyway.

"Don't break into her phone, we already talked about this. We gotta trust each other at least a little, right."

She sighs. "We gotta trust each other a lot."

"We'll figure it out. Put a dog show on TV or something for when she comes back."

"What will *that* do?"

"I dunno, make her talk about it? She's the manipulator, not me."

"We're all manipulators," Bits grumbles.

"Then what's the problem?" I laugh. I've got my new and/or temporary handgun taken apart at the coffee table and all laid out on a nice cloth. It's pristine, it's like a me of the past or a possible me of the future left it there, it's just a pleasure to work with. I'm not gonna start thinking about time travel bullshit, though, it's hard enough wrapping my head around some of the knots that Bits ties her brain into when she's super deep into the computer side of thing. "Oh hey did you look at the zappers?"

"Yeah they look fine," she said. "Turned up, like you thought. Really clever how they did it, actually, you wouldn't think you'd be able to get more juice out of one of those. Like they'd have all you could have." She pauses and I almost ask if it's the settings and I wait. "Of course, as it turns out, there are settings that limit it. That's how they keep the production costs down, there's really only one device, but the stronger one is for professionals, and they gate the voltage for civilians."

"Kinda like how on some semi-autos, all you need's a paperclip and some know-how to make 'em rock and roll."

"...yeah. Like that."

Clearly, we got our own niche interests. "Anyways, when she comes back we should just—"

The door chimes and Bristol comes in, checks her phone, and in about thirty seconds she's talking on it in French. Bits watches her flounce back and forth, I put the gun back together. I'm not the type who names my guns, but I wonder if its old owner did that. Am I using somebody's Matilda? I don't know what people name their guns. Somebody's Bruce? Hell I never even named the robot dog. There was a name sharpied on the white plastic when I got it, but I cleaned that off of there. Didn't seem necessary. Names are a funny thing anyway, though. None of us go by our real names, right? Birth names? Whatever you might call 'em.

"Problem?" I ask when Brisol sets her phone down and sighs.

"Our buyer is *exceedingly* nervous, or his intermediary is, and requires much reassurance. I did soothe his nerves, I think, and everything is still set. I just cannot conceive of why people cannot maintain a professional demeanor."

"Wonder what made him nervous," I say. "Something seem wrong with the dog?"

"No, that I've heard, she's just fine," Bristol says distractedly, looking in the mini fridge. "Oh I'm just going to be wicked and have one of these awful little wine coolers."

"You devil you." I holster the gun, tilt my head at Bitsy. She nods just slightly; she caught that. "Why deny yourself, anyway?"

"It isn't special if you make it into a habit." She comes and arranges herself on one of the wingback chairs. "What have you two been up to?"

"Weapons checks," I say.

"Maps and security," Bits says.

Bristol nods and sips the wine cooler and I get up and get a beer and then say "Bristles, should we have any dog stuff on hand? At least a leash right?"

She thinks about it a moment. "Well, I would think they'd have a leash and other...equipment right there. The handlers have been caring for it, after all. And we'll be going from the auction to the intermediary, so we don't really need anything at all, I don't think."

"Roger that." Bits looks and me, and I shrug. Probably, yeah, there's leashes or whatever there, but I'm also at least gonna put some hot dogs in my pocket. I'm pretty sure dogs don't like just going with strangers. I could be wrong, this could be a baby show dog who's used to being handed off to whoever. Maybe somewhere in the middle. "So we're golden, then, we just wait."

"We just wait," Bristol agrees.

"You, uh, you wanna talk about why you wanted to leave Dubai?" I ask. Bristol kind of waves her free hand dismissively.

"My skin was getting so *dry*, I'm constantly amazed at how adaptable you all always are. And I'd heard about the spas here being a world class experience but for less than you might pay in Europe." I'd say she was blowing smoke but she seems serious. Really, if Bristol's talking she's lying in some way or another, even though we got a rule about that, so there *might* be something bothering her other than dry skin, but dry skin's on the list too.

"Is that where you've been all day, the spa?"

"Are you going to get one of those fish pedicures?" Bits asks with what seems like genuine interest.

Bristol visibly shudders. "I am not."

"Fish pedicure?"

"Yeah, I guess instead of them using the foot grater thing on you, you stick your feet in a pond and fish eat the dead skin. Or maybe they use the grater to loosen the skin first, I don't really know." Bits looks at Bristol for help, and Bristol just raises her eyebrows and takes another sip of her wine cooler. "Anyway. It's expensive and kind of specialty."

"Oh it sounds special all right," I laugh.

"Dolly, you know, you'd be so striking if you'd just—"

"No, nope." I cut her off. "We're not playing Dolly Dress-up. We're here to steal a dog, to sell that dog, and be on our way."

"Bits…" Bristol turns her big innocent eyes for appeal.

"No thanks," Bits says, either meaning she doesn't want to dress up either or she isn't gonna help, I can't tell, but it works for both.

"We never do what I want to do."

"We're doing what you want to do right now? And we did with the diamonds job? You act like we're always against you, it's kinda weird."

"Yes, but you're always on about *equipment* and plans of action and it just does get tiresome, darlings, I'm sorry."

"Real talk with Bristol at two o'clock in the afternoon," Bits says dryly.

"Hey, you wanna do solo work, you can. Nobody's saying we can't have side projects."

"Oh, I know, but I do like working with you girls. I was just hoping for some teambuilding."

"Maybe next time," I say, still grinning. "There's always bungee jumping, why don't we do that?" We all laugh, and it clears the air. But could it be possible that Bristol is lonely? That'd be wild. Maybe her Dubai friend group was having some kind of drama that she got impatient with. Maybe the real heist is the friends we made along the way.

Chapter Seven

The night before the auction, Bristol's out partying with new friends or acquaintances or connections, it's hard to tell which or maybe to her it's all the same, and me and Bits go to the convention center or whatever it's called where the auction'll be. It isn't the convention center with the bungee jumping anyway. The only auctions I've ever been to before were at barns and stuff, what do I know. I stopped at 7-Eleven again, bought all the hot dogs that they had on the rollers, and cut 'em up with a combat knife in the back of a van that we rented for a couple of hours. Well, that Bits rigged the system to think that we rented, for a couple of hours.

"One of the guards is out tonight," she says as we drive over, lying on the floor in the back with her headset on. "So they added to the drone patrols."

"Good news."

"Yup. I rerouted them a little last night, to see if it would work and if anybody would notice. It did, and they didn't."

"Double good news," I say. See, I have the active camo, but it's not gonna extend to the dog. "So you figure the middleman guy is actually French or is that just a language they had in common?"

"Hard to say. It's possible. And with people who're rich enough to pay millions of dollars for one single individual dog, well, rich people get weird. They could be from anywhere."

"Literally anywhere." I wonder if she's thinking about tigers. I'm thinking about tigers. "Good thing we're not that kind of rich people, right?"

"Is it weird that I don't think of myself as a rich people?"

I'd turn around to look at her for a sec, but with the headset on, Bitsy's facial expression isn't gonna mean anything. "No, I guess I don't either. I don't really do different things." Other'n drop off money to family members. Other'n have the money for fancyass prosthetics and to see a doctor once in awhile to make sure all the enhancers the army gave me are working right. Which they are. And especially after we deprogrammed all that goddamn posthypnotic shit, I've been feeling fine. I typically feel fine; it's what made me such a fit for the program to begin with. "Not expensive-pet-buying things." The robot dog doesn't count; something me and Bits could slap together an approximation of doesn't count as a weirdo rich person thing.

There's a long pause and then Bits says "Yeah true." Of course, she built that bleeding edge VR rig that she let me beat apart with a hammer, that was kinda the rich people thing to do. The one she slapped together at the Dubai house isn't nearly as involved, but she isn't spending her time totally conked out either, so I guess it's different. "We don't have cheetahs on gold leashes."

I park next to the building, do a quick equipment check, and hop out. "Catch you on the flip side," I say, and Bits laughs quietly in my earbud.

"Roger that," she says. "Did you bring enough hotdogs?"

"If I run out, we got bigger problems than explaining to Bristol that we tried to steal a march on her."

The truck locks behind me as I go to the door and swipe her fake keycard. I don't know what she did to make it work, if she snuck out here a different day or what, but it goes green and the lock clicks and I walk into a blank hall and flip on the camo. Why are the back ends of these places always so goddamn boring? Money sure but is that the only reason. I've got the map in my head and it's just a couple hallways before I'm at the dog room. I hear a drone at one point, but around a corner, and I trust Bits to nudge it away from me, if necessary. It's fine right now, anyway. What I also need is Bristol on the map in my head, so I know what *she's* up to, but the chances of us seeing her before we're all back at the hotel are slim. Also I just like knowing where people are. That's the rough thing about doing what I do and not being home anymore.

I swipe my fake keycard here and it buzzes but the door doesn't open. The light's yellow. "So hey..." I mutter.

"They've got another layer of security there hold on," Bits says. The numbers on the keypad start to light up like somebody's pressing them. I pucker my lips to whistle while I wait, stop myself. It's too quiet here for that. Probably nobody else whistles while they're on security detail. Plus I don't want to get the dogs riled up; it's shadowy in the room, but I can see at least one dog head in profile in a cage, and some eyes reflected in the hall light. I hope to christ they don't go nuts once I get in the room, or if they do, that any other human personnel just ignore it because dogs just bark sometimes, right. Or maybe they don't have the code to come in here, just the handlers do, so there's no point.

Oh, the handlers.

The door goes green and I open it, and I have the gun in my hand and that surge of adrenaline where I expect the room to have people in it to handle, but nobody's in here. I don't want to shoot somebody so I can steal a dog, so I'm glad, and Bits and Bristol have the tasers. Not that taze or shoot are my only options, obviously. There are any number of varyingly terrible things that I can do to a fellow human being, when called upon. But again, for a dog? Sure it's for a payday but. We were having those in Dubai, and nearly legit. Okay some companies would sue the shit out of us but that's neither here nor there.

I turn off the camo but don't turn the light on and the dogs have all stood up, judging from where their eye glows are, but aren't making any noise yet. Wait, no, one of them is growling way deep in their throat and if I had animal sense I'd've noticed it before now. "Relax, bud," I say quietly, and get out a handful of cut-up hotdog that I toss at each of the cages. Kennels? They aren't right next to each other, and there's collapsible room dividers between them. The dogs pay attention to the hot dogs while I look for a leash, and a collar, and the female.

The cages have little AR labels on 'em, so it's easy to figure it out. Both of the males are black with tan eyebrows, like a hound dog, but that's really the only hound dog similarity. Well maybe earset a little, but all three dogs have big fuckin' heads like lions. The female is the smallest; probably maybe half grown I guess. She's kind of a reddish golden color, like when retrievers get darker, and when I get close I can see the broad leather collar that she's wearing, part hidden by her fur. She looks at me suspiciously, and I toss her some more hot dog as I look at the kit nearby her. A leash, some grooming stuff, in a duffle. I pull out the leash, let it jingle a little. "Hey puppy girl, wanna go for a walk?" She looks at me when I talk, still chewing, but doesn't do anything else. Probably doesn't speak English, but that's fine, we'll figure it out. She isn't the one growling, anyway, that's one of the males. Both of the males. Growling in stereo. We're cool, it's good.

I hold out some hot dog to the bars of the cage and she sniffs at it audibly, then licks them out of my hand and ducks her head to pick it up. Okay good. I undo the top latch of the cage door, unlatch the bottom, and swing it open with a little creak. Her head comes up but she doesn't move. I think about reaching into the cage for her collar, think better of it, step back and crouch down. "C'mere. I got lots more hot dog where that came from."

She takes a step towards me, head tilted one way, and I drop hot dog right at my feet. She comes out of the cage readily, and I find her collar, rotate it around to clip the leash on the ring. She must be trained for handling, at least a little, so this is okay. She looks up at me after the leash clips, and I get more hot dog out of my pocket for her, and then grab her little travel bag. Might as well; she's gonna be at least overnight at the hotel with the new plan. I look in the cage to see if there's a toy or anything there but no, just a hamster bottle of water clipped to the side. Kind of weird, don't puppies chew? Whatever. Bits hasn't said anything yet but she's letting me hear her breathe which means she's getting impatient.

"How's it looking, Bitsy?" I ask, and again, the dog looks at me while I'm talking.

"Still okay for now. They have people doing the auction setup in the big facility so there's more people here than when we scouted."

"But they aren't back here, it's fine."

"You've got the dog right?"

"Yeah, comin' out now. Keep our exit clear."

"I will." She's laughing at me, probably. But it's always at this point of a job that I try not to think of everything that could go wrong and just work on the exit. Nothing fancy, nothing flashy, nothing extra. Got the thing, get the thing out. Unless the thing doesn't wanna get out. I take a few steps and the leash goes taut, and the dog is still standing there looking at me.

"Come on," I say, trying to make my voice inviting, not impatient. I could carry her, there's lots I could carry, I just don't want my face gettin' bit off. Please no prosthetic replacement face. Though could you get modular ones, so you could switch 'em out? What a tool that would be, in our life of crime. She tilts her head and looks at me the other way. Do I know something in French that might get her moving? "Allez." Her dropped ears move a little, but I guess not. "Hey Bitsy, can you look up dog commands in Chinese for me?"

"What?"

"Nevermind." I get out more hotdog. Honestly, I don't want to feed this dog five pounds of hotdog and have her puke in the hotel and/or van but I also can't fuck around here for much longer. The hotdog works, the puppy follows along with me gently and happily as I manage the leash, the bag, and the hotdog pieces. I wonder how dog people do it, it reminds me of seeing people somehow wrangle toddlers and toddler equipment. Everything is still weirdly quiet and I realize that she doesn't have any tags on her collar, and wonder what all those tags are, anyway. In case a dog gets lost, I guess, so they can get found. But that's what microchips are for anyway. Ooh, I hope Bits has a microchip reader. "Bits, you got a microchip reader?"

"Can you just shut up and get out here please?"

"Just askin'," I mutter. I consult the map in my head and reverse the turns I took coming in and then we're at the exit door, the dog and me, buddies now and requiring less hot dog. I let the door close quietly and let the dog sample the air with her sniffer before I open the back of the van. Bits is sitting up now, VR headset hanging around her neck. "Okay, get in," I say to the dog, helpfully, as though she'll just hop up on cue. She looks up at me, looks at Bits in the van, looks up at me, and backs up a couple of steps. "Aw c'mon, here's more hot dog." I give her some, toss some in the van. Chewing, she considers it, paces back and forth a little as the leash allows. I wait. Bits inhales to say something and I shake my head. The dog gathers herself and hops up, snuffling around for the other hot dog pieces.

"Give me the leash," Bits says, and I toss the loop to her, put the bag down, shut the door.

"Hotel first and I'll return the van?"

"You'll...help me get her upstairs, right?"

"'Course I will."

"Yeah, then."

"Bristol still partying?" I roll us towards the road in neutral, keeping an eye in the rearview. Nothing going on. I start the van, turn on the lights, and a couple of blocks later we fade into traffic.

"Bristol's still partying," she says. So far so good.

Chapter Eight

The problem with stealing an auction item the night before the auction is set to go is they find out. I mean, they were obviously always gonna find out, but this many hours before the covert hand-off, the police and other interested parties have that much more time to organize their searching. Which does and doesn't matter to us. We're in a cushy enough room in a cushy enough hotel that nobody's gonna be doing a room to room search here. We don't need to go ramming around the city with the dog, gettin' ourselves caught. We just wait for the handoff time, go, get paid.

Of course, Bristol doesn't know yet. That we've got the dog. Who is happy to cuddle in with me and sleeps nice the whole time. Exactly the kind of companionship you want a dog for. She wakes me up whining and then I realize the flaw in the plan, that dogs, unlike robot dogs, have to put the hot dogs somewhere when they're done with them.

"Wait a sec," I say, and the dog stops whining. She's probably gonna pee the bed, at the very least. Maybe not. This might've been easier with a boy dog. I go out into the common room of the suite and wander around. Quickly. There's some big baskets arranged as decoration, and have some moss looking stuff in them. Good enough? Maybe? I haul it to my room and put it in the corner, the dog sniffing intently as I do. I kind of point at it once it's settled and she looks at it looks at me, and starts circling. Rad. I leave her to do her business.

"My, you're up early," Bristol says when I come through the door between the suites and close it behind me. She's wearing one of the complimentary bathrobes. Oh I should message Bits that the dog is...doing her business.

"So're you, you were out late." She has fancy waters that she bought at some point, and is pouring one over ice. Has she been back long enough to sleep? Her and Bits, I swear, sometimes they really don't seem to get the value of some shuteye. You'd think Bristol would love her beauty sleep, and I guess she does, until something else has her attention. At least she isn't one of those party girls who also gets coked up, or maybe she does, but not enough that you can tell by the time she gets home. But I don't think she's like that, I don't think she'd ever let herself lose control like that. I know I don't really understand who'd want to; drinking, fine, smoking, sure of course, but there's a line. Everybody's got a line.

"I was making connections," she says airily. "The girls I met are friends with some local politicos, it would seem. There's quite the scene here."

"Oh, politicos," I say, like that means anything to me. Politicos are just lookin' to fuck people in order to get ahead. Not like, literally. Though also I guess sometimes literally. It's like venture capitalists. "I guess they probably got a scene everywhere, though, huh."

"Well yes. Though different scenes." She sips some of her water, then cocks her head, frowning just a little. "Do you hear that?"

I assume any 'that' is gonna be the puppy and listen accordingly but actually no, I don't hear her. I go over to the fancy 'sunken lounge' area and Bits is sprawled on the couch, but she's got a...well it's some kind of computery thing that's not a phone, that's buzzing like a phone would if it was on vibrate. "Oh that's where she is."

"You didn't know she wasn't in your room?"

I shrug, go poke at the coffee maker. "Well I didn't check."

Bristol gives a little laugh. "Darling, your beds are right next to each other."

"Yeah that's kinda weird for a swanky suite deal, ain't it?" I think the machine's brewing. Bits' little tech thing is still makin' noise and I go and kick the couch leg. I know better'n to put hands on somebody to wake 'em up. "Hey, is that important?"

She inhales sharply, gives a little jerk, and paws the VR thing up off her eyes and I watch her pupils contract in the light. She blinks at me for a sec before feeling around, putting the buzzing right in front of her face. It's got a metal casing. "Oh."

"Oh, what?" Bristol asks, in a too-casual tone. I dunno if right now's when she caught on we were up to something, or if it's just when she decided let us know she knew we were up to something. Always hard to tell with her, she's got a helluva a poker face. The best bluffer I've ever known.

"Well I wrote some code that would route through a vpn that I don't use all the time and ping through...well okay that doesn't matter, but if a certain thing happens it sets off an alarm in this." She shakes the little box, as though we have any fuckin' idea what it is. "So that it wouldn't be traceable to any of the equipment I typically have up and running."

"Well okay what happened?"

She sits up, stretching, and the coffeemaker does a sputtering steaming thing that seems to suggest it's done. It smells done. I go and take out two cups, look at Bristol, who nods, take out a third. Let's see, Bits like sweet and black, Bristol likes pale and sweet, and I'll drink it any old way so I just leave mine black. Bristol probably also likes balloon animals or something made out of the foam but I'm not making foam.

The thing isn't vibrating anymore when I hand Bits her coffee.

"Okay, so—" she says and Bristol's phone rings.

Bristol looks at it, I assume to cancel the call, and then her eyebrows go up and she answers it, pacing away. The person on the other end is talking even as she gets it to her ear. Nope, I still don't speak French. Spanish, yeah. Maybe I should get like, those recordings you play when you sleep, or whatever, learn it subliminally. Couple of our buddies back home, they learned French to sign up for the French Foreign Legion, god knows where they even heard of it. Operator messenger boards or some shit. God knows why the French Foreign Legion is even still a thing, and why it accepts people who aren't French.

Bits looks at me and I shrug. "I assume the two are linked," I say dryly.

"Yeah," she says, then she lowers her voice. "The dog?"

"I brought her a plant so she could do her thing." Bits blinks and kind of frowns a little, but then Bristol comes back.

"Well, everything's ruined," she says cheerfully, taking a sip of her coffee and then setting it down. "Somebody stole the dog last night, the auction is off, and my contact is *freaking* out. I've never heard him like that before, ever. Just inconsolable, the poor dear, this really is more than he can bear."

"I thought he was an intermediary?" Bits says.

"Well excuse me for not having a map of their organization, being an intermediary doesn't mean it isn't still important to him, evidently."

"Organization?" Maybe we should've asked her more to begin with. Not that it matters much. We don't need to know why the dog, we just had to get dog from point A to Person B. Which we can still do.

She wave a hand, picks up her coffee again. "I don't know that there's an *organization*, I was just using it as an exaggeration. Family tree? Is that better?"

"Yeah, sure." I shrug. "But anyway, Bits?"

"Well I had this set for—"

"Bits, I'm dreadfully sorry, but now isn't really the time to talk about your gadgets, we need to find out where the dog is, and who took her, and why they knew that she's the one that was—"

In the adjoining suite, the dog must've finished her business, and we'll see how that went, or maybe she was just bored of hearing people's voices and not being able to see anybody. I should've left food out for her, there was food in that bag. But she barks and it is loud. Bristol stops midsentence, midgesture, and blinks slowly. Wets her lips. Takes a breath and gives her head a little shake. Looks at me.

"Dolly, what was that?"

"Oh that? It was—" I'm tryin' real hard not to laugh at the look on her face.

"Did you two steal the dog already? Is the dog in your suite?" Pretty soon her voice is gonna be a tone that only the dog can hear.

"Surprise?" Bits says hopefully and I can't help it anymore, I just laugh. I set down my coffee so I don't spill it.

"When did you...*why* did you?"

"Last night, and we were bored while you were at a party so we figured we'd just go scoop her up." I go to the door between suites and open it. The dog is standing there and swishes her tail a little when she sees me, but her head is down. "You hungry? Let me get a bowl for your food."

"You were bored," Bristol says faintly, and sits in one of the plush armchairs.

"Well we hoped it'd be a nicer surprise but the cat's out of the bag. Or the dog is out of the. Bag." That saying doesn't really work with a not-baggable animal. I get a bowl from the kitchenette and bring it over to the dog, who's still standing between the rooms. "I gotta get past you for your food."

"Oh but that's what the code was about, when people were sending out the alarm about the dog, so I can make sure it isn't tracking to us. And nothing is," Bits says helpfully.

"Delightful, I'm sure," Bristol says, still very quiet, looking at the dog. "I suppose I should call—"

"Yeah go call Pierre or whoever back and let him know he can stop losing his shit. Everything's fine." The dog hasn't moved. "Hey come on." She blinks up at me, and then backs up all the way into the room, then turns her head and yawns. "Let's see what they've got for you. Some kinda meat cereal I'm sure."

I wasn't sure Bristol could hear me, but she sighed elaborately, then paused, and then was speaking French again. Good. No need for the hullaballoo. Though I guess now whoever her guy is is gonna have to figure out how to act natural until we can meet up with him and do the handoff. There are little containers of varying things, but I'm looking for simple, and there is kibble that I pour into the bowl. The dog sniffs it, then looks up without moving her head and growls. You'd think, with all that fur, it'd be too heavy to see any of it stand up, but she manages.

I look where she's looking and Bits is standing in the doorway. "So I guess she's nervous?"

"Prob'ly definitely nervous. You got any idea yet why Bristol's buddy might want her? You figure she's got a microchip with CIA intel on it or something? Chinese government? Russia again?"

"I guess we'll find out when we scan her for a chip. Or chips. Not while she's eating though." Bits sits on the edge of her bed. The dog yawns again, and then she does start crunching her kibble. I wonder how much I should've given her.

"Yeah definitely not." I look through the doors, at Bristol with her phone smile on, soothing nerves and rerouting plans like a champ. "Well that went okay."

"It could've been a lot worse." Bits smiles a little, looking at something else. Or maybe not. Her mind is always on other things. "I assume we'll still do the handoff tonight."

"Yeah, don't see why not." I look through the door into Bristol's suite, where she's sitting again, still on the phone, and seems much more relaxed now. "Seems like things're smoothed over."

"I think so?" She shrugs.

The dog finishes eating and stares at me again. "Oh, water." I fill up the bowl in the bathroom sink, put it down for her, and she laps it up noisily.

Bristol comes to the doorway, still in her robe, now with her coffee. "Well I'm still going to the auction, because at this point it would look odd if I didn't."

"Plus you don't wanna waste the new dress."

"Plus that," she agrees, that sharp little edge in her voice that we get when she means business. "It's possible I'll make other useful connections there."

"Or see something else you like," Bits points out helpfully.

"Perhaps." So she doesn't expect that at all. I didn't look at the catalogue, really, I dunno what else is gonna be on the auction block.

"Gonna wear your special shoes?"

"Oh, no, they're for Paris next month." And she shuts the door and goes to change.

Chapter Nine

Of course we go as backup when Bristol goes to the auction. The windows of the car that she for-real rents are tinted enough that it doesn't matter I'm not dressed like a chauffer, and the back is spacious enough that it doesn't matter that Bits is sprawled in the footwells with her head in VR. She's got all the cameras before we're on site and feeds Bristol information about who's already arrived, about security, about media, because there is media. "This is gonna flag you, you realize," Bits says.

Bristol smiles a smile that only I can see, and says "Oh yes, darling, I'm well aware." Our eyes meet in the rearview and she winks at me. I got no clue what level of 3D social chess she's playin' and I'd just as soon be left out of that aspect of the festivities, please. I like things to be more direct, which again, isn't to say I'm in a real hurry to use this nice handgun I got. And while I've got a couple fast escape-from-Macau notions in my head, none of 'em involve also having a dog that isn't ours. Let's hope it won't come to that.

She gets out in the snowstorm of camera flashes and strides confidently up the walkway. I guess celebrities are expected to be at this gig, and I wonder who the photographers assume she is. Somebody's girlfriend or mistress probably. Somebody's go-between. They've latched onto her, fascinated by the mystery, and of course she fucking loves that. I watch for a sec, then drive away before the car behind us honks.

"I've got a stopwatch running on the first agency sort of communication I notice," Bits says from behind me.

"I expect nothing less." I think about making a bet, stop myself. No good borrowing trouble, no matter how fun it might be. Not like I'm very fucking cautious in my overall living. "Y'know, she mentioned that she had makeup that—"

"Messed with the cameras? Yeah that's the pictures that people are posting on local groups, it's like she's got a mask of light." Bits puts one of the images in the car's dashboard screen for a second, for me to see.

"Modern problems require modern solutions," I say dryly, fish the ecigarette out of my jacket pocket. I actually like real cigarettes better, it's weird to go around smelling like cookies and cinnamon rolls and stuff in my particular area of expertise. It's...the word isn't contradictory, Bristol would know the word. It's like naming your big dangerous killer 'Bubbles.' Or I guess like having your normal-sized dangerous killer named Dolly, so really I'm just provin' my own point. At least I don't have to figure out what to do with the cigarette butts, if I'm using an ecig. You'd think they would've come up with a better kind by now. Biodegradable. Eco-friendly. Edible. "You don't mind?" I ask, not thinking about how she can't see me, won't know what I'm talking about.

"It's okay." Okay, fair enough.

Macau's a nice place to drive around in, actually, especially at night if you get away from the main traffic. There's a good loop you can do that still keeps you close to where you need to be. In case you need to swoop in and give somebody a fast getaway. Or have a deep and sudden need for luxury goods shopping in an indoor mall that has gondolas and a painted sky. I cruise, keeping an eye on the vehicle's charge, wonder what I'd do to make money if I lived here. Could join one of those rideshare companies. Could do security for a club, or even one of the hotels, though I'm probably not polished enough in my appearance, in a manner of speaking. I haven't noticed a single mechanic's, but that doesn't mean they ain't here.

I think about the dog, but we put her in one of the bathrooms with food and water and a blanket from one of the beds, or a duvet Bristol called it. I don't know what the fuckin difference is between a duvet and a comfortor and a bedspread, but I guess there is one.

"How's it looking?" I ask after awhile. Place like this, you don't want the camera watchers watching you pass by too many times. Switching the route too much would take me too far away, but I don't want to be noticeably parking either. "How long's this shindig supposed to take?"

"They're almost to the dogs now, and they definitely didn't say that the dog's been stolen or missing or anything, just that she's no longer being auctioned tonight. Somebody left right after that and made a call, it bounced off a local tower. Bristol didn't comment on it, so it's fine, or she didn't know who they were. The paparazzi didn't say anything about them either." A long pause, but normal in Bitsy's way of doing things. "Okay that person went back to the auction."

"Okay." She puts him on the screen for me, a kind of sandy-haired white guy, maybe in a black suit or maybe it's a tux, who cares. Nobody I recognize, so that's good. "Send that to Bristol too."

"Already did."

"So what's the demographic of our buyers here?"

"Are you asking if he and Bristol are the only white people? They aren't."

"You really know how to put somebody at ease." I grin, take a different loop this time. Maybe I should learn how to blow smoke rings, that'd work for both real cigarettes and the e ones. Nothing too fancy, just a good old fashioned ring. I hope the dog is sleeping.

"It's what you wanted to know!"

"Naw, it is. Did she say anything when you sent it."

"No, but that could mean anything. She knows him, she's never seen him before in her life, they used to go out..."

"That's our girl." No telling how many notches Bristol has on her belt, or even what a notch on her belt means to her. Just a few dates or actually lettin' him run the bases. When the topic comes up she just kinda smiles mysteriously and says that a lady never tells, or something. Bits just always kinda shrugs, so I'm guessing she's never felt particularly inspired on the topic, and pretty much neither of 'em are interested in my range of conquests, from one of my closest road crew friends back home to a stewardess that one time in Berlin. Maybe those things are best kept quiet, who am I to say. It's kind of a pity the stewardess thing didn't work out, but she was too nervous about things, and I wouldn't've been able to be honest with her, and that's just no way to have a relationship.

"Looks like there are other cars pulling up," Bits says. "I don't know if it's a problem yet."

"Pulling up out front or out back?"

"Out back."

"That weren't there before?" I'm already turning around to take the direct route back to the conference center.

"I'm running their plates against the data I pulled before...no. They weren't there before."

"I don't suppose what they're packing is also wifi enabled."

She starts to say something, probably tell me that's not what it's really called, and I know that's not what it's really called. Then she says "I didn't scan for that, but I can see them on the cameras and it mostly looks like holstered handguns. They're in suits or street clothes and filtering into the building, this isn't geared paramilitary."

"Fair enough." The paparazzi have mostly cleared away when I pull back up. "Tell milady her chariot is here."

"I already did."

I tap my fingers on the steering wheel. "Soooo..."

"Give her a minute. Nothing's wrong yet inside, she doesn't want to Cinderella, she said."

"What, is she talkin' to a literal prince who might take her away from all this?"

"I am not going to ask her that," she sighs.

I laugh. "Surprised you don't already know."

"I don't background check everybody that walks past us." She sounds a little huffy but more distracted than anything else.

"Guess it would get tiring." Still no Bristol. I'm not the only car here at least, and I don't see anybody looking our way, not from the conference center side of things or from the across the street way of things.

"Yeah. And it's mostly boring. So many people are just really boring."

"Not like us."

"Mmmm." She's real quiet back there. It's amazing to me, how just effortlessly still she can be, and for how long she can do it. I can do it, but it takes a lot of concentration. And it's exhausting, the effort of doin' nothing. Or, doing nothing in anticipation of sudden and vigorous activities, typically of the violent sort. Maybe also with some running and lifting. Climbing, stairs or fences. "Here she comes."

"Thank Christ." We were none of us raised religious, but still. I adjust my rearview so I can see that front walkway, and when I finally see Bristol, I can't hear her, but in my head I can hear the sharp clack clack that her heels're making, at that pace. She's still moving too slow for my comfort, and stops for a painful thirty seconds to talk to one of the paparazzi, her head tilted just a little, nodding, laughing. "Tell her to—"

"I already did."

Then finally, finally, she's sliding into the back seat and I'm pullin' away about the second she's got the door closed, maybe a half

tic earlier than that but who's counting. There's nothing guarantee-
ing there's gonna be gunplay inside, or that the people attending the
auction even know that there's a whole buncha guys with guns cruis-
ing the halls that I cruised last night, but there's nothing guarantee-
ing that won't go sour, and we want to be well clear of that. We're all
well familiar with brushin' up against the law, and it doesn't make it
any sweeter with repetition.

"Y'know, we spend an awful lotta time drivin' you away from situations," I say.

"In a very large way, you caused this situation," she says, smirking.

"You didn't still have to come to the auction," Bits says, still on
the floor.

"Oh but I did, it is always such a learning experience, rubbing elbows with these types."

"I'm sure," I say. I'd ask Bits if anybody noticed us or is following
us, but that's why she's still on the floor. Just gotta trust the process.
Bitsy knows what she's about. Honestly, we're lookin' pretty good
right now. "Anything you want to share with the rest of the class?"

"From the auction? I don't imagine there was anything you were
interested in, no." I glance at her in the rearview, and she does seem
to be genuinely considering. "I did receive another message from our
intermediary, just confirming our engagement this evening."

"Again?" That was just this morning that they hashed everything
out again.

"He *is* rather nervous."

"Apparently. Not really so great for him, to be in business like
this."

"I get the sense it isn't his usual."

I let that ride for a little while, counting the streetlights. "Get the
sense? I thought you two were old friends." Wait a second, Bristol
treats everybody she meets like old friends.

She does one of those light little laughs, that make you think about blowing bubbles on a summer afternoon when you were a kid and you didn't have to do much decision making. "Oh heavens no, I first spoke to him about six months ago I'd say."

"Have you been...planning this for six months."

"No, the day he asked me about it was the day I told you girls about it. My friend in Tokyo might know him better; she thought well enough of him to refer me for the job."

"Alright then." Six more streetlights. "But he knew about us?"

"Of *course* not, not specifically. He knew that I had associates."

"And so does your Tokyo associate."

"Oh yes, she does. *You* remember meeting her that once, when we were all in London? Keiko?"

"At that Oxford party." Okay, yeah, I did remember Bristol's Keiko. Doesn't pay to second guess Bristol, but she leaves a hell of a lot out more than Bits does. "Okay, so we swing by the hotel for the dog, then we rendezvous and then, what, numbered bank account? Briefcase of cashola? Cryptocurrency?" I'm not second guessing. I'm just starting to feel real weird about this. Maybe not starting. Starting to acknowledge that I feel weird about this.

"Half numbered bank account, half cash." She's checking her makeup in a little mirror she pulled out of her little purse. "And anyway, Bits already has the bank account information."

"Yup. And already disseminated the funds."

"Oh, fair enough." I guess that says a lot about who I am as a person, that I haven't noticed a big ol' deposit into my bank account. Well. My business bank account.

"I don't imagine he'll be so gauche as to put it in a briefcase."

"No of course not," I say, thinking of the briefcases of diamonds we once emptied. "Nobody ever does anything like that."

Chapter Ten

There's still a ton of people milling in and out of the Venetian for the shopping experience, so it isn't super late. I park as close to an entrance as I can manage and saunter in, leaving Bits and Bristol to hash out who's gonna sit in the front and who's gonna sit with the dog. I've got my guesses about how that arrangement'll shake out, but I'll just have to wait and see. I make it up to the room and get the bathroom door open before Bits is in my earpiece. The dog actually seems kind of happy to see me, she isn't lifting her lip or anything. Lookin' at me sideways with all the whites of her eyes showing. I crouch down and she comes to me, slowly, and when I hold my hand out she sniffs it and then bumps it with her nose.

"The contact just called in a panic, we gotta go."

"Without the dog, I assume?"

"Yeah, leave her for now."

"Roger that." I give her a quick pat and say "Sorry, pup, I'll try to be right back," and I'm out the door again, making sure the do not disturbs are still up. They are, and there's another tag hung so that we can indicate when we do want service. I'll let Bristol handle that when we get back. "Bristol is this guy always so flighty?"

"No, actually, this has been an exceedingly odd situation."

"In the six months that you've known him."

"Yes, in the six months that I've known him," she snaps. "Please don't *harp*, it isn't as though it will help a single thing."

"Sorry." Not sorry but. Sometimes you gotta pay lipservice to peacekeeping, not technically a lie. I get outside and get back in the car. "Okay where to?"

"I put his location in the car's GPS," Bits says. She's still in the back seat, headset around her neck, and Bristol is up front, so I would've won money on that bet.

"You know, this might be the first time we're ever like. To the rescue."

"I think it is."

"Oh please don't call it that, darlings." I cut my eyes to Bristol, and while she isn't exactly wringing her hands, she's tense.

"If there's something else goin' on here, now might be a good time to fill us in," I say.

"I told you the entire story, cross my heart. My contact was paid to reach out to us to get the dog for his employers. Beyond the price these dogs go for, I don't know what makes the one we've dognapped special, and I *certainly* didn't know that other parties were interested as well."

"I feel like we gotta start making a mental note that other parties're gonna be interested. Just add it to the mission checklist."

"Yes that's all well and good but—"

"Bristol, cool it. We'll get your guy, he'll get the dog, we go our separate ways. Everything's copacetic. We don't need to know what's up with the dog, that's not what we're getting paid for."

"Looks like we'll be there in five," Bits says.

"Oh good," Bristol says, shifting in her seat, resting her hand lightly on the door handle. She's ready to roll out, which is great. Whatever you might think about Bristol at first or even second glance, there's always more to her. I haven't seen her actually have to hit somebody more than a couple of times, but she's definitely got a crafted capability. I wonder if she learned that in her little online classes too. Old videos. Some kind of combat yoga spa retreat.

I look at the GPS in the dashboard, at our little blip getting closer and closer to his little blip, and I've got the feeling that we won't be in time for...whatever this is. I still try, within reason, even pushing reason, trusting Bitsy to have an eye on things like radar and police and all that. It's late enough that there is and isn't traffic, are and aren't pedestrians, and I make the final turn sharply enough that all of the tires are gently singing, like if you run a wet finger along a glass rim. I hear Bits' teeth clack together when I stop and we all slam out of the vehicle and I've gotta hand it to Bristol, she actually can haul ass in high heels. It's a public garden or a park or something, and we go through a stone arch, and then up a whole bunch of stairs, and then we see him on a walkway, leaning on a railing, looking out across the little lake there. Reservoir, inlet, whatever.

And at first I think I was wrong. Just 'cause I go with my gut a whole lot doesn't mean I like being right about bad stuff. There aren't any lights up here, just some globe lamps in the park below, and the glow from the city. It isn't ideal but I let Bristol get to him first, he's her contact and he's already spooked, right? She gets to him and he doesn't react and I'm right behind her and she touches his shoulder and he's not leaning on the railing he's draped on the railing and starts to go over but I shove past her and grab a handful of his wet suitcoat and haul him back. He kathumps on the pavement the way no conscious person can and I was still holdin' out for unconscious but then I look at my hand and of course it's blood.

Bristol puts her hand to her mouth like she's shocked, just shocked, and maybe she is. It's just so quiet, even with the city all around us. Not even birds. Bits gets in there, though, kneels down and pulls his phone out of his inside coat pocket, blinks at it. "Can you turn him over? He's got something else, I think in a pants pocket." I oblige, and she pulls out a flat data pack or maybe another phone, it's not a gun so my expertise is limited. She pulls his wallet too.

Bristol walks past a few steps, as though maybe whoever did this is at the other end of the walkway just waiting and watching, but I can't see anybody, and if Bits picked up any electronics over there, she'd've already let us know. The internet of things makes it real hard to be sneaky sometimes. But if I was gonna shoot somebody here, I'd have my team spook them so they'd come out on this bridge and I'd drop 'em without them feeling a thing. Oh shit. Oh we are so fucking stupid.

"We need to get outta here," I say, but there's no time, all the hairs on the back of my neck standing up a split second before I tackle Bristol over the railing, hearing the rifle crack once, then again, feel the wind of a round right by my face and the white-hot sear of one creasing the side of my neck, but by the third crack we've plunged into the water.

I don't know if Bristol can swim. I assume she can. For me, growin' up, there were all kinds of lakes and things by us. And we had that stereotypical Southern Gothic swimming hole that all the kids went to. Rope swing, ancient tree, kids driving out there to neck, the whole nine. Shallow by the shore, with weeds and stuff that people would pull up periodically so you can wade in without gettin' all wrapped up, but it got real deep in the middle. No idea how deep, I'm sure there's records somewhere, but not that we had access to. But once, I jumped off the rope swing with a belt that I tied a buncha crap to, so I'd get to the bottom right quick. Just wanted to prove I could do it.

Grabbed a handful of silt and rocks there with my left hand, while I undid the belt with my right hand. Pretty much blacked out on the way back up. My oldest brother pulled me out, cursing a blue streak, and the last thing I remember before actually blacking out is looking up at our friend Butler and shoving my balled up fist of silt and rocks and stuff at him until he held his hands out. Then I opened my hand and let go. And then I let go. Might be the first time I ever blacked out, actually. Somethin' to put in the baby book. There was a super old coin in that wad of stuff, and he had it made into a belt buckle that I wore until I lost it, and there was a cowboy spur, and I had that made into a belt buckle he wears. I assume he still wears. I'm not sayin' he's carrying a torch but...

Anyway we don't hit bottom, and I keep a hand on Bristol as I swim off for where I think the right shore is, and where I hope cover is. I don't think my neck's too bad, just a graze, more on the meat than near anything vital. Stings like a bitch. I don't hear any more gunfire, and I have to trust that Bits'll keep her head down and get back to the car without getting aerated. Bristol seems to be doing okay, swimming, not dead weight that I'm dragging. I don't think she's hit, I didn't feel her shudder on our way down. You don't forget what that shudder's like. I'm not gonna forget what that shudder's like, not for all of my days. I hope Bits isn't hit. I gotta think about what the plan is, if one or both of 'em did get shot.

That first breath when I break the surface both burns and is sweet relief, and Bristol's trying not to sputter and cough but really needs to sputter and cough and I haul her up onto the shore where there's some bushes and stuff, and between that and the angle, that shooter shouldn't have a shot anymore. That shooter should've cleared out already, just discharging an unsuppressed rifle in a city like that at least three times. There's some distant sirens but honestly, when aren't there?

She finally gives in to the coughing, her face buried in her arms, and we lay there for awhile and catch our breath. She lost her shoes but not her purse, so I guess it's a good thing she didn't wear the fancy schmancy ones. "Bits?" I finally say, when things seem quiet.

"I'm at the car, I'm going to do a lap and then come back for you."

"Understood." I think we've got tree cover all the way back to the parking lot. We should probably even go further, up the road a little, before Bits stops. In case whoever that was is also doing a lap and coming back for us. "You okay?" I ask Bristol. Our earbuds and stuff, it all can work subvocally, if we bother to take that care. Right now, I'm botherin' to take that care.

"Yes," she says after a moment. Somebody could be standing a foot away and not hear us, other than our creep-on-the-phone breathing. "How did you—"

"Sometimes you just know," I say. Because while I can't explain my timing, I definitely understood the setup. There's honestly no good reason we aren't both dead or bleeding, unless the gunman was about done packin' it in when we arrived and had to set up again. But that's a weird decision to make. The world may never know. I got a bandanna in my pocket and hold it against my neck and I can see the flash of Bristol's eyes as she looks at me. Of course I'd get just a little bit shot where none of the gear covers.

We lay there awhile longer and then Bits says "Everything is clear, unless they've just gone dark."

"I guess we gotta take that chance," I say. Can't say why, but I'd lay money that they're gone, not hanging around waiting, not circling back go look for us. I'm laying our lives on it, I guess, and that's worth more than money. I squeeze out my bandana, figuring it's mostly the lake water, then twirl it and tie it around my neck. Not quite a right fit, but kinda on the right spot. "You ready Bristles?"

"I suppose," she says with a little sigh, pulling that carelessness around her like a shawl.

"Okay, I'll meet you just up the road from the parking lot," Bits says, and we sneak through the park until we get to path again. Wait. Look around. Then we keep going, cutting over where we probably shouldn't be walking until we get to the street, right as Bits pulls over onto the shoulder.

"Everything still clear?" I ask. Until today we've just sat around for awhile, but also the thought of breakin' down all my equipment and getting it dried out right when we get back to the hotel is exhausting. I'll ride it out, though, can't let stuff sit like that.

Bits shrugs. "Seems to be. None of the police even came through here."

"Makes sense."

"Does it?" Bristol asks from the back seat. She's leaned over, rolling off her stockings. I forget that she wears 'em, but she's also said they're protective in some way. Guess they must be, if they didn't shred right off her feet on our walk through the park.

"I'm not sure any of it does, but close enough."

"Do you want me to look at that?" She leans forward, but doesn't touch me.

"Nah, it's probably fine."

"Look at what?" Bits looks at me, then her eyes get big. "Dolly!"

"I'm okay, Jesus, look at the road won't you? Gotten worse than this slamming my hand in a door."

Chapter Eleven

We park at the hotel and Bits does something to extend the rental and we walk through the quiet lobby to the elevator. I'm sure that overnight guy has seen a lot wilder than whatever picture we make. He just kind of fades back away from the desk to the offices they've got, and I think he's been the same guy every time, gotta remember to leave him a good tip. We get into the elevator and somehow, other than not having shoes, Bristol looks...fine? She's got some kinda personal grooming magic, I tell you what. I very definitely look like I jumped in a reservoir with all my clothes on and then tramped through the woods and maybe bled a little. I think it's stopped already, the papercut of bullet wounds I guess. Bits looks like Bits. Normally I don't concern myself with the way we as a group appear to others, I'm not sure it's the best time to start.

When we're in the elevator, I can't help but ask "So there wasn't anything else about the dog that you knew of? Data in the microchip? Did she swallow diamonds or something that somebody's gonna want?"

"No, nothing," Bristol says. "She's just a dog that's important to them, I don't know why. We may never know."

"I'm hoping that there's something worth it in his phone, or on this," Bits says. I realize that the other thing she got out of the guy's pocket was a hard drive or something. But a hard drive on its own doesn't throw a signal, even I know that. "And I macgyvered something to scan the dog's microchip, I just thought we'd be done by now."

"Oh good," Bristol sighs, and fishes in her soggy purse for her keycard. The lock beeps and when she pushes the door open, the dog barks. She sounds a little closer than Bits and my bathroom, though, and I swipe our keycard and go into our suite in a hurry. I remember opening our bathroom door, petting the dog, getting the call, leaving. Not closing the door.

"C'mere girl!" I say from our suite which looks pretty okay. A torn-up fast food bag on the ground, whatever, the garbage can doesn't have a lid on it. Oh and there's some couch fluff, that's a little less okay. Oh and the pillows have feathers in them, should've expected that I guess. Well. Had feathers.

"Dolly could you come in here, please?" Bristol calls through our open dividing door, tone strained almost to the pitch that only the dog could hear. Again.

"Sure thing." I look around, grab the dog's leash from the counter where I left it. The door to the hall is closed, Bits must be with Bristol. Or she went back out to the car and just drove away. I wouldn't blame her.

The pillows didn't survive in Bristol's room either. Or the comforter or duvet or whatever the fuck it is. The dog is in the little sunken living room thing, in the corner near the sliding glass door, and she'd got enough hair standing up that she looks maned, like a lion. Her ears are pinned and she's growling deep in her chest. Bristol's standing closer to her than I would've expected, holding something I can't really see. I come a little closer, note Bits by the mini bar.

There's red stuff on the floor, and around the dog's mouth, which is hard to see with all the fur. "Hold up, is that blood? Did she bite you? Did she hurt herself?"

"It isn't blood, it's….it's a LeBoutin."

Ohhh the shoes. "That sounds expensive."

"Because it *is*," Bristol says, a real snap to her voice.

"Look maybe come away from there, she's scared. The shoes're toast, I'm sorry, that's on me. I didn't close her in the bathroom again when you called me."

"Scared? She's ready to tear my leg off."

"Because you look like you want to hurt her, come on. We took her from anybody she knew, then left her alone in an unfamiliar place. She's a dog, not a person, it's not like she knows what being a guest is."

Bristol does back away from the dog, and turns towards me. I may never have seen her so angry, red spots burning high on her cheeks. I guess I understand now why people use blush. "Just because you've spent so much time with that *robot* doesn't mean you know anything about real dogs."

I don't know why that stings so much, why it matters, but I guess we're all just bundles of nerves right now. To my credit, I don't step any closer to her, but my hands go into fists just on their own. I've hit people for far less. "Look. I get that those shoes were special for you. I get that a guy you kinda knew died, and that's a terrible thing. And I know not a whole lot of people say this to you, Bristol, but please. Shut the fuck up."

Bits makes a noise like choking and maybe she's laughing. Maybe it is funny, and I'll laugh about it later. Maybe Bristol too. Right now, though, she looks shocked. "Dolly, I think it would be best if—"

"Yeah, I'm gonna go next door and cool down. Come on, pup." I whistle like I trained her, and the dog comes right to me, her steps slinking as she passes Bristol, getting more normal when she gets to my side. I go back between the doors and close them. I don't mean to separate Bits, she can do whatever. But Bristol and I need that separation. It isn't the first spat we've had, it'll be fine. But boy howdy does it not feel fine.

The thing about having a dog around you when you're pissed, is you try to feel un-pissed real quick. You don't want the dog to think they're the reason you're mad. They just don't get it. This dog isn't cringing, she's got a very 'yeah what?' attitude, but still. She came to me, that's something. I guess a thing to do first is get out my first aid kit, disinfect what I've got going. It looks awful in the mirror, immediately much better once I get the blood and leaves and lake gunk cleaned off me. Not even a thing worth trying to stitch, it looks more like a hot iron got laid against my skin for a sec. I kinda shake out the gun and leave it on the bathroom counter for now.

After awhile, Bits comes in, using the hallway door. The dog is following me around as I pick up garbage and put it in one of the pillowcases that's also fucked. I've been party to cleanup from military-type parties that got out of hand, one kinda busy dog doesn't really compare. No, not even comparing where she shit on the floor. Things just get outta hand sometimes.

"Are you okay?" she asks after watching me for a little while

"Yeah." What a weird question, and then I realize she probably means the injury, not my feelings. "Yeah, it's fine."

"We aren't normally like this," she says.

"I'd guess having a team mascot is right out," I say.

"At least the kind that eats shoes." She pops the tab on an energy drink.

"Am I wrong, that we can just get her another pair?"

"Nope. I even just reserved them at the store here. She doesn't know that yet."

"Then what's the problem?" I look at the room, twirling the pillowcase shut so I can knot it. Looking good, I think. Bits shrugs, her eyes in that slightly off to the side way. She's still enough that the dog eventually goes and sniffs around her, then gets on one of the couches, lying down but kinda stiffly, with her head up.

"I don't really know," Bits eventually says. "I couldn't find anything we should be worried about, like anybody from an agency coming for us. Social media of her friends back in Dubai seems fine, and nobody's blocked or unfriended or anything. She's texting a normal sort of amount, I think, and doesn't have any meetings set up or anything that was canceled."

I stare at her and then just laugh. "*Elizabits*! What were we just talking about?"

"I only do it when somebody's acting weird." She blinks and looks at me with kind of a frown. "And anyway, the guy that died tonight, she really did only meet him like six months ago. And they weren't dating or anything, that's not the kind of upset she is."

"Well, we do what we can to not leave a body count, maybe it's just that." Bristol's as stone cold as any of us, but in different ways. It's possible. Though also, I'm real curious about Bits's metric for whether somebody's bein' weird or not. She must have a program that runs, and compares our actions against our new habits. That's how I'd decide it, if I was like. Surveilling somebody.

"I'm not sure yet who he was working for and who was going to pay us, but I'm getting there. And then later, or maybe tomorrow, I'll see about her microchip. There was a number listed in the auction catalog. Have you looked at her collar and tags, do they seem normal?"

"I have not investigated that, no." The dog is looking between the two of us as we talk, not moving her head really, just sort of raising one eyebrow and then the other. Well, what would be eyebrows on a person. Is it eyebrows on a dog?

"Tomorrow," Bits says. "You look tired and I've got these other leads to chase."

"Bitsy are you sendin' me to bed?"

"Maybe." She smiles a little.

"Well I'm gonna hit the showers first, anyway. I guess holler if you need me." The dog watches me go, but doesn't follow me, and I take a shower that's first as hot as I can stand, and use all the smelly things the hotel provides, just to say I did, and then as cold as I can stand, just to round things out. I remember Bristol sayin' once that cold water closes the follicles of your hair or something and reduces frizz, I dunno. I don't really care about frizz so much, other than that static isn't good for the weirdly sensitive electronics that equipment sometimes has. Frizz has been a losing battle my whole life, so I gave up caring. Plus the cold feels good on my neck.

There's something botherin' me, I've got that tip-of-the-tongue feeling like when you're trying to think of a word, except it's my brain both trying to ask and answer a question that I'm not really informed on. Maybe it's just that I'm tired; we've gone awhile without this kind of action, which is a good thing, but you can't let things like that go too long if you wanna stay sharp.

Bits is reclined and in VR land when I come out of the bathroom, and the dog is lying on the floor between the beds. When I lie down, I pat the bed for her to get up, and after a couple minutes, she does. She killed a couple of the pillows when we were gone, but good news, there's about a hundred of them, so it's not really a big deal.

Chapter Twelve

I wake up knowing exactly what's wrong, but no idea how to fix it. I roll over and Bits is still sleeping or still in VR, who can tell, but I lean way over to the other bed and shove the mattress a few times, until the frame creaks, hissing between my teeth at the stretch and pull of my new scab. "Bits, we fucked up."

"What?" She jerks bolt upright, pawing the goggles off her face. The dog raises her head and watches her. "What's wrong?"

"I know what's wrong with Bristol."

"Christ, Dolly, you scared me." She blinks at me, looks around the room, looks at the dog and then at me again. "Okay what."

"That time she spent with Homeland last year."

Bits blinks at me, slower this time. "Oh."

"Yeah. Yup." Bristol's all about maintaining outward appearances, but Jesus, we shouldn't've expected her to be okay after that. Or not so okay, so quickly. Maybe she's putting that expectation on herself too, I'd guess she probably is, but also I think I've got it exactly nailed, the weirdness, the tension.

"Okay but what do we...do?"

"Well I don't know. Clearly a puppy was not the right answer." I grin and she laughs, and I stretch and get up. "I also feel kinda awkward just like. Sittin' her down for an intervention."

"I think it would be an encounter session, in this instance."

"Whatever. Touchy-feely talking meeting." I give a big fake shudder to make her laugh again but I'm not really lying, I don't wanna

307

have a feelings conversation with Bristol. I don't wanna have a feelings talk with anybody. But I don't expect her to be a robot either, we just should've realized that this was too big, too soon. She's the one who got antsy. She also hasn't done anything wrong; none of this is her fault. "Lord knows she won't want to have that with us."

"True."

"Have you made any progress?"

"Well I think the reason this dog is so valuable is that she's from the old lines or types that were somehow saved when China ordered all these dogs killed a long long time ago, which means she's still a valuable outcross for the newer lines. And I think somebody stole her."

I laugh, loud enough that I'm surprised I don't hear Bristol reacting disapprovingly next door. It's not that kind of hotel, though. "Yeah, Bits, *we* stole her."

"No, no, I mean. Stole her in the first place to auction her."

"Oh! Huh." Does it make more sense now, that Bristol's guy got shot? Was Bristol's guy working for the original owners? "That doesn't exactly clear anything up."

"It doesn't."

"Did you tell Bristol?"

"Yeah, I texted her. She says she's going to do her morning routine and then she'll open the between door."

"Makes sense." A morning routine. She doesn't mean like, pushups or walkouts or anything like I do. We've spent enough time traveling together to know each other's routines. Bits blinks at me, and her eyes look like her eyes but I know she did the cornea implants things so that she doesn't have to mess with contacts anymore, and I can't help but always look for them to catch the light weird or something. I knew people who got 'em early, that looked like that, but tech sometimes progresses in months, not even years anymore. Even with stuff like this. Especially if you're willing to go to a country with different regulations than maybe the U.S. has. No comment on where my arm came from.

I drink one of the beers from the mini bar then remember it's morning and make a pot of coffee. The dog starts wandering around, sniffing corners and whining. "I need to get her outside, this ain't a good way to keep her."

"She's *so* recognizable, Dolly, I don't—"

"Yeah I know but you can't make a dog live like this. When it was like twelve hours, that was one thing. Just gonna go out to the grass in the parking lot and back again, it'll be fine. What're the chances anybody looking for her thinks she's still here? And what're the chances they'd cruise past here what, for some gamblin' or luxury shopping?"

Bits sighs. "Okay."

I pick up the leash and the dog comes over eagerly. "Will you keep an eye out?"

"Of course. I'm not a panopticon though, I can't catch everybody who sees you."

"Yeah I know."

"Okay."

"Okay." We blink at each other, then I leash up the dog, poke my head out into the hallway to look both ways, and we skulk to the back staircase. So far so good.

I light a cigarette and wander around a little with the dog. Not very far, and on high alert, but it turns out okay. Bits doesn't say anything, nobody seems to particularly notice, and when she finishes up, we go back inside again, same way. I don't want to say it's a letdown, it's not like I'm jonesing for action. It's maybe also a little weird that this dog is so good with me, but I guess those hot dogs really did make us friends, who's to say.

I also feel like I need to start callin' her something. A real dog is a real dog and needs a name, unlike the robot dog, and I consider as we get down the hall and back to the suites. Ours is empty, and I go through the between doors to Bristol's. She cleaned up, and I feel kinda bad that she did it on her own, but I guess maybe Bits helped her last night. I didn't ask. There's also a room service trolly, with a pitcher of orange juice, no, I'll bet it's a pitcher of mimosas. "How we doing?"

"Better today, thank you" Bristol says.

"Look, Bristol, I'm sorry," I say, and she sips her mimosa and raises her eyebrows. "Bits and I have replacement shoes waitin' for you."

"You do know how to be very sweet, Dolly," she says, and there's the proper Bristol shell again. "I've been able to move on from that *mishap*," she quirks her lips a little and glances at the dog "to consider what steps we ought to take next."

"Oh that's good." I take a drink of mimosa; it's funny how something like beer isn't an okay breakfast beverage, but mimosas are. I've seen people go off their asses on mimosas without really trying. Only since meetin' Bristol, of course, champagne was thin on the ground back home, other than what people scavenged from wine caves sometimes. "What're you thinking?"

"Well probably simplest is we could unsteal the dog. Sneak it back into the facility and then it's just out of our hands." Bits and I exchange a look, and Bristol sighs. "I didn't say I prefer that option, only that it *is* one."

"Bitsy did you tell her what you thought?" Bits nods.

"She did, and that brings me to the next option. We go through my contact's electronics, locate his employer, and deliver the dog to them. They're the actual ones who hired us, after all. Surely they'll still wish to honor the deal."

"Surely." I look at Bits again, who shrugs.

"Well, I've already been working on that. First off, he didn't have any money on him, which is kind of interesting."

"Not even a crypto wallet?"

"Nope." Bristol seems visibly surprised. Bits gets a real paper map out of one of her pockets, and unfolds it. Oh, it's an AR enabled map, that's better; it means she can zoom it around and put down markers and stuff. "Okay, so from his phone we know where he was in Macau for the last few days. Before then he was in Da Nang, which is where he bought the phone, or at least where he started using it."

I finish my mimosa. They're always in smallish glasses, maybe that's why it's so easy to get blasted on them. I investigate the covered things on the breakfast cart and grab a plate of steak and eggs. The dog is now *very* interested in me. "So what, we get on a plane to Vietnam?"

"We haven't the papers to fly with the dog," Bristol says.

"We don't have the papers to travel with the dog at all," Bits points out. "That bag Dolly grabbed has the vaccine records, which might be good enough. But if we get stopped on the road someplace in China, we're gonna have a problem, because of the auction."

"Look, I like road trips, but a road trip from Macau to Vietnam seems a little much."

"It'd be shorter than Macau to Tibet," Bits says, reasonably.

"Well yeah but—"

"I *do* have the growing sense that we ought to leave Macau very soon," Bristol says, with that deliberate idleness that means it's a pressin' thought that she maybe shoulda mentioned immediately, but also we do tend to blow town once we get shot at. "We could just...borrow a boat and go across to Hong Kong."

"I don't disagree. Actually, since Hong Kong's self-governing, we'll at least have some breathing room to plan." Hong Kong is the emergency exit strategy I had in mind, actually. Barring Disney sovereignty. Besides, any one of us might know somebody in Hong Kong that can help us out. And even if we don't *personally* know anybody, we can always friend of a friend it.

"You do know how to drive a boat, don't you?" Bristol asks.

"Well yeah, I can pilot a boat." We try anything else, we run into the same papers problem, even on the official ferry I'm sure.

"Oh or a helicopter!" She's got that sparkle in her eyes now, oh boy.

"I like the boat option better," I say, as calm and dry as I can. "Haven't been shot out of the sky yet, and I'd like to keep that record shiny." Granted a helicopter to Hong Kong is an even shorter trip than by boat but. Like I said.

"Seconded," Bits says.

"Okay, so we're all in agreement, we're going to pack and get a boat?" Bristol asks.

"Yeah, we'll pack and get a boat," I say. Bits nods. "And we'll see who we know in Hong Kong to get us elsewhere."

"I'm sure that will be the simplest thing," Bristol says airily, and as a thought exercise, I really would love to have everybody's mental image of 'a boat' laid out in little AR popups to see what we each expect we're dealing with. Just to compare notes, you understand. Just like everybody's mental image of 'car' is gonna be different, or 'dog,' or 'apple.'

"Bitsy, what'd you find out about the guy's boss?"

"Well I didn't really find a boss, per se. I'm still combing through the data. Well, I wrote a program to comb through the data. I'm figuring out who to contact, and where they are."

"But we're certain they'll want the dog, so we might as well get to the right country," Bristol says, smiling.

"We don't really know that Vietnam's the right country," I say.

"However, we *do* know that we've finished our time in Macau."

"We sure do." I look at Bits, who's looking out the window. I look too, thinking wouldn't it just be fucking dandy if a helicopter hovered into view just outside, ready to open fire, but that doesn't happen. This time. Maybe I'll just call the dog Honey, the way she's all gold. We need to figure out how to travel with her, though. She's pretty recognizable. And then I think of all the appliances and shit that both the bathrooms have. Hair dryers. Curling irons. Clippers. I mosey over to my room to look, despite the private joy of imagining the look on Bristol's face if I shaved a dog in her hotel room.

Chapter Thirteen

Of course, it's one thing to decide to shave a dog, and another thing to shave a dog. She doesn't want to bite me, or us, and that's a lucky thing because I'm not really into being shredded open by an angry dog. Or being shredded open in general. It's kinda sometimes one of those occupational hazard things, the kind of thing you consider maybe reconsidering when you're in the bathtub in a swanky hotel suite with a dog who's as big as a person and who doesn't want any part of what you're doing. Yeah I made this choice.

Also, the clippers are the smart kind that don't cut skin, so that's another upside. And they have a dog setting. It's probably fuckin' sacriledge, to shave a dog like this down even a little, but it'd make her less recognizable. It's probably not great for a dog like this, to have her hair shaved very much.

I think I had the idea that being in the bathtub would keep the mess minimized but instead it made the clippers louder and was slick so made Honey nervous and so we get out of the tub pretty quick. Once I just let her stand on the bathmat, she minds the clippers less, and really, who knew that being a dog groomer was such a specialized thing? I guess they use tables, they have the dogs stand on tables. But she doesn't look too mangled when I'm done. We're all used to quarantine haircuts by now. She also doesn't really look like the same dog, which was the whole point. She's also got a tattoo in one ear, which I never would've found otherwise, and I take a picture of that for Bitsy's files. And while we're still corralled in the bathroom, she comes in with the microchip scanner she kitbashed together from all her collected scraps, and we scan the regular place and then some ir-regular places lookin' for a chip, but don't turn one up. Which is in-teresting, because the auction catalog listed a chipped dog. Chips fail sometimes, sure, but I think all our guts're telling us this is something else.

"Dolly, I never would have expected you to be crafty like that!" Bristol exclaims while I'm doing the paracord, while Honey chews some apology jerky and Bits is, I assume, crunching on that dog tat-too data we got.

"It ain't exactly knitting," I say, because doing stuff with paracord is pretty utilitarian but also, we don't know everything about each other. Sometimes it's more obvious than others. Sometimes it mat-ters more than others.

"No, but you could probably, I don't know, do hair."

"I don't think you want me doin' your hair like this, Bristles."

"Well no, but..." she trails off, but she's smiling like she's learned a secret. And it's nice to see her have that kind of sly smile again, hon-estly. Bristol's attractive in any number of ways, but it's not for noth-ing that I never mix business and that type of pleasure. Besides not being her type. I've seen her devastate men across the globe.

"Anyway, we all packed? Anything else we need?"

"I think we're good," Bits says.

"You got us a boat picked out, Bitsy? Any last minute data finds that'll make us change our mind?"

"I have a few boats in mind." She pauses, I guess to scan through some stuff. "And no. It seems like we're maybe on the right track."

"Well okay let's hit it."

I'm actually impressed with how little luggage Bristol has, but I guess with her veteran traveler status plus the kinda money we got floating around, she doesn't actually need to carry much. And a lot of her dresses like, vacuum pack down into eggs or something. I dunno. I always just roll a few pairs of jeans and tank tops and stuff into a duffle and call it good. Riot gear's most useful when it's on you, anyway, no sense having to worry about packing it.

This isn't to say Bristol doesn't have more luggage than the rest of us, but we don't need to hitch a cart to the dog to get it to the marina. And she carries it herself. I wonder, sometimes, how she got and stays so fit, without ever letting somebody see her break a sweat. She doesn't run. She doesn't go to a martial arts dojo or anything. Could she have just watched enough krav maga videos or something and learned it that way? There's other ways to hands-off learn something like that, my time in the not-quite-legit area of the military taught me that, but is any of it something Bristol would do? I actually think it's real important to not let yourself get too comfortable in what you assume people are willing to do. Limiting your estimations can be hazardous to your health.

And yeah, I kinda think Bristol would do a lot of things. Whether I've seen her do them or not. She got this way on her own sheer determination. And now that I've finally realized what that brittle edge she's had is all about, I'm just trying to keep an eye out, without being too obvious about it. Which probably means she knew about thirty seconds into this morning.

The dog's happily perched near the front of the boat like a figurehead, barking at the chop and wagging her tail, and I look at Bits, and she's already got her VR goggles on, making sure we aren't being APBed and targeted by militaries and flagged for bounty the second we're in international waters or something. Not like we can do a whole hell of a lot, depending on who comes after us. I feel pretty bad about not being able to put that handgun back where I got it, but I'll treat it good so long as I have it, and hopefully it won't be at the bottom of the ocean before all this is through.

"Bristol, you gonna be okay?" I finally ask. Then fumble for a reason I'm asking. "You normally get seasick?"

"I'm sure I'll be fine," she says, smoothing her skirt. Because of course she's dressed as though she's yachting and not as though we almost got shot last night. Over a dog. I nod and I wait. "No, I don't normally get seasick, and you know it."

"Check the cooler, see if there's ginger ale."

"Dolly, you don't need to baby me."

"I just know that you really enjoy feelin' like you're in the lap of luxury," I drawl. "And we ain't got the room for staff so..." She laughs, finally.

"Yes, I hadn't gotten around to hiring a personal assistant yet. They always require such *hand holding* and I just can't abide it." We've got the smile again, and I think I've distracted her enough. Which makes me wonder, is she acting like this on purpose to distract *me* from something, but if that's the case, that isn't a game I'm gonna win so I might as well just quit or play along. And we're in the middle of the...what body of water is this. The South China Sea, and there ain't a lot of quitting options. Not unless some pirates swing by and I join up or something. We probably should've thought about the whole possibility of pirates. I don't think they tend to have rocket launchers out here, though, that's more of an Indian Ocean thing.

The dog gets bored with the waves eventually and makes her way over to Bits, who pretty much hasn't moved since we've come aboard, and curls up at her feet. I play some music in my earbuds, then I wonder if we can get any kind of radio signal out here and scan for that too. Mostly static, a couple blips from maybe submarines or other boats or something. It's hard to know, what it'll grab sometimes. Not like I listen to numbers stations as a hobby, the way some people do, but the fact that it's viable is truly a thing of beauty.

Actually, now that I'm thinking about it, submarines could be a thing we should worry about. Not 'cause of the dog people, but because of who we crossed during the business with the diamonds. Shit, wouldn't that be something, thinking we're home free to cash in on this reverse dognapping and then a sub surfaces with that Will guy coming out of the hatch.

We used to do that a lot, me and my...well if we were real sanctioned military we'd be called a unit. Me and the guys. The ones who were part of the black site, "what if we put these various cybernetics in people with a certain type of training?" and the "what if we gave people this kind of training?" and "what about these injections?" and "what about this muscle density without increasing any apparent mass?" Those guys. We'd be bored somewhere, doing exercises, because all we ever really ended up doing was training exercises, canned deployment exercises, for the people with clipboards and the brass whose faces we never saw. We'd be bored, and we'd come up with worst case scenarios in as much exquisite detail as we could muster, and we'd then turn to somebody and say like "Hey Cash, wouldn't it be something if..." or "Hey Trigger, do you think somebody ever..." and lay whatever it was out. And everybody'd be like "nah" or they'd join in. Good times.

So we're all within earshot of each other but I gotta pick one and Bitsy looks busy even if maybe she isn't so I say "Hey Bristol, wouldn't it be something if..." and she suddenly looks up and off to the side, and then shades her eyes even though she's wearing sunglasses, and she says

"Ladies, do we think that's going to be a problem?" in a deliberately casual tone and I wonder if I've conjured a submarine into existence by my habit of whistling past the graveyard. If that's what whistling past the graveyard even means. Does anybody know what that means? And anyway, it's hard to be anywhere that's never been a graveyard. There's probably sunken ships under us right now, even if there isn't a sub. What Bristol's pointing at isn't a sub.

I can't help it, and laugh. "We got problems with that, it's 'cause whoever's at the helm ends up blind," I say. Bristol looks a little hurt, and I realize my eyes're better than hers. I forget about that, despite everything else. The eye thing is more subtle; not all AR and stuff like Bits's, just...better. "Sorry, sorry. It's a cargo ship."

"You could have said so," she says, a little primly.

"Hey I said I'm sorry."

"You two will argue about anything," Bits says, blinking at us.

"Yeah, prob'ly." Actually, a cargo container ship would be a great way to do a whole lotta things. How many helicopters could take off and land on a cargo container ship, even if it appeared totally packed to the gills from our remove. "So, not right now, but do you think—"

"Please no," Bits says.

"You didn't even listen to what I was gonna say!"

She looks from me, to the ship, and back again. "Do I need to?"

"I guess not." I grin, and Bristol laughs softly.

Chapter Fourteen

We spend the day at sea, snacking on Bristol's canned caviar and some kind of cheese spread and a whole lot of crackers and yeah, some beers. The crossing from Macau doesn't really take that long, but when you're tryin' to be *clandestine*, sometimes it means screwing around for awhile to run out the clock. We find a quiet place to dock when it's just around sunset. I've actually never been up and about Hong Kong in the daytime; what an experience that'd be. Maybe someday. Bits does something that sends the boat away again, I guess maybe it can get itself back to Macau, or close enough, and make it so we really didn't put the owner out much. I dunno. Some people own a whole bunch of boats and never even use them much. They probably wouldn't've even noticed, until time came to pay rent on the slip and it was empty, and then they would've filed insurance, and that would've been that. Practically a victimless crime.

"Bitsy, see about an Airbnb or whatever for tonight. No hotel, I don't think." I rub my shoulder next to my neck; scab's itchy and I shouldn't scratch it.

"Only tonight?" Bristol asks. She's real careful, there's only a little bit of disappointment, or disapproval, in her voice. The shopping, the night life, the fish pedicures. Probably something else, but we gotta keep this moving. At least she had time to pick up the replacement shoes before we went to sea.

"We're still too close, and anyway, it's pretty possible that whoever took shots at us came here too. I'm just looking for our out."

"I'll look for a place near Disney," Bits says. "Less chance of snipers."

"Good call, House of Mouse has its own mercenaries."

"They do *not*." Now Bristol's a mix of scandalized and delighted.

"They do. I interviewed once but ultimately figured it wasn't for me."

"You did not," she says. I grin at her.

"I absolutely, one hundred percent did. But now you'll always have that doubt and it'll drive you nuts." It's true, I did. The Florida park did a combination of like, sea walls and moats that protected it when the water came up. And they've got a bunch of underwater rides now. They didn't call me back after the interview.

"You are extremely wicked and I have no idea why we are associates," she huffs, but she's still smiling.

"We show off each other's best qualities." Honey has been standing with me patiently through all this, looking up at us as we talk and panting a little. It is hot here, hotter than it was on the open ocean. Sea. Open water. Did shaving her down a little help with that? Or was the fur protective? How hot does it get in Tibet, anyway? I could look it up but really, I pretty much prefer to wonder, and talk it out with somebody. I know Bits goes and learns the answer to a question the second it comes across her synapses but it's nice to wonder sometimes, about some things. It's nice to not know. I wonder which Bristol does. Probably a little bit of both. See, with Bristol and me, even if we *do* look something up, it's in a totally normal search engine way. Bits can do that I'm sure, but she can also do the 'oh I found a closed door, let's see what's inside' way. And does.

"Okay, found one," Bits says.

"Good, I'll walk you over there and then see about our airlift."

Bristol arches an eyebrow like she's practiced it in the mirror. I'm sure she has. "Walk us over?"

"You wanna walk the dog? If you do, I can just..." She looks down at Honey and sighs.

"Not with *that* haircut, I don't. The poor thing."

"Aw, sorry, her usual hairdresser was otherwise occupied. I guess. Probably." I grin, and Bristol rolls her eyes elaborately. Bits hides a smile. "C'mon. I want to be able to take advantage of the night life."

Lodgings, check. They pick where to order delivery, check. And I've already got the weapons I found in Macau; the gun seems fine after our swim, and I had fresh ammo for it just in case. Pretty much as prepared as I'm gonna get, without a rolodex for criminal and criminal-adjacent pilots that I know who happened to be in Hong Kong just now who also have their own aircraft. I actually got a couple people in mind, and a couple places to look for them. I get a taxi over to one of the night markets, My Cantonese is *okay*, better than most of the guys' French ever ended up being. Better than my Japanese.

The market's crowded, but the market is always crowded. I look at the food stands and little bars and things as I pass them, try to gauge the types of people eating there. Most of them normal types, not like me. Not the kind of person I need. I'm really not expecting to see a familiar face here, so when I do, I just keep walking for a few steps, like in a comedy bit, and then I stop, ruining the flow of foot traffic. Dunno if it would've been wilder to see one of my sisters or brothers, who I haven't talked to in awhile, or if it's wild enough that it's Butler, who I was just thinking about last night.

I turn around, though, and he's coming out of the little restaurant just looking shocked, and I can't help but laugh. The other marketgoers just part around us rude people standing in the walkway lookin' at each other and I get my laugh and he gets over his shock and closes the distance between us with a couple of long strides, takes me by the shoulders and looks me in the face. "Dolly it's been forever."

"I guess it has," I say. "Feels like it, anyway." Couple years, maybe. "You could've called."

I pull back, punch him in the shoulder. "Oh don't pull that sad puppydog shit, *you* could've called."

He actually rubs the contact spot a little, and I try to remember what upgrades I had the last time we saw each other. Definitely not the new arm. Definitely most of the muscle and endocrine stuff. "Geeze, don't know your own strength." He's kind of grinning, kinda shaking his head, and I grin right back.

"Trust me, I know." I wonder if he's imagined a reunion. I wonder if he thought we'd run to each other like all those movies with people running to each other across a meadow. I'm imagining the love story Bristol thinks would be going on here, and really, all of those things aren't really very near to the truth. Maybe in another life, if we were different people.

"I'll always trust you," he said, voice a little too serious. I blink at him. Right this second isn't the right time to look and see if he's wearing that belt buckle. "But enough small talk, what's going on? What're you doing here?"

"I could ask you the same thing."

"So ask, it'd be nice to see you taking an interest. Come on, I'll buy you a beer." I follow him back to his table at the little restaurant, let him order me a beer, partake of the plates of food he's got. Bristol's at-sea picnic was awhile ago, and it's gonna be awhile yet before I get to eat whatever takeout they picked out for me.

"You're kitted out," he says after my beer comes.

"Course I am, I'm working." Granted, I'm not wearing the jacket while we're sitting here, have it hung on the back of my chair. It's hot as hell even at night. "And what about you, just being a tourist?" He isn't kitted out, just jeans and a tee shirt, same old boots. You can always recognize my crowd by our boots, I feel like. Laces that the plastic tips never stay on, but we always pick the plastic tipped ones, never the metal. That thing has a name, doesn't it?

"Kind of touring, kind of scouting. What's the job?" He drops his eyes to my neck, where I left a bandanna tied, which has never been my habit. Yes, it's a clean one.Or was when I put it on this morning.

"Mmm, well it's a long story. Know any pilots in town?"

"I might." He gives me that old appraising look, sips on his beer. "You need more hands?"

"We've pretty much got it covered." What are the outcomes, if I bring Butler into this? Helps us with the dog wrangling, Butler's always been good with dogs, though I think I've handled her pretty well. It gives Bristol fresh material to work with; she'd be just wild to meet him, actually. Even more so if she thinks we're an item, or thinks we were ever an item. Nothing that's more than just companionship.

"Who's we?"

"Nobody you know." That's the downside, he's a little too interested. And he's solid, of course, or else I wouldn't be giving him the time of day right now. Our crew worked well, with our after-army ventures. After we couldn't just go home again, 'cause what was home anymore. If the world was different, we'd be married already, have a house somewhere, normal jobs, maybe kids. Maybe that's still possible and maybe I don't care about that. Maybe normal jobs never would've been something I'm suited for. I don't really think so. But I can never tell, and don't give me any of that biological clock bullshit about the kids. God knows we can hack and adjust and replace about everything else, of course it's on the list. "But anyway, we need a plane to Da Nang and can't just get on an airline and don't want to just road trip."

"Must be serious, if *you* don't want to road trip."

"Butler, for the love of god." It's just banter and I'm not mad, but there's a time crunch here, real or imagined.

"Sorry, sorry." He's smiling in a way that says he remembers the old days, and that's bullshit too, it was five years ago tops. Six. Seven. We aren't grizzled veterans; for all our scars, we're still pretty shiny and new. Lot of us were still practically kids, back when. Is there an appropriate time to tell somebody you had to get an arm replaced? If there's etiquette for that, Bristol'd know. "I know a couple people, sure. I've been working some guys are running a bootleg helicopter joint, and doing some side projects along the way."

Bootleg helicopters, that's sure a thing people try sometimes. Plus I'm startin' to think that my brain was messed with more than I thought, there keep being more coincidences than I'm happy with. I been thinking about helicopters since we got here and now...this. They did test us for, what'd they call it, precognitive abilities. Put us in VR of being in a room looking at a door when the doorbell rings, and it was fifty fifty whether there was a man with a gun on the other side of the door. Most of us did worse than fifty-fifty, me included, except the one time, right before they cut that part of the program off, where the doorbell rang and I was convinced right down to my bones that there was a man with a gun on the other side of that door, 100%, it was real and he had a gun, and I was right. Well except it wasn't real it was VR. Oh I should tell Bits about that, I don't think I ever did. "That's real interesting and all but I don't think we can take a helicopter from here to Vietnam?"

"You might. Vietnam's closer than you think." I sigh and finish my beer. "Anyway, they're gonna know other pilots, even if you don't showcase one of their models."

"Okay, good. That's good. We'll pay them, of course."

"Of course." He gestures at the person behind the counter for more beers. "And what about me?" Aglets, that's what the things on laces're called. Aglets go through eyelets.

I raise my eyebrows at him. "What about you?"

Chapter Fifteen

I message Bits while me and Butler are walking to the helicopter place, or maybe just where the helicopter people live. Sure I've known him for a lifetime but, people change, so I wanna give her the space to check and see if Butler's actually got nefarious connections and aims, but everything seems on the level, or at least still our type of crooked. //Who is this guy?// she asks.

//Somebody I know from home.// I glance at him; he must assume I've gotta make contact with my people, but he's not even lookin at me, but out the cab window. //Look he knows some helicopter people, and even if one of their rides doesn't work, they know other pilots.//

//Sounds good.// And I think that's that but then Bits messages me again. //So Bristol is really excited that you're bringing a man home so I guess be prepared for that.//

//Great. Roger that.// I assumed she'd be like this, it's fine. I'd be more worried if she wasn't, honestly. //I'll let you know when we're done and heading over.//

"You just got in today, you said?" Butler asks.

"Yeah, I haven't even seen the inside of the place yet. I came right to the market after dropping 'em off."

"Over by Disney you said? Was prob'ly pretty pricey."

"Right?" I grin at him; he's fishing and it's none of his goddamn business. Bringing a man home. I never brought Butler home, at home. He *was* home, if that makes any kinda sense. All the families knew each other, at home, all the families worked together, at home, because survival was work besides the other stuff that we did to get money for what we couldn't just do for ourselves. All us kids just ran in a feral barefoot herd as we grew up, playing and scrapping and all of that, boys and girls alike. Sometimes people peeled off for more domestic pursuits and sometimes we got caught up in cybernetic super soldier programs, it's just how it is. How it was. Well. We signed up for it. We thought it'd be good for our families.

I assume he messages his guys too, and where the cab leaves us is definitely not a place where helicopters are stored or manufactured, it's still right in the city, an apartment building with stories and stories of rocking and crackling and humming AC units perched on the outside like the weirdest squarest pigeon problem. Seems like all the renewable energy people would be really into figuring out a better way for environmental controls planetside; they got it figured out in space after all.

The elevator's got an Out Of Order sign written on it on cardboard and we go up the stairs, and then up the stairs, and then up the stairs. The building's pretty quiet, probably everybody else sleeping. I don't really know where the time went but it's to that time of night where most decent people're sleeping and people like us have drunk too much, or done other things too much, and are going about our business in a way that we tend not to in daylight, even though we could I guess. Bothers me less than a lotta people. Bits isn't super into light in general, she's practically mole people sometimes. Not normally so bad as when we drove back up through Mexico, finished off that job with Bristol and Nicolai.

Butler's got a real actual key for the door and lets himself in. The door opens to a little hallway where shoes are lined up, and he kicks out of his unlaced boots, and I kick out of mine. I get a closer look, of course; they are definitely the same kind of laces. Old habits. Same socks too.

"Hello!" a gangly Asian guy in a coverall with the sleeves rolled up comes in the hallway and waves. I become aware of a repeating, high-pitched noise just at the edge of my hearing, maybe a fan, maybe some weird AC unit, but no, the AC units here are humming. "I'm Meatball."

"Dolly," I say, waving back.

"Scooter went out to get beers," Meatball says to Butler.

"Aw, they didn't have to do that."

Meatball scratches the back of his neck, shrugs. "Sure they did. *We* did." He's got mechanic's hands, scuffed and scarred, and his eyes have the replacement-glints that Bitsy's do now. I wonder if his are recent, or if they're post-market the way mine would've been, if I had 'em.

"Well I appreciate it," I say. In the apartment now, there's a couple closed doors but mainly this living room I think, and a row of 3D printers on a long low table against one wall, their arms all moving. That's the noise. None of 'em are really big enough to be printing big helicopter parts, but I'm sure there's lotsa small stuff that they can piece out here. Or other things that they can make faster and sell faster to support the helicopter habit. Everything's orderly, though. Tidier than I'd known Butler to be, so either he doesn't live here, or he pitches in. Or they let him take care of other things. Lots of possibilities. Lots of people willin' to do housework for you, if you take care of occasional necessary violence for them. As me how I know.

"See? Somebody knows about hospitality!" Meatball says, and Butler actually chuckles.

"Yeah, Dolly hung some manners on somewhere," he said. Did I? Kinda. Bristol's manners by osmosis, maybe. "When we were kids, though..."

"I don't think we need to revisit that era," I say. God we're gonna go over this again in the rental with Bits and Bristol, aren't we.

Maybe we'll be late enough that Bristol will be asleep, anyway. Then we can at least all face it fresh with the morning.

"You knew each other when you were kids? That's so cool!"

"Sure did! And Butler's the biggest mama's boy you ever did know. Every little bump or scrape, he'd go runnin' home from wherever we were, sometimes across the whole damn county, so she'd kiss it and make it better." I smile sweetly when Meatball laughs, and wander over to the printers as Butler defends his manliness.

"She's always been this mean, as you can guess."

"Sure have." They've got all kinds of little parts going on the printers. Valves and clamps and other fiddly things. One of them is definitely gun parts, not really a surprise. Gotta print what pays, I assume. Or maybe it's a one-off, maybe they started it when Butler called 'em because they didn't have any guns on hand. I guess that's possible. Scooter and Meatball could be wide-eyed innocents in this terrible world, just helicopter enthusiasts. With their good new friend Butler. Hmm.

There's a key in the lock and I glance at Meatball and Butler; Butler was looking at me already and our eyes meet for a moment. I don't know what his play is here, I shouldn't assume he's got one, and I shouldn't mess up whatever it is. We just need a ride, preferably sooner rather than later, preferably as discreet as a bootleg helicopter can be.

Scooter comes in cautiously, a little less vigorous than Meatball, but they do smile and hold up the beers. "I bought two six packs of Hong Kong Machine Men."

"Sounds exciting, thanks a ton," I say. Really, what I know about Hong Kong beers is that there's a bunch of breweries here, actually, and that Party is the one that people really don't like. There's probably more but no matter how fun it sounds, Party beer is not where it's at. Kinda like mandatory fun. Nobody wants that.

"You're welcome! Any...friend of Butler's is a friend of ours!" Scooter pulls out one of the bottles and hands it to me. Well that was a weird pause.

"Aw well thanks." I look at Butler, and look at Butler's belt buckle then. Yup, it's the old spur one. He sees me looking and grins. I lever my bottle cap off with the offered opener; probably a table edge would've been fine, but you don't do that when you're a guest in somebody's house unless they do it first. Plus, no sense showing off my cyber strength unless I have to, doin it with my bare hands. "So did he tell you why I'm in town?"

"Only that you need a ride to Vietnam and he offered one of our helicopters?" Scooter says, looking slightly worried. "Which, not that we *mind* really, except that—"

"I didn't offer to give her a helicopter, I said that we could maybe arrange a ride," Butler says with a laugh.

"And we'll pay," I say. "We're not lookin' to take advantage of anybody. Well. We're not lookin' to take advantage of *you*."

Scooter looks less worried, and Meatball looks even more delighted. "From here to Vietnam? Where in Vietnam?"

"We were thinking Da Nang, but really, if you can get us in-country, we can figure it out from there." We're all of us pretty good, directionally. For different reasons, I guess.

"If we're taking your money to fly you to Vietnam we aren't going to just drop you off *wherever*," Scooter says, just total genuine disbelief.

"Hey, I'm not castin' aspersions on your professionalism. I just know plans have to change midstream sometimes, it's how things go."

"Okay but how much money are you going to pay us to fly you to Vietnam?" Meatball asks, maybe with visions of new 3D printers in his head, who can say. Of the two, I think Meatball's the dreamer. Probably also the impulsive one.

"Oh I dunno. I think just an airplane ticket is a couple hundred bucks nowadays. Let's say we'll cover your fuel and refuel, and then..." I watch Butler watching them and wonder what his play here is. He isn't here out of the goodness of his heart, that just isn't how he operates. Which isn't to say there isn't any good in him, he isn't the villain of many stories that I know about. God knows none of us're without sin; that's not even Tragic Backstory, just plain hard truth. Where we're from, it's too far from the coast to've flooded and too far from cities to've benefitted and just the infrastructure crumbled when they built the hyperloop and stuff, and when factory farms kept buying out the family ones and then going vertical. Time marched on. "How about ten thousand dollars."

That might still be too little, we might be takin' advantage, I do have more than that liquid. But Scooter makes a visible effort to decide to play it cool, and for a second, I wonder what a whole damn helicopter costs to buy, anyway, bootleg or not. I think, of the two, Scooter's the worrier. The planner. "Well I think that sounds about right, between the fuel, and then the maintenance we'll have to do once we get to Vietnam, and after we get home again. Plus our discretion of course."

"Plus your discretion," I agree, then I hold out my sweating beer bottle. "Drink to it?"

Scooter and Meatball look at each other, and Meatball has far less of a poker face and grins. Scooter shrugs, and we clink bottlenecks. "Drink to it."

Chapter Sixteen

Me and Butler walk to the Air B&B a couple hours later, after we get the plan hashed out. The beers weren't enough to get us drunk, but the bottle of rice liquor Scooter and Meatball *also* poured to us sure helped a lot, supersoldier livers or not. It's a good buzz, we're still more than combat ready should that become a necessity. I have a brief image of gettin' in some kind of weird brawl with police along the way, but that doesn't end up happening. We see police, sure, but they go their way and we go ours.

It's a nice walk. It's cooler at night, I guess, but still humid, so it still feels like you're moving around in a big mouth. The street lights all have these condensation puffballs around them like dandelions gone to seed. It's nice to be walking with Butler again; I missed him, but also it wouldn't've been all that hard for either of us to find the other and reconnect. We're not a tragic love story, just a tired one. Another life, another situation, we'd already have the house and picket fence and 2.5 kids or whatever. Dog and cat and electric minivan and lake cottage for summers. Little league games and lemonade stands and dance recitals. That stuff all still exists, right? Maybe not lemonade stands; too many kids were gettin' tickets for not having food service licenses or whatever bullshit. Like come *on*.

Instead, we got injections, and replacements, and playing soldier. Found out later some people got VR training. Some people got memory training. I dunno what the control group was; the history of modern warfare to that point, I guess. We got training and testing and more training and more tests and war games that we were all actually real good at. We also assumed that doing all that would help our families, protect our town, let them keep on keepin' on. The program kinda petered out and we were cut loose and that's when we found out it wasn't really the case. Nothing big bad happened, just the usual kind of everything slowly dried up and everybody blew away. Usual now, anyway; I guess it probably didn't used to be. Or maybe it's always been there, when you peel back the gold foil wrapping of The American Dream. Who can say.

Butler's not much of a talker, even when buzzed, and I think he expects me to grill him on what he's doing with Scooter and Meatball, if he's taking advantage of them or actually really into this helicopter thing, and when I don't, just kinda settle into my own thoughts as we walk, he doesn't really know what to do with himself. Eventually, after time looking at me out of the corners of his eyes, he clears his throat. I wait, and he does it again, and then he says "So you like the kids?"

"Yeah, they seem good, real smart. How'd you meet them?" They seem...I don't want to say young, that ain't it. And Meatball's got a shock of gray in his hair. They still seem hopeful, I guess. They aren't all scarred up and jaded. Or anyways, not visibly.

"They were at a weapons expo."

"3D printed guns?"

"Yeah. They're really into the theoreticals of that, but real squeamish about the idea that guns, y'know, shoot things. People."

"I can imagine." I can't remember when I still had a problem with that, necessarily. It just always seems like it was part of our reality. I just think it's a responsibility, that one should take care with. I got the scars that say I've been on the other end of people not takin' so much care with it. Or, they thought they were, without a doubt, in the right. I can sympathize with that. "And so they thought of the helicopters or..."

"Well you know how those things are, they sell all kinds of things."

"They do."

"And we got to talking..."

"And drinking."

"Yeah, and drinking." He looks at me and laughs. "And we bought a helicopter, and they already had a pretty good scanner for the rendering software so..."

"So you kinda accidentally fell into the bootleg helicopter business."

"Kinda."

"Got tired of shootin' people?" Like I'm one to talk, really. It's not like I don't still end up shooting people. Just my choice now, typically. The category of people, the type of rounds. Not that our little group of playing pretend super soldiers did a whole lotta shooting but. Well we didn't always know where they put us, or whether the rounds were live.

"Didn't say I gave that up. But you know how it is." He don't look haunted, exactly. I'm not sure any of us have that capacity, not after. But yeah. I know, and I nod, and he takes that as good enough. "So tell me about who you work with, don't let me walk in there with no intel."

"Damn, I thought I'd get away with it." We both laugh, and I think about it. What does he need to know. "Bristol's a flashy one, and smart as hell. Don't let her fool you with any kind of airhead act, and don't let her get you hooked either."

"You know who my heart belongs to." He's being dramatic, but is he?

I roll my eyes, I can't help it. "Shit, don't be like that."

"Noted."

"And Bits tends to be pretty quiet, and she's the smartest person I ever met. And I like and respect both of 'em and I'll eat your liver and your eyeballs if you upset them in any way." We used to say that all the time when we were kids; the big threat, too ridiculous to really understand, too scary to risk.

He puts his hands up, grinning a little lopsided. "I didn't realize it was that serious, I'll be on my best behavior."

"You'd better."

When we get there, I go in first and Honey barks once, big boom, and then comes to greet me. It's a really nice place, actually, and I wonder what we paid for it. I wonder if it's actually somebody's home for any of the time, or if it would normally be a local rental that somebody just uses for the online short term rentals like this. I rub behind the dog's ears, surprised and kinda pleased with myself that she's happy to see me. I should've at some point thought about how I should be careful to not get attached.

"Dolly, aren't you going to introduce us?" Bristol asks a little coyly, and I give her kind of a 'well maybe' grin and then shrug.

"This is Butler. Butler, this is Bristol and Bits."

"Lots of B names," Butler says carefully.

"Oh, the A names were all boring," Bristol says breezily, and Bits just kinda shrugs. "It's nice to finally meet you!"

"Finally?" he looks at me.

"I might've told stories, I honestly don't remember. You know how I get to running my mouth sometimes." Or she's fishing. Whichever, there's not a lot of harm in it. Probably.

"Might've told stories," he says slowly, laughing a little. "Well there's lots of those to go around. I'm sure you've even got some of your own."

"I'm very certain we do," Bristol says.

Bits knows what I'm about, though, and brings me to the kitchen where my food is. Also a range of beverages, I guess the fridge was stocked. Or one of them went out. I grab a bottle of water, and whatever my bag of food is, and call "Butler, you want anything? Coffee? Soda? Water? Beer?"

"Probably good to switch to coffee," he says after a brief pause. He'd better be careful, Bristol's getting him mesmerized. I warned him.

"Sure thing." I start to juggle stuff around to get a hand free and Bits laughs at me.

"I'll get it," she says, and gets a canned coffee out of the fridge. He'll take it just however, prefers it black or at least trained himself to drink it black. We all did, at one point. Couldn't rely on sweetener after the bees were gone, or creamer for about forever. The powdered stuff is surprisingly good, anyway. Well I think so. Prob'ly just thinking about it'd give Bristol hives or the vapors or something.

Back in the other room, Butler's in a chair and Honey pressed herself against his knees and is grinning up at him as he scruffs his big hands around in her fur, her eyes half closed.

"What, I invite you here, you steal my dog?" I toss him the coffee and he catches it, pops the tab.

"*Your* dog?"

"Nah, not really. I've just been on animal handlin' duty since we got her."

"And you are indeed the one who got her," Bristol says pointedly. Butler catches it but doesn't understand, looks between us, drinks his coffee.

"Sure did." I grin until Bristol cracks a smile and then returns her attention to Butler.

"So how long have you and Dolly known each other?"

"Oh, just about forever," Butler says. I start shoveling food, nod with my mouth full. He isn't gonna say anything that embarasses me. There isn't anything that embarasses me. Bits must've remembered that I liked ramen, or they both remembered that it doesn't matter what I eat, because they got me some kind of bright yellow, spicy noodles with little shrimps in it. Other meats too. My lips go numb pretty quick and it's really great actually. Spicy food is great after beer. And whatever that other stuff was. "How long have you ladies known each other?"

"A few years now, I'd say?" Bristol glances at both of us and Bits kind of nods. I'm sure Bits has a datestamp of our first encounter. Maybe even recordings squirreled away on some server or another, encrypted from here to the moon.

"But I guess you don't base outta Hong Kong."

"You know we don't. Quit fuckin' fishing," I say. Honey folds her ears at my tone, and I rub her flank with the side of my foot.

"Sorry, sorry. Old habits, y'know. Plus, what we do? You want to stay informed."

I laugh. "What you do is bootleg helicopters."

"Right now."

"Fair enough." I'm a little surprised Bristol is satisfied to just watch this interplay, but of course she is, it's like she's a predator drone that needs to take readings and calibrate.

"So is that really all you need, a helicopter ride?"

"Sure is," I say. "Told you to stop fishing."

"Well if he's offering *help*," Bristol says sweetly.

"Bristles I already paid for the damn helicopter, if you wanna pay for whatever Butler ends up costin' us you can go right ahead."

Butler leans back in his chair, folds his arms behind his head. "Who says I wanted you to hire me?"

"There's other ways ya end up having to pay sometimes." He pulls a hurt expression, boo hoo. I finish my noodles, take the garbage to the kitchen where I think I saw a can, Honey padding along behind me. Bits has to have worked her magic, found Bristol's contact's contact by now. I can hear Bristol's tone of voice, less her words, but that rise and fall of diverting and soothing. If he was a riled up horse, he'd be eating carrots out of her hand by the time I got back. It's just the banter, always has been, but anytime we add somebody to the mix, the dynamic has to shake out and settle down.

"Okay, so the plan is we get our flight plan in, load everybody up, and take you away from all this," Butler says when I come back.

"Oh well good. Gotta love a cakewalk."

"You know better than to say that," Bits mutters.

"Sure do!" I smile big and Butler laughs. Bristol smiles, but in that brittle-edged way that means she doesn't particularly like where this is going, and I can definitely see how it'd seem from her perspective. "Anyway, when will we be in the air you think? I'd say wheels up, but..."

"It typically takes a day to get flight plans approved," Butler says.

"So day after tomorrow? Elizabits, you think you could..."

"On it," she says.

"Just like that?" Butler asks.

"Sometimes," she says, getting up and going to what I assume is a bedroom.

"Bristol, do we know anything more about the Vietnam end of things?"

"I put in a call to a contact," she says, maybe a little carefully. She doesn't know what I told Butler, and doesn't want to have to explain the whole thing I'm sure. I didn't want to have to explain the whole thing, so I didn't. "They're going to get back to me in the morning."

"Perfect." I stretch, and yawn. "Well I gotta go to sleep. I guess I'll empty the dog first, yeah."

I can't even describe the looks that cross Bristol's face in rapid succession, but she makes some noise of agreement and retires. I find the leash, get Honey hooked up, and she and Butler follow me outside. "So you're just reuniting this dog with the owner or what?" he asks, quietly.

"That's the plan!" I say. "We thought it'd happen in Macau but...lost our contact."

"Lost your contact," he says, like he's thinking about it. It doesn't take him long, though, I see it in his face when we pass under a streetlight. I see somethin' else there that makes me wonder a little. Side jobs. "Well that's rough."

"Only Bristol knew him, and only a little. Friend of a friend. But yeah it was a surprise, definitely." Dangerous as this line of work is, we don't lose people often, somehow. I guess if we did, we would've stopped before now, providin' we were smart enough. I'd like to think we're smart enough. Back doin' army stuff, we lost people a couple times. Officially, on the books, we were only ever experimental, and only ever playin' war games. In reality, they put us in the shit a couple of times. Very expensive, very expendable; a real weird combination, I always thought. Though I also always thought it was real weird that they just cut us loose, instead of pushin' some red button that made something self destruct. Though I guess with the posthypnotic stuff, we're considered mothballed. I should've thought of that sooner, that I'm deprogrammed but Butler ain't.

Honey does her business, and we walk back to the air b&b. He hangs out at the bottom of the steps like he's come callin' and is too bashful or too mindful of my dad with a shotgun to come up and kiss me, and I gotta smile at that. "You gonna ask me to stay the night?" he asks.

"You know, I don't think I am. But I'll see you tomorrow." I pull the bandanna off my neck to see the look on his face, then wave it and blow him a kiss. Yeah, he looks, has a little twitch of the lips, then he recovers and laughs, shaking his head.

"Goodnight, Dolly."

"'Night Butler."

Chapter Seventeen

Butler texts me in the morning, right around dawn actually, that we got our flight clearance for 1100. Sure we're programmed to be early risers, but he could've waited a little while. I go to roll over, but Honey's sprawled across my legs, and she doesn't move but she does groan. I lay back for a sec, and laugh, because what else are you gonna do if a Tibetan Mastiff is layin' on you and doesn't want to wake up? I can move her. I'm gonna move her. But there's no harm in lettin' her get a few more minutes of shuteye. We should probably look into some kind of doggie tranquilizer for the chopper ride, I'm pretty damn sure she isn't gonna just go along with it otherwise. I message that to Bits, she'll find me a pharmacy or something.

Eventually I just doze off again, and eventually Butler messages me again and it's a picture of a dog kennel strapped in the back of a helicopter, Scooter and Meatball giving thumbs ups from the open doors. This time I groan, and then I send back a thumbs up, and then I get to work gettin' Honey to move. She's more amiable this time, has to go out, and I smoke a cigarette while we're at it, for the up and at 'em and for the memory of...who was that? Butler's dad and one of his brothers, rigging up a trailer to bring home a steer they'd won at auction because they were the only bidders. Of course that particular steer had never been loaded on a trailer a day in his life, much less one held together with wire and future thoughts of barbecue.

When I get back inside, Bits is blearily poking at the coffee machine, and Bristol is breezing about the place in a cloud of flowery perfume. She's actually in riot gear, which is good, I didn't wanna have to fight with her about wearing high heels in a helicopter. Of course her boots are black velvet, but I know they're leather too, and a good brand. So long as it's fashion *and* function, I don't give a fuck. She isn't stupid; she's very interested in self preservation, so we're all on the same page there.

"We all packed?" I ask. "Tasers charged, dragonscale on?" Other than getting shot at, this whole thing has been a little too calm, actually. Other than bickerin' with each other. I won't say I got jitters, exactly, but the anticipation adrenaline has a little more edge to it. Hopefully it'll stay boring, we'll just have a big long chopper ride and then that'll be that. Whistle through your teeth and spit, I guess.

"Yeah, we're ready. Do you want to order breakfast or what?" Bits asks.

"If you're wondering if I'm hungry, fuck yes. If you think that I think we should wander out for street food with a stolen dog, no. So yeah, let's order in. Bristol can pick the place."

"How very generous of you," Bristol says cheerfully. She already knows what she wants, it's fine. We all know I don't care what I eat.

"Hey, I got my moments." I didn't really unpack in the first place, but I repack what I did. Make sure all the dog's stuff is packed. Give the house a general once-over, make sure we're not leaving anything vital. It's not like it's really feasible to do a forensic sweep or anything, remove all our fingerprints and loose hairs and stuff, but not leaving a big sign with flashing fluorescent lights sayin' who we are and why we're here is also good. If somebody on our trail looked around this apartment, would they find anything out, other'n what we ordered for food? What soap Bristol prefers? Doesn't seem like it. Leave only footprints, they say but...lotta times, you don't want to even do that.

//So where's the meetup?// I text Butler. Chances're about zero that Scooter and Meatball just have a helipad on their apartment building's roof, unless their bootleg helicopters are also stealth. He doesn't answer in words, just a set of coordinates, and I forward them to Bits.

//See you soon// he says after a few minutes and I just send him a plus sign because Bristol is making that 'can't we just have a nice meal for once?' face and no of course we can't, but sometimes we pretend for her. It's not the same as lying, exactly.

Breakfast is good, of course it is, and then Bits sends me a file that's part of the care 'n' feeding of this dog and for flying, that involves sedation sorts of pills that's in her kit that I also stole, and I haven't put pills in many things other than people, but I hide it in a piece of hot dog and it goes down fine. It's a double-edged sword, givin' a dog that big knockout pills. You need to do it early enough to take hold by the time it matters, but then you also have to get 'em where you're going. Honey's still alert when we get in the cab, the driver real hesitant to let us, but Bristol smooths it over, and then I really gotta urge her to get back out again, at an airfield. Not a lot of people around, that's good, and Bristol gives the driver a real good tip and I'm sure urges him to forget that he saw us. The standard.

As a team, we've only had a few helicopter rides together, but once Bristol's done something once, or studied it virtually with laser focus, she makes it look effortless forever after. She immediately greets Scooter and Meatball like they've been friends for years and sets them at ease, gets them talking about different things as they about fall over each other to stow her and Bits' gear. Butler helps me get Honey up into the chopper, and into the kennel that's strapped down and padded inside and honestly is probably the safest place on this whirlybird. Bristol's on a similar wavelength, I guess, 'cause she's got Meatball talking about the safety features, the ballistic parachutes that the thing has.

"Oh, don't *we* get parachutes?" she asks.

"No, that isn't how helicopters work," Scooter says. They look a little conflicted about whether to explain, or if it might be insulting, and Bristol just smiles graciously.

"I'm sorry, I didn't realize. Do forget I asked." She straps into one of the seats, accepts a headset. Our eyes meet briefly; yeah, this is gonna be her longest helicopter ride, and she wants to know what happens if the thing falls out of the sky. What we're supposed to do. I feel like I know, but not how to explain it in words. It's one of those trained things, and it'll kick in if I need it. I kinda shrug and flick my eyes to Bits and Bristol nods slightly. Bits can get her any intel she needs. We'll probably be over water for a lot of this; if we go down, I guess the chopper would float? I don't think normal ones would, but it seems like composite 3D printed ones would. Maybe we'll even have a shorter flight, less weight.

Honey's asleep before we're even in the air. I'm not sure yet who's piloting, Meatball or Scooter, but they take us up nice and easy, and I wonder where and how they got those chops, in addition to all the printing stuff. They've gotta be in their twenties. Good for them, really; we're all just making our way in the world. This is even legitimate. Or kind of. Legitimate enough that they're still getting flight clearance and operating in the open in Hong Kong.

I don't know if Butler was looking forward to around 12 hours of having me boxed in with him to converse or not, especially after I figure he's maybe the sniper from that night in Macau, but first order of business, really, is more shut-eye. Plus, the headsets aren't really noise canceling enough for good conversation. Bits could loop everybody in on our network and that might work out but, we'll worry about that when I wake up. Or nobody'll be worried and when I wake up it'll already be taken care of.

I don't know about anybody else, but I don't dream much. I did when I was little, I guess. Not so much after my experimental days. Maybe it's to do with them messing around with my programming.

Maybe I'm just not super imaginative, who knows. Any time I try to remember when I sleep, it's mostly just maybe different colors, or if I'm warm enough. But nothing bothers me and I wake up good and refreshed, open my eyes to Butler asleep bolt upright, Bristol looking out the window, and Bits might've not moved the whole time.

"Where we at?" I ask.

"A few hours left," Bristol says. "Meatball mentioned not too long ago."

"So what do we do for the next eternity? Play I spy?" I lean a little, look out the window. "Whole lotta blue. Ooh a boat."

"*Please* no," Bristol says, turning her ever-suffering gaze to Butler, whose eyes are open now. "Why don't you tell us a story about how you and Dolly know each other?" Everybody just wants to know that, when we're out in the world, it's amazing.

"I promise, playing I spy's better." I laugh. "Anyway, Bristol, I already told you."

"Well you told me *your* version," Bristol says dismissively.

"Aw, I don't know," Butler says, with a play-bashful grin. He's never been bashful a day in his life. "We've always known each other."

"If you've always known each other, and are depriving me of a meet-cute, then can you tell me, has she always been like this?"

He's smiling and not lookin' at me and he says "Like what? A being of sweetness and light? Yup, that's our Dolly. Just the sweetheart of our town, she was, readin' library books to old folks and gettin' kittens out of trees."

"Aw come on, my reputation's gonna be ruined," I say.

"Dolly, your softer side is *hardly* a secret," Bristol says, a little smugly.

"Really? I thought I was still pretty intimidating. Obviously a hardened career criminal. A bloodthirsty, remorseless killer." I'm running out of descriptives.

"Maybe strangers think that, though I'm not sure how many acquaintances would say so."

"Well damn." I'm watching Bits, because I'm pretty sure she started paying attention to the real world a little while back and is just waiting for things to be safe before she takes her headset off. It's like how you can tell when somebody's pretend sleeping; after awhile you're just familiar enough with a person's breathing. And anyway, it's not like *she* knows what she breathes like when she's asleep or concentrating on virtual stuff. "I just feel so bad anytime anybody has the misfortune to be in my care."

"Nonsense darling," Bristol says briskly. "You've always done a marvelous job, so far as I'm aware."

"Well there was that time…" Butler says with a wicked grin, and I kick his foot.

"There's gotta be a first time for everything, okay? Plus you can hardly see the scar so I guess it turned out in the end." I don't know if you can hardly see the scar; I haven't seen him with his shirt off since we reunited.

"You simply *cannot* torture us like that," Bristol says. Bits sighs and pulls her VR goggles down around her neck, blinks around at us.

"You did fine taking care of me," she says, bless her heart. That ain't gonna be enough to distract Bristol.

"Thank you, Bits. See that's two outta three. Let's pray we don't need any more examples just now, huh?"

Bristol does pout now. "But I'm bored and want a story."

"Well you know what happened. After the…" Bits trails off, looking at Butler, who is listening with interest, realizes she doesn't really want to explain. "Anyway, it wasn't until then that I knew you knew how to cook, Dolly."

"I'm not certain you could call what Dolly does 'cooking,'" Bristol says delicately, and Butler laughs hard enough that Meatball turns around for a second. Good thing he seems to be the navigator and moral support.

"Aw come on, I make a perfectly serviceable steak with cast iron or a grill."

"A hubcap too, at least once," Butler says thoughtfully. He's like me, though, with a cast iron gullet. Like all of us are. Or were, I guess.

"A hubcap."

I grin. "Yeah, you know how it is. Sometimes circumstance makes it so you don't always have the right tools on hand."

"And...circumstance...led you to have steaks, but no appropriate means of cooking them."

"Well we *washed* the hubcap, if that's your problem." I watch her struggle, and I assume she decides against askin' after the provenance of the steaks.

"I don't think that's her problem, Dolly," Bits says helpfully.

"Yeah, prob'ly not." I grin at Bristol and she gives me her very small, very disapproving smile particularly crafted for moments like these, and Butler laughs again.

"So you three are a team?"

"We are business associates, yes," Bristol says primly.

"How's that work out for you."

I shrug. "Pretty good, mostly. We have our moments."

"Like stealin' a dog in one country that you had no plans to get to another?"

Bristol bites her lip. "We hit a snag."

"I should fucking say so." His tone is off, just a little.

"You don't need to be *crass* about it."

"....Crass?"

"She means the F word," I say, leaned over like I'm tellin' him a secret. He looks at me, and I wiggle my eyebrows at him. Is now the time to tell him I know? Nah.

"He can curse in other languages," Scooter interjects. We weren't disincludin' them on purpose, it's just hard when you're not lookin' at a person, even if everybody's in the headset.

"You don't understand, Bristol smells swear words." I look at the back of Scooter and they give me a thumbs up. "Plus, there's no telling what languages she knows. She picks them up like adaptive camouflage." And what a handy thing that lil prototype adaptive camouflage box has been.

"I work very hard at it," she says.

"It's really impressive," Bits says, and Bristol looks pleased, so really, that's the best way this conversation could've turned, both me and Butler off the hotseat. For the moment. I'm sure the second I go find a bathroom or something once we're in Da Nang, she'll drag out his entire life story, and family history, and then mine, like how magicians pull knotted scarves outta their mouths. It's fine, it ain't new; I've resigned myself to my fate.

"Hey Meatball and Scooter, we're puttin' you up in a nice hotel, so you're nice and well rested for your flight back."

"Thanks!" Meatball says. Scooter nods in agreement, but yawns. I think they're the one that did the bulk of the flying and stuff.

"Not me?" Butler asks.

"Well I was under the impression you were interested in how this was gonna shake out," I say. "Or were you not?"

"Well I've got an interest," he says.

"I guess you might," I say, letting my tone slide a little off too, and he gets a little too still.

"Good, see, it's settled then," Bristol says. "It's possible we'll solve our little issue and we'll all be in the same hotel! Won't that be a treat, having a nice dinner together." Partway through that sentence, I see her rememberin' that nobody but her actually has nice dinner clothes, but to her credit, she soldiers on through to the end anyway.

"It'd be real keen," I say, grinning hard. "Lookin' forward to it."

"Real keen," Butler says slowly.

And it's banter all the way until landing, which really, there are worse ways to pass the time. It's been too long, since I've shared the same space with Butler for this long, and I'm not gonna be all starry-eyed about it. He's got more sense than to expect that, or he used to. After the job, though? We'll see how things play out. Especially after we talk about Macau, and his side jobs. Maybe the kind of rifle he's favoring lately. Business is business, he couldn't've known it was me, but I'm gonna let him squirm anyway.

Chapter Eighteen

Da Nang is dry and hot and I'm glad we aren't here for monsoon season, though I'm not sure which Bristol would find worse. She's the kinda person AC is made for. The airport's an airport, they're their own kind of places, y'know? Even walking off the tarmac from the helipad, we still gotta go through customs, and thank Christ Bits is as good as she is, we sail through no problem, everything stamped the way it needs to be, even the very sleepy dog's papers. She's a champ, though, just bumps into my leg as we walk, swinging her big head around to look at things.

Once we're outside again, Bristol immediately calling her new contact, mined from the old contact's phone, I just take a minute to look up at the night sky that we just came down from. We haven't been able to fly for all that long, people. It's kinda mind blowing when you think about it. Scooter looks a little nervous about leaving their helicopter, but I guess we arranged some kind of hangar and refuel for them, and they'll check it all over before they leave again tomorrow, so it's mostly the jitters from leaving a piece of equipment like that outta your sight. Plus they made every piece of it. That'll get you pretty attached.

Bristol drops her phone in her purse and looks off up the street. "Well?" I ask.

"He's at a hotel by the river, and after sitting for so long, I don't mind a walk. Shall we?"

"I think we'll find our own hotel, if you don't mind," Meatball says. "We're awfully tired after..."

"Oh I'm so sorry, what was I *thinking*? Bits, can you...?"

"On it," Bitsy says.

"I'll come along, if you don't mind," Butler says.

"Don't go thinkin' you get a cut," I say, grinning hard so he knows I really mean it.

"Nah, you already paid me. I just like seeing happy dog reunions, my phone is full of 'em," he says, grinning so I can't tell if he's serious or not, and we both laugh. Bits looks at us kind of wide-eyed, like okay weirdos, and then looks at Meatball.

"You should be all set, the place is right that way."

"Thank you," he says, grinning but also suddenly shy, and I think oh Meatball honey, Bits isn't gonna be any kind of interested, just go to your hotel. But maybe I read it wrong, and him and Scooter are an item, it's not my business, and Scooter is in the jaw-cracking yawn stage of things, so now isn't the time to try and puzzle it out. They stumble-walk off on their way, though not with enough stumble that I think they need a minder.

Honey looks around at more and sniffs at more than in Macau, her ears canted forward, or at least I think they are. But she sniffs and sniffs, and sometimes stops to sniff with her nose up in the air, not on the ground, and I wonder what she's after, or thinks she's after. I wonder if dogs sometimes think they recognize a smell, the way us people think we recognize a person or a taste or a sound. Or a smell too, I guess, but dogs're way better at that. Bits told me once that smell-memories are the strongest ones, and I believe it. A certain smell'll take you back to school, or to your dad's garage when you were eight and holdin' the flashlight for him, or to picking blackberries in the summer with somebody who maybe-kinda wants to be your beau, while the cicadas scream in the trees all around you.

Bristol gives me a knowing look over her shoulder, she and Bits walking a little ahead. On purpose, I guess, to make sure me and Butler get time together. So obvious even I know what they're doing. Though I guess also I want to spend this last little time with the dog; we've only had her for a few days, but I guess she and I understand each other pretty well. We managed not to take any chunks out of each other, that's a pretty big deal. Wonder if Butler's still got that scar on his back, or if it got fixed with one of his upgrades. It wasn't on purpose. Maybe we're actually square by now, after everything.

"So in Macau…" Butler says, kinda guarded.

"Side job, I assume?"

"You're not pissed? I was already part broken down when I took my other shots, and—"

"You could've killed me," I said. "Or Bits or Bristol."

"Well yeah, that's what I'm trying to apologize for, if you stop being an asshole about it."

"You did kill Bristol's contact."

"And I was supposed to get his electronics to figure out where that goddamn dog went." We stop walking a minute, look at each other.

"And?"

"And what?"

"You didn't get them. Did you still get paid?"

"Yeah I still got paid. Got over there, took his picture, said somebody rolled him while he was still warm, thinkin' he was drunk. Like I was going to try and track down a couple people I barely saw in the first place?" He's telling the truth, and talking faster than he normally would, and I think he's maybe just thankin' christ he didn't kill me. He never would've known. Maybe years from now, if news ever got back home. If he ever got back home.

"Well there, see?" I reach up, pat him on the cheek. "Coulda happened to anybody."

"Dolly..."

"Shut up about it, already? I'm feelin' magnanimous, givin' you a pass." I start walking again, and about five steps later he catches up again.

We're getting closer to the river, there's a nice breeze off of it, and that watery smell, and then Honey about yanks the leash out of my hand, hittin' the end of it for the first time in our association. I keep hold, but I'm surprised. She looks back at me like, what are you doing, why are you stopping me, and scrabbles a little on the pavement until I walk faster. Still not fast enough for her, but better. Up ahead, Bristol's already talking to a guy, but he isn't looking at her, he's looking at the dog, and he steps past her and crouches down and I take a chance and let go of the leash and she runs and piles right into his chest, wagging furiously, licking anything of him that she can reach. Hot dogs can't fake that reaction; Honey's his dog all right.

He wraps his arms around her, and then feels the leash and grasps it, and after a few awkward moments of the rest of us standin' around waiting, Honey calms down enough for him to get up again. He's got some tear tracks on his cheeks, and he doesn't bother to wipe 'em off; can't say as I blame him. "Thank you," he says to each of us, sincerely, looking us in the eye. "I don't know what we would have done without you. We would never have been able to find her."

"You're welcome," I say, just as sincerely, and Bits kinda nods, and I can see Bristol's surprise and disappointment, see her gears turning, can see the image of flyin' away dollar signs in her eyes. I'm tryin' to figure a way to beam my thoughts into that pretty head of hers when she seems to come to a conclusion and smiles.

"It was our pleasure," she says warmly. "If you ever find yourself in such a difficulty again, or your associates, do please call us. We'll see what we can do about it."

//Guess we're not getting paid// Bits texts me morosely, or maybe she's just trying to head me off from sayin' something real stupid. I catch her eye and nod. Really, I'm just trying not to laugh, now. It's honestly kind of funny. We can't possibly demand this guy pay us. This guy might not be able to pay us. Probably, there was never any three million dollars. Well we got that one and a half mil, however they scraped that together. And you know, that's fine. That's enough, for the look on that guy's face, and the look on the dog's face. I'm gettin' soft, must be. I hand him the bag of her gear, if it is even her gear actually or just what whoever stole her was using, and he says thank you again. He seems more than a little disbelieving. That it's really his dog. That we're really just giving her back. But just like that, we're walking away in one direction, and he's goin' back to his hotel. //If we got upset about it, there's a guy with a rifle in that window there. Not a sniper rifle, I don't know how well it would have worked but...//

//But they tried to have insurance, in case we were real hardcore mercenaries.//

//Exactly.//

//Good thing for them we aren't.//

//Sure is.// I get a glimpse of her face; she's smiling like she isn't sure if she should be.

Bristol marches us right to an outdoor cafe there under the starlight, well the city lights, but the stars gotta be up there someplace. She stares at a menu that I'm not confident she can read and then she orders so I guess I'm wrong again, and then she looks out over the water in silence for a long time. Butler reaches for my hand under the table, and I let him. His skin is warmer than mine at first, and then after awhile, our hands match temperature.

"Hey Bristol," I say, after the guy brings us drinks, and a plate of spring rolls, and a basket of what I think are snails.

"Dolly," she says, blinking at the water and then looking over at me with maybe the saddest smile I ever saw on her face. "Do you ever just want to feel *nice*?"

"Well yeah, I guess I do," I say, both 'cause it's true and because it's the only thing to say to her right now.

Bits picks up her drink; it looks like we have glasses, but they're actually all plastic, probably safest by the river and on the pavement here, and we clunk them all together in a rattling toast, smiling cautiously at first and then broader, like the end scene in a wholesome 1900s sitcom. Maybe there's scales we all think about balancing, sooner or later. But yeah. It really is good, sometimes, to just feel nice.

Epilogue

Butler comes with me to Chiba, and we shack up at a hotel we pick at random in center city. A 7-Eleven is practically in view from our room window, and I can only kinda explain why I think that's funny. Or I can explain, he just doesn't get it, and that's fine. We're there three days, just gettin' room service and spending time making up for lost time, and on the morning of the fourth day, I get the message that my robot dog is ready.

I get dressed, quiet, and leave a note on hotel stationery. I'll be back, probably. Unless the devil takes me once I'm out in the street again. Pretty sure I don't have the heart for that, though, even if he did kinda wing me in Macau. Other'n if it's like, the end of the war movie, and me going and doing whatever solo is what saves everybody. Even if I don't come back. I wonder how many goodbyes like that Bristol has pulled, just a note, maybe a *perfumed* note, I'd never think of that but she's so details-oriented, and then she's just a memory. Maybe zero. Maybe plenty. It's always hard to tell with her, always about appearances, and you gotta figure out what the reality of the situation is. I guess that's true of all of us.

They bring out the case with the white service tag still on the handle, but open it on the counter so that I can see proof of workmanship. I take the dog out of the case, crouch down and set it on the floor before I power it up. I almost feel like I cheated on it, goin' to play with a real dog while it was in the shop. The lights all come up, and it runs its usual boot sequence with wagging and head shaking, and it does a cute thing where it sits and lifts up a paw for you to shake. Then it's fully booted and it blinks at me, and starts wagging again, all on its own.

Acknowledgements

When I wrote the first Run With the Hunted novella, there was a lot I didn't know (including the character names; everybody had at least one switch, and Bristol two.) I didn't have a series in mind, it didn't occur to me that I'd rotate through narrators book by book. I didn't know that I'd make friends, and that strangers would read and review the books.

I'm very grateful for everybody who has taken that chance, picked up Run With the Hunted, and come with me on this brief near-future journey. I'm beyond thrilled that readers are invested in my characters, have favorites among the main trio, and also among the side characters we often see oh-so-briefly.

Thank you to Premee for being my enthusiastic co-cap'n on this writerly voyage, encouraging me, and yelling with me about things in DMs.

Thank you to Tori for encouraging me to self publish and looking at every iteration of every cover I have created (and sorry about that too.)

Thank you to Jazzi for loving these characters, reading through the stressful situations, doing book cover manicures, and being my patron.

Thank you to Ro for proofreading Run With the Hunted and Run With the Hunted 2: Ctrl Alt Delete. The way you nailed the character voices in your comments was invaluable to me.

Thank you to Lennon for proofreading pretty much everything I throw at you, and for being my friend for so long.

Thank you to my family for reading my work, even though it so often isn't really your thing!

Jennifer R. Donohue grew up at the Jersey Shore and now lives in central New York with her husband and their Dobermans. She works at her local public library where she also facilitates a writing workshop. Her work has appeared in Apex Magazine, Escape Pod, Fusion Fragment, and elsewhere. Her Run With the Hunted novella series is available in paperback and ebook, and her debut novel, Exit Ghost, is available in ebook and hardcover. She tweets @AuthorizedMusin and you can subscribe to her Patreon for a new short story every month: https://www.patreon.com/JenniferRDonohue

Other Works by Jennifer R. Donohue
Exit Ghost

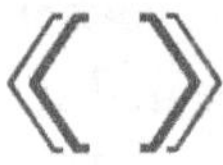

The Drowned Heir

Between the Blood and the Sun

Run With the Hunted (series)
Run With the Hunted
Run With the Hunted 2: Ctrl Alt Delete
Run With the Hunted 3: Standard Operating Procedure
Run With the Hunted 4: VIP
Run With the Hunted 5: Insert Coin to Play
Run With the Hunted 6: Burned Asset
Run With the Hunted 7: The Casino Job
Run With the Hunted 8: Neural Howlround

Learn to Howl (series)
Learn to Howl
Baying the Moon
The Company of Wolves